STAR VOWS

STAR VOWS

STARLING LEGACIES
BOOK ONE

MEGAN MOORES

For Sister J and Sister S

TRIGGER WARNINGS AND TROPES

Star Vows is a steamy romance meant for mature audiences.

Trigger Warnings:
Sexual Assault (referred to, not on page)

Tropes:
Fake Marriage
Millionaire/Billionaire Romance
Forced Proximity
Sworn off relationships
Childhood crush
Marriage Pact
Fake Relationship
Found Family

1

SUSANA

A perfect woman. A perfect life. A perfect future. That's the story you'd get about me if you typed my name into your search bar. Internet gossip sites loved to spin the tale that I, Susana Maddix Starling, was an American heiress, a descendent of a Hollywood Legacy, and first in line to inherit my huge family fortune. Perfect, right?

Wrong.

If you knew the real me, you'd see that the truth was a completely different story: I was an imperfect woman. No, imperfect was too nice a word. I was flawed, messed up, maybe had a screw loose.

I was thirty years old, chronically single, and barely making ends meet. I was effectively an orphan: my father died when I was eleven, and though my mother was still alive, my relationship with her was on life-support. I had a theory that my mother was cursed. Like maybe she'd sold her soul to a crossroads demon to get the perfect man—my dad—but once she lost him, she had to pay up by remarrying his exact opposite. My stepfather, Harry Hardin, was a monster, and his son, Tyler, was a chip off the old block. My mother and I had been estranged since I was seventeen, when my stepbrother tried to hurt me, and she'd sided with Tyler over me, her own flesh and blood.

I also had no boyfriend, husband, or lover. I'd never had the best luck with men, so while I wasn't surprised that I'd made it to thirty with no significant other, it was depressing. My friends tried to reassure me that I was pretty, but I'd never liked my appearance. My complexion was patchy, and I often chewed my nails. While my frame was slender, my breasts were designed for a 1950s pinup girl, and without other curves to compliment my boobs, I was top-heavy and out of proportion. My boring, straight hair refused to pick a lane—depending on the day it was either as dry as a scarecrow's armpit hair or so oily that you could fry up a batch of popcorn shrimp on my scalp.

I wasn't confident about dating and had trouble letting my guard down. There'd only been one guy that I thought might be "the one," but I was young and stupid when I knew him, and he didn't feel the same way about me. I'd built up a lot of walls since then, and had settled into knowing that I'd probably be single forever.

When I was little, I loved to try on my mother's wedding dress and pretend that I was getting married. I married my teddy bears, my Ken dolls, and even a life-sized Halloween scarecrow decoration. I was obsessed with writing out my vows, and each pretend wedding had a new set of vows that'd I'd recite, and my mom would sometimes read the vows for my imaginary husband.

I'd given up on the fake marriage thing but still had the habit of writing out vows when I needed to work something out or make a change in my life. My most recent ones were stuck to my refrigerator door, held up by a pink flower magnet. They read:

*Susana Starling, do you vow to make your own way in life
and not rely on your family name to become successful?
-I do.
Susana Starling, do you vow to never settle for a man who
doesn't fully excite you, support you, and enchant you?
-I do.
Susana Starling, do you vow to be a single, strong, indepen-
dent, and self-supporting woman?
-I do.*

THE SOUND of bubbling brought my attention back to my stove, and the pot on the burner. Food and cooking kept me distracted enough that I didn't linger on my dreary romantic life. I was a personal chef by day, and I moonlighted as a cooking instructor for kids. "Personal chef" sounded glamorous, but that was only if you were the wealthy client—my days in other people's kitchens were long and my earnings were mediocre.

I'd been trying to come up with a new menu for class, and it was such a pain in the ass that everything else was cleared from my mind. I was playing around with an insolent risotto that sputtered over the gas flame on my stove. It started out innocent enough: arborio rice, chicken broth, onion, garlic, olive oil, just simmering away, but it was a devil in disguise. This was my third attempt at trying to make a kid's version of a complicated and arduous dish and I should've known better; risotto was Satan's spawn in grain form.

The sticky mess might make an excellent wallpaper paste—I had a bathroom that needed a makeover. I was about to turn off the burner when the knock came at my door. Four clear knocks, not so loud that I'd think the visitor was in a panic, but not the casual knock of a friend. Authoritative. Unignorable. I rested the wooden spoon across the top of the pot.

I only had three regular visitors, if by "regular," you meant once in a blue moon. Two of them were my cousins, and one of them was Mrs. Jenkins from the house next door, who sometimes wandered over to show me one of her new tattoos. "Takes longer to ink this saggy skin than it did when I was your age," she liked to say, but really she wanted to know what I was cooking, and if she could have a taste.

My cousins Sebastian and Simon Starling dropped by less often than Mrs. Jenkins, but I was always glad to see them, even if they did annoy me. All of us were only children, but they were like brothers to me, especially because our fathers were identical triplets.

It couldn't have been Sebastian. Bash usually crashed right in, using his spare key if he remembered to bring it, but nine times out of ten he'd pound on the door with his fists and loudly sing my name until I let him in or until Mrs. Jenkins came over to investigate the ruckus.

And it couldn't have been Simon. He would've sent an email one week in advance of his visit. Plus a reminder text and maybe a last-minute confirmation via his secretary to make sure his scheduled stop-in was still on my calendar.

There was silence from the other side of the door. No singing, no more knocking, no friendly voice calling out. Goosebumps fanned out over my skin, my scalp tingled, and my pulse quickened. Whoever was out there, whatever was out there, it wasn't good.

I slid the chain lock out of its track, braced the toe of my Converse against the base of the door, and cracked it open. I saw a young man, probably twenty years old. He was standing at a polite distance, like a door-to-door salesman. I opened the door a bit wider but kept my foot pressed against it just in case. He wore a zipped up black leather jacket, dark tailored pants, expensive shoes. Skin soft, eyes bright, not a hair out of place. His pristine appearance was in stark contrast with my front porch and its peeling paint, broken rocking chair, and sun-bleached garden gnome. A document peeked out from between his fingers. My stomach dropped.

"Susana Starling?" he asked. Was I about to be served? If I didn't admit who I was, could I shut the door and avoid taking possession of that paper in his hand? My tongue was stuck, and my jaw refused to move. I nodded. "This is for you." He waved the letter and the paper flapped in the air like an injured bird. I recognized that stationery. Ecru cotton parchment with deckled edges. Handmade in Italy, and most likely embossed with a gleaming starling on the bottom right corner. It was folded into thirds and sealed with a petite golden wax bird. "It's urgent."

My fingers shook as I gave in and moved to accept the delivery. He pushed the note into my hand, gave a tiny nod, spun around, and hopped down my front steps. He disappeared into a sleek black car waiting at the curb which drove off as silent as a ghost.

I slammed the door and leaned against it for support, fanning myself with the letter as I tried to catch my breath. The smell of lemons and roses wafted into my face. My mother's scent. I wanted to drop the paper. Burn the paper. Drown the paper. I wanted to bury the paper in my garden, feed it to the birds, rip it into a thousand tiny bits and throw it up into the air like confetti. I was holding a note obviously straight from Starling Manor.

It looked like I'd be advancing right to the boss battle with this personal demon. Fine. I'd read the letter. Then I'd destroy it however I wanted, and I'd pour some wine. A lot of wine. Something dark red and heavy. Bloody. Maybe a Zinfandel.

I tore off the wax seal and let the little starling fall to my feet. The letter was thick and soft with a luxurious weight. I unfolded it and saw a handwritten message. The script was small and tight. Reserved. Not the exaggerated ornamental style of my mother's handwriting.

My Dear Susana,
I regret to inform you of the death of your mother. She died
in her sleep on Friday, April 27th. Please accept my condo-
lences. The reading of Helen's Last Will and Testament will
be May 1st at 10:00 a.m. at the Starling Estate. Your pres-
ence is strongly requested. Please.
Yours truly,
Edward Jagger
Head of House, Starling Manor

MY MOTHER WAS DEAD. I didn't know whether to cry tears of sadness or ones of relief. But no tears came at all, which was good, because I didn't want to trigger a migraine. I felt numb. I took a full breath, and then another. For the first time in a long while I felt like I could breathe all the way in, and all the way out . . . until I realized that this meant that I'd have to go back home to Starling Manor. Jag would be there, and I missed him. But so would Harry Hardin, and I'd rather pull out my fingernails one by one than see my stepfather again. Tyler might be there, too, but I wasn't scared of my asshole stepbrother anymore.

Something caught in my stomach. A rolling, twisting, slightly achy, slightly excited feeling. That was probably my gut wondering if Gabriel Green was still the groundskeeper on staff. I hadn't seen him since I was seventeen, and he was nineteen, and we'd planned to meet for our first official date. But Gabe never showed up, never followed up. We never spoke again. Sometimes I still wondered what I'd done wrong—but I suspected the wrong thing was just me. I was never Ms. Right, so there'd never be a Mr. Right.

A gurgling sound from my stove broke me out of my trance. I tossed the letter onto my kitchen table and returned to the risotto. It was clumpy and gluey and stuck to the side of the pot. Ruined. Forget the food—it was time for the wine.

2

GABE

Starling Manor was a goddamn madhouse. It hadn't been a well-oiled machine of riches and glamour for a long time, though the other staff and I kept it together the best we could. But once Helen Starling died, all hell broke loose.

Starling Manor, tucked into the hills of central Massachusetts, was called Maddix Mansion back when it was built at the turn of the 20th century. Even at a hulking 15,000 square feet it'd been considered a mere vacation cottage by the Maddix family who'd made insane money in shipping, then railroads, then publishing, or some combination like that. Eventually the house became the love nest for Quentin Maddix and Sadie Starling back in the 1950s, and the rest was history.

I was part of a skeleton crew of holdovers from the glory days of the estate. The grounds, gardens, and pool were my domain. I'd just turned thirty-two, and I was the youngest of the main staff. Arthur Jagger, a stately guy who never lost his cool no matter who was messing with him, was Head of House. Jeffrey Tan, ten years older than me and my best friend at the manor, was the chef. We had extra help depending on the time of year, and if there were any special events going on. Sometimes there were drivers, gardeners, waiters, and service staff. Last, and definitely least, was Mrs. Skinner, the head housekeeper. She had an eternal scowl planted on her face, and her upper lip was short and pulled tight, giving her the look of a deranged rabbit. A revolving door of maids shifted through her shit show of a service. Only the meanest and nastiest new hires made it more than a few weeks with Skinner; birds of a feather.

The most recent maid caught in Skinner's web was named Ella. She showed up in March, around the time of the last big blizzard of the season. I was clearing snow from the front walk when she was dropped off with two suitcases and an overload of positivity. I caught her gazing at the manor with such unguarded awe and admiration that I knew she was in trouble—Skinner always squashed the hopeful ones the hardest. Ella was super cute: honey blond hair that fell in waves over her shoulders, happy blue eyes that glittered in the bright light of the snow and sun, and a generous friendly smile. Not really my type, but she was definitely Harry Hardin's type, even though he was forty years her senior and married. None of that mattered to Harry, who took what he wanted, when he wanted it, with little regard for feelings or consent. Harry thought of himself as "the man of the house" but "maniacal despot" was more accurate.

"I'll get your bags," I told Ella as her ride pulled away.

"Thank you so much! I'm so excited to be here!" Her cheeks were pink from the brisk air. I wanted to tell her to get back in the taxi and run away while she still had the chance, and I should've. You'd think by now I'd know to go with my gut.

Because Harry was married to Helen Starling, who'd inherited her late husband's wealth and estate, Harry took that to mean that the whole Starling kingdom was his to rule, especially as Helen got weaker and sicker. He was sometimes accompanied by his son, Tyler, who fancied himself Prince Charming, but was more Lord Fuckhead in my book.

The worst part, though, and the part I'd never get over, never forgive, was that Harry killed my father. That night was seared in my memory. It had been storming and windy, and sheets of rain swept across our cottage windows, the sharp drops clicking against the glass like a thousand skeletal fingers drumming against the glass, waiting to be let in. Our phone rang and my dad, sore from a long day's work, groaned as he pulled himself out of his comfortable chair.

"You're sure about that? I just checked the satellite dish last week and everything looked good," my dad said into the receiver. I could hear Harry bellow something in response, and my dad sighed as he hung up the phone. "Gotta run to the main house, son. Be back in a few."

"In this weather? What's that asshole want now?"

"Says the picture is fuzzy on his TV."

"Screw his picture. Don't go over there, dad. I'll go." I stood up and went to get my boots that were thrown by the front door."

"I wanted to get something from the big kitchen anyway. You stay here, son. I'll be back soon."

But he didn't come back that night. He went to the hospital instead, after he'd fallen off the roof, broken two vertebrae, fractured his leg, crushed his collar bone, and sustained a brain injury that he never really recovered from. A few years later, he had a heart attack, and his body wasn't strong enough to survive it.

I'd hate Harry for the rest of my days. And for the record, the picture wasn't fuzzy. Harry was so drunk that he'd just forgotten to put on his glasses.

A WEEK AFTER ELLA ARRIVED, I was in the back hall on my way to the kitchen when I heard a muted crying coming from the linen closet. Mrs. Skinner was on her hands and knees in front of the closet door scrubbing away at a spot on the floor like her life depended on it.

"What are you doing?" I asked her.

"Don't you have some worms to feed?"

"My compost is coming along nicely, thanks for asking." I took a closer look at the floor. It was immaculate. Pristine. She was up to something. I heard another cry from the closet, and something bumped against the inside of the door.

Tiny beads of sweat popped up on Skinner's forehead.

"Torturing kittens in there?"

"Get out of here if you know what's good for you," she hissed through clenched teeth. Maybe she *was* torturing kittens.

I scooted her aside with my leg and she toppled over on the slick parquet floor. I grabbed the doorknob while Mrs. Skinner clutched my leg and tried to pull me back.

"Stop it, you ogre!" She was no match for me, and I opened the door. Harry Hardin tumbled out and the stench of scotch-sour breath settled on me like a toxic cloud. Of course.

"Jesus, Harry, were you jerking off in the closet?" It just took me a second to see what Harry was actually doing. In the back of the linen room, cowering between a pile of perfectly folded white towels and crisp sheets, was Ella. Her hair was matted against her forehead and a few buttons of her uniform shirt were undone. "Christ! Are you hurt?" I pulled Ella to me, and she buried her face in my chest.

"I'm ok," she said, the words catching in her throat. "I think."

I pushed past Skinner, who'd gone back to her scrubbing, and past Harry, who was lying on the floor like he'd just decided to take a leisurely siesta. His eyes were glassy and his mouth hung open a little; I could see his tongue rolling around like a lazy slug. I kicked at him as I passed, a little harder than I needed to, but he didn't seem to notice.

"Goodbye, Stella!" He gurgled, and then grabbed Mrs. Skinner's leg and snuggled up like it was his favorite teddy bear.

. . .

I STAYED by Ella's side as she went to her room and packed up those two suitcases. I gave her my number and the business card of a lawyer I knew in the city.

"I just want to go," she'd told me. "I don't need the numbers. Harry didn't put his hands on me."

"He trapped you in there! And he was going to put his hands on you."

"He was too drunk to even keep his balance. I'm ok, really. Thank you, though. Thank you for everything." The bright look in her eyes was long gone, replaced with a flat, hesitant gaze.

It was my fault. I should've kept a better watch. Should've protected her. As usual, I'd failed to keep someone safe.

THERE HADN'T BEEN any Harry incidents since that one, but Jag, Jeff, and I tried to keep a close watch. Helen never came out of her bedroom anymore, and Harry took off for a few weeks with his buddies for a trip to Vegas, or Reno, or some kind of sin city where he'd fit right in. Totally on-brand for Harry Hardin to leave his wife's side as she withered away. The word around the house was that it was lymphoma, but Helen didn't want to see doctors, seek treatment, or talk about it. She just kept drinking, kept popping pills, and kept herself locked away in her room.

Jag had knocked on the door of my cabin on Friday, so early in the morning that it was still dark out and no birds were singing.

"Jag? What's up?" I was groggy and hazy and rubbed my eyes to clear my vision.

Jag wore a dark overcoat, and he held up a lantern that cast a haunted glow over the scene. The lantern was battery operated, but it still gave him the look of some 19th century nobleman wandering the paths of his estate.

"It's Helen."

He didn't need to say anything else. I pulled on a hoodie and stepped into the pair of jeans I'd left on the floor before I went to bed, and then I followed Jag up to the main house while his little lantern light cast a spotted glow on the pathway. The manor staff gathered on the front porch and were silent in the low light. Two ambulances and a coroner's van were parked in the circle drive. The front doors to the house swung open as EMTs carried a covered stretcher to their rig.

"Things are about to change, aren't they?" I asked Jag.

The lines on his face seemed deeper and darker in the shadows of the night. "More than you know."

IN THE FOLLOWING DAYS, there was an endless stream of visitors, but none of them were Helen's people. Her friends had fallen away as she got more reclusive, and the ones that did still try to visit were turned away at the door by Mrs. Skinner.

Back when Helen was healthier, she hosted occasional gatherings for her friends, who all drove Audis, Volvos, BMWs, and a Japanese car here and there. But after Helen's death, it was just the pristine Bentleys, Cadillacs, Lincolns, and Range Rovers that snaked up the driveway. They belonged to Harry's asshole cronies who gathered, drank, toasted Harry, and even broke out in song like they were at a bachelor party instead of in the home of a bereaved widower.

ON THE SUNDAY after Helen's death, a hired messenger boy arrived at the manor. From my vantage point in the yard, I watched him hop up the front steps, two at a time. Jag handed him a paper and no words passed between them. The young man got behind the wheel of a house car that was running and ready, and drove away, quickly disappearing down the long driveway.

I walked to the front porch to speak to Jag and the pathway stones crunched under my boots. "What was that for?"

Jag rested his gaze on me, as if trying to decide whether or not to loop me in on the latest. "For Susana."

How could that one word, *Susana*, make me feel like I'd had the wind knocked out of me, like I'd had three double shots of whiskey, and like I'd had a thousand sweetly sharp fingernails scrape down every inch of my skin?

"Are you alright?" he asked.

Just the mention of Susana's name took me out at the knees. Most days I tried to push her to the back of my mind. It'd been a long time since I'd spoken to her . . . ok, it'd been twelve years, nine months, and maybe three days . . . give or take. I'd spotted her a few times at Starling Manor and had looked her up online from time to time. But I'd seen her more often than that in my mind, with her straight black hair that looked like it was spun from dark chocolate and fireflies; her eyes a sharp gray that was translucent in the sunshine and steely in the dark; her full lips which were slow to smile unless I got her laughing.

I could remember Susana in her green swimsuit when she'd floated on her back in the pool, years ago. Her body stretched out, her breasts pushing at the fabric, water moving in ripples around her perfect form . . . I felt my jeans get tighter as my dick started to stiffen. Great. This was exactly why I wasn't allowed to think about Susana.

"Gabriel," Jag interrupted my daydream.

"What?"

"I asked if you were alright."

"Sure," I lied. "Totally fine."

"Good. Because you need to be ready."

"For what?"

"Like I said last night, things are about to change."

3

SUSANA

What did one wear to the reading of one's estranged mother's last will and testament? I packed a suitcase bigger than an overnight bag, but smaller than what I'd take for a weeklong vacation. My hands trembled as I stuffed an extra sweater into my bag and tugged on the sticky zipper. I'd gone with a long sleeved emerald green dress that stretched across my chest and flared at the waist. Tall brown boots and a tan cardigan because the morning was still cool.

I wasn't exactly sure why I'd been invited back to the estate. In our semi-yearly phone calls, my mom always made it clear that I wasn't in the line of succession, especially if I was still single. She was obsessed with my relationship status, and it was always the first thing she asked about. I didn't know why she placed such a high value on marriage—she would've been so much better off without Harry, the stepfather from hell.

On Sunday evening, a few hours after I received the note about my mother's death, my cell phone rang. The main number for Starling Manor showed on my screen which sent a zap of adrenaline through my nervous system. My rational mind knew that it wasn't my mother calling, but it still felt like a haunting.

It was Mr. Jagger on the other end of the line, and his familiar voice was calm, even, and reassuring. As we spoke, my shoulders relaxed, my fists unclenched, and my pulse evened out. Talking to Jag infused me with a comfort I didn't realize I'd needed. Then I thought about my stepdad, and I went right back to feeling tense.

"Does Harry know I'm coming?" I'd asked Jag.

"He's been made aware."

"How'd that go over?"

"As one would expect."

"So, a lot of swear words, some stomping around, and maybe a broken plate or two?" I heard Jag exhale a small laugh.

"Something like that."

"Jag, you're not giving me anything here. Are you being held hostage? Are they forcing you to make this call? Clear your throat if I should call the police!"

"As entertaining as ever."

"I have a reputation to uphold."

"It's wonderful to hear your voice, Susana. I'll send a car to pick you up at eight AM on Tuesday. Why don't you plan on spending two nights here."

"First of all, I can drive myself. I'm a thirty-year-old woman now, not a panicked teenager. And why would I need to spend the night?" The last time Jag had arranged a ride for me, I'd been running away from home.

"I know you can drive yourself, but I'd rather you not have to worry about that. And there may be a few details to sort out after the meeting, so I wanted to give you advance notice."

"What kind of details?"

"I should know more in the next few days." Jag cleared his throat.

"I'm assuming you don't need me to call the police, but are there people nearby listening to this conversation?"

"That's correct."

I didn't want to get off the phone. Having him on the other

line made me feel safe. But it would be weird to ask him to just stay on the line. "Alright. I'll see you Tuesday. I've missed you."

"And I you. Thank you for agreeing to come. Goodbye, Susana."

TWO DAYS LATER, that conversation with Jag still echoed in my head. I rolled my suitcase to the front door and rested my shoulder bag next to it on the floor. I realized I was chewing on my fingernail, and I pulled my hand away from my mouth.

What I hadn't asked Jag was if Gabe knew I was coming. But of course Gabe knew, right? Everyone knew everything around that house. But how did he feel about it? Did he remember me? Did he think of me? Did he feel bad for standing me up for our date, leaving me alone and waiting in the gardener's shed, like a stupid sitting duck for Tyler Hardin? Sure, it was possible I was twisting the narrative a little—I'd replayed that summer so many times in my head that I was no longer sure what was fact and what was fiction. The memory had started out like a pencil sketch, but my rumination was like a heavy marker I used to trace those lines again and again. I'd created an indelible mental mess.

I had such fond feelings for Gabe along with so much anger. It was a strange emotional cocktail and it made me feel unbalanced.

Four sharp knocks on my front door snapped me out of my daydream. Mr. Spiffy Hair Messenger Boy was back on my front porch with his black jacket and idling car.

"You ready, Ms. Starling?" He lifted my ten-ton suitcase as if it only weighed a pound.

"Ready." It was a total lie, but I followed him down the steps and toward the car that would take me back home.

THE DRIVE PASSED QUICKLY. In the hour or so it took to get to the manor, I'd distracted myself with thoughts of food. I came up with recipe ideas for the kids' cooking class (risotto was not on the list) and I worked on my proposal for my *Green Kids Grow* project where I hoped to mentor a group of local kids and help them plant, tend, and harvest their own food in a community garden. There were only two lots available for service projects, and there were twenty applications. I wanted to get that started and develop it into a Green Kids Grow for schools, where kids could grow food in school gardens and serve it in their cafeterias. If I could get that plan off the ground, I'd run the cooking portion of the program and turn the gardening over to more capable leaders.

Despite my love of food, I didn't inherit my father's green thumb. I figured I could manage to keep a basic garden alive, so I'd give it my best shot. I sketched a plan for the plot—carrots, beets, and onions underground, broccoli, peas, and tomatoes above, three varieties of lettuce for greens, parsley, basil, and mint for starter herbs. Maybe add some marigolds, a pumpkin, sunflowers, and leave a spot open for extra ideas from the kids. I got lost in coloring the burnt orange leaves of a sunflower, and when I looked up from the page, my former home loomed in the distance. If I hadn't been full of mixed emotions and complicated memories about the place, I would've found it beautiful.

Fashioned after a seventeenth century English country house, Starling Manor was stately, but also warm. Three stories high, it sat proudly atop a rolling hill and was surrounded by acres of woods. The white stucco exterior was complemented by the dark green shutters that graced its sixty windows. Spring was in full bloom and the lushness of the grounds overwhelmed me as we approached the mansion from the long driveway. I'd spent so much time remembering all my bad times at the estate that I'd forgotten how enchanting it could be. The gardens, the paths, the pool—I couldn't think about that pool without also thinking of Gabe and our midnight swims and long talks. The winding halls, the secret dormers, the library—those were magical places.

The car pulled up to the front of the house and tears built up in my eyes when I saw Jag. He was standing by himself, handsome in a dark, perfectly tailored suit, waiting for me. The last time I'd seen him, his brown hair had flecks of white, but now it was pure silver. He had some extra lines on his forehead, but his eyes were still kind.

Jag opened my door, and I jumped into his arms and buried my face in his chest, trying not to get any tears on his very expensive lapel. I was realizing that so many of the feelings I'd flushed down the emotional toilet were not actually dead and gone. Jag was the closest thing I'd had to a father for the last twenty years of my life, and holding on to him made me feel a little less like the orphan I was—could you be an orphan if you were an adult?

Jag stepped back and offered me a handkerchief embroidered with a silver starling. I wiped my eyes, blew my nose, and dropped the cloth into my bag, which the driver had placed at my feet. He took my hands in his.

"It's wonderful to see you, Susana. You look lovely."

"You're sweet, but also a liar. How bad is my make-up?"

"You look perfect. Nothing out of place." Jag nodded at the driver, who got back into the car and drove toward the garage. We were alone on the driveway and the house cast a shadow over us in the morning sun. "I have something for you. We need to be quick." He was speaking quietly, and his voice was low and serious.

He reached into his jacket pocket and pulled out something shiny and small. "I'm going to put this on your finger, but don't look down. Keep looking at my face and don't draw attention to your hand." Jag held my gaze and slipped something onto my left ring finger. "This was a ring that belonged to your grandmother, Sadie Starling." The manor doors opened, and a few staff members descended the stairs. "I don't have time to explain. Just promise that you won't remove this ring while you're here. I'll tell you more when I can, but for now, follow my lead."

The ring had a brilliant pear-shaped diamond flanked by two

rubies. The band, white gold, or platinum, probably, shone brightly.

"I don't understand—"

"Well, if it isn't the little lost starling!" Harry Hardin was suddenly upon me and pushed his way between me and Jag. His cheeks were ruddy and his hefty belly pushed against his shirt, giving his buttons a real workout. His voice was thick and hot and tiny specks of spittle hit my face as he spoke. "Come give Daddy a hug," he said, opening his arms wide.

"Go away, Harry." I backed away, but he closed the gap between us.

Jag stepped toward him, but Harry pushed him in the chest, causing Jag to stumble backwards.

"I don't know why you're here, but I've read the will. If you think you're going to swoop in and gather up some kind of inheritance, you've wasted your time. There's nothing for you." Harry grinned at me, revealing teeth that were stained and tiny, like he never lost his baby teeth.

I retrieved Jag's handkerchief from my bag and slowly dabbed Harry's spittle off my face. I hoped that he didn't see how my hand was shaking. "Just paying my respects."

Harry leaned toward me, his breath was sour and sharp. "Nobody respects you, so why don't you get the hell out of—"

Harry swallowed his words with a ragged gasp. A new man had joined our huddle, had wedged himself between me and Harry, and by the looks of things, had punched Harry in the stomach.

"Speak to her like that again—," new guy growled. His back was to me, and he was so tall that all I could see was the back of his suit jacket inches away from my face. Fancy Italian wool. These guys had some nice clothes. "—and I'll pull out your tongue and stick it up your ass."

"Fuck you, Green," Harry spat. He grabbed his belly and tried to stand up straight but couldn't manage it.

Green? Oh shit. Oh god. Gabriel Green was standing inches

away from me and had just threatened to perform a glossectomy on my stepdad. I smelled sandalwood. And grass. And a touch of vanilla. My stomach flipped. It was Gabe alright. The scent of him woke up my memories and feelings and, oh Christ, he was turning around.

If any part of me had believed that my attraction to Gabe was gone, past tense, old news—that part was a filthy liar. His deep brown eyes. His hair the color of dark wheat kissed with gold. His broad chest under a crisp blue shirt. His lips . . . oh wow, his lips. Grown up Gabriel Green was a god, and I was in serious trouble.

Gabe touched my arm gently and leaned closer. The vibrations of his voice were still moving through my bones like some kind of aftershock. Everything about his face was utterly new and devastatingly familiar. "Hey there, Sunny." His voice was like hot honey over my skin. He remembered my nickname. He gave me a half smile and his eyes were soft and sweet. He dipped his head toward mine and a lock of hair fell across his forehead. He leaned in, close to my ear, and then he spoke again. "Long time no see."

4

GABE

*L*ong *time no see?* I was finally next to Susana Starling after years of wondering about her and that's the best I could do? My lizard brain was in charge after the confrontation with Harry, and I had to calm down and get my shit together. I'd promised myself that I'd keep my distance from Susana. My pride was still hurt from what happened when we were young. It was stupid to hold on to something for that long, but in my life as a loner, I'd had a lot of time to ruminate.

When I'd watched her arrival from the safety of a front window, the sight of her, in that dress the color of a perfect summer lawn, took my breath away. Sweat started to prickle all over—one look at Susana's long black hair and how that dress hugged her chest, and I felt those familiar sparks of attraction and arousal.

But when I saw Harry approaching Susana, all the promises I'd made to myself went out the window. I'd rushed outside and got there just in time to hear Harry spouting some vile bullshit. But now Harry was gone, and I was inches away from Susana and had kicked off our reunion with a vapid greeting.

She raised her chin and I got a look at her eyes up close for the first time in so long. They were still the color of the Atlantic Ocean —a ragged gray with flecks of green and blue. A few freckles dotted the bridge of her nose, and her mouth was so close that if I leaned forward just a little, I could—

"Hey there, Archie."

I felt blood rush to my face. She used to think it was funny that my name was Gabriel, like the Archangel. She called me Angel for a while, and then it slid into Archie. I always told her not to call me that, which only made her say it more. The wicked little grin on her face let me know that she knew exactly what she was doing. And, to be honest, it always delighted me that she'd made up a name for me, though I never admitted that to her.

"We need to go inside. It's time." Jag's voice brought me back to Earth.

Susana and I straightened up and pulled away, like we'd been caught making out. The three of us walked up the stone steps together, a trio of long-lost friends. The swell of emotion in my chest caught me off guard. We were finally back together in the place where it'd all started, but we were about to get wiped out. Rumor had it that Helen Starling had left everything to Harry Hardin. The estate, the accounts, the cars—all of it. That was insane to me, because all of Helen's money came from the Starling family, which was Susana's paternal line. How could Helen leave it to her second husband? Harry would destroy Starling Manor, either by letting it fall to ruin or selling it for parts. I only had one year left to work at the estate—once I turned thirty-three, I'd inherit my own little bungalow on the gulf coast, and I was out of here. But I'd given a lot of good years to this place, as had my father before me, and it sucked to think about it ending up in Harry's control.

WE FILED into the dining room and took our places at the long table where nine bottles of water were set out, one for each attendee. Helen's attorney, Yvonne James, was seated at the head of the table with her paralegal to her right. Harry Hardin sat at the other end of the table, flanked by his personal attorney. Mrs. Skinner and Jeffrey were on one long side, and Susana and I sat across from them, with Jag between us.

"We're all here, so let's get started." Yvonne's voice was smooth and confident. I'd seen her around the manor a few times in the year leading up to Helen's death, but only when Harry was out of town—probably didn't want to get hassled by that asshole. "There will be no formal reading of Helen's will today. It's not customary to have a full reading, and we have copies for each of you here." She pointed to a stack of folders. "You may go over them with your legal representatives as needed."

"I don't know why there are so many folders," Harry said. "Seems like there should just be one big one for me!" He barked out a laugh that echoed in the high-ceilinged room.

"Everyone here is a beneficiary or is directly involved in the terms of the will." Yvonne gestured toward the folders. "We'll pass these around in a moment, but I need to make a clarification before doing so." Yvonne cleared her throat and shuffled through a notebook like she was stalling for time. I rested my arms on the table so I could glance down at Susana, who was on the other side of Jag. Her hands were restless and as she tapped her fingers together, I saw the telltale jagged edges of a fingernail—she must've still had the habit of chewing her nails. Then I saw what Susana had on her finger. She was fiddling with a spectacular diamond and ruby ring. Clearly an engagement ring. My gut clenched. Fuck.

Yvonne continued. "I wanted everyone to be on the same page with these initial communications." She nodded at her assistant who stood and started handing out the folders. "You may be aware of Helen's will from December 2017, which names Harry Hardin as the trustee for the Starling Trust, which owns the estate, most of Helen's accounts, and other assets."

Harry smirked at Susana, who missed it because she was looking down at her hands. At that stupid ring on her finger.

"However, Helen filed a more updated will in September of 2023."

Susana stopped twisting the ring on her finger. Jeff froze with his water bottle halfway to his lips. Mrs. Skinner's mouth fell open, and mine may have done the same thing. Harry's eyes were bulging and his attorney was frantically leafing through his folder. Only Jag sat perfectly still.

"The newer will has been notarized and verified. It presents some drastic changes from the 2017 will, so I wanted everyone to be here so I could answer your questions in person." Yvonne took several sips of her water.

"How drastic?" Harry did not look pleased.

"It names Susana Starling as the sole trustee, but there are stipulations."

"What stipulations?" Harry stood up so fast that his chair toppled over. His lawyer tugged at his sleeve, but Hardin swatted him away.

Yvonne read from her copy of the will, "You'll see on page four, second paragraph, where it states,

'For my daughter, Susana Starling, to become the full and sole trustee of the Starling Family Trust, she must meet four requirements:

1. *She must be entered into a legitimate marriage within thirty days of receiving notice of my wishes if she is not already married at the time of my death.*
2. *She must remain married for one year following my death.*
3. *She must live, with her spouse, at Starling Manor for one year following my death. They must take up residence in the north wing.*

4. *She must keep all Heads of Staff employed for the first
    year after my death unless the staff members wish to
    resign.*

*If these requirements are met, Susana Starling will be the full trustee
one year and one day after my death. If these requirements are not
met, the terms of my December 2017 will and testament shall be
reinstated. If my husband, Harold Hardin, is still alive at the time
of my death, and my daughter, Susana Starling, agrees to my stipulations, Mr. Hardin may not reside at the estate while Ms. Starling
is in residence. Arthur Jagger will serve as interim Trustee until
either Susana Starling or Harold Hardin takes on the full role.'"*

Harry started laughing. He picked up his chair off the floor,
rolled it back up to the table, and sat down. He laughed so hard
that fat tears rolled out of his beady eyes. "Leave it to Helen to play
a joke like this." He pulled out a handkerchief and dabbed his eyes.
"Well, little Miss Starling. You're not married, and you never will
be, so I guess we can get back to business at the grown-ups' table."

Susana's chest rose and fell quickly—there was a chance she
was about to hyperventilate. She tried to speak, "I mean . . . I don't
. . . I'm not . . ." but she couldn't form a complete sentence.

"We know you're not married, Susana, but you are engaged. I
thought you might want to speak to your fiancée about moving up
the wedding," Jag said.

Susana looked at Jag as though he'd just sprouted a second and
third head. "What do you mean?"

"I know this is a shock. And it's a lot to take in."

"Did you know about this, Jagger?" Harry's upper lip trembled, making him look like he was snarling. I expected him to drool
at any moment.

"I was generally aware. Helen asked me if I would stand as
interim trustee if she filed a new will. I was not filled in on all the
specifics."

"Bullshit! This won't hold up in court! This is a scam, and you're trying to steal all my money!" Harry pounded both fists on the table, but no one jumped. "Right, Wilson?" Harry's lawyer refused to look him in the eye. He was still flipping through the pages.

"The updated will is legal and binding. It is up to Ms. Starling concerning whether she would like to accept the terms of the new will. You can take your time, and don't have to give an answer right now," said Yvonne.

"Clock is ticking, you little—," Harry stood up again, and I stood up too, ready for whatever bullshit he served next. "You're not even engaged, are you?"

Susana looked at Jag and then looked at her ring. He nodded just the tiniest bit. Why was this such a mystery? She had a huge ring right there on her finger. She was engaged—why was everyone acting so weird? Unless . . . that ring looked familiar. Then it hit me. The portrait in the library of Sadie Starling, Susana's paternal grandmother, after her engagement to Malcom Maddix. She was wearing that ring. Had Jag given Susana the ring this morning? I felt both elated and sick. Elated because maybe there was no other man, but sick because we were right back where we started with Harry Hardin slated to be the destroyer of everything we all held dear. Harry and I were still standing, and Susana took a big breath.

"No, I am." her voice was quiet. She tried again. "I am. I'm engaged."

"Oh yeah?" Harry wasn't going to let this go. "Who's the lucky guy?"

A dark blush spread over her face. I wanted to help her. I wanted to save her. I wanted to fix this for everyone. I felt a sharp pinch on my left leg. Jag's hand was near my thigh, poised to pinch again. He was looking straight at me, right into my eyes like he was trying to hypnotize me. Was everyone on drugs today? Then I figured it out. Maybe I wasn't firing on all cylinders, but I got there eventually: Susana wasn't engaged. And our only chance was me.

Maybe for once, I could make something right, and this time, I was going with my gut. Screw the consequences.

Harry yelled across the table again. "Cat got your tongue, Susana?

It was my turn to pound my fist on the table. I slammed my hand down, causing everyone to jump. "I warned you not to speak that way to my fiancée, Hardin. *I'm* the lucky guy. She's marrying me. So back the fuck off."

5

SUSANA

"I won't do it."

"You won't do what?" Gabe loosened his tie and ripped it off his neck like he had a personal vendetta against the thing. He tossed it onto an end table, shook off his suit jacket and plopped down into an overstuffed chair. Jag made sure the library door was shut firmly before joining us in the sitting area.

"I won't jump through these marriage hoops just to play whatever insane game my mom set in motion. And why'd you do that, Gabe?" My neck was itchy. I looked through my purse for a hair tie but couldn't find one.

"Why did I claim to be the future Mr. Starling?"

"You blurted that out and now you've made things difficult." I pulled my long hair off my neck and tried to twist it into a bun, but it slid out immediately. This was pointless. And also, no amount of messing with my hair was going to distract me from what had just happened.

"*I've* made things difficult?" Gabe's glare was intense.

I was panicking. Not on the outside, but my inner world was alarm bells, flashing lights, total freak-out mode. I could *not* get married. I could *not* live in this house again. And I could *not* commit to being with the man who'd screwed me over, even if the marriage was fake. I'd made vows to myself, and I couldn't break them. "You're *not* my fiancé." I sat on a sleek leather chaise lounge and yanked off my boots. My feet were sweaty and aching.

Gabe glanced at my legs as I took off my boots, but he quickly looked away. He stood and started pacing. "Right." Gabe crossed his arms. "Enlighten us on why you won't temporarily marry me to become, like, a gazillionaire? I know I'm not your type, but am I that bad?"

He *was* my type. And that was a problem. I had a blind spot when it came to Gabriel Green, at least in the past. I'd finally moved on from him, and from Starling Manor, and if I got dragged back in, would I lose myself?

Gabe stopped pacing and stood in front of me with his legs settled into a strong, wide stance. His thighs were prominent even in suit pants and I wondered what he'd look like in a pair of tight jeans. He was roughly unbuttoning his Oxford, revealing a gray undershirt that hugged his chest. No one told me that a striptease was on today's schedule. He stared at me. Why was he staring at me? Shit. He was waiting for me to answer.

"I just can't."

Gabe slid the button-up off his shoulders and the sight of his muscular forearms caused me to lose my train of thought again. Gabe huffed and balled up his shirt in his fist. Had his hands always been that large?

I needed to concentrate. I tried again. "It's not you. I just don't want to have anything to do with my mother's money. Or Harry. Or any of it."

"That's rich," Gabe threw the shirt onto the table with his discarded tie. "So to speak. I didn't know you were that selfish."

"Hey!" Hot tears sprung into my eyes. It hurt, but I wanted him to be meaner. Rougher. The worse he was, the easier it would be to leave this place again.

"Let's take a step back." Jag stepped into the middle of the room. "Susana, please share your reservations."

I smoothed out my dress and tucked my legs underneath me. I held back the tears that were threatening to fall. I took a breath to steady my voice. I couldn't tell them the whole truth, so I went with a partial one. "My mother made it clear that I was never enough. And I'm doing just fine on my own. I don't need . . . any of this."

Gabe clicked his tongue and rolled his eyes.

"Do you have something you want to say, Mr. Green?" I asked. *Be mean. Please.*

"Go ahead, Princess. Don't want to interrupt your pity party."

More words tumbled out of my mouth. I always talked too much when I was nervous. "My mom was always obsessed about me being married. When I was a kid, and when I was an adult. Whenever we spoke on the phone these last few years, all she wanted to know was if I was married. This must be her way of punishing me." My words sounded stupid as I said them, and I hadn't been totally honest. *I* was the one who was obsessed with marriage when I was little, not my mother.

"Is that so?" Gabe's eyes were darker, as if a storm was brewing in his irises. "Maybe I should tell you about the time that—"

"Gabriel. That's enough for now." Jag's voice was stern.

Gabe sat down in the chair again and dropped his feet onto the tufted ottoman. He rubbed his hands across his eyes and then moved them down to his jaw. I wished I didn't have to look at his face. It was hard to concentrate with Mr. Garden God spilling his handsomeness out everywhere.

Gabe spoke again, but in a softer tone. "It's not all about you."

"What do you mean?" My voice sounded pitiful, like I might burst into tears at any moment.

"Just what I said, Sunny."

"Don't call me Sunny."

"Whatever. *Susana.* Have you thought about your cousins?

Your uncles? The people who work here? If *that's* not enough to convince you, have you thought about how the world would be a worse place if Harry Hardin suddenly had this kind of money?"

My mouth went dry. Gabe was right and I didn't want to admit it. I hadn't processed anything other than the feeling of panic that rose up from my belly into my chest when I envisioned having to get married and step back into the Starling family, the Starling name, the Starling way of life.

"I'll take that silence as a no." Gabe sat forward and glanced around the room. "I need a beer."

"I'll get it." Jag crossed the room to the bar that took up the far corner of the library.

"You need to contact Simon and Sebastian, at the very least. They've been here several times over the winter, checking on things," Gabe said.

"They have?" My cousins hadn't mentioned anything to me about visiting my mother. And I hadn't seen my Uncle Miles or Uncle Mitch in a while. They were my father's brothers, and they'd reached out over the years, but they reminded me so much of my dad that it was easier for me to ignore them than to face that pain. I was a terrible niece.

"See? You're totally disconnected from your family. From this place." Gabe rubbed his palms up and down his thighs. Distracting. "Talk to your family. Talk to Jag. Think about this for a minute before you screw over people you love, people who work here, and anyone who has to deal with Hardin. Get your head out of your ass."

"When you put it like that, who wouldn't want to be your wife?"

"I was doing this for you."

"Such a humanitarian. And you don't get anything out of it?" Being shitty to Gabe was easier than letting myself think about liking him.

"I'd get a tender flower of a wife. What man could resist?"

"Piss off, Archie."

"Don't call me Archie."

"Fine, Gabriel Green. You're just taking one for the team."

"I get something out of it: my last year here would be a peaceful one, and Hardin finally gets thrown to the curb. Having the esteemed Susana Starling in the big house instead of that shithead is all the motivation I need."

"About that," said Jag, who'd returned with an open bottle of beer.

"About what?" Gabe grabbed the beer and took several long swigs. Pretty early to be drinking, but I kind of wanted one myself.

"Remember that you would also need to live in the main house for a year. And there are some additional stipulations."

"Stipulations on the stipulations?" Gabe raised his beer in the air. "Cheers to Helen Starling. Causing a stir even though she's dead."

"What do you mean, 'your last year?'" That phrase was echoing in my head and I didn't understand it. I'd assumed Gabe would always work at Starling Manor, just like his dad.

"I head to the Gulf Coast as soon as I turn thirty-three and the paperwork clears."

My stomach dropped. "What's on the Gulf Coast?"

"The world's most beautiful little ocean bungalow. It's been in my family for a long time, but my father rented it out to a corporation for twenty years because we needed that money to survive. Their lease will be up next year, and ownership will revert to me. I've been waiting for this all my life."

"Oh," I said, and tried to smile, but my cheeks weren't cooperating. Of course he didn't want to stay at Starling Manor. Working for an asshole like Harry and always doing someone else's bidding? When would I learn to stop making assumptions about Gabriel Green? I'd assumed he'd liked me and that was wrong. I'd assumed he liked working for my family—also wrong. Maybe I *was* that selfish little rich girl, after all. I'd left home, but maybe you could never take the Starling out of my blood.

"So, these stipulations?" Gabe asked.

"Let me find the paragraph. It's on page twenty-two, I think." Jag flipped through his packet until he found the page. "It says, 'Susana and her spouse must host the Starling Charity Snow Ball, and attend The Starling Christmas weekend at the family cabin. They must submit to approved photo events, accept invitations to social and charity gatherings (at least three in the year after my death), and they must travel to Boston for a minimum of three cultural events within the same year.'"

"I'm out!" Gabe finished his beer with a flourish and stood up. "You're right, Ms. Starling. This was a terrible idea. I rescind my proposal."

My stomach dropped again. This was what I wanted, right? I wanted him to walk away. But why did I feel more panicked than ever? "Scared of a little opera?" The words were out of my mouth before I could think about what I'd said.

"I'm not scared of anything." Gabe draped his jacket over his arm and grabbed his shirt and tie. "But if you're refusing to do this, why should I twist your arm? I do plants. Pools. Not people." Gabe put his empty bottle on the counter of the bar and walked towards the door. "I was willing to do you a favor—to do us all a favor, but it takes two to fake marry. Sorry, Jag. I wasted everyone's time."

This was happening too fast. He needed to wait. Wait until I could get my head around this. "What happened to saving humanity? Don't you want to make Harry Hardin suffer?" I called out.

Gabe stopped walking but he didn't turn around. My pulse was racing, and I wanted to cry, to scream, to punch something, and to run away.

Gabe spun around on one foot, took a few steps, and was suddenly in front of me again. "Stand up."

"What?" He was too close to me. I felt dizzy.

"You heard me. Stand up, Sunny."

"Thought I told you not to call me that." I stood up but we were face to chest, not face to face. I tilted my chin up and took in the sight of his neck, his jawline, his face, so stern. God, he was beautiful.

"I'm not the kind of husband you can boss around."

My knees threatened to buckle. I swallowed, and tried to speak, but my voice came out barely louder than a whisper. "What kind of husband are you?"

Gabe leaned in close and pinched a strand of my hair between two fingers. He slid his hand all the way down my hair, dragged his nail over my collar bone, up my neck, and then gently flicked my earlobe. His lips were close to my ear. "Fuck around and find out."

Gabe headed to the door and gave instructions on his way out. "Sunny, talk to your cousins, don't take that ring off, and meet me tomorrow morning. Nine o'clock, my cottage." He walked out of the library, shutting the door behind him.

I'd vowed to stay single. I'd vowed to never need anyone else. I'd vowed to stay away from all things Starling. I was not a vow breaker. So, what was I supposed to do with this new feeling I had? The feeling that I should run after Gabe, throw myself in his arms, and let him take care of everything? This was not good. Not good at all.

6

GABE

'm a liar.

That's what kept going through my head as I stormed out of the library and away from Susana. I'd said that I wasn't scared of anything. Total bullshit. I was scared of having Harry as my boss for my final year at Starling Manor. Without Helen to protect me, he'd harass me, at best, and more likely, he'd fire me on day one and fuck up all my finances.

I was scared of coming out of the shadows and having to live in the public eye. That went against all my instincts, and I didn't know if I could pull it off.

And most of all, I was scared that if Susana and I went through with this fake marriage, the next year would be pure torture because I'd have to pretend to love a women I really used to have feelings for—a woman who didn't have those same feelings for me, and who'd treated me like shit, in the end.

A few days ago I was confident in my identity as an eternally single, serial first dater, loner, possible hermit, cottage dweller guy. Now I was a maybe engaged, soon-to-be married, mansion magnate, socialite dude? Shoot me now. When I'd announced that Susana was my fiancée, I really *had* done it to get her out of trouble, but in true Gabriel Green form, I'd made more trouble instead.

I took the steps of the grand staircase two at a time. Escape, in the form of fresh air, birdsong, and solitude, was moments away, until Mrs. Skinner blocked my path and crushed my quest for freedom.

"Outta my way." I tried to push past her, but she blocked me with a long broom handle.

She wore her usual uniform: black sneakers, black pants, black tunic with a silver starling on a breast pocket, and an angry scowl on her face. Her hair, which was dyed an urgent shade of red, was coming loose from a painful looking bun that stretched her scalp as tight as a drum. "We know you're lying. Ms. Starling wasn't your fiancée when she got here this morning."

"Who's we? You and the mice that live in the walls?"

"Mr. Hardin knows."

"Harry wouldn't recognize love if it bit him on the ass."

"I'll find proof that you're lying, and we'll destroy you."

"Seems extreme, but you do you. Now, if you'll excuse me." I grabbed the broom from her grip and tossed it aside. A few more hops down the staircase and I was on the main floor, but Harry and his attorney were arguing on the front steps of the manor, so another exit was in order. I had no interest in being the focus of Skinner's surveillance or Hardin's revenge plot. I liked to fly under the radar. There was already too much attention on me, and this whole engagement fiasco was only hours old. I was sneaking past the kitchen with the service entry in my sights when I heard Jeff's voice from the back of the pantry.

"Gabriel Green, get your ass in here."

"Sorry, Chef. I need to get out of here before I lose my shit."

"We need to talk about what happened this morning." Jeff had his arms full of produce: celery, two bunches of carrots, some cucumbers, and a bag of snap peas.

"Not in here, we don't. If you wanna talk, you gotta walk." I opened the back door and the sweet warm air brought me instant relief.

"Wait up." Jeff dumped the vegetables on the counter and shouted some instructions to his kitchen assistant, Patrick. I couldn't make out the specifics because I was already ten paces away on the back sidewalk. "You don't make it easy to love you." Jeff jogged to catch up to me. He removed his apron and folded it over the back of a porch chair on the south patio. "If a bird shits on that, next round's on you."

"I'm not sure that I have many bar nights in the near future. I'll have to check with the missus."

"Shit man, so you're for real with that?"

"I think so. Maybe. I don't know. I'll get back to you."

"Good for you, Green." Jeff punched my arm a little too hard. "I know you've been hung up on that woman for years. Way to just rip off the band-aid."

"I'm not hung up on anyone. I'm a 'no attachments' kind of guy. I'm out of here in a year, and I couldn't fit a bride into that beach hut even if I wanted to. I fly solo, and you know it." We were on the path that led to my cottage, and with each step I felt a little more grounded and a little saner. Branches made a leafy canopy overhead and shrubs and ornamentals crowded in from the side; I felt protected and hidden. When we reached my cottage, I headed straight for the fridge for another beer. "Want one?" I asked Jeff.

"Sorry, I'm on the clock. Technically. And aren't you?"

"I don't know what I am. It's possible that I'm now the man of the house, and your new boss."

Jeff sat down on my couch and put his feet up on the coffee table. He ran his hands through his thick black hair, making it fluff out and stand on end. "When you put it that way, maybe I'll have a few sips of something."

I grabbed a bottle for him, set it down on the table, and sunk down into my favorite chair; a fat brown leather recliner that just screamed *bachelor pad*. "I don't know what I expected when I woke up this morning, but it sure as shit wasn't this." I took a huge sip of my beer. If I kept up this pace, I'd be trashed by dinner time.

"Tell me what's happening." Jeff took a tiny sip of his beer and placed the bottle back on the table.

I filled him in on my library chat with Susana and Jag, leaving out the part about what I whispered in Sunny's ear. If I lingered too long on that memory, of how close her body was to mine, how her lips parted when I flicked her ear lobe, and how I heard a gasp catch in her throat when I spoke to her—I'd make this whole friend chat pretty awkward by sitting here with a raging hard-on.

Jeff listened quietly and rubbed his chin like an old man contemplatively stroking his beard, except Jeff was clean shaven, so the effect was different. I could see that his wheels were turning. "So, if you're in, you're gonna have to go *all* in, right?"

"Right."

"And Skinner'll be around every corner, spying on you and trying to prove that this is all just a lie."

"Right again."

"And you'll have to live in the big house, eat at the big table, and go to the big parties?"

"Don't remind me."

"But it's only for a year, then you can abscond to Florida to live out your bachelor dreams while at the same time you save Starling Manor and stop Harry Hardin from building an evil empire?"

"Maybe."

Jeff raised his bottle to me. "Anything worth doing is worth doing well! And let me know about any dietary restrictions, sir. I speak for the culinary staff when I say that we welcome you to the helm of Starling Manor. Your wish is our command."

I STAYED AWAY from the big house for the rest of the day. Cowardly, but I had shit to do. Get my head straight was at the top of my list, but I also had to deal with some hanging chats on my dating apps. I had a second date planned on Friday with an accountant named Kari.

> Gabe: Hey

Kari: Hey yourself

> Gabe: I hate to do this, but I need to cancel. Late notice. I'm really sorry.

Kari: Hm. Cold feet?

> Gabe: No, really. I was looking forward to it.

Kari: Meet someone else?

> Gabe: I have an engagement that popped up

Kari: An engagement

> Gabe: Yeah

Kari: Raincheck?

> Gabe: Not sure. I might be getting married.

Kari: LOL. Right.

> Gabe: No, really. It's a long story

Kari: WTF

> Gabe: I'm sorry

Kari: Asshole

I'd stopped drinking after that second afternoon beer, but promised myself I could have another one at 9:00 p.m. once I'd finished my tasks for the day. At 9:01 p.m. I put my phone on *do not disturb* and poured a beer into a glass mug that used to belong to my father. As the head built up and then the foam bubbled and calmed, I remembered watching my dad pour his beer into the same mug after a long day's work. My father used to be the groundskeeper at Starling Manor—he took the job here when I was seventeen. We moved into this cottage, our bachelor pad, my dad always said. My mom died when I was six, and he never really picked up with another woman.

It was a modest two-bedroom house with a living room, dine-in kitchen, and one bathroom sporting an old clawfoot tub with a shower attachment. The best part of the house was the screened-in back porch where we'd spent our evenings from April through October, and where he and I used to talk, play cards, and listen to music in what felt like our own private garden.

Dad would tell me stories about the bungalow. How you could hear the ocean every night. How salt would cover your skin and lips and heal you two times faster than if you lived inland. He spun stories about fishing and surfing and boatbuilding. Those stories kept us going back then, and life was good. Until the accident.

Helen was kind, though, and after my dad's death she hired me as the groundskeeper, against Harry's wishes. She even set up an investment account for me. Not a fortune but enough to help me get started in my new life, and that's all I needed.

The porch was lonely without him, but it was still my favorite place. I had a hammock set up out there, and I climbed in and stretched out, my drink next to me on a table. A soft breeze pushed through the screens as crickets chattered and frogs sang to each other in the darkness. I fantasized about how soon I'd be hearing the crashing of waves in my own place, and I wouldn't have to answer to anyone ever again. Finally feeling calm for the first time all day, I started to doze.

"Archie!"

"Jesus Christ!" I struggled against the fabric of the hammock but was like a fly caught in a spider's web. I heard someone giggle a few feet away. "Sunny?"

"I'm sorry," she said, though by the way laughter laced her words, I didn't believe she was sorry at all. "We need to talk."

"Why are you in my backyard?"

"You used to like the porch at night. Thought I'd see if you were out here before coming around front."

"That's creepy stalker behavior. What if I was naked out here?"

"Are you naked?"

"Not currently."

"Good, because it seems like that'd be one way for a hammock to get pretty funky."

"Go to the front door."

There was a rustling of branches as she made her way out of my yard along the garden path. My heart was beating a little too quickly and I wasn't sure if it was because I'd been startled or because Susana remembered how I liked to be on the porch. I extracted myself from the death grip of the hammock, grabbed my drink, and opened the front door where I found Susana waiting. My porch light was off, and she was all shade and shadows out there in the night.

"Want a drink?" I headed to the kitchen to see what I could put together for her.

"Aren't you going to invite me inside?" Susana had stayed on the front step instead of coming into the house.

"If Mrs. Skinner turned you into a vampire since the last time I saw you, we're going to have to renegotiate the terms of this marriage thing."

She still didn't come in.

"Fine. I'll risk it. Susana Starling, would you like to enter my humble abode?"

"It would be my pleasure." She walked across the threshold and into the light. She was stunning. Judging by her damp hair and clean face, she was freshly showered. Her hair had a slight wave to it as it fell past her shoulders and she wore heather leggings, a long soft cardigan that ended at her hips, and a blue tank top.

It took everything I had to keep my eyes on her face, but I was about to break. She wasn't wearing a bra. Why the hell wasn't she wearing a bra? Susana was more than blessed in the chest department and for the sake of all things holy, was she trying to kill me? Even as I was concentrating on her eyes, which looked sleepy and relaxed, I could see her nipples at full attention under the thin fabric. I turned away quickly. "So, how about that drink?"

"Archie?" She stood in my entryway and didn't follow me to the kitchen. I glanced at her. Yep, nipples still there, loud and proud.

"Yes, Sunny?"

"We have a problem."

7

SUSANA

"You're right. We have a huge problem." Gabe pointed at my chest.

I looked down, expecting to see a stain on my shirt or a Japanese Beetle climbing up the edge of my sweater. But I saw nothing . . . other than the fact that my tank top was way more sheer than I'd realized, and my breasts were very prominent and, well, alert. "Shit. Sorry." I pulled my cardigan across my chest, covering up my peepshow. I'd been in a tight and binding bra all day, and after my shower I just couldn't bear to put one back on. That may've been a mistake.

"Oh." Gabe's face went a bright shade of pink. "No, that's not what I meant. Those aren't a problem. They're great. Perfect. Zero problemo." He cleared his throat and looked away. "I meant the drink," he said.

"What drink?"

"Exactly. You don't have a drink, and that was the problem I was trying to point out."

"Oh, right. Sorry." Off to a great start, Starling.

"Would you like a drink?" Gabe asked.

"Sure. Thanks." I sat on the couch while Gabe opened his fridge and stayed there longer than it should've taken to grab a beer. When he finally emerged, his skin was back to its normal shade of handsome.

Gabe put a bottle of hard cider in front of me and he settled across from me in a monstrosity of a recliner. "Ok, what's this problem?"

I would've loved to tell him the truth. That I was having an existential crisis, that I didn't know how to mourn my mother, that I was pissed at him for how he'd treated me when I used to live here, that I still thought he was sexy, and that I was petrified of living as a public Starling again. But instead, I went with the basics. "My cousins are going to be here tomorrow morning at nine. They want to talk to us about all this. I think we need to have our stories straight and our plan ready to go. Tonight." My mouth was dry, and my hand shook as I took a sip of my cider.

Gabe took a swig of his beer and stayed silent for a moment. "I've had a few drinks, so I might not be in the best state to have a complicated and rational discussion." His hair fell across his forehead as he looked at his hands. He'd been good looking when he was younger, but now that he was a grown man, he was impossibly hot. He'd filled out, and years of manual labor showed in his shoulders, chest, arms, and even in his hands.

I kept my cardigan closed against my chest; my nipples had already spoken their minds, and I didn't need them interjecting again. "So, what do we do?" It was an honest question. I had no idea what to do, and I was too weary to make a decision on my own. It seemed like something I should think about for days, or weeks, or even months, but it felt like I just had a few hours, and the sand had almost emptied out of the hourglass.

Gabe leaned forward, rested his forearms on his legs, and laced his fingers together. "We make a plan."

"Ok." I took another sip of my cider. "But how do we make a plan?"

"Let's start with the basics. We'll go over the essential questions and those answers will tell us what to do next."

He was just a regular guy with a regular face, but something about how all his features were arranged hit me in some kind of weak spot. Keep it together, Susana. Just act normal. "Sounds fine. What's the first question?"

"How about this: Do you want Harry to be the trustee of Starling Family Trust?"

"Absolutely not." Ok, that was an easy one. Maybe I could do this.

"A clear answer. That's what we need. Next question: do you want to be the trustee of the Starling Family Trust?"

That one wasn't so easy. "I don't know."

"That's fine. Let me rephrase." Gabe thought for a moment and tried again. "If there are only two choices for trustee of the Starling family assets, who would you choose: yourself, or Harry Hardin."

"Well, me, when you put it that way. But aren't there other options?"

"Maybe. But those are the two your mom put out there. Making new options could take a lot of time and money, and once Harry's at the helm, I think it would be hard to unseat him."

"Shit." Moisture was building under my arms, and I was going to ruin my shower-fresh feeling. "But I'd have to change my whole life. I feel like this is a trap. Like I'm the only one who can stop the evil mastermind from taking over the world."

"I don't think I'd endow Harry with that title. He's more of a pathetic sidekick than a main character. But let's approach this a different way." Gabe bit his lip. "Tell me something good you could do in your life if you had big money. Starling money."

The money. It'd been circling in my brain, but I felt guilty every time it popped up, so I'd buried the thought. But there, in Gabe's cozy cottage, half a cider in me, and comfortably braless, I let myself imagine it. "I could dump my private chef clients."

"That's a good start. What else?"

"I could fund my *Green Kids Grow* program, not just locally, but on a bigger scale."

"Great. Anything else?"

"Lots of things. A million things, I guess. That's part of the problem. If I had that kind of money, I'd have a lot of responsibility. To do the right thing. What if I do the wrong thing? What if I'm completely selfish and just hide in the mansion for the rest of my days and blow the money on massages, food, and books?"

"I could think of worse things." Gabe flipped out the footrest on his recliner, leaned back, and shut his eyes. "But I think if you're doubting yourself, you're probably well-suited to hold the responsibility. The best leaders are the ones who don't really want to be in power."

"I think you missed your calling as a life coach." I took advantage of Gabe's closed eyes to really look at him. His face was relaxed and the stubble that dotted his jaw gave him just enough roughness to balance out his angelic looks. I'd nicknamed him Archie because he shared a name with an Archangel, but also because he'd always looked heavenly to me—like he was a little too lovely to be purely human.

The chair clanked loudly as Gabe snapped the recliner back into its upright position, startling me, and knocking me out of my daydream.

"That chair is the devil."

"Don't talk bad about my baby!" He patted the overstuffed leather arm. "How about this: would you consider taking one year out of your life to meet your mother's terms and conditions, and once you're the official trustee, you'd have the power to set up a team of professionals to advise you and take on some of the responsibility of managing that kind of wealth?"

I let the question sit with me, and couldn't find fault with the idea, especially in light of the alternative, which was having it all land in Harry's lap. "I guess so. But what about the marriage—"

"One step at a time. Just answer that question, and then we'll move on."

I took a deep breath and let it out slowly. "Ok. Yes. I could do that. Yes."

"Excellent. Now on to phase two."

"Oh god."

"Don't worry. We'll break it down." Gabe noticed my empty bottle. "Want another?"

"Sure." I tried to look away as he stood up from his chair, but I couldn't help but watch him. He was graceful and his movements were smooth.

"Are you seeing anyone? Are you in a long-term relationship?" Gabe asked as he retrieved another cider from the fridge.

"Why do you ask?"

Gabe returned and held the bottle out to me, and I took it from his hand, letting my fingers touch his until he pulled away. "If you have someone you're thinking about marrying anyway, that could make this easier."

"Shouldn't you have asked me that before you announced that you were my fiancé?"

"It would've been nice to have a plan before we got blindsided in that meeting, but we didn't have that luxury. I made a last-second call."

"No. I don't have anyone. I'm not in a relationship."

"That makes it less complicated, then. I don't have to worry about backtracking on my statement or about getting beat up by a dude who thinks I'm trying to steal his woman."

A heat rushed into my belly, like someone turned on the pilot light for my desire furnace, which hadn't been operational for a long time. "What about you?"

"What about me? No, I'm not seeing any dudes, either."

"Very funny. What about women?" Please god, don't let him have a girlfriend.

"I'm not in a relationship."

"Seeing anyone casually?" Real cool, Susana.

"I only do casual."

"How so?"

"Because I'm not sticking around, and no need to break any more hearts than necessary. So don't worry. I don't get emotionally involved with anyone."

"Who's worried?" I crossed my arms and looked away, pretending to study Gabe's wall of family photos. I had the opposite problem. When I dated, I seemed to fall right in, but then I'd scare myself and sabotage the whole thing. "I do the same thing. Keep it casual."

Gabe raised an eyebrow. "Really? You seem like you'd be a serial monogamist."

"I'm at the age where a lot of guys want to settle down and have kids."

"But not you?"

"Settle down, maybe, but no kids."

"Do you hate kids?"

"No, I like them a lot. That's why I teach them how to cook. Just don't think I'm the right person to be a mother."

Gabe studied my face, and the attention of it made me squirm. "I feel like there's more to this story."

That nervous shaky feeling came over me, which meant I was about to cry or overshare. "Can't take the pill. Makes me super sick. The idea of implanting a coil in my uterus is a no-go. Had a scare with my last boyfriend and it didn't end well."

"Who was this guy? And what do you mean?" Gabe's nostrils flared.

"I kinda freaked out when I thought I was pregnant. He took that as an insult. He was a great guy—"

"Couldn't have been that great," Gabe mumbled.

"But I'm probably not cut out to be a mother. I don't have the right training or genes. So abstinence seems like a good decision for now. No sex, no babies." Guess I went with over sharing.

"That seems like a big jump."

"Multiples run in my family on both sides." We needed a change of subject. I looked away from Gabe and focused on his wall of photos. So many of his dad. I remembered Michael Green from my teenage years when he and Gabe arrived at Starling Manor.

When Gabe's dad took the groundskeeper job years ago, my life had instantly improved. Michael was kind and professional, and the landscape of the estate, which had been formal and stuffy, started to shift and bloom as he planted flowers and ornamental bushes. Suddenly there were more birds, butterflies, and bees, and everything felt more alive. Gabe was two years older than I was and I was drawn to him. Like any teenager with a little crush, I figured out his schedule and tried to "accidentally" run into him any time I had the chance. We struck up a friendship, which bloomed, just like his father's flowers. I'd hoped we could maybe be more than friends, but then—

"Hey, where'd you go?" Gabe had moved from his chair and was now next to me on the couch, blocking my view of the photo wall. He was so close. Too close.

"Just looking at the photos of your dad."

"I get it. He was pretty handsome." Gabe was turned toward me and put his arm along the back of the couch. So, so close.

"I'm really sorry that you lost him," I said. "I don't think I ever told you that in person."

"It's been ten years. So it's not as hard for me now. But thank you." Gabe's eyes were on me, but my eyes were on the empty bottle in my hand.

Wow, when did I finish the second cider? I felt like I was losing my grip on reality.

"Ok." Gabe shifted and scooted back on the couch, giving me some more room. "Let's finish talking about this plan. We could probably both use a good night's sleep."

That was a good idea. Because a lot of visions were jumping

around in my head, and none of them were about sleep. "Where were we?"

"We'd established that we're both single. Let's cut to the chase." Gabe took my hand in his. Chills shot up my arm, across my chest, through my belly, and spread out over my legs. "Susana Starling, will you marry me and be my wife for one year and one day?"

My heart was hammering in my chest. "Maybe."

Gabe laughed and did not let go of my hand. "Fair enough. What can I do to get a yes out of you?"

"Tell me again what's in it for you." I wanted him to say that *I* was in it for him, but I knew that was my inner rejected teenager talking.

"I'd get to work my final year at Starling Manor without that ogre in the big house,"

Gabe said. He let go of my hand and dragged his fingers through his hair again. "I'd be able to expand the grounds crew and get everything lined up for when I leave. I can help you get settled, and I think it would make your mom happy to know that you're here, so it feels like I'd be repaying a debt to your mother. That's enough for me."

"What kind of debt do you have to repay to my mother?" I felt a little sick. Jealous, maybe. I was having too many feelings. This emotional whiplash was exhausting.

"She looked out for me." He fiddled with his hands and looked off into the distance, sliding off somewhere where I couldn't reach him.

"Lucky you." My mother had probably liked Gabe more than she liked me.

"She loved you, Susana."

"She had a funny way of showing it." Why was I even entertaining this ridiculous idea? It would never work.

"We can make this work," Gabe said. Was he a mind reader? "We just need some ground rules."

"Like what?" I'd let him make his case.

Gabe adjusted his position on the couch and started picking at his cuticles. I remembered him doing that when he was nineteen when I'd asked him who was the prettiest girl he'd ever seen.

We'd been sitting on the side of the pool with our legs in the water. I remember the long wait as he thought about his answer. I wanted so badly for him to say that I was the prettiest girl, but he didn't say that. He didn't say anything because we'd been interrupted by Tyler Hardin, Harry's son, and my stepbrother. Tyler and a few of his friends came crashing through the bushes, drunk and rowdy, armed with rafts and a cooler.

"Is the help supposed to fraternize with the family?" Tyler shouted. Gabe jumped up. Laughter from Tyler's friends echoed over the pool. "Don't you have work to do? Stop flirting with my sister, or I'll report you to my father and you and your deadbeat dad will be out of a job."

"I'm not your sister!" I stood up and quickly covered up with my towel, but it was too late to avoid the ogling stares from Tyler's crew. Gabe was gone, having ducked out between a row of hedges. I grabbed my bag and tried to leave.

Tyler blocked my way as he and his friends made a circle around me. "Sure you don't want to stay and swim with us, Susana Banana?" He knew I hated that nickname. "You might have a good time if you let yourself." He pulled back the shoulder strap of my green bathing suit and let it snap back against my skin.

I pushed by him, praying that he'd let me pass.

"Raincheck!" Tyler had called after me.

"THIS WOULD BE A BUSINESS CONTRACT, not a romantic one," Gabe said. Jolted back to the present, I felt nauseous. *Where were we? Rules. Right.* "So no kissing, sex, or anything like that." Gabe peeked up at me and then looked back down at his hands.

"I'm not sure about that," I said. "I mean—"

"Listen, I know it's hard to resist this much man," Gabe interrupted, "but I have faith in you."

I couldn't help but laugh, and that little reprieve gave me the confidence to continue. "It's just that *if* we did this, and I'm just saying *if*, it would have to look real, right? The contract says it has to be a 'legitimate' marriage."

"Right. But I don't know a lot of real married people who have sex in public, so I think we're safe keeping a 'no sex' rule."

"Real married people, newlyweds in particular, kiss in public and show a lot of physical affection. So, it would be weird if we were, you know, asexual." I was sweating again. This was the strangest conversation I'd ever had.

"Fair point. What would you suggest? I mean, hypothetically," Gabe said.

"Hypothetically, we'd need to hold hands, kiss, flirt—stuff like that, in public spaces when we're under observation."

"Kissing. Check."

It had been my teenage dream to kiss Gabriel Green. But now it made me nervous and even a bit sad to think about kissing him just for show. Not that I wanted to be in a relationship with him. I was still pissed about how he'd stood me up. I'd thought he was a good guy, but I might've been wrong.

Gabe spoke again. "There's no danger of it getting personal, because like I said, I—"

"You only do casual."

"Bingo."

"And I've sworn off romance and sex for now anyway, so I'm not interested in that."

"Right. Sure." Gabe raised his eyebrow again.

We needed to move on from that little lie I'd just told. "No dating other people for the year. I don't want a cheating scandal. *If* we did this. Which I'm not saying we are."

"Right."

"You'd delete your dating apps."

"You delete *your* dating apps!" Gabe poked my arm.

"I don't have any."

"Perfect. What's next?"

"Have any other ideas?" We weren't going to do this were we? No, we couldn't. But then, if we didn't, Harry would win, my family fortune would get swallowed up by a terrible man, and Gabe's life would probably be derailed, or wrecked. Shit.

"I'd go to those stupid events. But the rest of the time I'd want to keep working in the gardens. I think if this were real, I wouldn't just marry you and quit doing the thing I loved. That would feel extra fake. You know. *Hypothetically.*"

I turned my body towards Gabe so we were facing each other. "So in this hypothetical scenario, our rules would be: no to sex, yes to PDA, no dating anyone else for the year, and you go to all charity and social events as needed."

"And," Gabe added, "I still get to work on the grounds."

"We'd have to sleep in the north wing every night. And live in the big house."

Gabe grunted. "Can I take naps out here?"

"I'd permit that."

"Thank you, oh benevolent wife."

"I'm not your wife yet."

"Thank you, oh benevolent fiancée."

"This is hypothetical."

"Fuck hypothetical," Gabe said.

"What?" My pulse was racing again.

"You heard me. I'm done with hypotheticals." Gabe hopped off the couch and shoved the coffee table out of the way, clearing a spot in front of me. "Take off that ring."

I looked at the ring I'd been wearing all day. The diamond and rubies sparkled despite the dim light in the cottage. "You told me to keep it on."

"Just take it off for a second." Gabe held out his hand.

I took off the ring and placed it in his open palm. He knelt in front of me. I felt flushed and dizzy. Maybe it was the cider.

Gabe cleared his throat. He studied the ring, and his hair fell across his forehead again, and I had to stop myself from raising my finger to his face to slide the locks out of his eyes. "Susana Starling, will you be my pretend wife?" Gabe lifted the ring like he was holding the Olympic torch.

I looked up at the ring. Then at Gabe's face. He looked serious. I looked back at the ring. "Really?" I felt tears in my eyes. They were fearful tears. Worried tears. Tired tears.

"We can do this. I've got you. All you have to do is say yes." Gabe lowered the ring so it was at the same level as my heart.

I closed my eyes and inhaled for four seconds and exhaled slowly. When I opened my eyes, Gabe was still there, in the same position, with the ring extended to me. It was decision time. I closed my eyes again and thought of my mother. How sweet she'd been when I was a child and how she'd helped me say my vows to a hundred pretend husbands. I thought about my father, who'd always been so patient and kind with my mom, just like Gabe was being with me. I thought about Gabe's mom and dad, both gone, too. And I thought about Jag, and what his life would be like if I said no. Time for a leap of faith.

"Yes."

Gabe jumped, like my voice had startled him. "Wait, what?"

"Yes. I'll be your fake wife for one year."

"You will?"

"I will."

"Oh, the ring!" Gabe took my left hand and slid the ring back on my finger, and I thought I detected a tremor in his touch.

"We can do this," he said.

"I hope so."

Gabe stood and brushed off his knees. He reached out for me, and I took his hand. He pulled me up and we were standing face to face—well, still face to chest, but close enough. He looked into my eyes and for just a moment, he ran his finger softly across the line of my jaw. My heart jumped into my throat, and I wondered if he was going to kiss me. His lips parted and he said, "I need you to leave."

8

GABE

Was I an asshole for proposing to Susana and kicking her out a minute later? Probably. But Susana had to get out of my arms, out of my sight, out of my house. If I had trouble resisting the urge to kiss her in the few seconds that she was close to me, how the hell was I going to survive a year of living with her?

I'd ushered her out the front door and into the night as quickly as I could, with the promise of meeting her at nine in the morning. I went straight to the shower as soon as Susana was gone and set the temperature a few degrees above icy. The freezing water wasn't just to calm my dick, which was letting me know that it would like a say in all things Susana, but to calm my mind. I couldn't think about her romantically—it wasn't allowed. This was more of a business transaction, or a humanitarian effort, if I took into account the bonus of cutting Harry off at the knees.

I needed to stay in the moment and not let my thoughts wander back to Susana . . . how she fit in so perfectly on my couch, drinking that cider, her hair damp and her sweater falling open again, giving me another glimpse of her dark nipples under the sheer fabric . . . shit. I tried to focus by naming four things I could smell: the sharp woodsy aroma of my soap; the shower water which was laced with a slightly metallic odor, probably from copper pipes; alcohol on my breath (that meant too many beers); the air of late spring, coming in through the open window, when the flowers were ripe and sweetly scented, but not as heavy as the musky perfume of late summer. Ok, that worked. I shut off the water, grabbed a towel, and quickly dried off.

I told myself that my feelings were just a lingering attraction from all those years of wondering and fantasizing about her. Once we were around each other on a daily basis, surely I'd end up seeing her as more of a friend than as a wife. We only had to be married for a year, and then Susana and I could live separate lives in whatever ways we wanted. If it meant ruining Harry's life, I would do anything, even shack up with the woman who tried to break my heart.

I set my alarm for six a.m. and I crawled into my comfortable, perfect bed. I was going to miss this bed. I turned on a podcast about the most boring topic I could think of. So, to the mind-numbing voices of two bros discussing crypto news alerts and trends, I fell into a fitful sleep.

I'D HAD four cups of coffee, and it wasn't even eight o'clock yet. This might not bode well for me remaining calm and relaxed but at least I'd be perky. Tired of pacing around the small rooms of my cottage, I walked the grounds until it was time for our meeting. Jag had suggested that we have our meeting in the stables, so we'd have a better chance of evading Mrs. Skinner, Harry, or any other spies. I had no idea how much Sebastian and Simon knew about this whole marriage plan, so we needed to play it safe.

It'd been years since horses had lived in the beautiful old building, which over a century ago had also provided storage for carriages and apartments for male servants on the second floor. More recently the stables had been transformed into an event venue where Helen and Harry hosted a polo-themed party every summer. When Susana still lived here the stables had three full-time occupants: a golden Quarter Horse we called Sandy, who charmed everyone with his glowing blonde mane and showboat manner; Dapple, a black and white Appaloosa who used to flirt with me for apples; and a Welsh Pony named Buster who, despite being the smallest of the bunch, was definitely in charge. Susana spent a lot of time with those animals—they were all very young, and she helped raise them, so I was surprised that summer when she disappeared that she'd left them all behind. A year after Susana had gone, the stable manager quit after too much harassment from Harry, and she and the horses relocated to another estate.

I came around the last corner of the garden path and stepped into the open field that led down to the stables. The sight of lush green valley never failed to relax me—maybe if I stared at it for an hour, I could counteract my caffeine overdose—but what I saw made my heart jump in my chest: Susana was already at the barn, leaning up against the antique Parisian lamppost that was our meeting spot years ago. The old oil lamp was still functional if I had the right supplies, but the last time I lit it was over a decade ago. She wore jeans, a pale yellow sweater, and black converse high tops that looked identical to the pair she used to wear in high school. Seeing her had definitely sparked some old feelings for me, but that didn't matter. I had to keep things professional.

I made my way towards her, hands in my pockets, trying to look cool and casual when I felt anything but.

"Hey." Susana greeted me with a small wave. The breeze blew her dark hair across her face and a few strands got stuck on her lips.

I resisted the urge to reach out and pull the hair off her face and tuck it behind her ear—I pushed my hands deeper into my pockets. "Good morning."

"Simon's inside." She gestured to the barn.

"Already? It's only eight-thirty."

"He's Simon."

"Right. Of course." We stood in silence for a few moments,

like a couple of shy teenagers. "Should we head inside or wait for Sebastian?"

"You know that Bash is always on his own timetable. Let's go in." She led the way to the grand arched double doors, pushed them open, and waited for me to enter first. "Age before beauty," she said, batting her eyelashes.

"Beauty's in the eye of the beholder." I made her laugh. Goal achieved.

Simon Starling was just inside the door, leaning against a wooden column. His pristine suit and $400 shoes clashed with the sloping dusty floor made from bricks over a hundred years old. Simon had the same black hair as Susana, but whereas she was small, like her mother, he was tall, like their fathers. I was no shrimp at 6'2", but Simon had several inches on me. He was slender, brooding, and cool, and if he ever won a role in a movie, it'd be a vampire part for sure.

"Nice of you to join us, Mr. Green." Simon gave me a onceover and didn't seem impressed by my jeans and button-down. Nobody'd told me that today's dress code for the men was Black Tie.

"You're early," I said to Simon.

"Hardly." Simon's phone buzzed in his hand, and he flicked his finger across the screen to check a text. "My father says he hasn't received the newest copy of Helen's will. Do you have her attorney's personal number? I'm not getting anywhere with her assistant."

"Shocking."

"I was speaking to my cousin, Mr. Green, not you."

"I think Jag has it," Susana offered. "He'll be here soon."

Susana, Simon, and Sebastian Starling were cousins, but closer than most, probably because their fathers were identical triplets. And not any old regular triplets, not that having three babies at once was ever regular. But the triplets, Malcom, Miles, and Mitchell Maddix-Starling were the sons of America's sweethearts, Quentin Maddix and Sadie Starling. Quentin was part of the Maddix Publishing family and had more money than God. Sadie rose to fame in the 1950s first as a singer and later as a movie star. Starling Acres, once part of the Maddix empire, was where the triplets were born. The arrival of the triplets was celebrated nation-wide, and the family became known as America's Royalty, like the Kennedys but without the politics. Susana and her cousins all had the same middle name, Maddix, and used Starling as their last name. Quentin and Sadie were no longer living, but Sadie Starling's music was still world-famous, especially her Christmas hit, "Stars in the Snow." Taking care of Starling Manor meant being a steward of the family legacy and everyone who worked here had to know the basic family history.

"Let's get this party started!" Sebastian burst through the door with his arms open wide. Susana and I just stared at him, and Simon went back to his phone. "What is this, a funeral? Everyone looks so depressed. Oops. Sorry, Sus." Sebastian used his yellow and black striped scarf like a lasso and looped it over his cousin's shoulder, pulling her in for a hug. Once she untangled herself, we all got a good look at Sebastian's colorful outfit: a silken green shirt, shiny blue trousers, and orange sneakers.

"What are you wearing?" Simon looked at Sebastian with naked disdain. Guess my clothes weren't so bad, after all.

"Spilled coffee on my first shirt. This was the only back-up in my car. Besides, I'm hot no matter what I'm wearing."

"Can we get to it?" Simon asked. "I have a meeting in the city this afternoon."

Sebastian rolled his eyes. "Sure, cuz. I hear congratulations are in order! How're you lovebirds doing?"

"We're great, thanks for asking." Susana punched Sebastian's arm.

Simon looked from me to Sunny, and then back at me. "This isn't going to work."

I felt a nervous tug in my stomach. "Why not?"

"No one's going to believe this is a love match," Simon said.

"Give me a break," I said. "This is all pretty new to us."

Simon didn't back down. "I've been watching you two since you walked in. You can't make eye contact, let alone give the impression that you're in love enough to be getting married."

"Not everyone marries for love." Susana added.

"Correct. But isn't everyone under the impression that you two are a loving couple?"

Susana shrugged. "Uh, I guess so."

"And if it's found out that this marriage is a sham, the deal is off?"

"Something like that."

"So you'd better show us what you can do, or I'll have to tell father to hire an extra team of lawyers to fight what's coming in Harry's appeal."

"Jesus, Si. We've only been in here for a minute." Susana's cheeks were pink.

"But there are eyes everywhere. Any time you aren't in private quarters, you'll have to be 'on.' Not just at social functions. Walking the grounds, in the hallways, at meals. Assume you're being monitored and recorded at all times, both inside the house and out."

"Yeah, what he said," Sebastian offered.

I felt sweat coming on again. I was going to have to buy my deodorant in bulk for the next year.

"We've got it under control," Susana sounded confident, but didn't look it.

Simon grabbed a small wooden chair that'd been pushed up against a wall. He carried it to the center of the stable and put it down on the center of the brick floor. It wobbled on the uneven surface. "Show us."

"Show you what?" I asked.

"Show us how in love you are."

"What's with the chair?"

"This is your prop. Let's see what you've got."

Sebastian went to stand by Simon. "I love a good show. Lights, camera, action!"

There was no spotlight, though I felt like Susana and I were burning under the heat of a thousand bulbs. We were frozen in place.

"Not good!" shouted Sebastian. "Clock is ticking."

"What are we supposed to do?" Susana looked like she might cry.

Simon sighed. "You're going to have to do this for a year. If you can't do this in front of us, I'm sorry, but you're fucked."

An angry heat boiled up in my stomach. Fuck these guys for giving her a hard time. I clutched Susana's hand and pulled her toward the chair. I sat down and spread my legs out to make my lap bigger. I squeezed her hand as she looked down at me with confused eyes. "We're on." She looked at me with a blank stare, but after a moment, she nodded.

"We're on," she whispered back.

"Come here, baby," I grabbed her around the waist and brought her closer. Susana fell onto my lap and buried her face in my neck. I was attracted to Susana, but I didn't want to do this. I didn't want to force things. I didn't want to let myself develop any feelings for her. And I sure as hell didn't want to perform for a bunch of rich assholes. But I'd agree to this charade, so I had to try.

"I'm already tired." Her voice was sweet and soft in my ear.

I put one hand on the back of her head and lifted her face so we were looking into each other's eyes. I ran the fingers of my other hand up and down her back. She smelled like lily of the valley and peaches. "You've got this. We've got this. Please don't worry." And before I could talk myself out of it, I leaned forward and kissed her softly on the lips. She kissed me back. She dug her fingers into the skin of my shoulder blades and opened her mouth. Her tongue gently pushed again mine for a moment, and then it was gone. Her mouth was full and soft and sweet. Ok, I was *definitely* not getting friend or sister vibes with this kiss—for a moment, I got lost and forgot that anyone else was there. Forgot that we were in an old stable filled with memories and ghosts. Forgot that this kiss meant nothing, because right then, it felt like it meant everything. We were still kissing when Sebastian's voice broke me out of my trance.

"Well, I'll be damned. That was pretty hot!" He slapped Simon on the back as Susana and I avoided each other's eyes but she stayed on my lap.

"Hmph," Simon grunted and then he gave us a slight nod. "A good start, I suppose."

"Well done, future Mrs. Green," I said to Susana.

"I'm not changing my last name. You know that, right? I'm a Starling to the end."

"I understand. Hope you're ok with me keeping my name, too. I kinda like it."

"Of course, future Mr. Starling."

We were on.

9

SUSANA

I tried to stand up from Gabe's lap, but he held me in place. "Just a sec." Gabe had a half-grimace, half smirk on his face. "I need a minute . . . to recover."

I thought I'd felt something underneath me, but I told myself it was his belt buckle. Or a set of keys. Or an awkwardly placed seam. But as Gabe shifted my weight off his lap but still kept me from standing up, heat rushed through my body, and I let myself admit that Gabe had been turned on. By me. It was probably a good idea for me to stay seated for a few moments.

My pulse was racing, I was short of breath, and my stomach was flipping—it wasn't because I'd had two cups of coffee and no breakfast—these were butterflies. I was both elated and horrified. I couldn't give in to my feelings for Gabriel Green. He was marrying me only so he could secure his future, and to help me secure mine. This was a practical partnership, not a love match. We'd tried our hand at dating a long time ago, and Gabe had changed his mind and left me hanging. That heartbreak still stung, and I didn't feel like risking a sequel. But I couldn't mess this up—a lot of people were depending on me to get it right.

"Apologies for my tardiness." Jag entered the stables holding a small stack of folders. "Simon, I have the paperwork you request-ed." Jag handed over the files and did a double take as he took in the sight of me on Gabe's lap in the center of the room. "What's going on here? Some kind of interrogation?"

"The happy couple was just demonstrating how hot they are for each other," Bash said as he threw his scarf toward Gabe. "You can cover up with this, lover boy."

I stood up on wobbly legs and Gabe placed the fabric across his lap.

"So crass." Simon shot Sebastian a glare laced with his usual cocktail of 80% annoyance, 10% respect, and 10% amusement. It'd been like this our entire lives. "They did better than expected. There's a chance they might fool a few people if they keep working on it."

Jag gave a small nod of approval. "Excellent. I'm glad they've given this a test run. It's shaping up to be a hostile environment, so the more practice the better."

"How hostile?" Gabe was back to 'all systems go' mode as he stood up and threw the bumble bee scarf back at Bash's head.

"Watch the hair, dude!" Bash tidied his locks. Sebastian was the only cousin with wavy hair, and he never let us forget it. If he'd inherited the gene for male-pattern baldness, I think he would've considered life unlivable.

Jag ignored the tension between Gabe and Bash. "Mr. Hardin hasn't moved out yet. I don't think he'll leave until the marriage is official. And Tyler's here this morning as well. If you add Mrs. Skinner and some of Mr. Hardin's friends, it's a hornet's nest."

Tyler Hardin was at Starling Manor? The name of my step-brother hit my butterflies like a firehose and drowned them on the spot. I could put up with a lot of things: the death of my mom, my slimy stepdad, a fake relationship, and changing my entire life for a year—but the idea of Tyler was one step too far and my resolve and composure felt like they might dissolve at any second.

Maybe Gabe noticed me wobble, or felt my energy change,

because he wrapped his fingers around my arm and held me steady. Sebastian was still messing with his hair, Simon was frowning at one of the documents, Jag was staring into space like he was trying to come up with a plan, but Gabe was focused completely on me.

"What's wrong? What just happened there?"

"Tyler's here," I started, but I had trouble voicing the rest of my thoughts. "He's . . . I . . . maybe—"

"Let's do it today," Gabe announced. Bash's hands dropped to his side, Simon looked up from his reading, and Jag focused his gaze on Gabe.

"Do what?" I felt a little woozy and the edges of my vision started to blur and sparkle.

"Let's get married today." The deep and sexy voice of Gabriel Green was the last thing I heard before everything went black.

WHEN I OPENED MY EYES, the scene before me was straight out of a cartoon. I was on the ground, maybe in Gabe's lap. Four heads were crowding my space, looking down on me like I was an alien lifeform or like the men were gathered around an altar and I was about to be the ritual sacrifice. "I'm fine!" I tried to shoo them away, but I felt dizzy again and closed my eyes.

"You're not fine," said Gabe. "Jag, call Jeff. We need juice, yogurt, toast. Maybe a hard-boiled egg. I'll have Susana up to the kitchen in a few minutes, but if she can't get there, we need some food delivered down here."

"I have a protein shake in my car!" Bash ran out of the stable doors while Gabe helped me sit up. Jag stepped away to call the kitchen. My sweater was dusty and streaked with dirt from the floor.

"Dammit." I tried to brush off the marks.

"It'll wash out." Gabe tried to wipe some dirt off my back. "Soon you'll be rich enough to fill your closet with a flotilla of yellow sweaters."

"Is that the name for a grouping of sweaters? I could've sworn it was a gaggle."

"Nope, that's for pants. Common mistake." Gabe helped me stand up and my head felt clear, but my stomach was groaning.

Sebastian was back and shoved a chilled glass bottle into my hands. "Drink up. Passing out on your wedding day isn't the best look."

"It's not my wedding day." I took a sip of the shake. Vanilla with a hint of cinnamon. Delicious.

"It's not the worst idea," Simon chimed in, "but there's a three-day waiting period between filing the *Intention to Marry* notice and getting the actual marriage license."

"Look at Mr. Legalese! I didn't know finance guys knew anything about marriage law, unless there's something you're not telling us," teased Sebastian. "Will we be meeting Mrs. Simon anytime soon? We could have a double wedding."

"There's no woman in my life." Simon's icy growl would've made me wither, but Sebastian shrugged it off.

"There *is* a workaround." Jag pulled out his phone and was scrolling through his contacts. "We can file a *Marriage Without Delay* form today at the District Court. I'm sure Judge Hart would approve it, and seeing as it's only 9:30 in the morning, there'd be plenty of time to make it happen. I have names of several licensed officiants who are ready to offer their services at a moment's notice."

I was no longer dizzy, but the conversation was making my head spin. These men could make a wedding happen in just a few hours. They could skip the line, easily pay the fees, and they had a long list of people willing to help them out of any jam. This was the life I was about to enter. Or re-enter. I knew it was stupid to take too much pride in "doing things the hard way" as my mother always accused me of doing, but it was what I was used to. Life was difficult for most people; even the relatively simple act of applying for a marriage license would take some research, travel, lines, money, and time, but here at Starling Manor, things were different. I'd vowed to be self-sufficient, and this was breaking my rules.

Jeffrey poked his head though the door. "Did somebody order breakfast?"

Gabe grabbed my hand and pulled me toward Jeff. "I'm taking Susana outside. We need to talk about this. We'll let you know what we decide after she eats."

The morning sun was much brighter than the dim light of the stables, and it took me a minute to adjust. I shaded my eyes with my palm as Gabe led me to the black iron bench that was near our old lamppost.

Jeff handed a picnic basket to Gabe. "You can leave this here when you're finished. I'll have someone collect it."

"Thanks, man." Gabe was pulling food and drinks out of the basket: a cranberry muffin, a small pot of Greek yogurt, orange juice in a mini carafe, a bottle of water, and a ham and cheese pastry.

"Keep an eye out." Jeff nodded slightly in the direction of the main house. "There are a lot of folks up there. Too many. And half of them are probably looking out the window or taking videos with their phones."

I took a bite of the pastry, and the flaky layers were buttery perfection. "Oh my god." I was talking with my mouth full, but I didn't care. "Did you make this?"

"Guilty as charged."

"This is amazing. Can I hang out in your kitchen sometime?"

"Of course you can. Just—" Jeff was interrupted by Gabe's moans of pleasure as he tasted the muffin. "Have you two not eaten in days? I appreciate the compliments, but this is getting a bit obscene."

"Sorry, dude. This is one hell of a muffin."

"Enjoy. I need to head back to the house." Jeff left us to devour our breakfast.

Gabe found a container of strawberries and mandarin oranges and we ate them quickly. I had the yogurt, and we shared the juice.

"You know how people talk about the difference between stage acting and movie acting?" Gabe asked me.

"What people?"

"People people. Just, you know. In general."

"Do I know these people?"

"Lord," Gabe huffed. "If you're acting for a movie, in front of a camera, you can make the tiniest movements with your face, and just that miniscule twitch can say more than a hundred words."

"Right."

"But if you're on a stage, you need to make sure that the people in the back row can understand what your face and body are trying to convey."

I nodded and looked around in the basket to see if anything else was hiding in there. No luck.

"We're on stage, Sunny."

I looked at Gabe's face and saw that he was focused and serious. "We're on stage?"

"Yes. I don't know for how long, but your cousins are right. We can't mess this up. We're going to have to do things big. For the people in the back row."

"What do you have in mind?" My stomach fluttered.

"Do I have your permission to step on stage? As your fiancé?"

I didn't know what exactly that meant, but I figured I'd give it a go. "Um. Sure?"

"Ok. I'm about to start. You ready?"

"Maybe?" This was all happening so fast. I liked that Gabe was so close to me, but I also had an urge to flee.

"Just like this." Gabe leaned forward and caught a piece of my hair between his fingers. He twirled it a little, and then tucked it behind my ear. "I might be talking to you about the most boring thing, but my body language has to speak to the watchers." He ran his other hand across my shoulder, down my arm, and then he grabbed my fingers, bringing them to his lips for a soft kiss.

I wanted to kiss him. I didn't want to kiss him. I didn't want to let him in, and I didn't want to let him go.

He kissed me, and then pulled back. "We have to get used to this. We need to build up the muscle memory. You try."

"Alright." I looked at Gabe's body, and suddenly forgot how a lover might act. Should I hold his hand? Nibble his earlobe? Sit on his lap again? Maybe I needed to run my hands across his thighs, sneak my fingertips under his shirt and explore the skin on his belly. It all felt foreign. Stilted. Scary.

Gabe waited, drawing little circles on my palm while he watched me survey his body. "Doing ok there? You look a little—"

I interrupted him by leaning forward and putting my lips on his. Maybe the direct route was the right one. Gabe let me lead the kiss and he was still when I was still and then moved his lips as I started to move mine. I opened my mouth to breathe him in, and the air from his lungs tasted like resin and flowers. A little groan escaped against my will, and I put one hand on the back of his head and pulled him closer. I caught his bottom lip in my teeth for just a moment before pulling back.

"Did you bite me?" Gabe ran his finger across his lip and then inspected it for blood.

Shit. I bit him. I couldn't let him know that the kiss moved me that much. "Just working on muscle memory and all that." I tried to sound casual, but my hands were shaking.

Gabe crossed his legs and picked up the picnic basket and put it in his lap. "I have one muscle that's going to have to work on forgetting."

My breath caught in my chest, and I wasn't sure if the swelling feeling in my chest was a laugh or a sob. My emotions were twisted up into a tangled mess.

"Sorry," Gabe said, pointing toward his groin. "I told him to consider himself a film actor, but I think he's going for a Tony award!"

That pressure in my chest bubbled out as a laugh, and the giggles came so rapidly that I was soon overtaken by hiccups. Gabe tried to get me to drink water, but I nearly choked twice. After a few minutes, the hiccups subsided, and my breath finally evened out. "You know I'm going to have to call your dick 'Tony' from now on, right?"

"He prefers Anthony until you're on more intimate terms."

I started to laugh again.

"Cut it out, you already drank all the water! Your hiccups are nightmare fodder."

"Then stop making me laugh."

"Fine. Let's talk about getting married. Today."

I quickly sobered up.

Gabe rested his hand on my arm. "You don't have to do this. Not today, not ever. You can still change your mind."

"No, we talked about it. Made up our minds." I watched his face for any sign of doubt or wavering.

"True." Gabe slid his fingers down to my palm and went back to tracing lines with the tip of his finger. "Do you want to wait? We have a few weeks before we're required to be married, by the terms of the will. We don't have to rush this any more than we already are."

God, he wanted to wait. He wasn't sure. This wasn't just about me. Gabe was about to be stuck with me, and he'd already decided a long time ago that he wasn't interested in me. "I'm worried that if we wait too long that we'll open ourselves up to something going wrong. I don't trust Harry, and now that Tyler's here—" A cold shiver overtook me.

"Do you want to try to go to the courthouse today? Jag is ready with that plan if you are."

"What do you think?" I felt vulnerable. Exposed. I was at the mercy of whatever words were set to come out of Gabriel Green's mouth. This was ridiculous. This was fake. It was a business deal. But my heart may have had some other ideas—I had a muscle that was overdoing it, too.

"I understand your worry. I have it too. I'm not sure what the best thing is, but I think I know what the worst thing is." Gabe cleared his throat, crossed his arms, and looked out over the estate.

I sat as still as I could, hoping not to let him know that I'd just realized that I'd be crushed if he called off our plan.

Gabe took a big breath, and let it out fast. "We should do it. Let's get married, Sunny. Today."

My heart felt like it was soaring and flying and twisting and spinning. I grabbed his hand and squeezed, and he squeezed back. I wanted to speak but I knew the words wouldn't come out right. So I just nodded. Gabe seemed to realize that I needed to stay silent.

"Let's tell Jag," he said.

10

GABE

A few days ago, I was a single guy with a decent dating life and my biggest day-to-day concerns revolved around pool chemistry, pruning roses, and keeping Harry Hardin away from the younger staff. Now I had my own personal chauffer who was driving me and my bride-to-be to our wedding. What the hell.

Susana was resting her head against the car window, which was cracked open to let in the late spring air. Sunlight danced across the sleek length of her hair, making it shine like the blue-black feathers of a raven. My feet were cramped in my leather dress shoes, I was sweating underneath the shirt/suit jacket combo, and I was about ten seconds away from cutting off my tie and throwing it out the window.

"You're going to strangle yourself if you keep pulling on that," she said.

"I've worn a tie more in the last three days than I have in the last three years. Your fault."

"Blame my mother. That strategy usually works for me." Susana wore a gauzy white dress dotted with pale blue flowers. She looked so soft and lovely that all I wanted to do was touch her. So, I did. I took her hand in mine and squeezed it gently. She turned her face to me, her brow furrowed. "We aren't being watched, so you don't have to do that. The car is most likely our one safe space."

We were hot and cold, up and down, but that was no surprise. Neither of us were entirely sure about this plan—we were jumping out of the airplane of doubt and hoping that our parachutes would open before we slammed into the ground. I needed to be patient with her moods, and with mine. "Just practicing. Muscle memory and all that, remember?" I asked.

"Speaking of muscles, how's Tony holding up this afternoon?" A tiny smile pulled at the corners of Susana's mouth.

"Behaving himself. Thanks for checking in. I gave him a stern lecture before we left."

"Would've liked to be a fly on the wall for that little chat."

I pulled at my tie for what must've been the hundredth time.

"Here, just take it off." Susana let go of my hand and shifted to face me. She grabbed my tie and slipped a finger into the knot, loosening it. After a few tugs, the tie was undone, and she pulled it off my neck. She unbuttoned the top two buttons of my shirt and slid her hand across my collar bone. "Just breathe. Close your eyes. You're ok." She kept her hand on my chest, and the skin-to-skin contact relaxed me.

I hadn't realized how agitated I'd been until the knots in my stomach followed the example set by my tie and started to loosen. I leaned my head back and closed my eyes and counted to five with each inhale and exhale.

"That's better." Her voice slid over me like hot oil spread over my skin, where all my pores just absorbed her and sent her straight to my bloodstream.

I let myself imagine her undoing all my buttons and sliding her hand across my chest, over my stomach, and down to my waist-band. How would it feel if she slipped her fingers slowly under the fabric of my boxers and followed the trail of hair that led from my belly button to my—I felt her lips brush against my jaw, and I opened my eyes and sat up. "Hey, I thought no one was watching."

Susana shrugged and went back to looking out the window. "Just practicing." The heat of my fantasy stayed with me, and it felt good to let that warmth spread through my body. It gave me some relief from the feeling of my stomach cramping from nerves, my jaw aching from clenching my teeth, and the throbbing of my knuckles from having my hands balled up into fists.

After a few more minutes of driving, the three cars in our caravan pulled up to the courthouse. I inhaled but felt like I couldn't get a full breath.

"You ok?" Susana had the door handle halfway pulled, but she paused, waiting for my answer.

"Fine and dandy." I extracted a handkerchief from the inside breast pocket of my jacket and dabbed at my temple. "How about you?"

Her gaze softened and she looked like her thoughts were a million miles away. "Cannot predict now. Ask again later."

"My own Magic 8 Ball." I held on to her shoulder and gave her a gentle shake. "Ok, I've cleared you. Next question: Are you ready to get married?"

She pulled on the handle, pushed the door open, and smiled at me—a soft smile with closed lips, and the sunlight caught her eyes and made them sparkle. "Better not tell you now."

I GOT out of the car, hoping that the fresh air would calm my nerves, but no such luck. Doubts started to pelt my chest like hailstones, and I started a mental list of my worries:

1. This was a mistake
2. My motto was "keep it casual" and marriage was anything but casual, even if it was fake.
3. Could I stomach those social events?

4. Would I suffocate in the big house?
5. Would we be found out?

I contemplated puking in the petunias near the courthouse sidewalk.

"You're completely green, Green." Sebastian dug around in his fanny pack man-purse and offered me a mint. "Have one of these. Walk it off." He slapped me on the back a few times and led me toward the building entrance.

While Sebastian took care of me like I was one of his hungover fraternity brothers, Simon and Jag stood on either side of Susana and escorted her up the courthouse steps.

It was quiet inside the building, and our footsteps echoed among the cold tile floors and concrete walls. Jag led us straight into a private room where a clerk was waiting. Jag had emailed our *Marriage Without Delay* form a few hours ago, and everything was signed, stamped, and approved by the time we got there. Susana and I signed some more forms.

Jag looked at his watch. "The officiant should be here in about twenty minutes. Why don't we take a break and meet back here in a few."

Jag, Simon, and Sebastian pulled out their phones and disappeared into the hallway. Susana was chomping on a fingernail and bouncing her leg so aggressively I could feel the vibrations of it through the floor. Guess I wasn't the only one with some wedding jitters. I put my tie back on, but made the knot a loose one so it wouldn't strangle me.

"Let's take a walk." I held out my hand and she took it to stand up but then let go. "We can wait outside." I didn't want to stand in the parking lot, so I led us to a back exit. I pushed open the door and was hit by the heady scent of lilac. We'd found a secluded stone patio with a bench surrounded by dense lilac bushes filled with white and lavender flowers.

"Whoa." Susana went a little pale.

"What's wrong?" I took her arm and guided her to the bench, where she flopped down and put her face in her hands.

"Lilacs were my mother's favorite flower." She kept her face hidden, and her voice tripped over the words.

"They were? I thought roses were her favorite." There were only a few lilac bushes on the Starling Manor property. Some by the stables, and a few others in a meditation garden near the pool. "She was always telling me to put in roses. How can I be a good groundskeeper if I didn't know the lady of the house loved lilacs above all other flowers?"

Susana sat up and wiped away a few tears. "It's probably because they reminded her of my father. Their first kiss was near a lilac bush, and they always said that every time they smelled that flower they were reminded of that kiss. They were crazy about each other." Susana's words hung in the air like the drunk bees floating from stem to stem gathering nectar and pollen. So many bees. "She used to say that roses reminded her of death. And funerals. So maybe that's why she had you plant them—because surely being married to Harry was like a kind of death." She laughed, but it was a dark, sad sound. "I like roses, though," she added. "Pink ones, with big petals."

"Pink roses. Noted." I put my arm on the bench behind her, not touching her, but still close. "What was your father like?" I asked. "I've seen pictures, of course, and videos, and I've read articles about him. But what was he like for you?"

She sniffed and swiped her finger under her nose. I found an extra handkerchief, this time from my waist pocket, and offered it to her. "Thank you." She dabbed at her eyes and blew her nose. She folded the fabric. "Sorry for getting snot all over it."

"Not a problem. I have a never-ending supply of these. One of the employee benefits of Starling Manor."

She laughed softly, then continued talking. "My father was wonderful. Gentle. Funny. Had a temper, I guess, but mostly with himself. He'd get frustrated if he messed up or didn't get something exactly the way he wanted it. I wonder if that's one reason my mom married Harry after my dad died. Harry was the opposite of my dad in so many ways. Maybe she didn't want to risk actually loving someone again." Susana picked a blossom off a bush and rolled the bloom around in her fingers. "When I was little I'd always stage these pretend weddings. I'd be the bride and one of my toys would stand in as my groom."

"Did you have these marriages annulled?" I asked. "Or do we need to consult an attorney about the legality of our union?"

Susana smiled and gently elbowed my ribs. "And I'd always write these intricate vows, and my dad would listen as I recited them, and would tell me how thoughtful, or smart, or funny they were. I think one of the reasons I had so many of those weddings was because I loved having his attention like that." Susana's voice got shaky, and she stopped her story.

"Need another handkerchief? I have one in my back pocket." I stood up.

"I'm ok. Just distract me. I can't believe I'm about to get married. And that I'm going to live back home. And that neither of my parents are here to see this."

"Well, it's a fake marriage," I said, instantly regretting my word choice, but pushing ahead anyway. "Maybe it's good that they aren't here to see this."

She shrugged. "I guess. But I miss them anyway. It's hard to stay mad at my mom knowing she's gone forever. It's like I'm already forgetting the bad things and I'm just left with sad feelings."

"It does create a kind of amnesia when you lose someone. I've felt that. All those little fights and conflicts that felt like everything; they become ghosts. It's disorienting."

"Did you feel that with your dad? And your mom?"

"My mom's been gone so long that I don't feel haunted. But with my dad, there are a lot of those ghosts. What about you?"

"It's still pretty fresh, with my mother. So, I don't know how I feel, exactly. And hey, I thought I told you to distract me!"

I rubbed the back of my neck, working out the tension in my muscles while trying to think up something to get Susana's mind off her worries. Maybe the best way to evade the fears was to dive right in. "Let's play *Worst Case Scenario.*"

"You must be popular at parties."

"It's not as bad as it sounds."

"You sure about that?"

I took off my jacket and placed it across the back of the bench. It was heating up outside and I didn't want to get any sweatier than I already was. "It's something that makes me feel better when I'm stuck in my head or stressing out. I come up with outlandish worst-case scenarios, and then I ultimately feel better about my actual situation." I paced around the patio, kicking a little rock across the stone pavers. "Do you want to go first, or should I do one so you can see how it works?"

Susana stood up and stretched and the fabric of her dress strained against her ample chest. I tried hard to keep my eyes on her face, but I wanted to ogle every inch of her. She crossed her arms like she was cold and looked down at her feet. Suddenly she looked young. And sad. But still so beautiful. I opened my arms, and she stepped forward, kind of falling into me. She pressed her face against my chest, and I held her lightly. She took a deep breath and then let it out slowly. She fit perfectly against me. I felt her push backwards and I released my grip.

She wiped her face again, and then tossed the handkerchief toward her bag. "You go first."

"Ok. How about this one: it turns out that we're both deathly allergic to bees, and your cousins and Jag find our dead bodies out here in this garden, and a few months later, all that's left of us is a memorial plaque on this bench."

"Wow. This game is even weirder than I thought."

"It's supposed to be! You know, a 'so dark it's funny' kind of thing."

"Well, I *am* deathly allergic to bees, so I don't find that scenario all that funny."

"What the hell!" I grabbed her arm and started to drag her to the door.

She doubled over in a fit of giggles. "I'm sorry. I'm just kidding," she said between laughs. "You set yourself up for that one."

"Damn, Sunny. That was low."

"You're the one who turned this wedding day into *My Girl, The Sequel.*"

"More like *Romeo and Juliet, Take Two.*"

"Shakespeare. Nice. To bee or not to bee, that is the question."

"Did you just hit me with a bee pun? That was awful."

"Ouch, that stings," she said.

"Quit it."

"Listen, the beauty of puns is in the eye of the bee-holder."

"One more of those and I'm going to toss you into the bushes, and you can live out the rest of your life among your beloved bees."

"Oh Gabe, don't take it personally. I'm just pollen your leg."

"That's it!" I grabbed Susana and swept her up into my arms. She screeched and held onto my neck. She had tears in her eyes but this time they were from laughter. I started to heave her back and forth as if I was going to toss her into the flowers. "One . . ."

"Don't do it!"

"Two . . ."

"Put me down!" She was still laughing.

"Thr—"

The courthouse door opened, and Simon stood on the threshold, staring at us as if we'd gone insane. "It's time."

11

SUSANA

Gabe put me down and I straightened my dress and caught my breath. I was dizzy, but not from him spinning me around. Even though the words *this isn't real, this isn't real, this isn't real*, echoed through my head, a lightness filled my chest and for the first time in a while, I felt the whispers of hope flutter around my heart.

Bash poked his head out of the door, pushing Simon aside. "Hey, it's nice out here! Way better than the stuffy office we're supposed to take you to. Lemme see if we can do this thing out here." He whacked Simon on the back, causing him to stumble out onto the lilac porch, and went back inside.

"Christ." Simon straightened his jacket and brushed some invisible dirt from his sleeves. "He's an eternal child."

"Just now figuring this out?" I straightened his tie, or really, I just went through the motions because it was already perfectly tied and tidy. "Thank you for being here. I'm sorry I've been so out of touch these last few years."

Simon nodded and his posture stayed stiff and straight. He wasn't one for emotional displays, but he did reach out and pat my shoulder, which was the equivalent of a hug from a normal person.

"I'm glad to be here. And you're sure about this? We can try to find a different way if you're not comfortable with marrying—" Simon shot a critical glance at Gabe who looked glorious in his shirt that was unbuttoned at the top and clung tightly to his chest and biceps.

"—this perfect specimen of a man?" Gabe struck a pose like Michelangelo's David, and I couldn't help imagining how his naked form might look high up on a marble pedestal.

Simon rolled his eyes. "Not exactly what I was going to say, Mr. Green."

"I'm not comfortable with anything these days, but I think this is the right decision."

"Let's step over here." Simon placed his hand on my back and guided me to the back corner of the garden. He turned his back to Gabe, looked intently at me and frowned. "Hm."

"Do I have something on my face?" I ran my fingertips across my cheeks and lips, trying to find what Simon was seeing.

"Your make-up is just a little smudged." He pulled a handkerchief out of his jacket pocket, took my chin in his hand, and ran the fabric under each eye. "Have you been crying?"

"Isn't a girl supposed to have a few tears on her wedding day? Between you and Gabe, I think this is the fourth handkerchief appearance in the last hour." Simon raised an eyebrow, as if surprised, but not displeased to hear that Gabe had come prepared with his own Starling-branded nose-wipers.

"They're out here!" Sebastian boomed from just inside the courthouse, and a second later he flung open the door and hopped out onto the patio. "Looks like Simon has the maid of honor duties covered, so that means you get me as your best man!" Bash pulled his arm back, preparing to launch one of his signature back slaps, but Gabe was too quick for him and caught his arm in mid-swing.

"Thanks, dude. You can be my best man, but there's no need for violence."

"This is indeed an improvement from the clerk's office." Jag was surveying the garden, and behind him was an older woman. "This is Jane Murray, your officiant." We could've gone with a court clerk to marry us, but the plan was to have things seem more official and a little more romantic by bringing in our own officiant.

Jane smiled and gave a small wave. "Nice to meet you." She was quite short, maybe five feet tall. Her hair was a mass of short silver curls, and a shiny butterfly bobby pin was tucked in over her ear. She wore cream slacks, a gray sweater, and had a silk rainbow scarf draped loosely around her shoulders. "Is everyone ready?"

"Ready!" I said a little too brightly and a little too quickly.

Gabe watched me, as if waiting to see if I'd change my statement. I pushed a big grin onto my face and gave him a thumbs up. I was making *myself* cringe, so I was surely mortifying everyone else with my awkward behavior.

Simon covered my hand with his and pressed my thumb down. "No need to be tacky."

"Locked and loaded!" Gabe arranged his face into a ridiculous expression of exaggerated joy and gave Jane a double thumbs up.

I almost teared up at the realization that Gabe was making himself look like a fool to ease my own embarrassment.

Maybe Jane Murray was used to nervous couples because her smile was warm, and she seemed unfazed. "Wonderful." She beckoned for Gabe and me to move toward her. "If you'll join me here, we can begin."

"Just a second." Gabe dove into the nearest lilac bush and gently snapped off five purple stems. "Doubt anyone will miss these. Except some of the bees." He reached over to a bush filled with smaller white blooms and plucked one stem. He tucked the white flower into his lapel pocket and then arranged the purple flowers into a small bouquet. He brought the bouquet to me and placed it in my hand.

My mouth was suddenly dry, and my knees were wobbly. Gabe escorted me the few steps to where Jane was standing, and kept my arm laced through his as we stood before her. Simon stood to my left side, and Sebastian shuffled over to stand on Gabe's right.

"Welcome." Jane's voice was low and smooth and felt like a cozy blanket—it soothed my frazzled nerves. "We are gathered here today to honor the marriage of Susana," Jane paused and looked into my eyes as she said my name, and then she turned her attention to Gabe, "and Gabriel."

There was something about the use of Gabe's full name that made everything feel real. I was marrying Gabriel Green. Actually, really marrying him. Officially. In the eyes of God. Or Goddess. Or at least the state of Massachusetts. Holy shit. I swayed a little, and Gabe scooted closer and braced my shoulder with his.

"You are making a commitment to share in each other's joy during happy times, and to support and comfort each other during difficult times."

Now it was Gabe's turn to sway, and I tried to press into the side of his arm to offer support. But if he went down, we'd both be goners.

"You ok, Green?" Bash looked ready to jump in and catch Gabe if he were to collapse.

"Yep. All good. It's just hot out here." Suddenly three Starling handkerchiefs were thrust forward, one from Bash, one from Simon, and one from Jag.

The sight of all those little white cloths and embroidered birds struck me as funny, and some giggles started to bubble up into my chest.

"Oh, thanks, guys." Gabe grabbed the one offered by Bash and dabbed his face and neck.

Some of my laughs escaped, and then some more, and within a few seconds I was overcome with a fit of giggles.

"I hope someone has water, because I know where this is headed, and it isn't pretty."

Gabe's warning only made me laugh harder, and as predicted, the hiccups hit. Jane kept her composure, unlike me, and Jag produced a small bottle of water. I took a few breaths and my laughter subsided, but the hiccups endured.

Simon peeked around to see my face. "Your make-up." Simon offered up his handkerchief to wipe my eyes, and I felt the urge to laugh again.

"Oh no you don't!" Gabe pushed Simon's hankie away. "She's going to hyperventilate if she starts laughing again." He swept both thumbs under my eyes in an attempt to remove what was probably a mess of smeared mascara. "Perfect."

"It's beautiful for a marriage to be ushered into existence on the wings of laughter," Jane said. "Let your joy be seen."

I tried to wipe my eyes again but nearly stabbed myself in the face with a lilac stem, so I gave up.

"Are you ready for your vows?"

Oh god. Vows. This used to be my favorite part in all my fake childhood weddings, and in the marriage ceremonies I'd attended. What kind of vows would we have to say? Probably just some canned standard ones, but still. Everyone was staring at me. "Oh, right. Yes. Ready," I sputtered.

"Turn and face each other and take each other's hands."

I handed my bouquet off to a set of waiting hands and did as instructed.

"Do you, Susana, take Gabriel to be your husband from this day forward, to honor and cherish him, in sickness and in health, for richer or poorer, for as long as you both shall live?"

For as long as we both shall live? Someone should've vetted these vows. Was I about to lie? Would I be struck down? Attacked by a swarm of bees? Couldn't we have ended the vow after the word "poorer?" Apparently, I'd taken too long to answer because I heard Simon clear his throat behind me.

"Oh. Sorry. Yes. Yes, I do."

Jane still seemed unworried, and she turned to Gabe. "Do you, Gabriel, take Susana to be your wife from this day forward, to honor and cherish her, in sickness and in health, for richer or poorer, for as long as you both shall live?"

"I do." Gabe's answer was strong and polished and timely. Show-off.

"Do we have the rings?" Jane looked to my cousins.

Rings? A hot flush spread across my chest and face. Would this marriage count without rings? This was going to fail before it even started.

But both Simon and Sebastian handed a ring to Jane—simple platinum bands, one thin, and one thicker and more masculine. I slid the fake engagement ring off my finger, leaving it naked and ready for the wedding ring.

"Thank you, gentlemen. Susana and Gabriel, your wedding rings are an outward and visible sign of your commitment to each other. As you look upon them every day of your marriage, may they remind you of the promises you made to each other." Jane handed me the larger ring. My fingers were trembling. "Susana, place this ring on Gabriel's finger, and repeat after me: with this ring, I thee wed."

Gabe spread out the fingers of his left hand, and I glanced at his face. His eyes were dark and his lips were full and slightly parted. A ray of sunshine filtered through the branches and dappled his face with light. He looked rugged yet elegant, chiseled but smooth, serious but with a playful sparkle. He looked perfect.

I slipped the ring on to his warm finger, and it was just the right size. "With this ring, I thee wed."

Gabe held my gaze and I thought that for a moment I saw tears in his eyes, but he looked away and took the smaller ring from Jane's hand.

"Gabriel, place this ring on Susana's finger, and repeat after me: with this ring, I thee wed."

Gabe took my left hand and massaged my palm, then slowly ran his fingers up my ring finger, which sent a tingle down my spine. Looking into my eyes the entire time, he slid the wedding ring smoothly over my knuckle to its final spot at the base of my finger. Another perfect fit. "With this ring," his voice had a hint of emotion. "I thee wed."

"Susana and Gabriel, because you have now both declared your intention to marry through the vows you have declared and the rings you have exchanged, with the authority granted to me by the state of Massachusetts, it is my honor to pronounce you husband and wife. You may now kiss!"

I knew how to do this part. No delay, no holding back, no fears. And if I was being totally honest, there was no acting involved. I was ready to kiss him. I put my hands on either side of his face, my fingers brushing against the fresh stubble beginning to roughen his jawline. I pulled him to me, and he let himself be pulled and I kissed him. Soft lips, open lips, hot breath, the tip of my tongue on his. I let myself taste him. Gabriel Green. Gabe. Archie. My husband. He reached his hand around my back and pressed my body to his as we continued to kiss. I never wanted to come up for air. Sebastian let out a low whistle of appreciation that broke the spell, and Gabe and I pulled apart.

Gabe's cheeks were ruddy, and he moved his lips so close to my ear that only I could hear when he whispered, "This is going to be one hell of a ride, Mrs. Green."

12

GABE

I'd only been a married man for seven hours and thirty-four minutes, but I was already wrecked. It was just this morning that Susana and I had shared our first kisses in the stables— staged, observed, calculated kisses, but it felt like a lifetime ago. Then there was the wedding, which shouldn't have moved me as much as it did. I'd agreed to a platonic business arrangement of a marriage, with rules and everything, and I was confused, annoyed, not to mention a bit horny, with no relief in sight for any of my ailments.

"Earth to Mr. Starling." Jeff waved a baguette in front of my face to get my attention.

"Don't call me that." I grabbed the bread out of his hand and put it on the snack platter to take up to my "millionaire's honeymoon suite," as he called it.

"Will she be taking your name then, Master Green?" I picked up a cheese cube and launched it at Jeff's head. It bounced off his hair and onto the counter. "That was a delectable slice of sheep's cheese from the French Pyrenees, and you're tossing it around like Colby Jack. You're in the big leagues now, Your Majesty, and you should behave as such."

I didn't want to be in the big leagues. I wanted to be alone in my beach bungalow, sipping beer out of a can and listening to the ocean crash in the distance. "You're fine to refer to me as King Gabriel," I told Jeff. "And Susana is keeping her name, and I'm keeping mine. Is this plate almost finished?" I picked up what looked like a giant raisin. "What's this?"

Jeff slapped my hand. "It's a fig, and you're messing up the presentation. Let your bride have a look first, and then you can destroy it." The tray had a selection of meats, cheeses, fruits, bread, crackers, nuts, and chocolate. "We'll have champagne brought up, and I'm still fine to have this delivered, even though you've insisted on taking it yourself. Why aren't you upstairs with your wife? It's your wedding night and you're in the kitchen with me."

I shot him a look that I hoped conveyed what I was thinking, which was something along the lines of *shut up, we don't know who's listening, and we've got to keep up appearances at all times.*

He dropped a few candied violets onto the plate for final touches, and then lowered his voice to a whisper. "But really. Why are you not upstairs?"

I was nervous as hell, that's why. And I didn't know the wedding night protocol for fake marriages. Susana and I had to sleep in the same room, and right now there was just one bed in there. A big bed, at least, but we had to share it. I couldn't go back to my own place, have a beer, and relax. I was starting to get anxious about how stressful the next year was going to be. "She wanted to take a bath. It was a long day. We had the meeting this morning, the wedding, a late lunch and meeting with her cousins and Jag after the ceremony, the drive back, and she wants to get settled."

"But don't you want to be in that bath with her?"

Another glare from me.

"Fine. I won't question Your Royal Highness. You're all set to go with the food."

"Thank you, Chef."

"When you hear three knocks on the door in a few, that's the champagne delivery. We'll just leave it outside the door."

I lifted the platter and started the long walk to the north wing of Starling Manor. I took the back stairs and corridors, usually reserved for the staff so they could get around the house without interrupting the family. It was our job to be invisible. But I was technically the man of the house now. Should I have been taking the grand staircase? Probably not while carrying a tray of food.

Jeffrey was right that meal delivery should be left to a staff member, but I still felt like the groundskeeper, and I felt nothing like the former man of the house, Harry, who treated the manor employees like shit, at best. And it was an act of chivalry to bring food up to Susana, but this was all a show. I felt a headache coming on. There was no way I wasn't going to fuck this up at some point.

"Well, if it isn't Mr. Romance himself." A sharp voice cut through the air and startled me. It was Mrs. Skinner looming in the shadows of the back hallway.

"Always a pleasure." I picked up my pace, hoping to convey that I had no interest in talking to her.

She shuffled alongside me, not taking the hint. "So I hear you've signed on the dotted line. Officially married and all that."

"You heard correctly."

"You won't get away with this." She matched my pace.

I ignored her and kept walking. I only had one more staircase and two more hallways to go before I reached the master suite.

"Did you hear me?" Mrs. Skinner's voice splintered the air and assaulted my ears.

"I heard you, but I have nothing to say to you. I'm just trying to bring some food to my wife."

"Your *wife*," Skinner spat out the words.

I stopped walking and she ran into me, causing a few grapes to roll off the tray and plop onto the wood floor. "You work for me now, Mrs. Skinner. And I'll ask you to not take that tone with me. I can't fire you for the next year, but I can reassign you to bathrooms and baseboards. If you'll excuse me, I have somewhere to be." My voice was steady, but my heart was pounding. I had to assert my authority now, or the next 364 days might be unbearable.

Skinner tutted and huffed but turned around and returned the way she came. I climbed the final staircase and turned down one hall and then another and arrived at the entrance to my new bedroom. The door was slightly ajar, and I could hear movement from inside the suite. This was it. The start of my new life for the next year. I pushed open the door and stepped across the threshold.

"I have food! And wow, that's pink." I put the tray down on a table and took in the sight of Susana sitting on the edge of the bed, an oversized fluffy pink robe drowning her small frame.

"I know. It's awful, but it was the only robe in there. You should see the one for you. Hope you like blinding blue."

"I think I'll just use a towel until I get my own clothes from the cottage."

"Joke's on you. The towel is the same color."

"Maybe I'll drip dry."

She laughed and ran her fingers through her damp hair. "Your suitcase is over there in the sitting area. I think the rest of our clothes and stuff will be delivered tomorrow, but I'd like to get my own stuff from my house. Do you want to go with me?"

The invitation caught me by surprise. "Oh, sure. I'd be happy to go along." There were three knocks on the door. "And that would be our champagne."

"You trying to get me drunk and take advantage of me, Archie Starling?"

"Archie Starling sounds like some kind of detective character in an old comic book." I retrieved the drink cart from the hallway. "And, no, I'm not trying to get you drunk, Sunny Green, and is 'take advantage' the right term to use when it's our wedding night?"

"Sunny Green sounds like a health smoothie or some kind of

lawn care company." Susana walked over to the food. "Is this sheep's cheese? This is my favorite!" She took a few slices and looked around for a plate. I collected a plate and napkin from the drink cart.

"Read my mind. See, you're good at this husband stuff already."

I wasn't good at it. I had no idea what to do. I wanted to take a shower and watch some tv or read and get some sleep. Well, I wanted to do other things, but those weren't on the list of possible options. But there were so many unknown steps between where I was and sleep and I wasn't sure I knew how to navigate the situation. I got the champagne from outside the door, opened it and poured her a glass. She took it from my hand and drank it down all in one go.

"Whoa, steady, tiger." Had I just married someone with a big drinking problem?

"Another, please."

"Only if you sip it slowly. And have some more food." I poured another glass.

"You can't tell me what to do, my dear husband." Another gulp of champagne down the hatch. "Which side of the bed do you want?" She shoved a cracker in her mouth.

"Uh, that side's fine." I pointed to the side where she hadn't been sitting when I came in.

"Cool. I like this side." She sat on the edge of the bed, bouncing up and down like a kid. "It's closer to the window and the bathroom."

"I guess I'll change. Maybe take a quick shower."

"Go for it. Apologies in advance if I finish off all the food."

I stopped as I was walking past her on the way to the bathroom. I leaned down, putting my face close to hers. She smelled like soap and cherries. "Do that and there'll be hell to pay. Don't mess with a hungry man."

She raised an eyebrow and smirked. "We'll see." She popped

several grapes into her mouth and looked like a chipmunk storing food for the winter.

"Don't choke on those." I headed toward the bathroom.

"I can take it. No gag reflex."

Thank god my back was to her so she didn't see how that got an instant response below the belt. I shut myself in the bathroom and ran the water for the shower. Hot. I stripped down and got under the stream—it was one of those rain shower heads that shot the water straight down on you. There were also some other heads in the wall of the shower at different heights, but I didn't feel like figuring out the complex plumbing, when my own plumbing was already giving me problems.

I couldn't get the image of Susana in her cotton candy robe out of my mind. She was naked under there. One pull of a belt and she'd be exposed to me, fully. And what she'd said about putting things in her mouth—my dick was at full attention. I couldn't walk back out to the bedroom, my cock leading the way like a soldier heading to battle, but I also didn't want to jerk off in the shower on my wedding night. What the fuck had I gotten myself into? I switched the shower handle to cold and let the brutally freezing water pelt my body until I was shivering and not as visibly aroused. When I couldn't take it anymore, I turned off the water and grabbed an obnoxiously huge towel the shade of cartoon blueberry. Shit. I'd left my suitcase in the bedroom. I didn't want to walk out in just the towel, which left me no choice but to change into the baby blue bathrobe so large it must've been custom-made for an NBA center. Feeling foolish, but having no other options, I exited the bathroom in my terry cloth monstrosity.

Susana was on the bed, still bundled in the fuzzy pink robe. She glanced over at me, and then sat up, her eyes wide. "Oh my god. You're wearing it!"

"Don't hate me because I'm beautiful." I headed toward the platter of food. I was famished, and maybe if I ate something, I'd be clearer headed. But the tray was gone. "Where's the food?" I looked around the room, but the tray was nowhere to be seen. Only the champagne bottle was there on the table, and it was half empty. "Did you drink half of this?"

Susana raised the glass that was on her nightstand and swallowed what was left. "Maybe."

"Where's the food?" I asked again.

"I told you I was hungry."

"You did not eat all of that. And the platter itself."

"Prove it."

I'd never been one to back down from a challenge. I approached her and gently pulled on the front of her robe. "Show me where the food is or take your punishment."

"It's hard to take your threats seriously when you're dressed like that."

"You're one to talk, pink princess."

"Let's see what you have up your sleeve, Papa Smurf."

"Last chance. Where is it?"

"You want to know where it is?" Susana's gray eyes flashed, and she pulled her bottom lip in with her teeth. She lowered her head and looked up at me through long eyelashes. I was close enough to her to smell the champagne on her breath.

"Tell me. Now."

"It's right. Here." She pulled away from me and untied the belt on her robe. She let the pink fabric fall open. I saw skin. Lots of skin. She pulled it open a little more, exposing her stomach, and she scraped her fingernails across her belly button. "I ate it. It's all here." She leaned back on the bed and the robe fell of her shoulders. Her breasts were free, and they were breathtaking.

I'd been imagining them for years, but they were more perfect than I ever could've conjured up in my mind. They were full and round and heavy, and her nipples stood out darkly against her pale areolas. Her stomach was soft and smooth, but I couldn't concentrate on that because she'd opened her legs slightly. And what I saw was so close to heaven that I didn't know where to start, though my dick had about a thousand ideas and the massive weight of the robe was no longer enough to hold me back.

Susana pointed. "I see Anthony came out to play." She flipped over on her stomach and her robe was gone. She pushed her ass up in the air and looked at me over her shoulder. "I'm ready to take my punishment."

13

<hr>

GABE

I'd been in some sexy situations before, but this one took the cake. My *wife*, Susana Starling, out of nowhere, was naked and almost begging me to take her, to "punish" her. I stepped forward and ran one finger across the skin of Susana's ass, and it lit me up like someone flipped a breaker and turned on the electricity for an entire city. She half sighed, half moaned, and pushed back so her whole cheek was shoved into my palm. My cock had broken free from the confines of the bathrobe from hell, and it knew exactly where it wanted to be. If I took one step forward, I could push myself between her warm folds and I'd be inside her—a place I'd dreamed about. I could do that. She was asking me to do that. But the "out of nowhere" was pulling on me. I took two big steps back and closed my robe, trapping my dick once again.

"Hey, Sunny?"

"Yes, Archie?" She'd relaxed onto the bed and was lying flat, her eyes were closed, and her voice was sleepy. She was still fully exposed, and I couldn't look away.

"How much champagne did you drink?"

"I dunno. Just a little."

"More than the one glass you had before I showered?" I

noticed a pink bath towel draped over the back of a chair near the bed. I reached for it and then placed it across her, covering her up.

"Only two."

"Only two all together?"

"No, only two after the one you gave me." She rolled onto her back, but shifted the towel so she was partially covered.

"That's a lot."

"That's a lot," she repeated.

"I wasn't in the shower for *that* long."

"I was thirsty."

"Did you have any food?"

"I hid the food." She opened her eyes and was staring at the ceiling like she was trying to decide if she should pass out or sober up.

"Did you eat before you hid it?"

"Just grapes. One cheese. Maybe cracker."

"Where did you hide it?"

She lifted her arm straight up and then let it flop down, her index finger extended and pointing toward the sitting area.

I walked in the direction she was indicating.

"Warmer . . ." she said as I approached the easy chairs.

I didn't see the tray. I walked back toward the bed.

"Colder . . ."

I turned back around.

"Warmer . . ."

I headed toward the curtain that separated the sitting area and what was probably a dressing area.

"Hotter!" Susana chirped.

I pulled back the curtain.

"You're on fire!"

The tray, untouched except for the missing grapes, was resting on a dressing table. I brought it back to the bedside. "Let's get you dressed."

"Too tired." Susana was still under the pink towel, but it wasn't doing the best job at fully covering her breasts.

I tried to avert my eyes. Kind of. "Do you have some pajamas? Where's your suitcase."

"Bathroom." She sat up, wobbled, and then lay back down. "Have you noticed that the room's a little spinny?"

"Stay there until the room stops spinning. Might take a bit."

"Still spinning."

"Close your eyes."

Susana followed my instructions and closed her eyes. She was on top of her robe and the towel wasn't cutting it, so I folded over one side of the comforter, so she'd be warm and covered. I stretched out on my side of the bed, on top of the sheet, and waited.

Five minutes turned into thirty, and an hour later I was still staring at the ceiling, hungry but not wanting to wake her up. I went through an inventory in my head of all the orders I needed to make, the new staff I'd need to hire to take over when I was off doing my insane public appearances, and I tried to think about new gardens I could plant at the south end of the property. Anything to keep me from wondering if this marriage idea had been a stupid one. I'd finally started to doze when I felt Susana stir on her side of the bed.

Her head popped up and she blinked and looked around as if she was seeing the room for the first time. "No more spinning."

"Excellent." I hopped off the bed and went to find her something to wear.

"How long was I out?" She rubbed her eyes.

I checked my phone. "Ninety minutes, I guess?"

"My stomach feels weird."

"You need to eat something." I found her suitcase in the bathroom and riffled through some clothes until I found something that resembled sleepwear. I also grabbed a thin teal cardigan in case she was cold. "Is this ok?" I held the silky black thing up for her approval.

"Yes, that's fine. Could you help me sit up?"

I sat on the bed next to her and supported her back as she slowly sat up. She clutched the towel to her chest. I slipped the fabric over her head, and she reached her arms through the straps, one at a time. I thought about giving her some privacy so she could finish getting dressed without me seeing her naked, but one, I wasn't sure about her steadiness, and two, that ship had sailed. "Ok, let's see if you can stand up." I really hoped that our wedding night wouldn't end with one or both of us covered in vomit.

She scooted off the end of the bed and stood up inch by inch, while holding onto my arm. I slid her nightgown down her body as she stood, and by the time she was all the way up, she was fully covered.

"Want this?" I offered her the sweater.

She put it on and pulled it closed across her chest. "I forgot."

"You forgot what?"

"I forgot that champagne immediately and irrevocably fucks me up."

"You just used the word 'irrevocably.' How fucked up can you be?"

She huffed a little laugh and rolled her eyes. "Did I ask you to punish me? Please tell me that champagne also makes me hallucinate."

"Don't ask questions if you don't want the answer." I let go of her to see if she could stand on her own, which she managed.

"Oh my god." She hid her face in her hands.

"You seem to be sobering up nicely."

"I don't know about that. You're right. I should eat, or I'll get a migraine for sure. Can you walk with me to those chairs?"

I escorted her to the sitting area. We'd only been in the master suite for a half hour or so, but strangely, I was actually feeling like —a husband. And a helpful one at that.

Susana sunk into a chair and I went back to the platter and loaded up a plate of food for each of us, and grabbed some bottled water. Settled into the obscenely comfortable overstuffed chairs, we ate our food. We were silent for several minutes, but it didn't feel awkward or uncomfortable. It just felt—quiet. Peaceful, though after a bit, something about the lack of noise in the room did strike me as unnatural. It felt like we were in a padded cell, locked away from the world. Realizing what was missing, I went to the window, pushed back the thick curtains that hung from the ceiling to the floor, and opened the window. A cool night breeze rushed in, along with the sounds of crickets, frogs, and wind moving through leaves.

"That's better," Susana said from across the room. "Can you open the other one, too?"

I pushed the other window open, and a nice cross-breeze moved through the room. I sat back down.

"I'm really sorry."

"No need to apologize."

"Unfortunately, I have a clear memory of my peep show, and to say that I'm mortified doesn't cover it."

"In good times, and in bad, right?"

"I don't think that clause was in our vows."

"I'll file for an addendum."

"I can't believe we're married." She took a long sip of her water, leaned her head back, and closed her eyes. Her hair was mostly dry and it fell across the soft fabric of her cardigan and across her chest. She was so lovely.

"It doesn't feel real quite yet."

"A week ago, my biggest worry was getting some recipes right for my kids' cooking class. And now, I feel like I have the weight of the entire Starling legacy on my shoulders."

"Was that really your biggest worry a week ago?"

"I guess not." She opened her eyes but still had her head back, so her gaze was directed at the ceiling.

"What *were* your biggest fears last week?"

She twisted her rings around her finger as she considered the question. "That I'd never talk to my mother again. That I'd go bankrupt. That'd I'd accidentally get pregnant. That I'd never make anything of myself. And that I'd never find love."

"Those are a little bigger than recipe worries."

"What were *yours*?" She lifted her head and made eye contact with me, and the intensity of it unmoored me.

I felt like I was adrift on a choppy ocean. I looked down at the plate on my lap so I could concentrate. "Probably that Harry would attack another staff member, that Helen would die and this place would cease to exist. Maybe some of that 'never find love' stuff."

"Never find love? Seems like you had a busy revolving door when it came to dates."

"Oh yeah? Who'd you hear that from?"

"I don't reveal my sources."

"I think you've been spending too much time with Jeff."

"What's said in the kitchen stays in the kitchen."

I went to the drink cart and poured myself a glass of warm champagne. "None of this for you, Mrs. Starling-Green."

"If I'm keeping my last name, how does that work? Am I Mrs. Starling even though there's not a Mr. Starling, by name, at least?"

"I have no idea. It's only for a year though, so it shouldn't be a big deal." I sat back down and took another sip. Not cold, but still bubbly. "And I may have had a lot of dates, but that doesn't necessarily mean a lot of love—I told you, I'm not sticking around these parts past next May. So my dates are always casual."

"You and I didn't have a lot of dates." She'd dropped her eyes and the tone of her voice had shifted. It somehow sounded both softer and sharper than it had before. Thin ice territory.

"True. Don't think we even managed one proper date."

"It's rude to stand someone up, you know." Her voice caught

at the end of her sentence, and I could tell that tears were some-where nearby, threatening.

A spark of injustice ignited in my chest. I didn't want to argue, but I couldn't let that one slide. "It sure is, which is why I'd never do that."

Susana made a huffing noise like someone had hit her in the stomach. "Didn't take you for a liar."

Now I was the one who'd taken the punch to the gut. "Excuse me?"

"We made a date. On August 30th, almost thirteen years ago."

"We sure did. But you decided you had better plans." She had a lot of gall to give me shit when she'd been the one to screw me over.

My memory of that night was still crystal clear. We'd decided to meet in the garden hut at sunset. I was a few minutes late because Harry had seen me as I was leaving my cottage, and he gave me a job to do.

"You," Harry had said. He never used my name back then. Just called me 'you' or 'boy.' "I need you to put out some pool chairs. My son is having some pals over later and the chairs were left stacked up by some idiot."

"I believe they're power washing the deck in the morning, sir," I'd said.

"I don't give a shit what's happening in the morning. The party's happening tonight. Do it now." I hadn't wanted to leave the job for my dad, so I ran to the pool and unstacked the damn chairs as fast as I could, and then sprinted to the garden hut, hoping Susana was still waiting for me. It was our first official date, and I didn't want to ruin it before it even got started. I saw the flicker of lantern light through the windows of the hut as I approached. I remembered how I'd felt flutters in my stomach at the sight of that. How I'd thought it was romantic that she'd lit some lanterns for us. She wanted things to be nice, too.

I'd spied a flash of movement through the window and I put my hands up against the glass to get a preview of what she'd set up. But I didn't see Susana waiting alone for me in the hut. I saw her in the arms of another guy. Her back was to me, but it was obviously her. Her long black hair was in a braid, which I'd never seen her wear before, but I *had* seen that blue dress she was wearing—it was one of my favorites.

But I also saw that she was in an embrace with someone else. Some asshole had his arms tightly around her and was kissing her. He had on a red baseball cap, and I couldn't make out who it was in the dim light. My stomach jolted, and I felt like I'd been stabbed right in the belly. I remember doubling over and thinking I might vomit. And then I started to run. I ran back to my cottage and burst through the door, startling my dad who had his feet up, a beer in hand, and the TV on.

"What's wrong, son?" he'd asked me. "I thought you had a date with Susana."

"Can I have the keys to the truck?"

"Why the hurry? Are you taking Susana somewhere?"

"Date got cancelled." I didn't want to break down right there in front of my dad. I needed to get away. Fast.

"Are you alright? Maybe you shouldn't be driving—"

"I'm ok, dad. I'll be careful. Won't go far. I just really need to drive. Please?" He nodded and pointed to where the keys lay in a bowl on the kitchen counter. I grabbed them and headed back out the door. "Thanks, Dad. Love you."

"I love you too, Gabriel."

"WHAT DO you mean I 'decided I had other plans?'" Susana asked. "I was there. You were not."

"I was there. Just a little late. But it looked like you weren't in the mood for waiting for me and found a better option."

"What the fuck are you talking about?" Her tone was dark and furious. Scary, almost. Why was *she* so mad?

"Our date. When I got there you were making out with some dude."

"Excuse me?" Her words came out in a choked whisper.

"I looked in the window and saw you kissing another guy. So I left. Left town for several days, in fact, on a job for my dad. And when I came back, you'd moved out. Figured you'd decided to run off with your new Romeo." So much for keeping my cool. I was being a dickish man-baby. But the sting of that day still hurt.

"My Romeo?"

"Yeah. Mister red baseball hat."

"Do you know who that was?"

"Nope. Don't know, don't care."

"That was Tyler Hardin." She spat his name out like it was acid in her mouth. My fury lit up again.

I jumped out of my chair and kicked the ottoman hard enough to wonder if I'd broken my toe. "You were making out with fucking Tyler Hardin on our first date?"

Susana stood up and came within inches of my face. I was so mad that I needed to walk away. Run away. Punch a wall. I tried to back up, but she grabbed both of my arms and squeezed. Hard.

"I was not making out with Tyler Hardin on our first date. I was waiting for you when he came into the hut and tried to force himself on me. I only got out of there because I grabbed a trowel off the table and slammed it into his nuts. I ran out while he was writhing around on the ground like the snake he is. And I went to my mother, and she said I should've been nicer to him. That it was a 'misunderstanding.'" Tears were sliding down her face.

My gut twisted like it was stuck in a rusty vice. *No, no, no. Don't let it be true.*

"So I left home. I always thought if you'd been there, you could've saved me. But now I—you *were* there. You saw him. And you walked away and left me." She wiped her face with the arm of her pink robe. "I can't believe you left me behind."

14

SUSANA

Everything was swirling, and this time it wasn't the champagne making my world spin. Stories I'd told myself about Gabe and about what happened that night so long ago were twisting and tumbling and turning inside out. I wasn't sure what was truth, what was fiction, and what was some kind of mutant combination of both, built up by years of rumination, regret, and grief. I sat back down in my chair and wanted to roll up in a ball and cry. And then I wanted to sleep for, well, a few weeks might be nice.

Gabe looked just as shell-shocked as I felt. He was still standing, but was swaying, as if he'd just taken a brutal punch in the ring and was caught in that moment between either pulling it together or losing the match to a knock-out blow. His eyes were glassy. His hands were balled into fists. His breathing was fast and shallow.

"I'll kill him." Gabe's voice rumbled through the air like thunder in a threatening storm. He turned, walked over to his suitcase, and started pulling out clothes. He threw off his robe and stood there naked before pulling on underwear, jeans, and a t-shirt. He yanked on his socks and had his shoes lined up.

"Gabe."

"What?" He was loosening the laces on a boot.

"Sit down."

"I'm going out. I'll be back."

"You're not going anywhere. It's the middle of the night."

"Less traffic."

"You just going to pop in and pay Tyler a little visit? Do you even know where he is?"

"I'll find him."

"Gabriel Archibald Green, sit your ass down, right now."

"That's not my middle name." He was patting down his pockets, maybe looking for his phone or keys. He found his phone on the dresser. "Keys are in my cottage. I'll be back later."

I lifted myself out of the chair and tested my balance. Seemed good. Room was steady and upright. I walked to the door of the suite and put my back against it, right as Gabe was moving to exit the room.

"Excuse me. I need to leave, please." His eyes were cast downward.

"That was a long time ago. He's not a danger to me now."

"But—" his voice broke, and then he pressed the heels of his hands into his eyes, as if to hold off tears.

"Smashing your eyeballs into the back of your head is not going to improve the situation, not even a little."

He removed his hands, and his eyes were red and wet. "I failed you. I knew better. Or I should've known. You wanted to see me that night and I just . . . I didn't even stop to check. Or talk to you. I fucking left. Left you with—" Gabe squatted down, ducked his head, and he covered himself with his arms.

I didn't correct him, and I didn't comfort him. Even though the world was still a little hazy to me, now I could see how it all happened, from his point of view. I gave him a few moments to collect himself, and I needed a little time, too. I could feel it pushing on me—the memory of that night. It was bubbling up, pressing at my memory and my stomach. I'd worked so hard to put it to rest. Time and distance had helped, and so had years of ther-apy, but this had all caught me off guard. I felt steadier since my sleep and the food, but I was probably still a little drunk, and I was in no position to process all of this tonight.

Tyler's attack had only lasted seconds, but the aftershocks had been with me for years. It infected so much, but I didn't want to let it in tonight. This was *my* night. My wedding night. And even if the marriage wasn't traditional and the situation was messed up, it was still mine, not Tyler's. He couldn't have me, and he couldn't have Gabe's attention. Not yet. I'd deal with it tomorrow. "Stand up."

Gabe sighed and wiped his face with the back of his hand. He stood, slowly rising up to tower over me. He was standing inches away from me, but still couldn't look me in the eye.

I placed my palms on his chest. "This is a lot. For both of us. It's messy and I feel like I have to rewrite all my stories of the past, and I'm not sure exactly how to do that. But what I do know is that I don't have to do that tonight, and neither do you."

Gabe glanced up at me, and then lowered his eyes again.

"And I certainly don't want the primary memory of our fake wedding night to be your arrest for the murder of Tyler Hardin, though it would make my drunken strip show less of the focal point. Maybe it will look different in the morning?"

"Maybe." He moved his free hand to my shoulder and pushed aside the fabric of my cardigan. He slipped a finger under the strap of my nightgown and caressed the skin over my collar bone. His touch sent a jolt of electricity down my spine and all the way to my toes. He finally made eye contact with me, and I almost forgot what we'd been talking about. Forgot about the memory of Tyler, about the champagne, about the wedding, and about the whole reason for this marriage.

In that moment, all I could focus on was the intensity of his eyes on mine. How his lips were full and parted and I could see a flash of his teeth and his tongue. I wanted to taste him. Touch him.

"I'm sorry, Sunny." He swept me up in his arms and lifted me off the ground.

I wrapped my legs around his waist. He slipped his hand under my nightgown to support the weight of me, but I had nothing on underneath, so he was palming my bare ass. What were we doing? We were ragged and raw and out of words. It was like I weighed nothing. He carried me to the bed, spun around, and sat down with me still straddling him. He pressed his forehead against mine and the heat of his breath moved across my skin. He snaked one hand up the back of my neck and into my hair. He spread his fingers across my scalp and then clenched his fist, grabbing my hair in the process. He pulled my head gently back, exposing my neck.

"I like that," I whispered.

"What do you like?" He pressed his lips against the vein in my neck like a vampire playing with his victim.

"When you pull my hair."

"Like this?" He squeezed his fist even tighter, and I felt the tension on my scalp.

It made me whimper and I wiggled against him. My legs were spread, and his shirt rode up when I moved, so my pussy was pressed against his belly. I knew he could feel my heat. My wetness. "Just like that."

Gabe growled and he bit my neck, his teeth lingering on my skin.

"Harder."

He bit me again and he wound my long hair around his fist. He was hard under his jeans and his cock was poking my ass. I wanted him. For an insane moment I didn't care about condoms or babies or rules or anything at all. I just wanted Gabriel Green. My husband.

"Susana." Gabe turned his face away like he was afraid if he didn't, he would consume me. "Our rules." He let go of my hair.

Right. The rules." I dug both of my hands into his hair and

pulled his head to me, against my chest. Our breathing was heavy and in-sync.

"Let's see how we feel in the morning." He untangled my fingers from his hair and then grasped my waist and scooted me back a few inches. "Once we break the rules, we can't go back."

I tipped over onto the bed, removing myself from his lap. He was right. "Sorry about that."

"Not as sorry as I am."

MY FIRST TEN seconds of morning wakefulness were blissful: comfortable bed, sweet breeze floating through an open window, and the scattered songs of birds singing me awake. But then my stomach twisted and the memories from last night swarmed me: the champagne, our argument, how Gabe almost murdered Tyler, and how we'd come so close to breaking the rules. I peeked out from under the covers to see if my husband was still asleep next to me, but the other side of the bed was unoccupied. I'd passed out almost as soon as my head hit the pillow, thanks to the champagne. It was the right thing to stick to our rules, but I would've broken them if Gabe hadn't stopped me.

Some squeaking coming from the door caught my attention, and I sat up and caught sight of Gabriel wheeling in a food cart.

"Had I known that room service was a regular thing here, I might've moved home sooner," I said.

Gabe jumped a little, as if surprised to hear my voice. "Good morning, Sunshine."

"How long have you been waiting to use that phrase on me?"

"Thirteen years, ten months, and two days. Give or take." Gabe was wearing a tight t-shirt from a local brewery, and athletic shorts. His feet were bare, and his hair was damp and the color of golden sand at sunset. I still wasn't used to the sight of him; he'd been walking around in my head for years, but the real Gabe was so much more than anything I'd been able to pull up in my fantasies. "Hungry?"

"I think so?" I threw off the covers and swung my feet over the bed. Usually after a night of drinking I didn't have any ill effects, but my reaction to the champagne was so intense that I didn't trust myself yet. Even hard liquor didn't affect me quite like that. Maybe I had a grape allergy.

Gabe hopped to my side and put his arm out for me to grab, which I did. I felt steady and normal, thank god. "I'm good. Just gonna use the bathroom."

"Susana?" Gabe didn't let go. The pressure of his fingers on my arm reminded me of how he'd grabbed my hair last night. "Are we ok about last night? Do you need to talk about any of it?"

"Which part? ChampagneGate, the Tyler fiasco, or our brush with the rules?"

Gabe kept holding on to me. He'd better let go soon, or we'd get ourselves in trouble sooner as opposed to later. "Any of it, but I guess I meant the last one. The rules."

"I don't need to talk. But I do need to pee."

He released my arm. "Don't let me stop you. And if you're good, I'm good."

"Temporary insanity, right?"

Gabe shrugged. "Maybe." He turned back to the food cart. "Join me for breakfast when you're done."

In the bathroom, I came face to face with my horrifying reflection. My straight and boring hair usually came with one benefit: it was hard to mess up. It was also impossible to curl, fluff, and style in any cool way, but whatever happened last night possessed my hair like an unhinged demon and it was tangled, matted, and sticking straight up in a few spots. I had circles under my eyes, my lips were chapped, and my nose was pink. There was no way Gabe could've found this attractive. Surely I didn't look this awful last night. Right?

I brushed my teeth for several minutes, and then took a quick shower. When I stepped out of the shower, I spied a fresh stack of white towels and two normal white spa robes hanging on a wall hook. The pink monstrosity was gone! There was also a new addition of fuzzy slippers that looked just my size. The bathroom fairy must've paid us a visit. I dried off, put on a robe, slipped on the slippers, and went back out to join my husband for breakfast.

Gabe was relaxing on a chair by the window, a cup of steaming coffee in his hands. He stood up as I approached. "What can I get you to eat?"

"I can get it. Thanks, though." I started lifting lids and checking out the offerings: scrambled eggs, sausage, strawberries, kiwi, and pineapple slices, plus an assortment of baked goods like muffins, croissants, and some apple cider donuts. "This is enough food for ten people." I put some eggs, fruit, and a donut on my plate.

"Jeff said that newlyweds need a lot of food to refuel after their wedding night."

"Some more than others." I sat down in the chair across from Gabe's and took a bite of the donut. Then another. I was ravenous.

"So, you're feeling better? Not hungover?"

"My stomach seems fine, no headache, and I'm not dizzy. Knock on wood, but I think I'm okay. Is there any more coffee?"

"The carafe's on the table by the door." He hopped up. "How do you take it?"

"Cream and sugar, please."

"I took you for a black coffee type."

"Because I'm bitter and have no taste buds?"

"No, the opposite. Figured you for a 'purity of taste' kind of person."

"I guess you're not totally wrong. But most places have sketchy coffee, and I usually play it safe."

"Jeff roasts his own beans."

"Ok, just cream, then."

"Coming right up." Gabe poured my coffee then brought it to

where I sat. "Champagne and rules aside, how's your headspace regarding our misunderstanding? I mean, I get it. It was a long time ago, but still. It changes things."

I took a deep breath and let it out slowly. Then I sipped my own coffee. It was bright and warm with notes of honey and cereal. "I'm not sure about the term 'misunderstanding,' and I'm not sure how I feel."

"I wasn't sure what to call it."

"Our 'plot twist'?"

"That works. How do you feel about our plot twist?"

"Twisty. How do *you* feel about it?"

Gabe ran both hands wildly through his hair like he was trying to shake something free. "I feel lots of things."

"Give me a few."

"I'm angry, frustrated, confused, concerned, disappointed in myself. Embarrassed. Your turn."

Sometimes the memory came in sharp and hot like a spinning blade, tearing up everything in sight. Other times it dropped heavy and suffocating, just snuffing out all my emotions and my ability to breathe. Right now, it felt defanged and distant, so maybe I was safe to explore it just a bit.

"Take your time." He was studying my face as I spoke, but I felt too shy to make eye contact. I watched the waving branches of the Tulip tree outside the back window.

"I feel disoriented." I closed my eyes and tried to center myself and find the words to describe my feelings. "There were different layers. There was the event with Tyler. Then what happened with my mom. And then what had happened with you. And now I have a new narrative about you, and that adds some relief, but also, I'm mad at myself. All of it is tangled together. I thought I had it all figured out, but now I'm not sure."

Gabe sat forward and clasped his hands together. I wanted to get back on his lap and just wrap myself in his arms and fall into a deep, forgetful sleep.

His mouth was set in a straight line. "Would it help if we talked about any of it? Tried to untangle it? It's ok if you aren't ready."

"We can try. I don't know how far I'll get."

"That's totally fine," Gabe said. "Where would you like to start? You choose."

"The part I'm most clear on right now is the Tyler part. I can tell you about that."

"Okay." Gabe's words were calm, but he was wringing his hands, and his leg was bouncing. His muscles were taut and tense.

"I was in the gardener's hut, and it was getting dark. There was no electricity in there back then. You know that. I lit a few candles. I had a lighter with me—I'd nabbed a few of my mom's cigarettes, in case you thought that would be cool, to smoke one. The door opened but it wasn't you."

Gabe sat back in his chair and swiped his palms down his face and then returned to the wringing of his hands.

"You sure you're ok to hear this?"

"You had to live it, Susana. I can take hearing about whatever you need to tell me."

I'd done enough processing of the memory that it usually didn't bite to recall it. So I went on with my story. "He'd been drinking. I could smell it. He said something stupid like, 'Hey sis, fancy meeting you here.' I told him, for the millionth time, that I wasn't his sister. He said, 'that's right, you're not, which is why we can do this' and he grabbed me and pulled me in and tried to kiss me.

I think I froze. He slobbered all over my face and it was just so disgusting. I tried to push him away. He was too strong, though, and he shoved me toward the worktable and was trying to suck on my neck. There was a trowel on the table. I grabbed it. He'd kind of lost his balance and stepped back from me for a second, and I took that moment to knock him right in the nuts as hard as I could. He didn't see it coming and he fell down, screaming. I threw the little shovel at his face, and it hit him right on the nose.

He called me a bitch, a whore. Some other stuff. I tried to run out and he grabbed my ankle and held on, and I almost fell. I remembered the lighter in my pocket. I flicked it open and held the flame against his knuckles. He screamed some more—"

"That tracks." Gabe tried to smile, but it looked forced.

"He let go, and I got out of there. Ran all the way back to the big house, found my mom, who was half-passed out in the library. Looking back, I realize that she was high or drugged or something. She was out of it. She kept telling me to 'calm down' and that it had been a 'misunderstanding.'

"Ah. That word." Gabe had stayed still during my story but he looked like he was taut and ready to jump out of his skin.

"I finally gave up on my mom and found Jag. Told him I had to leave but wouldn't give him any details. He found a safe place for me to stay, got me set up, called me every night. I never did tell him specifically what'd happened. And I guess that's how my life as an emancipated minor began. Then I turned eighteen, eventually went to school, stuff like that. But you don't need my whole life story right now."

"You can tell me any story you want, no matter how long it is."

"I'd rather eat some eggs. But mine are cold."

Gabe jumped up and took my plate from me. He got a fresh plate and spooned out some hot eggs from the warmer. He added a sausage link and broke a blueberry muffin in half, giving me part of it, and taking the other half for himself.

"Thanks." I bit into the sausage which was smokey and sweet and tasted slightly of maple syrup.

"How are you feeling? After telling me all that?"

I shrugged. "A little numb. Sometimes I go on autopilot. But I'm ok."

Gabe leaned forward, hung his head, and clasped his hands behind his neck. He stayed in that position for almost a minute, and I took that time to finish all the food on my plate. My mood was lifting. Maybe because of the food. Or maybe it was telling my story to Gabe. He hadn't meant to abandon me, at least not in the way I'd always thought.

"Susana, I'm so sorry."

"You don't have to—"

"Please let me finish, if that's okay."

"Okay. Go ahead."

"I'm so sorry. I'm sorry that I was late that night. I'm sorry that I assumed the worst. I'm more sorry than you'll ever know that I walked away—no, that I *ran* away that night. And that I never had the courage to reach out to you. I got so many things wrong, and so much of this is my fault. And I'm so sorry that you got hurt. By Tyler, by your mom, by me. You didn't deserve any of that." He reached out his hand but pulled back quickly when someone knocked at the door.

"Yes?" Gabe's voice was tinged with annoyance.

"Gabriel." Jag was on the other side of the door. "It's urgent."

15

GABE

Susana and I should've been luxuriating on some kind of fake honeymoon, but instead we were rushing through the halls of Starling Manor to try to avert a crisis that was brewing on the front steps. I wished the troublemakers had decided to make a scene in another spot, because the front of the house was closest to the road, and according to Jag, reporters had been trying to drive up the front boulevard since five o'clock in the morning. It was private property, so they'd been escorted out, but the house was surrounded by wooded acreage, and the forest was dense enough that someone with a big lens could hide out and get some pretty clear photographs if they wanted to risk it. I thought Susana and I would have some time to acclimate to the public nature of our marriage, but we'd had to hit the ground running. Literally.

"Hold on!" Susana was breathless and trying to slide her flip-flop back on. We'd been in such a hurry that she grabbed the closest clothes in her suitcase, which were a strapless sundress and slip-on sandals. She was trying to keep up, but by the looks of how she was grabbing her chest as she tried to jog along with me, she'd forgotten a bra, and the dress wasn't very supportive. "Good lord." She was tugging at her dress as it threatened to slide off her breasts.

"The press are going to get an eyeful this morning if I'm not careful."

"Let me help you." I slowed down and put my arm around her and balled up the bodice of her dress in my hand, holding it tight to her body. "Just walk with me and look like you're having a good time when we go outside."

"How can we be having a good time when there's some kind of labor dispute on the front lawn? I don't think I've ever heard Jag say the word 'urgent.'"

"You've been gone too long. He says a lot of things he doesn't want to say when Harry's around."

She stopped short. "Harry's out there?"

"Isn't that what Jag said?"

"I was in the bathroom getting dressed. I didn't hear the whole thing!" She was still clutching her chest.

"You don't have to hold on," I said in a hushed tone. "I won't let go." A staff member held the front door open for us and Susana and I stepped out into the bright May morning.

"If you forget for even one second, my boobs are going to end up as America's favorite breakout stars. People are still talking about Janet Jackson at the Superbowl, and that was just a nipple."

"You're pretty popular, darling." I said, kissing her on the cheek for show, because we were now in the public domain. "But you're no Janet." Playing for the folks in the nosebleed seats, I grinned at her like a madman.

"That's Starling, if you're nasty."

"Why doesn't this dress have straps?" My hand was starting to cramp, but I held on tight.

"It does, sugar blossom." Susana stood on tiptoe and planted an awkward kiss on the side of my neck. "But they're detachable, and I didn't have time to attach them, love bug."

"If it isn't the newlyweds," Harry boomed from the driveway.

"All packed up and ready to go, Hardin?" I wanted to march

down the steps and stuff him into his car, but I was still holding up Susana's dress.

"I thought I'd stick around for a while, wait and see what happens with this sham of a marriage." Susana broke free of my hold, mercifully grabbing tightly to the front of her chest as she descended the front steps.

My whole ground crew was out there, but they all still had their travel jackets on. No one had started working. I waved one of them over, a young guy named Logan, and motioned for him to give me his windbreaker. He slipped it off and I rushed to Susana and held up the jacket.

"Thank you, Gabriel," she said so sweetly, so theatrically, that surely everyone knew she was faking it.

I fought back the temptation to tell her to can it, and instead I silently helped her into the jacket like a good husband, even zipping it up for her. Renegade breasts were contained.

"You have no legal right to be here, Harry. You need to be on your way," Susana said.

"Just had a little business to do before heading out." He smiled, but with those teeth, he looked like a shark planning to chomp a school of fish.

"And what business is that?" Susana asked, all the sweetness drained out of her voice, leaving nothing but sharp edges.

"Just had to fire these fuckups, but they won't leave." Harry nodded toward my crew. "I've called the cops to remove them from the premises, and they demanded to see you while we wait for the paddy wagon."

Nothing like a few words from Hardin to make my guts feel like they'd been doused with gasoline and set on fire. There was no wind that morning, but I saw some branches tremble in the woods just to the west of the property. My guess was that Harry had a photographer planted there and they were all waiting for me to lose my shit. I couldn't give them the satisfaction. "You don't have the authority to fire my crew. They were hired by me, and you don't live here anymore," I shouted at Harry.

"I fired them yesterday morning, when I still had the 'authority' to do whatever I damn well pleased."

"We don't know what to do, Green." Gilbert was my crew leader, and he looked worried. "I don't want to go, but I don't want to get arrested."

A police car turned up the driveway and headed toward us. This was just a publicity stunt by Harry—one last hurrah to shit on the people of Starling Manor while he was still on the grounds, and I really, really didn't want him to win this one. A lot depended on what kind of officers were in that cruiser. No one made a move as the car came to a stop about ten yards away. The doors opened and two female officers stepped out. That was a good sign.

One officer was short and compact, and her biceps were barely contained by the tight sleeves of her uniform. She may have been a bit over five feet tall, but she had the presence of someone much larger. Her partner was almost as tall as I was with a soft face and sharp eyes. No way would I fuck with either of them. All of us, with the exception of Harry, took a step back when the officers approached us.

"Took your sweet time, ladies." Harry huffed out an exaggerated sigh. "Guess they sent us the B-Team." Another step back. Hardin might dig his own grave.

"What seems to be the problem?" The small officer had a big voice.

"I called you because I've fired these workers, and they refuse to leave. They're trespassing on private property." Harry gave a smug little shake of his head to punctuate his sentence.

"The actual situation is that Harold Hardin," Susana nodded in Harry's direction, "is trespassing. He is no longer a resident of this estate and he's been asked to leave. This crew has been hired by me, and I am the legal owner of this property." The officers looked between Susana and Harry.

"And your name is?" The tall cop asked.

"Susana Starling."

Pretty sure they already knew her name.

"I'm not going anywhere." Harry stomped his foot for added effect, nearly smashing Susana's toes in the process.

She jumped aside just in time but something on the ground caught her attention. Harry's feet?

"This is my house, and these fakers are just squatters. Arrest them!" No one wanted any trouble, but Harry was about to drag this out as long as possible. The officers exchanged a look, and then stepped back to their car to collect notebooks, I assumed. I glanced at Susana who suddenly had the most wicked expression on her face. She winked at me, and then turned back to Harry. She pointed at his feet, which were unusually small and stuffed like plump sausages into a pair of overpriced dress shoes.

"You know what they say about the size of a man's feet," Susana said, just loud enough for only Harry and me to hear.

A scarlet wave started at Harry's neck and slithered up to his chin, his cheeks, his eyes, and landed on his forehead. He was an impressive shade of fire-engine red!

"You little whore!" Harry lunged at Susana, grabbed hold of her hair, and yanked her toward the ground.

He sure moved fast for such a slug. I jumped forward to save my wife from the clutches of that cretin, but I was pushed back by the cops, who had the situation quickly contained. Harry was cuffed and in the back of the police car so fast that I almost missed it. Susana's hair was a mess, and she had some dirt on her cheek, but looked otherwise unharmed.

"Pick me up, Archie." Susana whispered. "We're on."

Shit, our PDA. I gathered her up in my arms and held her tightly against my chest. I cradled her cheek with my fingers as I visibly searched her for bumps and bruises. She flung her arms around my neck and gazed up at me so adoringly that I almost believed she'd fallen head over heels in love with me in the last two minutes.

"Are you ok, baby?" It felt weird calling her baby, but it was better than 'sugar blossom.'

"I'm ok." She snuggled in close.

Jag had approached the officers, and while Harry kicked at the windows of the cruiser, Jag gave the cops the information they needed about their latest perp.

"I don't know if you were really fired, but you're all rehired." My crew, some of whom were standing shell-shocked with their mouths hanging open, were visibly relieved.

"Will we get docked for the hours we couldn't work? He wouldn't let us work yesterday, either." Gilbert twisted his hat in his hands. "He tried to lock us in the pool house."

"You'll be paid double for the hours he made you miss," Susana offered, her arms still around my neck. "I'm so sorry and thank you for staying. You've made Starling Manor such a beautiful estate, and we're so fortunate to have you here."

My guys all smiled and a few of them looked starstruck.

"I'm going to change clothes, and then I'll come find you," I told them.

"But it's your honeymoon, boss," Logan said. Whoops. It was my honeymoon.

"I can spare him for a few hours," Sunny said. "Just don't wear him out," she added sweetly, making all the guys laugh. Then she kissed me square on the lips, lingering longer than she needed to, for sure. "Can you take me inside, Archie?" Did she just bat her eyelashes at me?

"Your wish is my command." That got some "awws" from the guys, but also some eye rolls. I walked back up the steps and carried my bride over the threshold of our mansion. I had no idea what to expect next in our marriage, but if our first morning had started like this, I knew to expect the unexpected.

16

I tried to concentrate on the road, but my mind kept wandering over everything that'd happened in the last forty-eight hours: I'd returned to my childhood home, gotten engaged, married, and drunk, I'd dissected my teenage trauma, uncovered information that changed a major life narrative, almost had sex on my wedding night, and I'd wrapped it all up with being assaulted on the steps of Starling Manor.

On the plus side, I'd managed to push Harry's buttons and any hidden photographers would've gotten some good footage. Overall, much more exciting than my normal mid-week activities, which usually included menu planning and making batches of freezable dinners for picture-perfect families. Now I had my own chef but wasn't sure that this was the life I wanted. To be honest, I didn't know what the hell I wanted, but I did know that I was glad to have Gabe with me as we drove back to my house to get some of my things. Maybe I'd feel more grounded once I was around my own stuff.

"Wasn't that our exit?" Gabe pointed to the off ramp that I'd just passed.

"Shit."

"That's the second turn you've missed. You sure you know the way back to your house? Should we use the GPS?"

"I don't need the GPS to get home." I spied a U-turn spot in the median and put on my turn signal.

"You're not making a very convincing case for that."

"I'm just distracted." We were already sounding like an annoying married couple. At least this would help us keep up appearances as a legit Mister and Missus.

"We should've taken the driver Jag offered. Then you could've daydreamed all the way to your house, and I could've caught a much-needed nap." Gabe touched my arm briefly. "Stop here. I'll take over."

"You don't know the way to my house." I pulled into the median and put the car in park.

"There's this crazy newfangled invention called Google Maps. Let's switch seats."

I didn't resist. I got out of the car and got back in on the passenger side while Gabe climbed into the driver's seat.

"I love this car." He slid back the seat of the Audi Q7 to make room for his long legs. It was one of the Starling fleet cars, because I'd left mine at home when I got a ride to the manor last week for the reading of my mother's will. "You know we could've sent someone to pick up your stuff."

"I want to get my own things. And I'm hoping my neighbor will be home—I need to touch base with her."

Mrs. Jenkins texted me yesterday and said that she was about to file a missing person's report. She had no idea all that'd happened in the last few days.

Gabe typed the address into his phone and pulled back out on the highway.

I reclined my seat and stretched out. "Sorry about the detours."

Gabe kept his eyes on the road, and I let myself fall into a daydream—back to last night when I'd been on his lap and he had my hair balled up in his fist, and I'd really wanted to break our rules immediately. I felt his desire swell underneath me. How would he feel in my hand? My mouth? My—

"Sunny?"

"What?"

"I asked what your neighbor's name was."

"Sorry. Mrs. Jenkins."

"I'm glad I took over the driving."

So was I. I couldn't be trusted to drive when I was this tired, this confused, and this distracted by a daydream that had to remain just that—an unlived fantasy.

Twenty minutes later, we pulled up into my driveway. I hadn't expected the pang of homesickness that hit me as I walked up to my little house, and I couldn't help wondering what Gabe was thinking as he looked around. He was used to beautiful, lush gardens, perfectly planned landscapes, and residences where one chip in the paint called for immediate maintenance. My place wasn't run down, but it sure looked lived-in. As I got my keys out of my bag, I noticed some movement in the curtains next door. Gabe stepped onto the front porch and waited patiently for me to unlock the door.

I put the key in the lock. "Incoming. In five, four, three, two—"

"Well, howdy stranger!"

Mrs. Jenkins' voice caused Gabe to startle. He jumped and he kicked over a small bowl of water that was tucked into the corner of my porch.

"Didn't mean to scare you, big fella! Looks like you'll need to replace Mallory's water, though." She pointed at the bowl.

"It's good to see you!" I reached out for a hug and Mrs. Jenkins gave me a big squeeze. "And who's Mallory?"

"Your cat."

I didn't have a cat.

Mrs. Jenkins had her eyes on Gabe, looking him up, down, and then up again. "I like the look of you."

"I like the look of you, too. Your art is incredible."

She held out her arms for him to admire and nodded toward a large colorful tattoo of a Russian nesting doll on her upper arm. "This is my newest one. Part of it covers up a horrible flower I had done years ago, but now you'd never know it even existed!"

Gabe leaned in for a closer look. "Stunning."

"Got any tats?"

"Can't say that I do. I've thought about it, though. Just have trouble deciding on what to start with."

"Let me know if you decide to get one. I'll get you the name of my artist, and I have thousands of ideas, and not enough skin to make them all a reality." She took his arm and ran her hand from his wrist up to his elbow. "Miles of virgin skin. So many possibilities!"

"Can we revisit what you said about a cat?" I opened the door and they followed me inside.

"I leave food and water out for your cat." Mrs. Jenkins wandered over to a window and pushed it open. "Need some fresh air in here."

"I don't have a cat."

"You *didn't* have a cat. But now you do." She sat down on my couch, still ogling Gabe. "It also looks like you have a new friend. Aren't you going to introduce us?"

"Oh, yes. I'm sorry. This is Gabriel Green. Gabe, this is Jacinda Jenkins."

"Nice to meet you." Gabe waved from his spot by the door.

"Likewise. You a new cousin I haven't met? You're just as handsome as those other two, but you have a whole different look."

"No, I'm not a cousin. I'm Susana's—" Gabe stopped short and looked at me for help.

"He's my husband."

"Sure he is." Mrs. Jenkins scoffed and then stood up from the couch and went to explore my kitchen. "Have any snacks?"

"I haven't been shopping since last Saturday, so I'm not sure what my snack status is."

"Why've you been gone?" She opened the fridge and started pulling out cartons of milk and cottage cheese, opening lids, and sniffing the contents.

"Because I got married."

"Sure you did. This cheese needs to go." She tossed a block of cheddar onto the counter and reached in to grab a container of yogurt. I pulled a trash bag out of a lower cabinet and handed it to her, with my left hand. She saw my rings and stopped mid-sniff. "What are those?"

"My engagement and wedding rings." I held my hand closer to her face for inspection.

"I don't understand." She looked at Gabe again, who gave another wave. "He's really your husband?"

"He is."

"But was he your boyfriend, like, last week?"

"He was not."

"You just met him? I don't know if I can stand by this. You're handsome and all," she shot Gabe a sorry/not sorry look, "but for all we know you're some kind of scam artist or serial killer."

Gabe held up his arms in a gesture of surrender. "I understand why you're wary, Mrs. Jenkins. Though I do promise that I have the best intentions with Susana."

"That's what you'd say if you were a scam artist."

"Good point."

"I've known Gabe since we were teenagers. And I knew his father. He's a good guy."

Gabe blushed and looked down at his feet.

Mrs. Jenkins crossed her arms, narrowed her eyes, and raised her eyebrow. "What are you two up to?"

I sat on the couch and Gabe froze for a few seconds, like he was trying to remember how he was supposed to act. He shook his head, ever so slightly, as if trying to get his mind straight, and then crossed the room and joined me. He put his arm around my shoulders but it hung there awkwardly, like he was a bad actor in a junior high play. Mrs. Jenkins kept her arms crossed and didn't look impressed. I needed to say something to break the tension.

"My mother died."

Her expression changed from one of suspicion to one of sympathy. Mostly. "I'm very sorry to hear that. That must've been hard on you." Mrs. Jenkins knew some of the stories about my mom and Harry. She'd been one of my only friends over the last few years.

"THERE WAS A STIPULATION IN THE WILL," I tried to figure out how to explain without overdoing it, "regarding the estate."

"Go on," she perched herself on a barstool and leaned forward. Mrs. Jenkins loved a good scandal.

"I needed to be married within thirty days, or the entire estate went to Harry Hardin—"

"That asshole?" she jumped off her chair and pounded her fist once on the counter. "I'd make you marry me before I'd see that man inherit anything!" She pounded the counter again and then studied Gabe for several seconds. "Though I see you've made a more appropriate choice."

Gabe planted a small kiss on my neck. He was getting better at the role of fake husband.

"I think she made a good choice." Gabe kissed me again. "No offense to you, of course."

"None taken." We were interrupted by a scratching at the front door, and the sound of something crying. "Mallory!" Mrs. Jenkins crossed the room, opened the front door, and let in a scruffy black kitten with golden eyes.

"Whose cat is that?"

"I told you, yours!" She scooped up the kitten and plopped her on my lap. The cat collapsed, stretched out on its back, and promptly fell asleep.

"It's obviously not mine." I put my hand on the kitten's soft belly and felt a rumbling purr vibrating her whole body.

"The day after you left, she showed up at your door. I tried to bring her to my house every day, and she was very polite, but she always wanted to go back outside, and then she'd camp out on your porch. I gave her some food and water and told her you'd be back to get her sooner or later. And here you are."

I glanced over at Gabe who was looking at the cat with an expression of . . . terror? Repulsion? Shit. Had I just married a man who hated cats? That was a huge red flag in my book. I'd never felt it was the right time to have a pet, but it wasn't because I didn't like animals. "What's wrong?"

"I don't do cats." He turned his head away as if avoiding looking at the kitten would make her disappear.

"Uh-oh. Guess you didn't vet him well enough!" Mrs. Jenkins snickered.

"Do you hate cats?" I asked him. "What about dogs? We might have to rethink this."

"You don't have any pets, and I'm not accusing *you* of hating animals." Gabe stood up and ran his hands through his hair. He was agitated.

Mrs. Jenkins hopped back up on the barstool, settling in for the show.

"I didn't want the responsibility of one, but the way you were looking at Mallory here, it seemed like you wanted to throw her out the window." Mallory had awakened and was sitting up on my lap, staring at Gabe.

"I don't hate cats." Gabe was pacing and still wouldn't look at me or the kitten.

"Then what's the problem?"

"Hey, I've got a cat tattoo! Check this out!" Mrs. Jenkins pulled up her shirt, showing off a hissing cat on her flank.

I shook my head at her to indicate that this wasn't the right time. She shrugged and lowered her shirt.

"The problem is . . . Pebbles." Gabe had his back turned to us and sounded like he might be choking.

"Did you say 'Pebbles?' Are you ok? Are you having an allergic reaction? I can put her outside." I stood up and Mallory let out a meow in protest.

Gabe spun around and his eyes were bright red.

"Oh god, you are allergic! Sorry, buddy." I gave the cat a kiss on the head and went to put her back outside, but Gabe blocked the door.

"I'm not allergic." He wiped his eyes.

"Then what's wrong?"

"This is ridiculous. I'm sorry." Gabe took a deep breath.

"Out with it, hot shot," Mrs. Jenkins added from her spot on the stool.

"I had a cat. When I was a kid. Her name was Pebbles. And she looked just like . . . that." He was pointing at Mallory. "It just brings back a lot of memories." Gabe turned away. I placed the kitten on the floor and put my hand on Gabe's back. He collected himself and turned back around. "I'm sorry. Mallory just looks so much like her. She was my best friend for a lot of years."

"Only child?" Mrs. Jenkins asked. Gabe nodded. "Figures."

I gathered Gabe into a hug, and he put his face on my shoulder and held on tight. "I think that's my cue to leave." Mrs. Jenkins was back on her feet and heading toward the exit. "Check with me before you leave. I have some cat food for you!" And then she was gone.

Gabe lifted his head, and his eyes were clearer. "Jesus. I have no idea why I'm losing it over a cat."

"Maybe it's not about the cat."

He glanced at me, and then pulled me into a hug. "You're probably right about that," he said into my hair.

His body was warm against mine. I wanted to tighten my grip, pull him closer, maybe even kiss his forehead. His jaw. His mouth. Shit. "Maybe you're hungry," I offered.

"Maybe I am." He closed the already small distance between us and his chest pressed against mine.

My body was getting used to the public displays of affection, but I had a hard time remembering to stop once we were alone. I needed to get out of this embrace. "Want a tour?" I asked.

"Wouldn't mind seeing your bedroom."

17

SUSANA

My bedroom. The way I felt when he said those words was problematic. Gabe was my husband, but on paper only. I had to keep my eye on the prize, the prize being not letting my family legacy fall into the hands of the vile Hardin family. One thought of Harry's slimy face was enough to get me back on track.

"You can tell a lot about a person from their choice in bedroom decor." Gabe let go of me and stepped back. "Are you a duvet girl, or a comforter kind of woman? Sheer curtains or blackout blinds? Three hundred pillows or one floppy old blanket that you've rested your head on for a decade?"

"Let's eat first. I don't want you bursting into tears if you see something in there that reminds you of your childhood."

"Keep it up, Starling, and you'll be sorry," Gabe grumbled, but he walked toward the kitchen and examined some of the containers Mrs. Jenkins had left behind.

I kind of wanted to "keep it up" to see exactly what he meant by me being sorry, but instead I opened the pantry and retrieved some protein bars for both of us. Gabe unwrapped his and ate it in two bites.

"Want another?" I asked.

"If you have one." He ate the second one just as quickly.

I wandered in the direction of my bedroom. "Not sure you'll find the answers you're seeking, but my room's over here." I almost never let men come into my home—if I was on a date and had a "let's go back to my place" moment, I always chose his. Female friends rarely came over, either, except for Mrs. Jenkins. I'd kept my house and my heart on lock down for a lot of years, and not only was I letting a man step into my bedroom, but that man was Gabriel Green.

He followed me, crossed over the threshold, and put his hands on his hips. "Huh."

"What?"

"Not what I expected." He walked a few steps and touched the wall. "Is that wallpaper?"

"It is." My walls were covered in a slate-blue wallpaper that was sprinkled with a pattern of fern fronds. Two large windows let in warm bright light, and they were flanked by white curtains hand-printed with grey diamond shapes. A plush shag area rug covered most of the wooden floor, lush plants hung from the ceiling near the windows, and a few more succulents sat upon an antique dresser I'd found at an estate sale. An eclectic mix of paintings, framed embroidery, photographs, and mirrors hung on the walls, making for a crowded but cozy vibe. My bed had a few layers of quilts and throw pillows, plus a stuffed panda named Poppy. "What exactly did you expect?"

"Honestly?"

"Unless you'd rather lie."

He sat down on my bed and ran his fingers across the blanket. "Like, neutrals. Minimalist kind of stuff."

I sat down on the other side of the bed. "So, you mean boring?"

"Your words, not mine." He kicked off his shoes and stretched out on the bed, and I did the same. "Is this a weighted blanket?"

"Yes. I love that thing."

"Are you some kind of masochist?"

"What do you have against weighted blankets?"

"Nothing, if you don't mind the feeling of sleeping with a boa constrictor. They make me feel like I'm trapped and dying."

"To each her own."

He studied my room for a few moments more. "I just thought of you as more . . . buttoned up than this. And you have a shit-ton of plants."

"I have some secret sides you don't know about."

"That became apparent once you got a little champagne in you."

"Can we put that in the 'never to be spoken of again' file?"

"I'm waiting to see if I have any bargaining power with it."

"You're not supposed to hold things over your wife!" I whacked him with a pillow.

"Oh, no?" He rolled over on his side so he was facing me. "What *am* I supposed to do with a wife, then?"

"Love, honor, cherish. That kind of stuff." The words just popped out of my mouth before I thought about what I was saying. And yep, I just used the L-word. I could feel my cheeks burning. "Or you could eat lunch with your so-called wife. Hungry?" Food was a universal subject-changer.

Gabe pulled on my shoulder and rolled me back on the bed, preventing my escape. "Not really hungry yet." He moved closer to me until our bodies were nearly pressed together.

My heart was pounding, my mouth was dry, and my fingers were shaking, so I balled my hands into fists and rested them against Gabe's chest. His chest. That's where I kept my gaze. Not that I minded looking at it, though I was getting distracted wondering what it would feel like to run my fingers through his chest hair.

"Is this making you uncomfortable?" He backed up a few inches. "We can go eat if you want."

"Nervous, yes. Not uncomfortable."

He combed his fingers through my hair, which sent tingles down my entire body. Maybe he didn't have the best control around me, either. This could be dangerous. We had to keep this above board. That's what I kept telling myself, at least. I closed my eyes, hoping that if I couldn't see him, I wouldn't be so attracted to him. Slow deep breath in, slow exhale. Slow deep breath in, slow exhale.

Gabe kissed my forehead, but lingered long enough that it didn't feel very chaste. He kissed my closed eye. Then the other. He ran his fingers down my neck, over my bone, and down my arm and then jumped them to my hip where he found a bare spot of skin and he traced soft lines up and down the skin of my waist.

Don't kiss him, Susana. Don't you dare. Do not escalate! My pulse pounded in my ears. *Thump, thump, thump . . . THUMP, THUMP!* The last two thumps didn't belong to the blood rushing through my veins—they belonged to some maniac who was pounding on my front door and didn't plan on stopping anytime soon.

18

GABE

Whoever was banging on the front door was on my *Top 10 Most Hated People list*, and I didn't care if it was friend or foe. The asshole had interrupted what could've been a magical moment between me and my wife, but now Susana was on her feet, straightening her clothes, and I was left abandoned on her bed with nothing but a kitten to keep me company. A pretty cute kitten, but still.

"Maybe it's Mrs. Jenkins. An emergency or something. Have you seen my phone?" She swept up her hair into a ponytail and secured it with a tie from the nightstand. She rifled through the blankets looking for her cell.

"Why don't you just call her Jacinda? What's with the formality?"

Susana tilted her head as she thought about the question and the noise at the door continued. "I don't know. I don't think of it as formal. It's just how she introduced herself and it's what I call her."

"Your phone's on the dresser." I hopped off the bed. "And I'll deal with the door."

"Wait!" She rushed after me, her feet bare and her shirt twisted and rumpled. "Mrs. Jenkins just texted me. It says: *Make sure you're dressed when you open the door. Paparazzi. Hide the cat.*"

"What does that even mean?"

"No idea." She was sending a text in reply, but the banging on the door had become intolerable.

We were both dressed. Screw it. I flung open the door, and a sweaty rotund man toppled toward me. I broke his fall and his slick skin slid over mine like a greased pig in my arms. I shoved him out, causing him to stumble a few steps until he steadied himself on the porch railing. I'd need about twenty handkerchiefs to wipe off that dude's perspiration.

"Do you know this guy?" I asked Susana, who was hovering behind me.

"I don't." Her body was behind mine, and she had her hands hooked into the back of my jeans. I didn't like the situation, but I liked the feel of her finding safety behind me.

I spread out my arms within the doorway, blocking the man from Susana and from entering the house again. "Is there a problem?" The man was much shorter than I was, and he looked up at me, his face ruddy and blotchy. He was around sixty and wore a sleeveless t-shirt, cut off shorts, and flip-flops that looked to be near the end of their lifespan.

"Yeah, there's a problem." He ran his tongue along his mouth in a full circle, top and bottom lips, making his face even wetter than it was before. "You stole my cat."

"Excuse me?"

"You heard me. Give me back my cat, or I'm calling my lawyer." He pronounced it *law-yur* and put his hands on his hips for emphasis.

"I look forward to hearing from your counsel." I started to shut the door in his face.

"Now hold on a minute." He shoved his foot in the door but yelped as his toes got pinched. "I'm always open to a little negotiating!"

Mallory chose that moment to sprint out the door and dart across the lawn toward the Jenkins residence.

"Tater!" The man turned and hobbled after the cat but didn't get very far after a strap on one of his sandals snapped in two.

"Did he just call Mallory 'Tater?'" Susana whispered from behind me.

The cat sprung onto Jacinda's front steps. The neighbor's door cracked open a few inches and shut again, securing Mallory safely inside.

"Mrs. Jenkins texted again. She said to look across the street," Susana said.

While the mystery man limped across the lawn, Susana and I looked for anything suspicious on the other side of the road. I saw a few parked cars, some trees, and a cluster of mailboxes.

"There!" Sunny hissed. "In the car!"

Parked on the side of the road was a dark SUV with tinted windows, one of which was lowered just enough for the photographer inside to fit his giant zoom lens through the opening. He wasn't *that* far away, and with a lens that big, he was probably taking pictures of my pores. I shut the door and secured the chain lock. "What's happening?"

"What's happening is that you're a Starling now." Susana made sure the curtains were closed and dropped onto the couch with a sigh. "And so am I."

"You've always been a Starling." I yanked aside the blinds on the kitchen window and saw another photographer behind a tree, and one standing in the middle of the yard, taking photos of the house like she was a real estate agent preparing to make a listing.

"In name only. I was out of the family, and boring. And here, in this boring little house. Why bother with poor reject Susana Starling when you can stalk the playboy Sebastian Starling and the Ice King Simon Starling?"

"The Ice King?"

Susana shrugged. "Just one of the many nicknames bestowed by the tabloids upon my wealthy bachelor cousins."

"I've never seen anything like that."

"Do you read *Press Play, The Tattler, Everyone Now,* or *World Weekly?*"

"Can't say that I do."

"And those are the more 'upstanding' publications. Don't get me started on what gets printed in *Inquiring Minds* or *Talk to Me.*"

"But why are they here? If they haven't bothered you before, what's so exciting now?"

Susana looked exasperated, and as soon as the words were out of my mouth, I realized how stupid they sounded.

"Ok. I realize that a few things have changed."

"Yes, just a few." She stood up and headed into the bedroom, and I followed. She pulled a suitcase out of the closet and started opening drawers. "My mother is dead, and I've stepped into the role of head Starling of the estate. I've married the sexy gardener—"

"That's sexy *groundskeeper*, thank you very much."

"The sexy groundskeeper," she continued, "and am set to inherit millions, out of the blue. Harry could've tipped them off, but it doesn't matter. They would've been here on their own within another day or two. We need a publicist. Maybe Simon's guy can recommend one."

"Why the hell do we need a publicist? I don't even get what you're talking about."

Susana gave up on the bag and crossed her arms. "We need a publicist because now we're a public commodity. I'm the granddaughter of the rich and famous Quentin Maddix and the even more rich and famous Sadie Starling. I'm a 'Stars in the Snow' legacy. Every time that song plays, the Starling family gets a royalty payment, and people remember the fairytale story of my grandparents. I'm the daughter of Malcom Maddix, one of the precious

Starling Triplets—America's babies. And he was the one who died too soon, so I'm an extra juicy piece of meat."

"I know your family history. I've been working at Starling Manor for years. I probably know some things you don't."

"Then why does any of this come as a surprise to you?" She whacked her fist against her suitcase. "Can you close this?"

I pulled it toward me and zipped it shut.

Susana fell into the soft chair in the corner and drew her legs up under her chin. "I knew this would happen. But I don't feel prepared."

"How bad can it be?"

"You know better than to ask that. Knock on wood or something." She started typing a message on her phone.

I rapped my knuckles against the side of her dresser. "Who're you texting?"

"Simon. We're going to need to schedule an interview with a premiere publication, just to get ahead of this. If we can tell our own story, provide our own pictures, then there will be less of a market for the tabloid stuff. So if we can get a publicist right away, maybe we can get this published before the week is out—"

"I don't want to do any interviews. And I don't want to do photo shoots." It was my turn to cross my arms. That shit was my own personal hell.

"I don't want to either, but this is what you signed up for."

"I signed up to be married to you, to live in the big house, to put on that ball, go to the opera, and attend whatever Christmas nightmare your family has in store, but this?"

"Do you need me to pull out the contract? There's something about photo events in there. But also, you have to take what comes to you, and publicity comes with the territory."

She was right, and I knew it. But I didn't like it. Not one bit. A restless anger filled up my chest. Not toward Susana or her family, but toward goddamn society. I liked being anonymous. I liked plants and trees and the outdoor air where the voices of others were muted and blew away in the breeze. Where I could hear myself think and my feelings stayed simple and contained. I didn't want to be caged and poked and prodded and watched like an animal in the zoo, which was exactly why I'd worked sixteen-hour days for more than a decade, so I could move to the beach and enjoy a quiet, solitary life when I turned thirty-three.

"I don't like it either, but with any luck, they'll get bored with us after a few weeks and move on to something more exciting. But buckle up, because the next few weeks could get bumpy."

There was another knock at the door, but this one was less urgent, and was coming from the back of the house.

"I'm gonna rip that guy a new one." I stomped off toward the back door, happy to have something to do with my anger.

"That's the back door. And I have a fence with a combination gate. Only Mrs. Jenkins has the code." She pushed ahead of me. "I'll get it."

"No, I'll get it. Stay behind me, please."

Susana sighed but followed my instructions and stepped aside. I braced my foot against the door and opened it just a crack. It was Jacinda, but she didn't look the way she had an hour ago. She was wearing a baseball cap with the brim of the hat pulled low over her face. Huge aviator sunglasses covered her eyes, and she was also sporting a rain jacket that was zipped up so far, I thought it might be strangling her.

"Let her in." Susana poked my back.

I moved aside and Jacinda stepped in and shut the door behind her.

"Thanks, kids." She unzipped her coat, revealing Mallory, who looked smug and a little sleepy. "I think Ted's gone. One of the photogs threatened to call the cops on him, and he's probably got a few warrants out, so he skedaddled."

"Why are you dressed like that?" Susana asked.

Jacinda looked like someone wearing a homemade spy costume for a last-minute Halloween party. "I have a few warrants out myself," she answered. "The eighties were an amazing time for me, but I might be on some 'Most Wanted' lists. And these tats stand out in a crowd if you know what I mean. Brought your cat back." She deposited the kitten at my feet, and the cat just sat and stared up at me. "And I'll be a monkey's uncle if Mallory belongs to Ted. Pretty sure she's from the litter of that tabby down the block at the Wilson's house. Ted just knew there were some famous folks here and he wanted his fifteen minutes."

"We're not famous." I scooped up the cat and held her to my chest. Her sandpaper tongue brushed against my neck. I was already in love with the Pebbles reincarnate and was relieved to see that she hadn't been kidnapped by the flip-flop bandit.

Jacinda's laugh rang out loudly. "Just keep telling yourself that, cowboy. You're about as famous as they come. Don't you fancy folks check the internet?"

"Shit. Not recently." Susana pulled out her phone.

"Well don't worry about it now. Just get back to your mansion, get a cheese plate and some champagne, and then check your feeds."

"I'll skip the champagne," Susana said, shutting her phone off. "And the internet. For now."

"Good idea. A nice double IPA trumps champagne any day." Jacinda pulled off her aviators and winked at me. "You two ought to head back to the castle, though. Word's out that you're here, and I need to keep on with my low-profile living. You're cramping my style."

"I have a few more things to pack." Susana headed toward the bedroom. "I'll just be a minute."

Mrs. Jenkins waited silently until Susana was in the bedroom, and then she beckoned for me to follow her out to the back patio. I put the cat down on the floor, not willing to risk losing her outside again.

Once we were out of the house, Jacinda looked around and then spoke in a loud whisper. "I'll keep an eye on things here, but you keep your eye on your bride." She was making such intense and direct eye contact with me that I wished I had my own aviators to cut the heat. "She likes to act like nothing gets to her, but she's just bottling it up inside. She never wants to talk about being a Starling, but I know her family is important to her, and she's gonna have to reckon with that legacy at some point. Her cousins have tried their best to protect her, but she'll need more than they can offer now. Sebastian will be in to check on you both in a few days, and Simon will stop by next week."

"You're in contact with her cousins?"

"I'm a lot of things," she said. "Don't worry your pretty little head about all that. Just keep Susana safe." She paused. "And cared for, if you've got the inclination."

"I'll do my best."

Mrs. Jenkins nodded at my response, and I had the feeling that even though her mother was dead, maybe Susana wasn't without caretakers after all.

The back door creaked as Susana came to check on us. She was holding the cat and had several suitcases lined up behind her. "Ready when you are, Mr. Starling."

19

SUSANA

"Return that creature to wherever she came from." Jeff was in the kitchen, pulling rustic round loaves of bread out of the oven. The smell of it made me realize I was famished.

"I'll do no such thing." Gabe held the kitten in his arms like she was his newborn baby. "Jeff, meet Mallory. She lives here now. Mallory, this is Jeff. You have full access to his kitchen."

"Like hell she does!" Jeff pulled off his oven mitts, tossed them on the counter, and crossed his arms. "No animals in the kitchen! They're fine outside but—"

Mallory must've decided that this was the perfect time to get better acquainted with the chef. She broke free from Gabe's grasp and leaped onto the counter.

"No! Off! Shoo!" Jeff waved his arms around like he was being attacked by a swarm of insects. The cat wasn't fazed—she hopped over the hot loaves of bread and glided like a flying squirrel towards Jeff, landing on his shoulder. Jeff screeched. "Get it off me! Help!"

While Gabe laughed and let his friend suffer at the paws of our newest family member, I tried to figure out how to steal some of that bread.

With no one offering to help, Jeff began to walk to the back door, slowly and stiffly, his arms straight out, zombie style. "Nice kitty. Good kitty. Don't bite me."

"She's not going to bite you," Gabe said. "And we'll keep her in the north wing. She won't bother you in the kitchen."

"Then will you kindly remove your feline?" Beads of sweat were forming on his temples. "And Susana, I see you eyeing that bread. Hands off. It's for dinner."

Gabe retrieved Mallory who seemed quite content to keep sniffing Jeff's ear. "You know, she could be helpful to you." Gabe nodded toward the kitten. "She could keep mice out of the kitchen—"

"There are no mice in my kitchen!" He sliced off the end of a loaf with a huff and handed it to me. "To tide you over." The bread was soft and steaming. Perfection. "And your new crew is waiting in the library if you want to meet them before we eat."

I'd just stuffed my mouth with bread, so my sentence came out as, "Frhat mew grew?"

"Your publicist, your stylist, and an assistant, I think. They've been here for a half hour."

Gabe's expression turned from amused to stormy. "For Susana, not me, right?" Gabe scratched Mallory under the chin and moved toward the back staircase like he was planning an escape.

"I assumed for both of you since you're a package deal. Only one way to find out."

"I'll get Mallory settled upstairs. I think one of the porters already brought up the supplies from the car. See you at dinner?" Gabe was backing out of the room.

"Gabriel Archibald Green." I grabbed the sleeve of his shirt. "You're coming with me. We've already talked about this."

Jeff shot Gabe a smug look as he wiped down all the surfaces that Mallory had touched with her cute little paws. "Being the man of the house comes with certain responsibilities, your highness."

"Whatever. Let's get this over with." Gabe clomped out of the kitchen and headed in the direction of the library.

I grabbed an apple off the counter and followed my husband, who seemed to be singing a lullaby to Mallory as he walked.

THE THREE INHABITANTS of the library jumped to their feet as Gabe and I entered the room.

A woman stepped forward, her arm outstretched. "Good afternoon. I'm Shelly Alsbrook, your assistant." Shelly was at least six feet tall, with icy blond hair cut in a sharp chin-length bob, and she wore large pink-rimmed glasses. Her skin was so pale that she looked like she might get a sunburn from a lightbulb. I shook her hand. She gestured to the man next to her. "This is Embry Nolan, your publicist."

Embry, who looked familiar to me, nodded in greeting. He was about my height, and because of his clothing, I'd assumed he was the stylist. He wore a very tailored short sleeved button-down shirt that nicely accentuated his muscled brown arms. His pants were perfectly pressed, and his shoes probably cost more than an average mortgage payment. "Nice to see you again, Ms. Starling. I believe we met at Simon's office in the city."

"Oh yes! I thought you looked familiar."

"I was on his PR team for the 'Stars in the Snow' anniversary campaign."

"That was an intense project."

"Indeed." Embry nodded again and kept his face neutral and professional.

"Embry has a lot of Starling background, so we thought he'd be perfect for this assignment." Shelly introduced the final member of the new team. "This is Indy. They're your stylist, and they'll be working for both of you, as well."

I didn't know what color Indy's hair was originally, but it was now electric blue, short on one side of their head, and longer on the other. They wore a black t-shirt, a kilt over a pair of jeans, and silver combat boots.

They were eyeing Gabe, who seemed nervous about the whole situation. "Hey there." Indy stepped toward Gabe and openly sized him up. "Mountain man meets boy next door with some Richie Rich sprinkled in. I can work with this." They turned their attention to me. "Not bad as is, but I have ideas." Indy grabbed a sketchbook out of their bag and started jotting down notes.

"How did you get here so fast?" Gabe asked. "Susana, didn't you just text Simon a few hours ago?"

"This team was assembled days ago." Shelly handed me a folder that she'd been holding. "We were just waiting to launch, and we got here as soon as the call came in from Simon."

Gabe shook his head and put the cat on the floor and went to close the door to prevent her escape. Mallory jumped up in the window seat and promptly passed out.

"How should I address you?" She asked me. "Ms. Starling? Mrs. Starling? Mrs. Green?"

"Susana is fine. And my last name is still Starling." I thought I spied a look of relief cross Embry's face over that disclosure.

"I'm Gabe. Or Gabriel. Last name's still Green. Just call me whatever."

"What's your inseam, Whatever?" Indy asked.

"Uh . . ." Gabe looked down at his jeans as if they'd have a number printed on his thigh.

"Don't worry about it. I'll take measurements. Shoe size? 12.5?"

"Usually 13." A whole new world was about to open up to Gabe, but was he ready for it? It was a lot, even for people who knew what to expect.

"Can you take Mallory up to the north wing?" I plucked the cat from the window seat and gave her to Gabe. "There's no litter box in here, and I'd rather not get into a situation where that's a problem."

His face lit up in a smile, revealing one dimple that only showed up from time to time. The team was seeing the same thing

I was—Shelly's cheeks were suddenly pink, Embry nodded (must be a signature move) in apparent approval.

Indy seemed to like what they saw. "I think 'Golden Boy' is my final verdict."

Gabe blushed and gave an awkward little bow. "It was nice meeting you all." Gabe and the cat made their exit.

I crossed the room and sat on the couch and the team followed and sat down. "He'll warm up. Maybe. But I'm not sure he's going to be the easiest guy to work with."

Indy snorted. "He's like a baby lamb compared to our average client. If he stays this sweet, I'm not sure we'll know how to behave."

"We're prepared for anything, Ms. Starling—Susana." Shelly had an agenda to tend to and she got right to it. "Pending your approval, we have a photo shoot set for the day after tomorrow, with an interview session to follow that afternoon. Your folder has the proposed schedule for a few other phone interviews and some possible meet and greets. The back section has some suggested publicity events and ideas for branding and some ideas from Embry for three months, six months, and one year into the marriage story, with contingencies for different outcomes and paths."

"And what is your view of my 'marriage story?'" Her wording had caught my attention, and I wanted to make sure they saw things in a way that lined up with my own vision of my story. This might be a fake marriage, but it needed to look completely real, and I needed a team with flexibility and sensitivity.

"We've been briefed by Simon and by Mr. Jagger."

Embry leaned forward in his chair. "We understand this is a special situation." He had the kind of speaking voice that made everyone relax but also pay attention. "We know your relationship with Mr. Green goes back a long time, but that you had a long gap between seeing each other, and your relationship and marriage are very new. We know a lot's at stake and we are prepared to support, promote, and protect you, your marriage, and the Starling name."

"He's saying we've got your back, and we won't let anyone mess with you." Indy added without looking up from their sketchbook. "Though some of that is the job for your security team."

"My security team?"

"We're still putting it together and we're not ready to brief you on it yet." Shelly shot Indy with a fierce glare that was completely unnoticed—or maybe willfully ignored—by my new stylist.

"I need to get measurements ASAP." Indy produced a tape measure seemingly out of nowhere and stood up. "Can I get you now, and then you lead me to Mr. Golden Boy for his?" I stood for my measurements and Shelly gave me a few last-minute instructions while Indy ran a tape measure around me and scribbled numbers in a notebook.

"All of our numbers are in the folder. Put them in your phone, and in Gabriel's. We'll be in touch about security, and other issues as they arise. If you need to change the schedule, please contact both me and Embry as soon as possible. If you have any ideas, questions, or concerns, you can text or email us at any time. For the next few weeks, we will be staying in the East Wing, and after that we'll see what works best, so you can meet with us at a moment's notice, if necessary."

This was intense. My old life, though I'd just been living it a few days ago, seemed light years away, and hard to grasp. I'd been alone, and not unhappily so, for a long time, and now I had a husband, a cat, Jag, Jeff, and a whole staff of people tending to me. Protecting me, or so they said. The whole thing left me feeling a little queasy, but maybe part of that was hunger and fatigue.

"Let's find Gabriel." Indy gathered up their things while Embry and Shelly settled in at a desk to go over some scheduling issues.

After a few flights of stairs and several minutes of walking, Indy and I turned toward the north corridor when I saw a figure lurking near a linen closet right outside the master suite and my stomach filled with dread.

"Heads up," I said to Indy. "Spawn of Satan at twelve o'clock." The lighting was dim, but I could tell by the slinking stature and the bad vibe that it was Mrs. Skinner.

Indy stopped short and put their arm out to stop me, much like a mother who is about to brake hard in the car and wants to keep her child from flying out the front windshield. "Who is it?"

"Mrs. Skinner. Housekeeper. Totally out to get me and Gabe."

"Should I call security?" Indy started to walk backwards, pushing us toward the staircase.

"I thought I didn't have a security team yet."

"Not fully assembled, but you have Anton, team lead. Texting him now."

"No, it's fine. I think she's harmless. Just really annoying and kind of aggressively hateful."

"How aggressive?"

Mrs. Skinner, broom in hand, began walking toward us.

"You're about to find out."

"How do you feel if I need to get tough with her? Or should we go back downstairs and wait for Anton?"

It was a strange feeling having another person stick up for me. Protect me. And it also felt strange to be in a position where I needed to be protected in the first place. I was used to a pretty solitary life, other than dealing with my cooking classes, my chef clients, and visits from Mrs. Jenkins. "You have my permission to unleash your inner demons on Skinner."

"You might not say that if you knew what I was capable of." Indy began walking again but positioned their body in front of mine and guided us to the far right of the hallway.

Skinner made a beeline for us and tried to block our way with her broom. "Where do you think you're going? And who're you?" Mrs. Skinner's second sentence was accompanied by some vicious spittle, which I was pretty sure sprinkled across Indy's nose, though they didn't even flinch.

I opened my mouth to speak, but Indy had other ideas.

"Is your last name Starling?" Indy was right in Mrs. Skinner's face.

"Ha!" Mrs. Skinner barked. "You couldn't pay me a million dollars to take that cursed name. My name's –"

"Did I ask for your name?" Indy grabbed Skinner's broom and yanked it, hard, causing Satan's bride to spin around in a circle.

When she'd found her balance again, Mrs. Skinner's face was red and blotchy. "I'm the head housekeeper here. How dare you—"

"Once again, I didn't ask," said Indy. "And if your last name isn't Starling, I think that means you don't ask Susana where she's going, what she's doing, or who she's with."

Behind Skinner, down the hall, I saw Gabe peering out our bedroom door.

"Are we done here, or should I call security?"

"We don't have security here." Mrs. Skinner had a haughty tone, but she backed up a few feet.

"We do now." Indy opened the voice recorder app on their phone and recorded a memo. "Note to request security detail outside master bedroom in North Wing."

"Ridiculous." Mrs. Skinner rolled her eyes but scurried past us and down the stairs.

"I don't need a security detail outside my room." We'd started walking again and were almost to the suite.

"That's for Anton to decide, but mostly I just made that note to let her know that she's being watched and that you're being protected."

"That was quite a show," Gabe opened the door for us, and Indy and I entered the suite. "Thank you, Indy. That was brilliant."

"No problem. Keeps my day interesting." Indy looked around the room. "Nice place you've got."

Gabe pulled me into a hug. "You ok?"

"I'm fine."

Indy seemed unfazed by the whole production with Mrs. Skinner. "I have orders to make. If you really want to thank me, Golden Boy, take your pants off."

"Excuse me?" Gabe cocked his head to one side and a half-amused, half-confused smile played on his mouth.

"Keep your skivvies on, though—we don't need to see the family jewels. Those jeans are just too thick for me to get a perfect inseam measurement." Gabe considered the request and then unbuttoned his jeans. "An enemy of Skinner's is a lifelong friend to me. Your wish is my command."

I sat on the bed next to Mallory and watched as my husband, god, it felt weird to call him my husband, but I was trying to get used to it—submitted to having his measurements taken. My stomach, which had been in some state of knotted and nervous for days, felt like it was relaxing. Unclenching. I leaned back on the overstuffed pillows, took a deep breath and put my hand on my warm purring kitten. Maybe I could get used to this life after all.

The handle on the bedroom door started to rattle and there was a bang as the door swung open and smashed into the wall behind it. Indy jumped, stabbed Gabe in the armpit with a pin, and Gabe cried out. There, in my bedroom doorway, out of breath and with a murderous look in his eyes, stood Tyler Hardin.

20

GABE

When your arch enemy, nemesis, dude whose head you'd like to rip off, shows up on your doorstep, you'd really prefer to be wearing pants. But I wasn't. I was standing barefoot, in my boxers, my arms held above my head while Indy pinned my T-shirt to get an idea of how closer-fitting clothes would "drape" on me, or something like that. To say I was unprepared was an understatement.

Susana screeched and rolled off the far side of the bed to hide behind it, which caused the kitten to startle, fly through the air, and roll like a tumbleweed under the bed.

"What the fuck are you doing in here, Hardin? Get out!" I had no control over my voice or its volume, and I sounded like a rabid snarling animal, even to my own ears.

Indy, reading the room from my obvious rage and Sunny's fright, raised their smart watch to their face, punched a button, and connected with someone. "We need Anton to the north wing suite immediately." Indy threw my jeans at me and quickly pulled the pins out of my shirt.

I wanted to slam Tyler against the wall and let out all my anger, but Indy was removing the last of the pins, and both of us could get hurt. Tyler's eyes were red, and his face was puffy and distorted.

"Done," Indy backed away, setting me free.

I grabbed my jeans and pulled them on.

"You're the one who shouldn't be here, Green." Tyler's voice was gravelly and strained. "You should be slumming in the servant's quarters where you belong. You can play the role of rich boy if you want, but no one's buying it, and once my dad's attorney is done with you, you'll be lucky to have a roof over your head at all."

Barefooted, but more or less clothed, I stepped forward, but Indy moved with me, like an annoying defender on a basketball court. "Excuse me," I said with every ounce of patience I had left in my body. I needed to get my hands on Tyler, and I had about zero restraint left.

"No can do, Champ." Indy put a hand on my chest and guided me back a step.

"As for you, you little—," Tyler said to Susana, who was still half-way hidden behind the bed.

I couldn't think, couldn't see straight, couldn't hold back. I jumped around Indy and shoved Tyler against the wall. His face was so close to mine that I could smell beer and onions on his breath. I pinned him with my forearm and wondered if I should punch him in the stomach or start with a good knee to the groin. Indy ran out of the room and yelled something down the hall. I heard a cry at my feet, and I looked down to see Mallory meowing and clawing at my jeans.

Tyler heard it, too. "There it is." Tyler was looking at the cat like he wanted to smash it to smithereens. He tried to slide across the wall, toward the door, but I kept him where he was. "I knew there had to be a fucking cat here somewhere. I have to get out of this room." He kicked his foot in the direction of the kitten but I pressed my arm harder against his chest and he stopped. "I'm deathly allergic. My face is swelling up and now my throat feels tight!"

"You aren't even supposed to be here. This isn't your home." I was only slightly worried about his allergy.

"I came back to get some of my shit. The north wing is my place, not yours."

"It's not yours. You've always been a squatter here." Susana was back on her feet, her dark hair tousled and framing her angry face.

"Says the little girl who ran away." His nasty mocking tone made me want to punch his teeth in.

"Mallory!" Susana screamed. Tyler had one foot raised over the head of my new fur baby. There was no reason left in the world not to take him out. I sideswiped his support leg, causing him to hit the floor, hard. I jumped him and was about to achieve my dream of knocking his teeth out when Susana and Indy pulled me off him. There was a flash of a bald head, oversized biceps, and some commands shouted in a Slavic language, and Tyler got dragged out of the room, presumably by the infamous Anton.

"Let go." I ripped my arms out of the grip of Indy and Susana. I was a caged animal, filled with rage. "Have you seen my shoes?"

"Stay here. You don't need shoes." Susana reached out as if to hug me, and I dodged her touch.

"I'll be back."

"Where are you going?"

"I need some air." I jammed my feet into my shoes and was sloppy and quick with tying the laces. The cat crawled out from under the bed and slid onto Susana's lap.

"Be careful, Archie."

"You don't need to go after him." Indy was putting the tape measure and notebook back into their bag. "Anton has that more than covered."

"I understand. I just need to . . . move." Indy nodded but

Susana kept her eyes cast down and focused on running her fingers through Mallory's fur. For a moment, I thought about staying. But my anger was still trying to claw its way out of my gut through my skin, and if I stayed in the room, I might pace a hole in the carpet.

Surely Tyler had been escorted down the main staircase, so I headed for the service stairs. As much as I wanted to continue that confrontation, it probably wasn't a good idea. If I could avoid all people, I might be doing everyone a favor, including myself. I made it down the stairs, through the hall, and out the back exit without seeing anyone. The sun had gone down, but the sky was still shades of purple and pink, and it was too early to see any stars. The air was muggy and thick, and it pressed into my skin, warming my body and relaxing my muscles.

A drive. That's what I needed. My truck was in the back garage, and there was a spare set of keys on the pegboard in the garage. In my former life, as an unmarried, non-famous groundskeeper, I went for drives at the end of my day. It cleared my head and settled my nerves.

The garage was behind the back garden, and I felt my rage loosen and cool as I moved through the green paths that looked almost blue in the waning light. I'd go out the back driveway, drive a few miles north on highway 57, then head to the reservoir where I could watch the moon rise over the water. I'd text Susana and let her know that I wouldn't be home for dinner. Fuck, already like a husband, having to tell the wife that he wouldn't be home. On autopilot, I rushed around the final bend in the garden path and almost ran right into Tyler Hardin. Again.

He was loading a box into the back of his Range Rover and a hulking man watching over him. Anton's baldness was so complete that I thought I'd be able to see the reflection of the sky in his scalp, if I had the right angle. What he lacked in the hair department on his head was made up for in spades by his over-ambitious eyebrows. Bet he needed a barber just to tame those buggers.

My rage reignited at the sight of Tyler, but fuck him. He wouldn't get the better of me. "What are you doing?"

Tyler jumped and knocked his elbow against the side of his vehicle. "Shit, Green. Where'd you come from?" Tyler rubbed his arm and pouted. His face was a little less puffy, but his eyes still looked weird.

"He's leaving now." Anton's voice was thickly accented and came from a spot so deep in his chest that I was intimidated, even though he was supposedly there to protect me.

Lucky for Tyler, Anton was a buffer between my ire and Tyler's face.

"I don't want you anywhere near Susana," I said.

"Why? Think I might steal her away? She had her chance with me and she blew it."

Time to rip off some Hardin limbs! I'd tried to pounce on the little prince, but Anton was too skilled at his job and had me contained before I'd even moved from my spot. "You attacked her. You don't get to say shit like that." I might not have been able to punch Tyler, but I could still yell.

"I never attacked her! Is that what she told you?"

"You know what you did."

"I know that she knocked me so hard in the nuts that I saw stars for days."

"And she did that for fun?"

"I may have gotten a little handsy, but she really overacted." Tyler seemed so casual. I wanted to knock him and his nuts into the next galaxy.

"How many beers did you have that night? How about pills? You and your dumbass friends were always fucked up back then. You assaulted Susana—consider yourself lucky she didn't call the cops that night."

Tyler shut the back door of his car and kept his back turned to me. Then he stood there, eerily still. For five seconds. And then five more. Was he stroking out? Then he turned around, his eyes on the ground. His shoulders were slumped, and he was trying to pop his knuckles, but his joints were silent as he pressed on his fingers. "I was probably drunk. Maybe high, too. She said I assaulted her?" He looked like a different person. Deflated. Weak.

"You tried to force yourself on her." Even though nightfall was coming on quickly, I could see that Tyler's face had dropped its color.

"It's all a bit fuzzy. That whole time. I was on a lot of stuff and my dad—" Tyler stopped talking and his gaze was focused on something behind me.

Someone, actually. Susana, holding a picnic basket and looking like she might throw up or pass out. I put my hand on her arm and her skin was warm, but she was shivering.

"I don't—I didn't remember it like that. I thought—but it's probably right—I just—" Tyler's sentences were disjointed and ragged. "Shit."

"Let me see your hand." Susana said.

We all turned to look at her.

"Who're you talking to, Sunny?"

"Tyler." She took a few steps toward Hardin.

"My hand?" He held out his hands to show they were empty aside from a set of keys.

"Your burn."

Tyler's eyes narrowed and he turned over his right hand so we could see his knuckles. "How did you know about that?"

Susana walked to him and took his hand in hers. She ran her thumb over his skin, but there was no tenderness in the gesture. "I know about it because I'm the one who burned you, remember?"

Tyler snatched his hand away like she'd just burned him again. "What? No, you didn't. That's from—"

"I burned you when you grabbed my ankle."

"When I—" recognition washed over Tyler's face. "Oh. Like I said, that night's pretty fuzzy."

"I wish it was fuzzy for me," she said. She walked back to me, and I put my arm around her shoulders.

Tyler kicked at the pavement and wiped his forehead with the front of his t-shirt. "Fucking shit." He kept his eyes down as he opened the driver's side door of the Range Rover, slammed it shut, and turned on the engine. He idled for a few seconds, and then put the car into gear and started down the driveway. Susana, Anton, and I watched his car drive away until we could no longer see Tyler's taillights.

"Let's go back to the house." Anton started walking.

Susana didn't follow. She just stood there like a statue, holding the picnic basket, and staring down the driveway.

"Why're you down here?" I asked her.

"Jeff saw you leave through the back garden. He said you were probably going out for a drive. He already had this food packed up to go to our room, so I just brought it out here, in case I could catch you."

I'd been so busy with weddings and neighbors and paparazzi and kittens and PR and Tyler that I'd temporarily lost sight of why I was here in the first place. I was here to help Susana. Hurting Harry was a bonus and maybe the reason I agreed in the first place, but Susana and her legacy were now my priority. Her beauty was undeniable, but that wasn't the only reason I was drawn to her. She was gentle one moment, and fierce the next. I'd seen her be brave and vulnerable, silly, and serious.

I had the urge to kiss her, but I stopped myself. *Only in public*, I told myself. Wait, we *were* in public. Someone could be watching from the stables, the house, the garden, or the woods. Erring on the side of PDA, I leaned in and kissed her. She jolted with surprise. Anton and his eyebrows politely looked away. The kiss was longer than it needed to be. She smelled like orange zest and lily of the valley.

I wanted her close to me. I wanted to be on the road, in the moonlight, but with her. "Want to go for a drive?"

21

SUSANA

The fragrant night air rushed through the open window of the truck, tangling my hair, and carrying with it the summer songs of spring peepers. My thoughts were tripping and tumbling through my mind, and I kept my eyes closed, hoping to starve any anxiety that might be brewing.

Gabe stayed silent as he turned the truck off the smooth pavement of Starling Manor's winding driveway and onto the rutted county road. "Want to talk about it?"

I knew what he meant, but I wasn't ready to talk about Tyler's revelation. I shook my head, careful not to let any emotion escape me.

"I'm here for you when you are. Or not. You don't ever need to talk about it if you don't want to."

Dammit. Why did Gabe have to be so perfectly sensitive? The picnic basket rested on my lap and my fingers curled tightly around the handle—until I released my grip and opened and closed my fists, trying to relax my hands. A flurry of unexpected dissonance fluttered in my stomach. I felt that familiar sense of running away—the familiar escape from fear, worry, trauma, and the unknown, but this time, I wasn't alone—Gabe was by my side, fleeing with me. Even more strange was the melancholy tug that felt like . . . homesickness? Starling Manor had never felt like home before, but now, even though I'd be away for just a few hours, part of me didn't want to go. Would anyone feed Mallory? Would her litter box be set up? What kind of dinner were we missing? The bed was so comfortable, and I was exhausted. I opened my eyes and lifted the lid of the picnic basket.

"Think there's any booze in here? I could use a drink."

"Is that the best idea?" Gabe gave me a sideways glance as he navigated the dark and twisty highway. "Not sure we want a reenactment of 'Wedding Night Sunny' though she *was* pretty entertaining."

"If it's champagne, I won't touch it. And this time I won't drink an excessive amount on an empty stomach."

"How much *did* you drink that night when I was in the shower?"

"Let's not talk about it." The basket held slices of that heavenly bread, cheese, warm baked chicken, a container of salad, molasses cookies, and a mini bottle of chilled white wine which I held up for Gabe to see. "It has a screw top!" I opened the wine and sniffed. Fruity. Crisp. "There are little plastic glasses in here. Want one?"

"Open containers and drinking while driving? It would be just our luck to get pulled over, and I'm not sure that kind of publicity would be considered 'on-brand' by your PR team."

"By *our* PR team. But yeah, guess I have to think like a Starling." I screwed the lid back on and returned the bottle to the basket.

"How's a Starling supposed to think?"

"A Starling who's in the headlines should be thinking about behaving. About appearances. About how something will look when it pops up in the tabloids."

"Is that how your cousins think?"

"Simon, maybe. It's hard to tell with him. He's got himself so buttoned up that I'm not sure he ever relaxes or lets his guard down. And Sebastian . . ."

"I don't follow the tabloids, but even I know that Sebastian doesn't seem to be wasting much time on that kind of thought."

"True. For Bash, any publicity is good publicity.'"

"Do you think you'll be held to a different standard because you're a woman?"

"What do *you* think?"

"That's fair. As for the wine," Gabe made a right turn and the truck bounced and bobbed as the road beneath us got rougher, "we can pour some when we get there. Only about five more minutes."

"Where exactly are we going?"

"To one of my favorite places."

As Gabe drove the final miles to our destination, I closed my eyes again and let myself revisit the scenes with Tyler. How I felt numb but also like my insides were burning when he was in the master suite. But when I saw him at the truck, and what happened there—I'd just felt steady. Calm. Things were changing—I was changing.

"We're here." Gabe parked the truck in a clearing where gravel crunched under the tires. The headlights illuminated a grove of trees, but beyond that, everything seemed dense, dark, and unseeable.

"So . . . here is nowhere?"

"It's somewhere. Somewhere special. I'll show you." Gabe crossed over to my door and opened it for me.

I got out of the truck and grabbed onto his arm. He was hot and all, and I didn't mind some more touchy-feely stuff, but the truth was that the remoteness of this spot made me uneasy. Walking into the wild night was exhilarating but scary. I was the kind of person who studied maps of a place before I ever set foot there, be it a new city or a shopping mall. I liked to know the layout, the scope, and the best routes and quickest ways to exit. I was flying blind here.

"There's a short path up there to the left." He pointed at what looked like a dark blob to me. "There are a few switchbacks and then we'll reach the clearing. I can do it with my eyes closed, but I did bring a flashlight. Got the food?"

I let go of his arm and retrieved the basket. He dug around in his backpack and found the flashlight, clicked a button and a jumpy stream of light stretched out before us. I grabbed his arm again. Just in case. I rested the basket in the crook of my free arm. The woods were alive with sounds, and I didn't know if nocturnal creatures were louder than their daytime counterparts, or if I'd just never paid enough attention.

"Is this where you take all your dates?" My foot caught on a tree root, and I stumbled but Gabe quickly steadied me, and I regained my balance. "I hope they lived to talk about it. Seems like a perfect place to—"

"To what?" Gabe sounded edgy.

"Sorry. Fair chance I listen to too many murder podcasts."

"It flattens out here. Should be a smooth walk to the water."

"What water?"

"This is a little cove of the Maple Creek Reservoir."

"I didn't realize it reached all the way up here." The reservoir was off limits to me when I was growing up. My mother warned me against it so many times that I came to fear it. I'd imagined that the shores of Maple Creek were filled with discarded needles, pot smoke, and naked teenagers fighting or fornicating.

"It's a hidden spot."

We headed into a clearing where the shimmering lake spread out in front of us. The moon, previously tucked behind a cloud, made an appearance above our heads, while its watery twin danced a blurry golden reflection on the water.

"And for the record," he slid the basket off my arm and placed it on the gritty sand, "You're the first person I've ever brought here."

"Really?" My voice cracked and what I'd meant to sound cool and casual ended up sounding like a seagull who's just been strangled.

"Yes, Sunny, really." He looked at me for a few seconds longer than seemed normal, and I thought he might kiss me, but he only lingered a moment and then turned away. "Let's eat."

"Where will we sit—"

He pulled a blanket out of his backpack and spread it on the tiny private beach.

"Wow, you packed a bag and everything."

"This is my truck bag. In case I go for a drive and need some supplies."

"So, flashlight and blanket. What else do you have in there?" I watched as Gabe smoothed out the blanket, brushed some sand away, and then settled into a seated position. I loved watching him move. His body was firm and muscled, but he was flexible and his movements were lovely and graceful. Was it possible to be attracted to someone's gait? Their cadence? To how their body just took up space in the world?

"Bottle of water, compass, little first aid kit, and a few other necessities."

Our whole marriage contract had been such a quick affair that we'd skipped over a lot of the "get to know you" questions. How many women had he slept with? Was I really the first person he'd brought here? Had he been in love before, and if so, please let her not be some perfect gorgeous genius.

"Sit," he said.

I forced the image of Gabe entangled with some anonymous blonde beauty to the back of my mind and sat down next to him. And it wasn't my business. He could love whoever he wanted to love. I mean, he couldn't date for the next year, but after that, he could have whatever woman he wanted, and I'm sure there'd be tons of ladies to choose from down on the Gulf Coast, and they'd want him. He was handsome and kind and funny, and—shit. I couldn't do this to myself.

Gabe poured me a small glass of wine. "I'll give you more after you have some food in you, and I reserve the right to stop wine service if you start asking me to punish you."

"I'm going to pretend I didn't hear that."

The wine was cool and smooth with sweet notes of smoky grapefruit and green apple. Gabe popped open the food containers and the aroma kickstarted my appetite. We stuffed ourselves with chicken, bread, cheese, greens, and cookies. He refilled my wine and poured himself a glass, and in between sips, he anchored the base of the glass in the sand to hold it steady. Chirps and clicks from the trees buzzed around us as crickets and cicadas made themselves known. A breeze pushed through the limbs and leaves, adding a fluttering melody to the night song, and the water of the lake pushed gently against the shore, lacing the evening air with romance. I was nervous. I felt like I was seventeen again, sitting with the boy of my dreams, and hoping against hope that he liked me back.

"Need anything else?" Gabe snapped the lid on the salad bowl and placed it back in the basket. I needed his attention. His hands on my skin. His lips on my lips. His tongue in my mouth. His—

"Susana?"

Whoops. Rein it in, lady love. "I'm good. Thanks." Liar, liar, pants on fire.

I fantasized about Gabe's fingers as he pushed the lids back onto the containers. I admired his body as he stood up and stretched and then sauntered over to the water. Maybe he'd get naked. Maybe I could convince him that photographers might be spying on us from the far shore, and he'd kiss me. Or, maybe I was one degree away from deranged and obsessed. I drew my knees up and pressed my forehead against them, an attempt at *out of sight, out of mind*, but it wasn't really working.

I heard Gabe's shoes crunching against the rocky sand. Coming closer. Closer. I looked up, and there he was, down on his knees, right in front of me. "Hi." There I went again with the brilliant conversation.

"Hello." He raked his hand through his hair, but his gorgeous locks flopped right back onto his forehead.

"Hey there." I felt ridiculous, but I couldn't come up with anything other than these vapid, silly greetings. How many synonyms were there for "hello"?

"Howdy." At least three, apparently. "I was just testing the water temperature." Gabe leaned in so close that I could feel his breath on my lips. "I thought I saw a flash of light on the far shore. Photographers, maybe?"

"I saw that, too." White lie.

"Maybe they're watching us."

"Maybe they are." My lips were dry. Dry lips were bad for kissing. I ran my tongue across my mouth. I would've killed for a little lip balm and a breath mint.

"Better safe than sorry?" Gabe was so close. A few inches stood between me and the sexiest man this side of the Mississippi.

The heat of his body bounced off my skin and lit me up like a thousand fireflies landing on my skin. I raised my hand and dragged my finger across his temple, his cheek, his lips. He nipped at my finger and pulled it into his mouth, his full lips closing around it and his tongue pulsing as he sucked. I gasped, and as I pulled the star-kissed lake air into my lungs, Gabe released my finger and pressed his mouth against mine. On my exhale, he embraced me, pushed his fingertips into the small of my back, and kept kissing me, pulling in my breath like we were sharing the most exquisite smoke.

We kept kissing. Longer than we needed to for the sake of appearances. I moaned into his mouth as our tongues and teeth and lips took turns exploring each other softly, then roughly, then soft again. He moaned back, a lover's call and response. This was more of a show than we needed to put on even if there was an entire press corps camping out on the shores of the lake. Gabe pulled away and the noise of our heavy breathing joined the cacophony of the night chorus.

He stood up, grabbed at his shirt, pulled it up over his head, and tossed it aside onto the rough sand. Was my naked wish coming true? He stared at me while he kicked off one shoe, then the other. His socks were tossed aside with his shoes, and then he unbuttoned his pants and pushed them down, pulled them off. Oh yes. It was coming true, alright. It was dark, but not so dark that I couldn't see the muscles in his legs, the power of his chest and shoulders, or the bulge in his boxers. He turned away and started walking toward the water. Then he stopped, pulled off his boxers and tossed them toward the pile of his discarded clothes. Bingo. Dream achievement unlocked. Gabe was gloriously, unashamedly naked. And he was perfection.

"Come on, Sunny. Swim with me."

22

GABE

I was naked. It was dark enough that maybe she wasn't getting an eyeful of a full moon other than the one above our heads. I wanted Susana to get naked *with* me, even though I knew she shouldn't. I'd seen a light on the far shore, but the chances of it being a camera flash were slim to none, though I wasn't complaining about having to keep up the show.

Back on the blanket I was about to consume her. I wanted to breathe her in, eat her up, soak in her waters. If she could see the scenarios playing out in my mind, would she realize what a dirty bastard I was?

Maybe the lake version of a cool shower was the right move for the moment. This cove of the reservoir was my escape spot. My thinking spot. My dreaming spot. For over a decade I'd been coming out here, no matter the season, when I needed to be alone, decompress, or come back to myself. I only swam here in the summer, but those were some of my favorite memories. The feeling of floating in dark water, unable to see what was around or beneath me—my troubles would soak, loosen, break off, and wash away. It hadn't been the plan to bring Sunny out here, but once we hit the road, I realized that it didn't feel wrong. As we got closer to the reservoir and the roads grew rougher, nervous and giddy bubbles bounced around my gut. I was taking someone to my secret place. Not just someone—I was taking my wife.

The water was cold, but not jarring enough to take my breath away. I didn't pause to acclimate to the temperature—I needed to get waist-deep so I didn't feel so exposed, but the water hitting my balls and then my belly was enough to make me gasp.

"A bit chilly?" Susana called from the shore. She was still on the blanket but was standing up.

"Brisk." I tried to sound casual, but shit, that cold water was enough to make a grown man cry. Or at least whimper. Screw it. I had to dunk myself, or this would be slow torture. I fully submerged myself in the lake and popped back up like a dolphin breaching the ocean waves. I could feel my body relaxing, my mood loosening. "Gonna join me?" All I needed was Susana's warm body close to mine, and all would be right with the world.

"I try to avoid hypothermia, so maybe I'll just watch from here."

"Where's your sense of adventure?" *Stop it, Gabriel Green. Don't invite her to get in the water with you. She said no. She's being sensible. You do not have good intentions.*

"Left it back at the house." She'd stepped off the blanket and was a few paces closer to the water. The moonlight was faintly reflected in her smooth dark hair, which was fluttering as the night breeze moved through it.

"Have you ever done this before?" I tried to keep the conversation going. I wanted her closer.

"Swam in dark, arctic waters?"

"Skinny dipped at night."

"Can't say that I have."

"You have to try it. At least once. It's life changing." I had an angel on one shoulder and a devil on the other, but I was pretty sure my devil had my angel bound and gagged.

"I think my life's seen enough changes for the time being." She took another step, wobbling a little as she navigated the rocky shore bare-footed. "And if there are photographers, I'm not sure I want them to get those kinds of pictures of me."

"It's too far away and too dark to get that kind of detail." I had no idea what I was talking about, but I didn't care. "Take your clothes off. Get in." My inner demon was large and in charge.

"Who's gonna make me?" She was standing at the edge of the water and her bare toes were probably feeling the coolness of the lake.

Don't do it, Gabriel Green. Don't you dare. "Your husband." I did it.

"Oh yeah?"

"Yeah." I moved towards her, into more shallow water, revealing my body, or most of it—everything above my knees.

"I'd like to see him try." She put her hands on her hips but didn't back away.

"Would you?" I took another step.

"I sure would." Susana kicked at the water, sending up a tiny splash.

I waded slowly but steadily toward my wife, giving her a chance to back up or change her mind, but she did neither. Seemed like her devil was doing the talking, just like mine. Three more steps and I reached her.

I caught the fabric of her flowy summer shirt dress between my fingers. It buttoned up the front. I kept my body close to hers just in case there really *was* a random shutterbug in the woods. That way they'd just get shots of my ugly ass and not this gorgeous woman. Neither of us spoke as I started with the top button, then the second, then the third, as I moved my way down her dress. With the last one unfastened, her dress opened, revealing her breasts pushing against the fabric holding them in. I slid the dress off her shoulders and reached around to her back to unfasten her bra. There were no hooks or clasps—it was pull-on style. I raised both her hands over her head and held them there. She tilted her head up and looked into my eyes, her gaze intense and steady as I pulled the fabric up and then off and tossed it on the beach with her dress. Released from their confines, her breasts bloomed like full, ripe summer blossoms. I wanted to lift one in each hand and run my thumbs over her nipples until they hardened and raised under my thumbs; I wanted to bring her to my mouth and suck and tease and nibble and taste until I brought her to her knees—but I didn't.

I slid my fingers under the waistband of her underwear and lowered them to her ankles. She stepped out one foot, then the other. I lifted her up, one of my arms under her knees and the other behind her back. She circled her arms around my neck and huddled in close as I carried her to the water—up to my calves, then my thighs, then my waist. The temperature didn't faze me the second time around. All I could focus on was Susana in my arms and the goosebumps that rose in waves on her skin and how I still wanted to consume her.

Susana fluttered her legs and slipped out of my grip—she tried to stand in the water, but because she was so much shorter, she was up to her chin. She let out a squeal and jumped back into my arms. My hands were on her ass and I had no complaints about that, but now that I had her here, what was I going to do with her?

She took matters into her own hands, or, her legs, as she circled them around me and straddled my waist. God help me now. My hands were busy holding her up, so my erection was free to make itself the main character in this story, and my dick pressed up against her pussy, which was excruciatingly perfect.

"Good evening to Anthony," she said.

"I think you'd better start calling him Tony."

No amount of joking about my dick was going to distract me from my intense desire to fuck her, and the fact that she was rocking her hips against me did not help *at all*. I wanted to kiss her, but once I did that, I'd have an even harder time controlling myself. Something about her mouth on mine drove me wild, and maybe if I kept her lips away, I could keep myself from sliding my dick into her.

Susana maneuvered her hand between us and let her fingers linger on the head of my cock and then she swept them down my shaft and back up. Christ, this was not helping. I was so hard it was painful, and it didn't matter that the water was cold or that we were shivering, or that we'd promised not to have sex—Susana was stroking me, and it took every ounce of willpower I had not to plunge into her. I curled my toes into the sandy bottom of the lake and tried not to come into the palm of her hand. She was teasing me, and fuck, it was hot. She was gripping me harder and was rubbing my tip against her folds. Everything was wet and soft and fluid and I'd never wanted anything more than I wanted to be inside her right then.

"What's happening on the blanket?" Susana whispered.

It took me a second to shift gears. She'd let go of my shaft and was pointing to our stuff on the shore. There were a series of flashes from two different spots. Light, then dark, then light again.

"Are those our phones?" she asked.

Susana pushed out of my arms and started swimming to the shore, and I trudged along behind her. Tony hadn't gotten the memo that the party was off, so he was still at full attention. I stayed in the waist-deep water while Susana went all the way to shore.

"There's a towel in my backpack!" I shouted. She ran to the bag and dug out the towel and snuggled up in it.

"It's our phones!"

Of course it was. There was no escape, not even out here. She was distracted, so I used that time to get to shore without putting on too much of a show. I shook off the picnic blanket and covered up with it. I grabbed my phone and saw that texts and notifications were coming in one after the other and illuminating my screen.

"My hands are too wet."

"Get dressed and then we'll see what the problem is."

Susana skittered over to her clothes. She slid her arms into her dress and buttoned it up, not bothering with any of her undergarments. As she slipped into her shoes, I found my own clothes and had my underwear and jeans on and was untangling my shirt when I heard her gasp.

"Shit," she hissed. Her face was illuminated by the glow of her phone. "Gabe, this is bad."

23

SUSANA

I flipped through the notifications that were piled up on the home screen of my phone. Even just glimpsing the text previews, I could see that things weren't good:

Simon: Call me

Sebastian: Where r u

Simon: Don't google yourself

Shelly: Please contact me as soon as you get this. What's your ETA?

Sebastian: Answer me

Embry Nolan: Please call me ASAP.

Sebastian: It's yr turn 2 go viral HAHAHAHA

Shelly: Everything is fine. We can handle this. Text when you're on your way back.

Indy: If you're going to be front page news, we need to talk wardrobe.

> Jenkins: There are people taking photos of your house. They're stepping in your flower beds. Thinking of setting booby traps. Any objections?

> Sebastian: Text me if u aren't dead.

> Sebastian: If ur dead does that mean Hardin gets all the goods?

> Sebastian: Please dont be dead

> Simon: You need a smart watch ASAP

> Sebastian: U can still text me if ur dead. Never got a text from a ghost

> Simon: Sebastian and I are headed to SM

"Christ. I have like ten missed calls and a million texts." Gabe was dressed but his feet were still bare, and he was scrolling through his notifications.

"I'm about to send a group text telling them that we aren't dead."

"I'll text Jeff and tell him we're headed back."

"We've not even been gone two hours!" My neck was itchy, and my stomach was cramping up. I knew this was the life of a Starling, but I'd been in denial. I couldn't ignore it any longer. All the attention that came with fame and fortune was part of the deal, and it wasn't always pretty. I composed a text to my cousins and the PR team:

> Susana: Gabe and I are together and fine. Headed back to SM. ETA 11:00.

> Sebastian: Is this your ghost texting?

> Embry: We will have updated info for you when you arrive. Don't make stops on the way back. If you need gas, we will send a car.

I also sent a text to Mrs. Jenkins:

> Susana: Booby traps approved.

> Jenkins: Roger that.

"Do we need to stop for gas, or can we drive straight back?"

"We left with a full tank, so we're fine. Why?" Gabe was tying the laces on his shoe.

"Embry said we shouldn't stop, and if we didn't have enough gas, they'd send a car for us."

Gabe's face darkened. "I don't like this." He walked to me, put his arm around my shoulders, and pulled out his phone. "I'm calling Jeff."

"Put him on speaker."

Gabe hit the speaker button and we heard just a blip of a ring before Jeff picked up.

"Well, if it isn't the famous fugitive!" Jeff's voice was familiar and warm, and my stomach started to unclench just a little.

"What the hell's going on?" Gabe's voice was not relaxed or warm at all. "I have you on speaker and Susana is here."

"How was the food?"

"Jeffrey." Gabe wasn't in the mood for playful small talk.

"Sorry. I'm not clear on the specifics, but I guess a bunch of stories and photos hit the interwebs, and a lot of it is bullshit."

"Ok, but why the intense response from our team and all that?"

"I think—hold on. Let me step outside." There was silence while Jeff relocated and then he spoke again. "I think there may have been some threats."

Gabe's body tensed against mine. "What kind of threats?"

"Uh...well, very vague threats of violence, maybe?"

"Against whom?"

"Listen, I don't know the specifics, and I'm not sure I want to go poking around the internet to find out. Just get home and—"

Jeff cut off and I heard another man speaking in the background. There was a rustling and then I heard Jag's voice on the line.

"Gabriel?"

"Hey Jag. Yes, Susana and I are here. You're on speaker."

"Please return immediately. Where are you?"

"Up at the res, off highway 57."

"Do you need law enforcement to escort you home?"

"Jesus. What kind of threats are we talking about?" Gabe barked into the phone.

My stomach dropped and suddenly this swimming spot felt very remote and very dangerous.

"We're just acting with an abundance of caution. Your team will brief you when you return."

"We're heading out." Gabe ended the call and looked left, right, and then behind us toward the trail. His mouth was set in a hard line. "Ok, Sunny. Let's get to the car. I'm sure everything is fine." He'd pasted a lame smile on his face that didn't come close to reaching his eyes.

"I'm not a child. I understand the situation." I grabbed the blanket and the picnic basket.

"Sorry. Just didn't want you to stress out."

"Too late. Let's go."

All romance and magic and sweetness had been stripped out of the air, and every noise I heard as we went up the trail felt threatening and out of place. Gabe couldn't decide whether to stay in front of me or protect me from behind, so we ended up walking side-by-side. We didn't speak because neither of us had anything to say, and I think we both wanted to concentrate on listening for sounds of an approaching stalker. We walked quickly and were both out of breath by the time we reached the car.

Gabe inspected the truck with the flashlight. He aimed the light underneath the vehicle, in the bed of the truck, and made a visual sweep of the interior. Everything seemed normal. He unlocked my door with the key, apparently not wanting to unlock the driver's side door at the same time, just in case someone was out there, ready to pounce. I climbed into the passenger seat and Gabe shut the door and locked the vehicle while he crossed to the driver's side. He unlocked his door, hopped in, and immediately relocked it. He started the engine, and we headed towards home.

Ten minutes into the drive, I couldn't stand the silence anymore. A half hour ago we'd been in a very intimate position, and now we were silent and grumpy and scared. "I'm sorry about earlier."

Gabe kept his eyes on the road. "Sorry about what?" He sounded like a robot.

"About, touching you in the lake and all that."

"You don't have anything to apologize for." His voice was softer.

"I know I crossed the line. And we'd agreed to no sex and—"

"We didn't have sex."

"I know, but I shouldn't have gotten so close to it, and we didn't have a condom and I don't want to—"

"You don't want to get pregnant. I totally understand, Sunny. Really." He took one hand off the steering wheel and rested it on my arm.

"Water sex is terrible, anyway. Everyone knows that."

"They do?" Gabe shot a side glance at me to see if I was kidding.

"Weirdly, it's too dry. Probably a better land activity."

"Sounds like some kind of late-night skit: *Tony and the Land Shark.*"

A laugh broke free from my chest, relieving some of the pressure built up from worry. We drove the rest of the way in silence with his hand on my arm.

THIRTY MINUTES LATER, we were back at Starling Manor. It was late, but lights shone out of most of the windows of the mansion, making it seem like a lighthouse on a hill, beckoning us to safety. I had mixed feelings—the estate had never been a source of comfort for me, but at the moment, it seemed like the most protected place to be.

We'd driven up the front driveway which had more security and more gates to pass through than the back entrance. As we pulled up to the front of the house, a group of people were assembled and waiting on the front steps: Jag, Jeff, my cousins, Anton, the whole PR team, plus a driver and a few other staff members.

Gabe groaned when he saw everyone. "It's going to be a late night, isn't it?"

"Could be." I was already bone tired, and thinking about security and media briefings made me want to pass out right there in the front seat of Gabe's truck. I was weary and worried.

Gabe put the truck in park but didn't turn off the ignition—a driver was waiting to take it back to the garage. Anton was at my car door before Gabe even had a chance to get both of his feet on the ground, and he and all his over-zealous muscles ushered me into the house and directly to an interior parlor which had no windows.

Everyone followed us into the room where the wood paneled walls were comforting and warm, the chairs were plush and welcoming, and the softly worn area rugs made me feel at home. A small but well-stocked bar occupied one corner of the room and a gas-powered fire flickered away in the fireplace, not putting out any heat but adding a nice touch of atmosphere.

"How are you?" Jag asked me. "Need any migraine medicine?"

"Not tonight. But thank you." All I needed was a whiskey in a heavy-bottomed glass to make the picture complete.

Apparently a mind-reader, Jag placed a crystal Old Fashioned glass on the table next to the chair I'd dropped into. It was filled with an amber-colored liquid and one large ice cube. Perfect.

"Got another one of those?" Gabe asked Jag. Gabe started pacing but wouldn't take his eyes off me.

Simon stood stoically near the fireplace, his arms crossed and his expression serious. Shelly, Embry, and Indy were huddled over some printouts, Sebastian was making himself a huge cocktail at the bar, and Anton was standing with his back to the main door —I pitied anyone who tried to get past him. The service door swung open, and Patrick entered carrying a tray with a teapot, cups, and right on his heels, Jeff carried a basket which hopefully held some snacks. I couldn't get enough of Jeff's baking, and I hoped that once all this shit calmed down, he'd let me play around in the kitchen. I couldn't remember when I'd ever gone this long without making food for myself or for someone else. I caught Jeff's eye and pointed to the basket. He brought it over and I peeked under the napkin where six beautiful madeleines lay.

"Take one," Jeff whispered. "Sugar helps with stress."

I grabbed three.

"The gang's all here!" Bash called out after taking a swig of his drink. He raised his glass into the air. "Cheers!"

Simon rolled his eyes and everyone else ignored him. Jag put a drink in Gabe's hand, and he took a sip but still didn't take his eyes off me. This was all so weird.

Shelly walked to the middle of the room and cleared her throat. "I apologize for the dramatic evening. I think once we get systems and protocols in place we can prevent this kind of mayhem."

"I'd like to know what kind of threat was made against my wife." Gabe was intense and imposing as he made his demand. Even Anton raised his eyebrow.

"We're all in the know, Gabe. You don't have to play the role of protective lover in here." Leave it to buzzed Bash to say the quiet part out loud.

"To answer your question, Mr. Green," Shelly continued, "A lot of posts and articles have popped up over the last twenty-four hours. We expect a good number of trolls and bogus posts, but this one caught the attention of our technology team because of the photos that accompanied it."

"What photos?" My mouth went dry and my heart rate sped up.

Embry handed me a printout and gave another to Gabe. Everyone else in the room must've already seen the posts because none of them seemed curious about what was on the page. I flipped through the pages and saw several photos of myself. I'd expected to see pictures from my house, where we'd seen the photographers across the street, but these were from Starling Manor. A few were taken of me, Gabe, Anton, and Tyler as we stood in the driveway. A few more were of Gabe and I kissing by the car.

"See, we *were* in public!" Gabe whispered. But the final photos were just of me. Close-ups. "What the fuck! Who took these?" He shook the pages in his hand. "And where's the threat? All I see are the pictures."

Embry stepped forward. "We've not printed out the written threat. While I know that you or Ms. Starling can look these up online on your own, I'm a strong believer in not exposing yourselves to every vile post. If you did that, you'd end up overwhelmed, anxious, and fearful. It's our job to screen these and come to you with what we feel are viable threats to your safety or well-being."

"I want to know what someone is threatening to do to my wife!"

"He's edgy." Bash added, in a mock whisper.

"The threat was vague but troubling. It said, '*The brightest stars fall the fastest. Time for a supernova*,' followed by a skull emoji and a knife emoji." Embry's voice stayed clear, calm, and steady, which was helping me not panic.

Gabe threw his arms in the air. "Great. My wife's getting death threats from astronomers?"

"For now, we're looking into who took the photos, and was

that the same person who made the threat or were those separate individuals. Because the photos were taken right before the two of you left for an undisclosed location, we felt it was best that you return to the estate."

"Because this psycho could've been in the house with us?" Gabe started to pace. "Have you checked with Skinner? I'd put money on her."

"I interviewed her personally," Indy said. "But I had to find her, first. She was cleaning out the pool house and security camera footage backs up her story. She was there for several hours and couldn't have taken the photos herself."

"Then who did this?" Gabe demanded.

Embry kept his cool. "We hope to know by this time tomorrow. What matters now is that you're both here and safe. By morning we'll have the security team fully assembled and we should have the safety protocols set. In the meantime, the tech team will be monitoring social media and other internet traffic. You two need to get some rest. Don't forget that you have photo shoots and interviews coming up."

Gabe let out an exasperated sigh. "Fine. We can revisit this tomorrow."

I took another sip of my drink and stood up. In moments of stress, my first reaction was usually to freeze, and the processing came later. Even though I knew I should probably be shaking with fear, I was oddly calm. Maybe it was the sugar. Gabe crossed the room, slid his hand around my waist, and kissed the top of my head. Simon and Sebastian exchanged a look, but I didn't care. I just wanted to shower, crawl into bed, and forget about all of this, at least for a few hours. I grabbed a few madeleines to go. I was also aware that when I got tired and stressed, I tended to get more impulsive once I got in touch with my feelings. Surely I could keep myself out of any more trouble for the time being.

"Ready to go up?" The heat of Gabe's breath in my ear made me immediately question if I had any will power at all.

24

GABE

We were safe and alone in our suite, the door closed against the rest of the world. A security guard was posted outside our room, but that didn't stop my anxiety. My head was spinning, and I wanted to collapse on the bed, but I needed to wash the lake off my skin. Susana was cuddling the kitten who now had a whole slew of her own belongings set up in the lounge area, including a cat tower, scratching post, several toys and a fluffy bed.

"We should shower." Susana interrupted my thoughts.

"You can go first, Sunny."

"Are you sure?"

"I'm sure. You go ahead." I was having trouble shaking the dread out of my gut. The thought of someone threatening my wife made my whole body tense up. I could feel my teeth grinding, my fists clenching, and my jaw tensing. *Relax, Green. Relax.*

Susana moved toward the bathroom. "I don't have to go first, we—"

"It's ok. You look tired."

She went into the bathroom but left the door ajar.

Fuck the "no looking it up on the internet" advice. With Susana gone in the bathroom, I googled her name immediately.

Lots of hits popped up—most were from gossip sites, social media, and one or two news outlets. Once the PR team really got rolling, I assumed there'd be more official profiles and stories.

I clicked a link from *The Tattler* website that had an older photo of Susana where she looked to be attending a fundraiser for the Starling Foundation. She was younger, her hair shorter, and her face rounder, but I felt such strong recognition and affection when I looked at her face. So close to the Susana I remembered from so many years ago.

WILL THIS NEW STAR SHINE? STARLING MARRIAGE STUNS!

Starling heiress Susana Starling, the formerly MIA descendent of the famous show-biz family, has rejoined the flock! Susana Starling dropped out of the spotlight thirteen years ago when she walked away from her family and the good life. Her cousins, the dashing and deliciously naughty Sebastian Starling, and the mysterious and always stunning Simon Starling have been soaking up the spotlight in her absence, but move over, boys, the lady bird is back, and she's not alone. Sources close to the family say that Susana Starling has married former Starling groundskeeper Gabriel Green in a rushed courthouse ceremony. Shotgun wedding maybe? Will they be adding some baby birds to the nest? Can we hope for a set of triplets?

Triplets? Oh *hell* no. The contract didn't say *anything* about babies, and with Susana's pregnancy phobia, it for sure wasn't happening. Sorry, Tattler. No babies for you. But I was glad they were sniffing around a shotgun wedding angle, rather than the inheritance angle, though it was probably only a matter of time.

I clicked through a few more articles, most of them saying the same thing: Susana was back, married, and suddenly in the spotlight. Nothing shocking there. Maybe I'd be able to sleep peacefully after all. Just in case, I searched for images, and most were that older photo of Susana from the fundraiser, a few photos grabbed from her kids cooking class social media sight, and even a photo from her high school yearbook. Maybe the PR team got the threatening post taken down—but then I saw it. The same photo Embry had shown me earlier: a photo of Susana holding the picnic basket in the back driveway with Tyler, Anton, and me cropped out.

I clicked on the link. Shit. It wasn't the threat itself, but it was a screenshot of the threat with the caption "Did anyone else see this earlier? Crazy shit. #Starling #starlingstalker." A slew of comments followed, and I scrolled through a few of them, knowing full well that reading comments was an activity guaranteed to make me lose my mind.

"WTF! DID SOMEONE CALL THE COPS?"

"I WONDERED WHAT HAPPENED TO HER. I READ SHE JOINED A CONVENT IN SWITZERLAND."

"CHECK OUT THIS POST BY @STARLINGFANATIC888 – HE HAS SOME GOOD THEORIES."

"DID SHE KILL HER MOM? WHY SHOW UP NOW?"

"NICE TITS."

I hated humanity. I searched for the hashtag #starling, which was trending at number twelve, and there were thousands of posts. After a little exploration, I concluded that the original threat post had been removed, but people were reposting screenshots and starting conversations. I wanted to know if more people were making threats, but I also didn't want to know. Maybe letting the team deal with this was the best decision after all— they were professionals and they'd let me know what I needed to know . . . right? Where had the photo been taken from? Judging by the angle, it seemed like it was from the west side of the mansion. I should go there and try to find that exact vantage point. Ask the other staff again if they'd seen anyone or anything suspicious.

"What're you looking at?" Susana's voice startled me.

I flipped my phone over so the screen was pressed against the bed, making it obvious that I'd been doing something I didn't want her to see.

"Nothing." Right, Gabriel. Now you look twice as guilty.

Susana had one towel wrapped around her body and another atop her head like some kind of twisted terrycloth tower. I tried not to let my mind jump to the thought of tearing that towel off her, but it was already there before I could stop it.

"Right." She opened a dresser drawer and pulled out a nightgown far too silky and sexy for my liking. I mean, I liked it, but I wasn't sure I wanted to sleep next to her if she was wearing that because I'd already proven I was not the best at showing restraint when it came to Susana. "So, porn or Google?"

"I wasn't looking at porn!"

"Ok, Google, then. Find anything good?" She carried the nightgown to the sitting area and started to open her towel.

I spun around before I saw anything I shouldn't have . . . or did she want me to see? "Nothing great. The usual stuff, plus some screenshots and comments about the threat. I think the original post has been removed." I tried to sound causal and upbeat, but it rang false even to my own ears and I was sure she wasn't buying it.

"You read some of the comments?"

"Unfortunately."

"That's the number one rule: *Never read the comments*."

"I thought the number one rule was *no sex*." Why the hell did I just bring up sex?

"Fine, the number two rule is *never read the comments*, but I guess neither of us are great with rules, though, so I get it."

Was she flirting with me again? My dick thought so, and it was at full attention, just in case Sunny was interested in throwing the rules out the window. It was a good thing my back was turned.

"You don't have to turn around every time I change."

"Just giving you privacy." And giving my erection time to rethink its strategy of pitching a very obvious tent.

"If I wanted privacy, I would've changed in the bathroom. We have to sleep in this room together for a year. We can't always hide from each other. And besides, it's just bodies. No big deal."

Just bodies? She must've had no idea what kind of pin-up body she had. It tortured me when she was fully clothed, let alone nearly naked and still soft and warm from a shower. Christ. This was a nightmare. Maybe I'd have to figure out a way to stay in my little house on the estate property. Or maybe I could change my schedule, like a night shift worker. I could sleep when she was awake, and I could be up when she was asleep. Though it would be difficult to check in on the conditions of the grounds in the dark.

"I'm done. You don't have to keep your back turned."

She was right behind me and had brushed my shoulder with her hand, which caused me to remember her hands on me when we were in the lake, and my boner problem was back. She tried to circle around to face me, but I kept pivoting so she was behind me. We did two ridiculous revolutions of that dance before she finally grabbed me and spun me around.

"What are you doing, Archie?" But she caught sight of the bulge in my pants and her cheeks went red with recognition. "Oh. Wow. I'm sorry." She didn't seem *that* sorry because she continued openly staring at my erection.

"No, I'm sorry." I had to get out of there, and fast. I locked the bathroom door behind me and then leaned against the sink, angry, exasperated, overwhelmed, and aroused. I was angry that anyone would make a threat against Susana, or that they would even think to make crass comments about her body in a post online. But of course they would—so many people were just fucking morons. I was exasperated that I couldn't do anything to stop the threats, to help Susana, or to find out who took that photo. I was over-whelmed by my new life and was aroused, far too easily, by my new bride.

I turned the shower on as hot as I could stand it, and let the spray pound my skin. My cock was still swollen and aching with need, and I didn't want to go to bed like this. Check that, I *couldn't* go to bed like this. I soaped up my hands, my chest, and my torso, and then I covered my shaft in slippery suds. I slid my hand up and down my length first slow and gently, then faster.

I indulged a fantasy of Susana getting in the shower with me:

She'd open the shower door and slip in. I imagined her nipples fully erect and puckered as the hot water rushed over her skin.
"I'm dirty," she'd say. "Wash me?"
We'd find a rhythm for washing, taking turns with soap, shampoo, our hands covering each other's bodies, exploring.
"My turn to rinse." She'd put her hand on my belly and push me gently to the side so she could get under the shower stream, but once she was under the water she wouldn't remove her hand. She'd close her eyes and tip her head back and let the water flow through her hair, down her back, over her perfect ass, and then onto the shower floor. She'd put her other hand on the small of my back and pull me to her. My hard cock would press into her stomach, and I'd kiss her ear, her jaw, and her neck and then I'd reach around and put my hands on her ass. I'd lift her, her back sliding up the shower wall, until she was high enough and perfectly positioned. She'd hold on to my neck and brace her back against the shower wall. I'd push her legs wide, and her pussy would be so wet and slick and ready, just like it was at the lake, the difference being I'd enter her in one hard thrust, my dick pushing all the way in. I'd pull back just a little, and thrust again, staying deep in her cunt as I fucked her against the shower wall. Her velvet folds would clench around my shaft as she bucked against me, saying my name over and over and over until she came hard all over my shaft. Her pussy would spasm against my cock, and

I'd plunge so deep inside that I'd lose myself and explode inside her, filling her as she cried out and spread herself open to take all of me.

I climaxed in the shower and stifled the moan I wanted to release along with my cum. I was dizzy and spent, and the orgasm had aftershocks which rippled through my body. I felt relieved of the pressure, but also a little empty—it'd been the thought of Susana that drove me so wild, and to end up alone and just jerking off in the shower was depressing. But if it helped me keep up my end of the deal, and keep my hands off my wife, then that's the way it had to be.

I shut off the water and wrapped a towel around my waist. I'd been in such a rush to get away from Susana that I hadn't brought in a change of clothes. Now *I'd* be the one doing the towel promenade through the bedroom. I cracked open the bathroom door to scope out the situation before entering our room, but things were dark. Susana had turned off the lights and gone to bed, and the only light was a soft glow coming from a nightlight in the sitting area. As I walked quietly across the room to my dresser, I could make out the shape of my wife on her side of the bed. She was still and covered by the blankets. I doubted anyone could fall asleep that fast, but I'd go along with her charade of sleep; we'd have to get used to pretending, both around other people, and each other.

The kitten was fully awake, however, and glad to see me. She pounced on my feet as I tried to walk, digging her tiny sharp claws into my toes whenever she would try to strike.

"Stop it, kitty!" I whispered, but she ignored me and had now made it her life's mission to murder my feet. "Ouch! You're a beast, Mallory!" I remembered how Pebbles used to attack my feet like that. It had been one of our favorite games. I knew I was setting myself up for heartbreak by letting myself fall for this furball, but I couldn't stop myself. I pulled on some clothes while Mallory continued her assault, and once dressed, I picked up the cat and carried her to bed.

Susana was on the far edge, her back turned. The bed was so large that there was room for at least one other person between us, or about twenty more kittens. I stayed on my side of the mattress, though I longed to reach out and just make contact with Sunny— the warmth of her skin was such a comfort to me—but I knew I shouldn't. I snuggled with Mallory instead, even though she was trying to bite my nose and wasn't a very relaxing companion. I stared into the darkness and longed for my old bed, my old house, and even my old life. Everything was so much simpler a few days ago and now, I felt lost and disoriented.

Mallory eventually wore herself out and collapsed on my chest. With her purr rattling against me, I let the wave of fatigue overtake me and wash me out to the deep sea of sleep.

25

GABE

Susana snuggled up to me under the covers. My eyes were still closed but I could feel her body against mine, all her softness and warmth as she put one leg over my stomach and draped an arm across my chest. I ran my fingers all the way from her wrist to her shoulder and back again, and a trail of goosebumps followed my touch.

"That tickles." She nipped at my ear with her lips and then sucked on my earlobe.

"How does this feel?" I let my hand drop to her breast and I caressed the edge of the curve before moving over to her nipple. She let out a quiet moan and pressed her pelvis into my hip.

"It feels perfect, Mr. Green."

"Why so formal, Mrs. Starling?" I gripped her arm again and she started rubbing herself on me, using my outer thigh as a source of friction.

"Mr. Green," she said again as she picked up the pace, the wetness between her legs making her slip and slide along my side. It took everything I had not to flip her over on her back and enter her. I tightened my grip on her arm as she rode me. "Mr. Green!"

"Mr. Green!"

I opened my eyes to the vision of an unknown face just inches from mine.

"What the fuck!" I jerked back from the intruder, realizing I'd been gripping her arm quite tightly. As the face came into focus, I recognized it as belonging to one of the newer members of the housekeeping staff. Lori? Kori?

"I'm so sorry, Mr. Green. I couldn't get you to wake up." She looked tearful and nervous and was holding her forearm where I'd been digging my fingers into her. I pulled the blankets up to cover my chest and tried to get my bearings. The room was bright, and I was alone in the bed.

"No, *I'm* sorry. Did I hurt you?" I sat up and tried to clear my head. "Where's Susana?"

"She's been down with the Public Relations team for an hour. She asked me to come get you because you weren't answering your phone."

"What time is it?" I reached for my phone on the nightstand, but it wasn't there. Had I left it in the bathroom last night?

"A little after nine o'clock." Lori/Kori backed up a few steps like she'd just lit a firework and wanted to get out of the direct explosion range.

"Fucking shit." Our morning meeting started at eight. Where was my alarm? Why had Susana not woken me up? "Thanks . . . I'm sorry, could you remind me of your name?"

"Rory," she said, taking another step backwards toward the door.

"Thanks, Rory. Is your arm okay?"

"It's fine. Thank you, Mr. Green. The team is out on the south veranda." Rory dashed out of the room, leaving me to sort out my disorientation and dream hangover on my own. After a minute of letting myself come to consciousness, I got up, brushed my teeth, found my phone, (dead, and in the pockets of yesterday's pants), and got dressed. Only 362 days until I could put this all behind me and start my new life on the beach. I could do this.

. . .

I FOUND Susana and the team out on the veranda, sitting in old-fashioned rocking chairs but talking about the very modern problem of cyber stalkers and press releases. Not quite ready to talk strategy, I made a beeline to the coffee pot.

"You're alive after all," my wife said. "Thought you might be dead."

"My apologies." I avoided eye contact with everyone as I poured my coffee into a large white mug and stayed standing. "What did I miss?"

"No developments in discovering who made the post last night, but there haven't been any more threats, so that's a good sign." Embry looked like he'd just walked off the pages of a men's fashion magazine.

Next to him, I felt a little sloppy in my jeans and t-shirt, but I prioritized comfort over polish.

"We've moved up the first photo shoot and interview to today at noon. We need to get ahead of any grassroots stories or gossip sites." Shelly had a tablet resting on her lap, a laptop on the table next to her, and a phone in her hand, on which she was tapping away like her life depended on it.

I nearly spit out my coffee, which would've been a shame, because it was like the nectar of the gods. "Noon today?"

"That's right, Captain America." Indy was eyeing my outfit with disdain. "Your style crew will meet you in the east parlor at 11:00."

"And I'll have someone there to brief you on your talking points." Embry added.

I wanted to run, scream, hide, throw a giant tantrum right there on the veranda. But instead, I just sipped my coffee and willed myself to calm down.

Susana was staring at me as if expecting me to erupt at any moment. "You good?"

"Yep." Lie number one for the day, and I'd only been awake for a half hour. "Any breakfast around here?" I was used to a giant bowl of cereal, grabbing some granola bars for breakfast, and getting to work. This standing around in meetings was making me itchy.

"You missed that. Jeff said he'd hold some for you in the kitchen." Susana was clearly annoyed that I'd slept in, but she could've woken me up if she wanted, so I didn't feel too guilty.

"Great. I'll circle back after I grab some food." I hopped off the porch steps and hoped that no one would try to stop me.

"But we have a schedule to go over with you!" Shelly looked up from her twenty screens in a panic. "And I need to know your dietary preferences for some upcoming fundraisers, if you can travel to Boston for—"

"Just schedule it, and I'll be there," I called over my shoulder. If I stayed around any longer, I was going to snap at someone and say something I'd regret. "If it's ok with Susana, it's ok with me." I practically sprinted to the kitchen where I found Jeff working on a shopping list on a clean counter. "No food?"

"Well, aren't you demanding? What happened to your trusty granola bar habit?"

"I don't have my own kitchen anymore!" My voice was gruff and a little too loud.

"Simmer down, princess. Somebody's hangry."

"Sorry."

"Then a little food might help. Have a quiche in the warmer, and you're lucky enough to get one of Patrick's signature muffins. He's tweaking his recipe, and this might be the best yet." Jeff pulled a towel off a tray to reveal a giant blueberry muffin, a jar brimming with ripe strawberries and three homemade granola bars. Maybe it was the fatigue, the hunger, or my jacked up emotional state, but I'd be lying (for the second time that day) if I said the sight of those granola bars didn't get me a little choked up.

"Thanks, man. This is perfect."

"You're welcome. It's my job, you know."

"I know—" I wanted to say more, but there was a damn frog in my throat. Jeff took pity on me and pointed to a chair at the corner table.

"Sit there. I'll plate up the quiche for you. Need some coffee?"

"Desperately." I settled into a seat and bit into the muffin which was bursting with giant fresh blueberries and hit my taste-buds with a tart twist of lemon.

"How're you holding up?" Jeff placed a slice of vegetable quiche in front of me along with some orange juice.

"I have no idea." I popped a handful of the little strawberries in my mouth, and they left a red stain on my palm. "Like, I think I'm ok, and then I'm positive that I'm not, and then I don't know what I am."

Jeff nodded like he totally understood the insanity of my life and my mind. "And you're getting along ok with Susana?" He kept his eyes on the coffee pot as he asked his question.

"Are there rumors going around about us or something?" No doubt the staff were talking about. I was used to being on the staff side, not the family side, and I liked it better before.

"No rumors really. I'm not hearing much. But I do have eyes." He poured the coffee into a stainless steel travel mug.

"And what are you seeing with those eyes?"

Jeff just gave me a look. One that included a raised eyebrow.

"Ok, she's attractive," I admitted.

"Go on."

"But the romance is just for show. Nothing happens off-stage."

"Nothing?"

"Mostly nothing."

"I sense chemistry."

"Good. That's what we need people to see so the marriage seems on the up and up."

"So you don't want anything more?"

"That doesn't matter. What matters is that Susana saves this place from Hardin, and I get to retire to my beach house in a year."

"You know you're going to have to work a little. You don't have that much cash stashed away."

"You're a buzzkill, chef. And I don't mind working. I just need a major change of scenery. Too many ghosts here, anyway."

"And you can't enjoy your wedded union for the year that you're here?"

"You've got a lot of questions."

Jeff waited, not willing to be pulled off topic.

"I can enjoy her company, but it stays platonic. Besides, she has some massive fear of accidentally producing some baby Starlings, so I think 'enjoying' my marriage like that is off the table no matter what."

"You know, I've heard that there are ways to prevent pregnancy—"

"I'm not going there. Not with you, and not with her. That's what she said, so that's that." I shoved the rest of the muffin in my mouth.

"We'll see. How'd you escape that serious meeting I saw on the veranda?"

"I overslept and then said I needed to eat. Which was true. I just don't know if I'm ready for primetime."

"You'd better get ready. I hear there's gonna be a steady stream of journalists and photographers here for the next few days."

My stomach dropped at the thought of it. "Don't remind me." I reached for my phone to check the time but remembered that I'd left it charging back in the room. "What time is it? I have a date with destiny at eleven."

Jeff checked his watch. "Coming on ten o'clock."

"I'm going to see if I can check out the grounds before I'm due back for my fitting. Clear my head and all that."

"Enjoy. And don't forget these." Jeff handed me a few granola bars which were sealed in a reusable pouch.

There was that damn frog in my throat again.

TEN MINUTES later I was hiding out in the middle of the rose garden, enjoying the rest of my coffee surrounded by thick bushes and hundreds of blooms. If the PR team wanted to hunt me down, they'd have to battle the thorns to get to me. I deadheaded a pink blossom. I held the withered pink petals in my palm and thought about how Susana liked these flowers, but for Helen, they'd made her think about death.

I liked Helen, even though she was hard to connect with, especially in her later years when it felt like she'd disappeared into a haze. Being married to Harry Hardin had to be its own kind of hell. He was such an asshole to the staff, and I'd bet a lot of cash that he was even shittier to his wife.

How much time had gone by since I got to the garden? I'd left a trail of plucked petals behind me. Maybe ten minutes' worth? I needed a watch or a better phone charging system. Sometimes I had my phone with me, and sometimes I didn't, but it looked like that was about to change. Speaking of changing, I had to change clothes with my "style crew," and it had to be getting close to eleven o'clock.

"You got this, Green," I said aloud to no one but myself and the roses. At least the plants didn't care if I was a loser. And talking to flowers was better than talking to the press. Bloody hell. The press. Something like panic bubbled up in my throat when I thought about the hours of interviews I had coming up. "How the FUCK did you get yourself into this? This is fucking miserable."

"Glad to know how you really feel."

I spun around and came face to face with my wife.

26

SUSANA

"So, I make you miserable?" I could tell my face was flaming red because of the flash of hot anger that'd shot through me like fierce lighting in a summer storm. The whirlwind of the last few days had gotten to me, and I had a massive headache coming on. I'd tossed and turned all night and then woke up at dawn. I spent the morning worrying, planning, strategizing, and meeting, while Gabe slept like some kind of hibernating bear, in such a deep slumber he didn't even notice me shaking his shoulder to wake him. And he came down late, not apologetic enough, if you asked me, and then ran out of the meeting after about sixty seconds.

He'd probably had a nice leisurely breakfast in the kitchen. Why did he get to do that? It wasn't fair. I had to eat with a plate on my lap and a phone in my hand while coordinating photo shoots and interviews that I had no interest in doing. And now Mr. Free Spirit was off smelling the literal roses while I hunted for him in garden after garden. It was almost eleven and I didn't know Gabe well enough to know if he was punctual or airheaded, but I didn't want to take any chances.

"Don't twist my words." Gabe crossed his arms to match mine, putting us in a standoff.

"Fine, 'THIS is fucking miserable,' is what you said. Would you like to back out of this marriage while you still can?"

"What's wrong?" His tone was soft, but his position was defensive: he held his ground and had his legs set in a ridiculous wide stance that was just asking for someone to kick him in the nuts. Not that I'd ever do that.

"I'm in a bad mood."

"I see that."

I wanted him to argue with me, or push against me, or be a jerk to me so I wouldn't feel so bad for being a jerk to him. "You know what, this morning you've been a real piece of—"

"Well, hello hello!" a saccharine, sing-songy voice rang out from behind an especially thorny rose bush bursting with magenta blooms. "I heard this garden was to die for, and it's even more gorgeous than I imagined!" An over-coiffed head of honey-blonde curls popped into view, and the lipsticked, eyelash-extended, pink cheeks to-the-max face that went with it belonged to none other than Sawyer Lacey, our local "Hard-hitting Lifestyle Reporter."

I had no idea why a lifestyle reporter would want to be "hard-hitting" but that was Sawyer's tagline. Sawyer had an exaggerated Southern drawl that slipped when she was caught off-guard, revealing a native Boston accent underneath, missing r's and all. It was a mystery why Sawyer thought putting on a Georgia Peach act would endear her to New Englanders, and maybe it hadn't, but her quirky and over-blown style had made her an internet sensation, and well, here she was. Our interview with her was scheduled for noon. How much had she heard of our argument? Was she recording? We were not off to a good start. If Embry heard about this, he'd be unhappy, to say the least. Did Gabe recognize her? I hoped he had enough sense to not be an ass to a random stranger, no matter how dark his mood.

"Sawyer Lacey in the flesh!" Gabe was beaming at the reporter, his body language completely changed from a moment earlier. His stance was narrower, and his arms were outstretched to her in greeting. He'd pasted a blinding smile on his face that somehow looked genuine and warm. Gabe was in the wrong line of work—he must've had acting in his DNA. He'd transformed from grumpy pouty face to grinning Greek God in about two seconds flat, and Sawyer was not immune to his charms.

If she'd heard us arguing, she'd forgotten about it, at least for the moment. Her smarmy smirk gave her the look of a maneater, but no way would I let her gobble up my man, even if our marriage was a sham.

"Looks like you caught us!" Gabe said in a weird gleeful voice that I'd never heard. He lunged for me and lifted me up, knocking the breath out of me. He planted a big wet kiss on my neck and nuzzled me like a deranged Labrador Retriever.

"Put me down!" I wheezed. Gabe let me slide to the ground but kept his arm around me in a way that felt like an affectionate chokehold.

"Susana's kind of shy, but she'll warm up! I was just telling her that she's stuck with me, because I'm her husband! And—"

"And I was telling him he's a real piece of work. Speaking of work, we're late for our eleven o'clock, Mr. Starling," I said in such a sickly-sweet voice that I almost made myself nauseous. I topped the whole performance sundae with a kiss by pulling his face down to meet mine and planting a soft but very lingering smooch on his mouth. Which, I had to admit, was pretty enjoyable.

"Are we, Mrs. Green?" Gabe nuzzled my neck again, nipped me with his teeth in some kind of showy love-bite, grabbed me, and spun me around like I weighed nothing.

"Oh my GAWD!" Sawyer drawled. "Y'all are adorable! Can we take a selfie? Just for my socials. People love candid shots."

I had no idea if this would be approved by the PR team, but Gabe stepped in and pushed through my moment of hesitation.

"A selfie with Sawyer Lacey? You don't have to ask me twice! Get over here!" Gabe waved Sawyer over and put his arm behind her as if he was hugging her shoulders, but I noticed that he wasn't actually making contact with her—his arm hovered behind her, and his palm, near her shoulder, was open and empty. Who was this perky giant who spoke only in exclamatory sentences and who'd pulled out Keanu Reeves selfie skills? He tugged me in with his other arm, causing Ms. Lacey and I to make a Gabriel Green sandwich, and by the looks of the goofy grin he sported when she took our photo, he didn't mind at all being the meat between us. So to speak. "We'll see you soon!" my perky husband said. "Have to get ourselves cleaned up for the likes of you!"

Sawyer clapped her hands like she was a baby seal about to receive a bucket of fish. "I can't wait! See y'all in a bit!" She waved with two hands and then skittered off down a row of rose bushes the way she'd came.

The cyclone of rabid cheerfulness had passed, and Gabe and I stood shellshocked and out of breath.

"Who are you?" I asked Gabe.

"I have no idea what happened back there. We might need to schedule an exorcism."

His good cheer started to melt my icy gut, despite my resolution to stay grumpy.

"Come on, time to get gussied up for everyone's favorite Hard-Hitting Lifestyle reporter." He grabbed my hand as we started to walk back toward the mansion. "People are here. So, it's game on until bedtime."

"You mean we have to turn on the PDA?"

"You got it. Even if it looks like no one's watching. Because apparently people are everywhere, even in the fucking gardens."

"Well, then maybe you should carry me back to the house?"

"Carry you how?" Gabe gave me a suspicious side-eye.

"A piggyback ride would be fine." I'd take advantage of him while I had the chance.

"You're really milking this, aren't you?"

"Who, me?" My innocent routine wasn't fooling Gabe, but he took it in stride.

"Fine. Hop on." He stooped down so I could climb onto his wide back. I leaped toward him and he grabbed my ass with his hands and scooted me up until I was securely situated. "You're going to pay for this, you know."

"Sorry," I giggled unapologetically. "If you tried to ride on my back we'd have to call an ambulance. Starlings are precious commodities, you know.

"Oh my GAWD! Look how adorable they are!" Sawyer's voice carried over the front lawn.

"Can you even see where she is?" Gabe was huffing and puffing like he was an ox pulling a cart.

"I'm not that heavy, so stop the theatrics. We're almost there. And no, I can't see where she is. It's like she's everywhere. Maybe this is like the *Hunger Games* arena, and everyone is watching us from the command room.

"Are you smiling?" Gabe asked.

"Why?"

"Just act like you're having fun. She's probably taking photos. Or that creepy stalker in the window is taking them, and I want us to look fucking elated. If we're gonna do this, let's do it right."

"Wait, we're not elated for real?" I kicked at his hip with my heel.

"Keep it up, cowgirl, and I'm going to tell everyone that your idea of fun is a pie throwing contest, or some shit like that."

"Ok, sorry, no more kicking."

Gabe hauled me up the steps to the front porch, set me down gently, and then turned to face me. He ran a finger along my hairline, down my jaw, and then across the delicate skin of my neck. "See you soon, my beautiful wife."

"Uh," I felt weird, like we were putting on a performance for no one.

Gabe leaned forward and kissed my ear and then whispered, "There's a photographer standing right inside the front door. Kiss me like you mean it."

So, I did.

I SPACED out for most of my style session. I felt like a Barbie doll as I was dressed and twirled and primped and brushed. Shelly reviewed notes with me when I was in the make-up chair but that mostly consisted of her monologuing and me nodding. My mind was back in the piggyback ride, the rose garden, the lake swim, his hands on me, the scene in my bedroom at home, the morning after our wedding night, the barn where we'd kissed for show, and the night in Gabe's cottage where we made our rules. Meaning, my head was everywhere but in the present, and I wasn't taking in a word Shelly was saying.

A half hour in, I realized we were in what used to be my mother's dressing room. Once adorned with perfume bottles and scarves and bright baubles that hung from hooks on the walls and ceiling and clinging to weird mannequin heads. This room had been chaotic and manic, but it'd had a touch of magic. Now it was bare and sterile.

"Where are all of my mother's things?" I asked.

Shelly looked up from her phone, the make-up artist pulled the eyebrow brush away from my face, and the hairstylist stopped mid-brush. My fashion advisor peeked out of the closet, and Ethan, a member of the housekeeping staff who was carrying in bottles of water and some snacks, froze mid-step.

"Which things are you looking for, Ms. Starling?" Ethan asked.

"All of them. Any of them. Where are all the things that used to be in this room?" I realized that my memory of the dressing room might've been very different from the reality of the last decade. I hadn't been in this room since I was twenty, when I came back once to see my mother in a visit that didn't go well. I felt self-conscious and like an obnoxious brat. "Never mind. I'll ask Jag later. I'm sorry." A vase of flowers on the dressing table caught my eye. Red roses. "Can someone take those flowers out of here? We need lilacs instead. You can find those bushes on the east side of the house. Gabe will know if you can't find them."

Ethan swiftly whisked the flowers off the vanity. "Not a problem at all, Ms. Starling. Would you prefer we not have roses in the house?"

"Roses are fine." I felt my voice catch in my throat. The rush of emotion caught me off guard. "Well, maybe pink instead of red. But just not in here. This was my mother's room and she preferred —" I couldn't finish the sentence. If I said "lilacs" again, tears would spill over and ruin all the work that'd been done on my face.

"Not a problem." Ethan zoomed out of the room, maybe in search of lilacs, and most certainly glad to be away from me.

There were a few moments of silence while everyone pretended to be busy so I could collect myself. I felt the tears recede and my throat opened back up.

"I'm fine. Carry on." I hadn't even taken a good look at myself in the mirror until that moment. I'd been transformed. My hair was pulled back into a loose ponytail, with a few dark strands left out to frame my face. And wow, my face. I usually went without make-up, and somehow Leah, the cosmetic artist, had made me look both natural and glamorous at the same time. My skin was glowing, my eyes looked huge and intense, and my lips were positively luscious, thank you very much. "Wow."

Leah laughed. "We had a great canvas to work with. I think we're done?"

"Just the shoes!" a stylist called from the closet.

And after a flurry of movement, tweaking, and turning, I was done. Ready to go and speak to some interviewers, pose for photos, and officially go out in the world as Susana Starling, wife of Gabriel Green, and new face of this particular branch of the

Starling family tree. My stomach was flip-flopping, and my palms were sweaty, but I knew that once I had Gabe by my side, I'd be able to breathe.

SCRATCH THAT. Seeing Gabe took my breath away. He was standing alone outside the stables, which was where a neutral backdrop was set up to conduct some of the interviews. Whoever styled him had taken him from homegrown handsome to iconic heartthrob. He was wearing higher-waisted pressed trousers the color of sandstone. They looked fresh, sharp, casual, and very expensive.

He had on a black short-sleeved luxury t-shirt a size or two smaller than he usually wore, which meant it clung perfectly to his strong chest and accented the visible muscles in his upper arms. And in a stroke of fashion genius, the outfit was completed by navy suspenders sprinkled with small white polka-dots and attached to his pants with brown leather ends that must've been holding onto hidden buttons inside his waistband. Was he wearing black Italian leather sandals?

Someone had trimmed his hair, and it looked casual yet perfect and I could see that he still had some stubble on his jaw. Forget *me* being the center of attention—when the world saw Gabriel Green like this, he'd be on the cover of every magazine. And he was probably uncomfortable and miserable. He was so lost in thought that he didn't notice me approaching until I was just a few feet away. When he did see me, he did a double-take and his mouth fell open for a moment.

"Holy shit, Sunny." He moved toward me and placed his hand softly on my waist. Then he seemed to remember that we were on display, and a big smile replaced his look of shock.

"It's just me."

"It's you, but it's . . . wow."

I decided just to take the compliment. "Thank you. As for you, have you looked in the mirror? I expect the movie offers to start rolling in, especially after your impromptu performance in the rose garden earlier."

"I clean up pretty well." He snapped one of his suspenders. "And don't tell anyone," his voice lowered to a mock whisper, "but these clothes are actually comfortable."

"I won't tell a soul."

27

SUSANA

We were spent. Wiped. Drained, strained, and weary. But we'd made it through the day. We'd finished four interviews, three photoshoot locations, and one meal on the veranda with Sawyer Lacey, who'd somehow wormed her way into getting a dinner invite and dominated the conversation by asking Gabe about everything from his favorite ice cream flavor (cookies and cream) to his thoughts on a higher power (agnostic but open) while mostly ignoring me. We lied and told her we had an evening meeting, and she'd reluctantly left Starling Manor, escorted gently by Anton, who'd realized that our guest had overstayed her welcome.

We were splayed out on the bench under the lamppost, blissfully alone, probably looking like two haggard travelers who'd just disembarked from a stuffy bus after a cross-country journey. Gabe's suspenders were hanging by his side and his shirt was untucked. He'd kept his hands off his hair for as long as possible, but at dinner he gave in to the urge to run his fingers through his hair and ended up looking like he'd seen a ghost. Obliterated, my sleek ponytail was now "bird's nest chic," I had a wine stain on my skirt, I'd been barefoot for the last hour, and ten bucks said my mascara was smudged and smeared, but I didn't care—put a fork in us, we were done.

"Is it going to be this intense all the time?" Gabe ruffled his hair, trying to remove the excess styling product, which only made him look more electrified. He was going to have to wash it out.

"I hope not. It shouldn't be. But I don't want to jinx us."

"Shelly said that we're 'setting the stage' and after this we should just have to do this once in a while, right?"

"That's what she said."

"If I never see our local Hard-hitting Lifestyle reporter again, that'll be fine with me."

"I think she'd be happy to steal you away from me."

"She kept touching my arm." Gabe stretched out his forearm as if to inspect it for any leftover marks from Sawyer's two-inch pink fingernails.

"Seventeen times."

"You were counting?"

"Maybe." I'd told myself that I'd intervene once she got to twenty touches. Lucky for all of us that she stopped short. The sun had just set, and the estate was cast in a warm purple glow. This was my favorite time of the day—the time between day and night when everything seemed softer, warmer, and laced with magic. I took a deep breath in, inhaling the floral musky scent of the evening. "I love the gloaming."

Gabe wrinkled his nose and cocked his head. "The what?"

"The gloaming."

"Is that one of those cozy British mystery shows?" He made an 'oof' sound when I elbowed him in the ribs.

"I mean this. Outside. This time of day, between daylight and night."

"You mean *dusk*?" Gabe emphasized the word and drew it out slowly.

"Sure, if you want to be pedantic about it."

"Wait, aren't you the one being pedantic?" he said.

"I like the word 'gloaming.'"

"It's a great word." Gabe paused. "If you're from the year 1892."

I gave him a little shove and held onto his arm a few seconds longer than I needed to. He bumped me back and I retaliated by poking his armpit. He clamped his arm down on my hand, trapping my fingers, and he was so strong that I couldn't even wiggle a fingertip. At this rate, the blood flow to my hand would be cut off in seconds.

"Let me go!"

"You started it." Gabe had a naughty half-smile on his lips, and I could tell he was enjoying having the upper hand. "Call it 'dusk' and I'll release you."

"Never! 'Dusk' sounds like a body odor problem."

"Then I guess you'll be stuck here forever."

"Then my fingers will be dusky with your armpit stink!" I tried to pull my hand away, but he had his arm locked down tight against his torso.

"I think you mean 'musky' or 'musty.' I'm fine smelling like sunset. Has to be better than having 'the gloaming,' which sounds like a sexually transmitted version of consumption."

"Release me, you dusky monster, or I'll go after your other pit." I wiggled my free hand as a threat, but Gabe didn't seem afraid.

"Go for it, gloam girl."

I extended my arm toward him, but with cat-like reflexes (no wonder Mallory liked him so much), he released my trapped hand, grabbed both my wrists in a meaty grip, and threatened to tickle me with his free hand. I'd been had.

"Don't tickle me!" I was extraordinarily ticklish and was likely to lose control if he so much as brushed the skin under my arm.

"Then say 'dusk!'"

"Can I say twilight?" I squirmed and twisted, but he easily kept my body close to his. "Can we have a twilight truce?"

Gabe took a step closer to me while pulling me in another few inches. He let go of my hands but captured me in a bear hug. He put his cheek against mine and spoke gruffly into my ear. "Tell me I win. Tell me you're giving in."

Gabe's sentence lit a fire in my belly, and I pressed against him before I'd even realized I was doing it. "You win, Archie."

Gabe let out a breath that carried a groan with it. "We're still in public, you know."

"I suppose we are." I could feel that he was hard against my stomach, and I kept the pressure of my body on his. I didn't want the embrace to end.

"Have to keep up appearances." Gabe scraped his stubbled cheek against my jaw and then kissed me. Hard, open, and rough. He put one hand on the back of my head as he stooped to reach me, holding my head as he moaned into my mouth.

I kissed him back, loving the taste of him, the feel of him, the heat of him. He felt familiar in a way that made my knees weak.

He released me from the kiss and from his grip. "That ought to do it."

"Do what?"

"Keep any onlookers satisfied." He looked out over the estate. "Want to walk in the field? Like we used to?"

"We had the horses back then. It won't be the same."

"Let's go anyway." He held out his hand to me.

I let it hover for a few seconds, and then I grabbed it, interlacing my fingers between his and we walked toward the meadow where Sandy, Dapple, and Buster used to graze. A wave of sadness rushed over me, and tears pricked my eyes. I had to stop walking, and I put my hands on my knees so I could concentrate on not crying.

"What's wrong? Are you in pain?" Gabe kneeled in front of me, trying to catch a glimpse of my face, probably worried that I had sudden appendicitis or something.

"Not in pain," I said, which technically was a lie. I'd tried not to think about my pony and horses, because I knew this would happen. I knew I'd be overcome with grief and loss and all the feelings I never let myself feel about my mom, or even my dad, really. The thought of my lost animals opened the floodgates, and I slumped to the ground, put my face on my knees and started to sob. "I'm. Ok." I said between sniffing. "Sad about the horses. And everything else."

Gabe lowered himself to the ground and placed a hand on my shoulder. After a while, my tears slowed to a trickle and when I looked up, I saw that the gloaming, twilight, dusk, whatever you wanted to call it, had passed, and darkness had fallen.

"Have another handkerchief in those fancy pants of yours?" I knew, without question, that I looked horrendous.

"I thought you'd never ask!" He whipped out a fresh white cloth with the starling embroidered in the corner, and I wiped my eyes and blew my nose.

"I've utterly destroyed this." I waved the hankie like a white flag of surrender.

"I know a girl who can probably get me some more." Gabe ran his palm up and down my arm, soothing me. "What can I do for you? Anything?"

"Maybe we should go to bed." My words hung in the air and Gabe didn't flinch or visibly react.

"Like go to sleep? You were up early and had a long day."

"Sure. Sleep. Or whatever." I was feeling impulsive and edgy and grumpy, and I just felt like his company in our bed. His skin on mine.

"Is that really what you want, Sunny?"

"I asked, didn't I?"

"Yes, you asked." Gabe was so close to me, but he wasn't making eye contact. "Sometimes you ask things. Or do things . . . that are a little impulsive." He wasn't wrong. And he was giving me a door so I could exit the conversation.

"True."

"And we have the rules, and your sex paranoia."

A little snort of a laugh escaped my throat. "Well, I don't know if I meant sex . . ."

More silence from Gabe. Why did he have to be such a good listener? I'd take a real over-talker right now.

"Maybe I'm just lonely. I'm sorry. I'm awful."

"You're not awful." Gabe lifted his face so he was looking directly into mine as we sat on the grass together. "You're not awful at all." Gabe took a deep breath, and then spoke again. "Tell you what. I'll do what you want. Whatever you ask. But I want to make sure that you really want what you're asking, and that you won't have second thoughts tomorrow, or the next day."

"I—"

"Think about it, Susana. Before responding. Let's just sit here for a minute while you think."

This was new. And uncomfortable. Sitting and thinking and feeling. Acknowledging what I felt, really, and making an informed decision about what I wanted to do. I wanted to know what it felt like to touch Gabe in private, not just for the prying eyes of someone else. But I also knew that other things were at play: the marriage, the contract, the inheritance, and our ability to keep up our public image. And Gabe was leaving at the end of our contract, and I'd have a whole new life to explore. A fresh start.

And I was lonely. But maybe I had time to process these feelings and this situation and Gabe would be patient with me. No one had ever done that, but then, I'd never given anyone the chance. I was so scared to test out the theory, but somehow, it felt like the right thing to do.

"How would you feel if—" I was scared to ask for what I thought I needed. Which was different from what I wanted.

"If . . ." Gabe prompted

"How would you feel if I went back to the room by myself and got cleaned up?"

Gabe kept holding my hand. His kind expression hadn't

shifted. He didn't look mad or surprised or relieved. He just looked like he was listening.

"And you cleaned up in your cottage, maybe?"

"I can do that. I need to pick some things up from there anyway." He paused. "What else?"

"And we'll stick to our plan." Maybe part of my desperation to take Gabe to bed was tied to my desperation to run from my grief. And it was probably better to run toward something than to be running away. "I think I should clear my head before I—"

"I understand."

"It might take a while. I'm not sure." I wanted to be honest about this part, and it was what scared me the most.

"You have time, Susana. A lot of it."

"That's ok?" I could hear the desperation in my own voice.

"That's just fine."

28

GABE

A "no sex summer" wasn't what I'd had as one of my New Year's resolutions, but it was my reality, and it didn't bother me as much as I thought it would— I felt less worried about getting tangled up in things that would bog me down when it came time to leave town. I couldn't believe August was almost over —I was used to the warmer months consisting of work from sun-up to sun-down, but it wasn't just the landscape that kept me busy this time of year. Plants and pools were still part of my day, but I'd had to squeeze them in around publicity, press, and public appearances.

Luckily, our early days of talking to journalists paid off. The public went crazy for Susana's re-entry into society, and her presence reinvigorated international interest in the legacy of the Starling family. I'd taken to printing out snippets of articles and taping them to walls and mirrors around the master suite. I'd wait for Susana to discover one and the inevitable "Archie!" would ring out in mock irritation. Usually, she pulled them down and read them aloud in amusing voices, but she'd left up one or two of them, including the one taped to the bathroom mirror that I was currently re-reading as I brushed my teeth.

. . .

RISING STAR REIGNITES A DYNASTY

Susana Starling, granddaughter of America's songbird Sadie Starling and publishing magnate Quentin Maddix has warmed hearts in her new role within the Starling Foundation. Starling, 30, and her husband, Gabriel Green, 32, have taken over at the helm of Starling Manor after the death of Helen Starling last April. "It's a breath of fresh air," said Gwenyth Owens, Starling Foundation Board member. "The Starling Foundation was in peril during the Hardin years, and this has been a rebirth for our mission and our work. People are already benefiting from the change of leadership. We have several new initiatives set to launch this fall, and we hope to make positive contributions at local, national, and even international levels."

Starling and Green have been seen enjoying each other's company this summer at the Manchester Drama Festival, the July Opera Institute, and most recently at the Polo Ponies on the Point fundraiser. Starling plans to join forces with her cousins Sebastian and Simon Starling this winter to revamp the Stars in the Snow gala, the highly anticipated benefit that's expected to be the event of the year.

I SPIT my toothpaste in the sink, rinsed, and went back into the bedroom to check on Susana. Still asleep. A gap in the curtains had allowed a ray of morning sunlight to fall across her cheek, making her look even more angelic than usual. I shut the curtain fully to keep out the light, and I quietly left the room.

Mallory, twice the size she was in May, was right on my heels and bounding down the hallway with me as I headed down to breakfast. I tried not to linger too long in the bedroom, ever. Sunny and I still shared a bed, but we tried not to go to bed at the same time. If I needed to stay up late, Susana went up early, or we'd reverse it if she had a midnight meeting. Same with waking up. We found that if we didn't linger in bed together, awake, that we wouldn't be tempted to break the rules of our union.

We'd been able to find a routine that worked for us, and I didn't want to disrupt our fragile ecosystem of a marriage by staring at her for too long and letting my desire get the better of me. I enjoyed our public displays of affection, and it had become second nature to pour on the PDA any time others were present. She accepted my touch, and reciprocated it, and we were the picture of romance when it came to the public eye. In private, we were platonic, at least in our actions, though I had less than pure feelings bubbling under the surface. She said she needed time, and time was what I was giving her.

My phone buzzed in my pocket, and I stopped walking to pull it out and check the incoming text. Mallory, who'd been about to bound down the stairs and enjoy her daily sardine from Jeff (who had reluctantly fallen in love with the cat), stopped short and waited.

Cal: Gonna be here? It's the day

Gabe: It's the 17th!!

Cal: Save you a seat?

Cal Cartwright was one of my oldest friends, and every August we went to Summer Hops Fest in town where beer flowed freely, local bands played on the main stage, and exotic rabbits were on display to raise money for Homes for Hops, a bunny rescue organization.

Gabe: Gotta check my schedule. BRB.

I checked my calendar app, which was constantly updated by Shelly, and there were no meetings, interviews, or events today. I still had groundskeeping duties around the estate on which I wanted to check in, but if I got my to-do list done, an evening with Cal would be just what the doctor ordered. I turned back around to check with Susana. The cat, baffled by my change in direction, paused at the top of the staircase, not willing to go downstairs without me, but also not willing to let me forget that she had a treat waiting for her in the kitchen.

I opened the bedroom door—Susana was on her back with her arm thrown over her eyes.

"Good morning," I said quietly from the doorway so I wouldn't wake her if she was still asleep and wouldn't startle her if she was awake.

She responded with a groan.

"You alright?"

"My head is killing me. Would you mind getting me a migraine pill from the medicine cabinet?"

I got her the medication and a glass of water and waited by the bedside while she swallowed the pill.

"Can I get you anything else?"

"A new brain? This one's a lemon."

"How about your sleep mask to cut out all the light?"

"Yes, please."

I found her mask in a bathroom drawer and brought it to her.

She slipped it on and groaned again. "Too much pressure on my head. Never mind." She tossed the mask aside.

"Cal has invited me to Summer Hops Fest today. The schedule looks clear. Any problem if I head over there later?"

"The same Cal from forever ago?"

"The one and only."

"Sounds fine. I'll be here researching the latest on head transplants."

"I'll let Jag know and I'll have him send someone to check on you in a bit."

"I'll be fine. Meds should kick in soon. Say hi to Cal."

"Will do." I closed the bathroom door so extra light from there wouldn't seep into the bedroom. "Need any earplugs?"

"No thanks." She pulled the blanket over her head. "And Gabe?" Her voice was muffled.

"Yes?"

"Don't adopt a rabbit. I'm not sure Mallory would like that."

"What if it's a really cute one?"

"Make a large donation. But no pet bunnies."

I HAD on my most comfortable jeans, Summer Hops Fest '07 t-shirt, and a baseball cap and sunglasses for some extra anonymity. Cal was running late but I had a cold pilsner in hand, a table with a great view of the stage, and nowhere else to be for hours.

"Gabriel?" a woman's voice called from behind me. I turned to see a blonde woman heading toward my table. She wore a t-shirt that sported a drawing of a cartoon rabbit along with the words SORRY, I CAN'T. I HAVE PLANS WITH MY BUNNY. She looked familiar, but I couldn't immediately place her, and being in the public eye had made me jumpier when it came to being recognized. "It is you!" She came in for a bear hug and I put my hand on her arm in case I needed to pull her off my neck, but she stopped when she realized that I didn't recognize her.

"Oh god, I'm sorry!" She pulled off her sunglasses. "It's me, Ella!"

The housekeeper who'd been harassed by Harry last spring. "How's it going?" The last time I'd seen her, she was traumatized, but now she looked great. Amazing how Hardin could dim even the brightest light. "How're you doing?"

"I'm doing well. May I sit down for a second?" She looked around to make sure I wasn't with someone else.

"Sure. I'm meeting a friend but he's running late."

"I was meeting a friend, too, but she just texted to say that she's not coming. So, I'm on my own. Anyway, I've been wanting to contact you, but I wasn't sure how to go about it now that you're a celebrity!"

"I think I'm married to a celebrity. I'm celebrity adjacent."

"I had something I wanted to tell you, and I didn't want to put it in writing." She lowered her voice, and I leaned in so I could hear her better. "I did contact a lawyer, like you suggested. There are criminal charges being brought against Hardin. But not just because of me. There are a lot of women who've come forward. I'm actually the only one so far from Starling Manor—there are women all over the country who've been victims of Harry's harass-ment. I can't give you a lot of details—in fact, I don't know a lot of details, but I wanted to give you a heads-up, and I also wanted to thank you." She put her hand on my arm for just a second, and I was grateful that she had short, plain fingernails, as opposed to those claws on the paws of Sawyer Lacey. "You really helped me that day at the Manor."

"I'm sorry you were ever in that position at all—"

"Did you start without me?" Cal pulled back a chair and it scraped against the surface of the concrete patio. The crowd had grown, and the band had started, so he had to shout a little to be heard, but then again, Cal was always the loud and boisterous sort — a friend to everyone. Cal whacked me affectionately on the shoulder and then held out a hand to Ella. "Cal Cartwright."

"Ella McFarland. Nice to meet you."

"Ella used to work at Starling Manor," I added.

"I hear that place is a real dump." Cal flashed a smile at Ella, and she blushed, suddenly shy.

That was fast! Cal had always been better with women than, but this might've been a new record. As Ella and Cal continued to chat and laugh, I ordered another beer and relaxed into the evening, glad to not be the center of attention for a change. The three of us hung out until the bands were done, the beer had stopped flowing, and all the bunnies had been adopted.

"Want to continue this at my place?" Cal directed the question to both Ella and me, but I had a strong suspicion that he'd be fine if just one of us accepted his invitation, and that one person wasn't me.

"I've got to get back to the estate. How about my driver drops you two off and then I'll just head home. I don't think any of us should be driving."

"Perfect!" Ella said quickly. "Let me just go to the bathroom first." She stood up from the table and had to steady herself for a second before heading to the restroom.

"I owe you one." Cal smiled.

"Don't do anything I wouldn't do."

Cal rolled his eyes. "That would make for a boring night. You were always so demure."

"I like to call it discerning."

"Avoidant might be a better term."

"Well, I'm married now, so, new chapter and all that."

"So, you aren't avoiding things anymore?" Cal knew me too well. "We still haven't had a chance to talk about this. I was hoping to do that tonight, but—"

"Ready when you are!" Ella was back, also looking happy and a bit drunk.

"To be continued," I told Cal, but he was too distracted by Ella to pay any attention to me.

"Wake up, Archie." Susana poked me in the ribs and woke me out of an extremely pleasant dream where I was swimming in the ocean with pink and purple dolphins, a talking whale, and maybe a mermaid?

"God. What?" I sat up and rubbed my ribcage.

Susana tossed an iPad on my lap, and it landed right on my dick.

"Ouch, Jesus. You maimed Tony."

"Sorry. Bad aim. Looks like you had a nice night on the town last night."

After I uncurled from the ball I was in and wiped my eyes, I picked up the tablet. The screen was dark. "What are you talking about?"

She snatched it from my lap, tapped the screen, and threw it back at me. This time I was awake enough to catch it.

"Jesus, Sunny. I don't know what you're—" but I stopped short when I saw the images on the screen. They were of me. And Ella. Ella hugging me, Ella touching my arm, Ella laughing at something I'd said, and Ella getting into my car as I held the door for her. My stomach dropped as I swiped through each photo on the gossip website—they were accompanied by the headline:

GABRIEL GREEN CAUGHT CHEATING!

"I can explain these."

Susana's voice was flat and stern. "You can explain once to me, and then again to the team. They're on their way and will be set up in the library in a half hour." She couldn't look at me and her nostrils flared. Her arms were crossed against her chest.

"That's Ella!" I poked a finger at Ella's image on the screen. "Who's Ella?"

"That former member of staff that I told you about."

"I have no idea what you're talking about." Susana's voice was shaking.

I knew the optics were bad, but she seemed pissed about more than how this looked. This was personal. I swiped through the photos, hoping to see one with Cal included, but there were none of him. This was bullshit. "She's the one who got trapped in the broom closet."

Recognition flickered on Susana's face. "The one Harry had trapped in there?"

"Yes."

"Why did you meet with her last night? And why is she all over you?"

I threw the covers off and stomped to the bathroom to pee. Susana followed me. "Can I have some privacy?" I was standing at the toilet but didn't feel like having an audience.

"No, you cannot. Where was Cal?" She wasn't moving, so I relieved myself. She didn't seem to care one bit.

"He was there! They just picked the photos without him." I marched back to the bedroom, and she followed.

By the time I'd explained the entire situation, texted Cal to ask if he or Ella had any selfies from the evening, and gotten my clothes on, Susana had calmed down and softened.

"You just have to expect that photographers are stalking you." She held one of my shoes for me while I tied the laces on the other.

"I thought about that, but also, I didn't do anything but drink beer while Ella and Cal flirted all night long!" I put on my other shoe as Susana grabbed the tablet and headed toward the door.

"Ready to tell your story all over again?"

"Not really."

"Too bad. We've got work to do."

29

GABE

We did have work to do. It took a week of intense PR and finding other photos and stories from 'witnesses' to stomp out the false story about me and Ella. Then August and September had zipped by in a rush of fundraisers, events, and foundation meetings. Susana and I attended some things together, but she had a lot of solo gigs, too, and while she was off doing those, I tended to affairs around the estate. Nothing had prepared me for how exhausting it was to live in the public eye, and though I was getting used to my new lifestyle and duties, I was seriously nostalgic for those quiet nights in my cottage.

Sunny was gone for the day, and I'd taken advantage of the unseasonably warm October morning to relax in my old hammock and hide out from the world. Even an hour hiding away like a hermit was better than nothing. I needed some solitude to recharge. That was one reason the dream of living in that beach bungalow had always sounded like paradise. Just enough room for me and my surfboard, and though it wasn't an oceanfront property, the beach was just a short walk down a few sandy trails. My dad had planned to retire there, and part of me felt like I was living a dream for both of us.

"Excuse me, your majesty."

"Shit. You can't sneak into people's houses like that, Jeff." My beachy daydream dissolved.

"My apologies, your honor." Jeff held up his hands in surrender.

"You know, you can drop that joke any time now. It's worn out its welcome."

"As you wish, Your Grace."

"Did we establish why you're breaking and entering?"

"I knocked. And your door was slightly ajar. And you weren't answering your phone."

"I have like two hours a week to myself. I have it set to *Do Not Disturb*."

"So say your notifications. But I need your help, or rather, Susana does."

My stomach lurched at the thought of Sunny in trouble, and I sat up too quickly, causing the hammock to sway dangerously. "What's up? Is she okay?"

"She's fine. But she won't be once she realizes she left her box of dessert decorations behind this morning. Her students will be making the cupcakes after lunch, which means if you leave now, you'll make it in plenty of time."

"What is she doing today?"

Susana had so many functions and appearances that I'd stopped keeping track.

"Cooking class for kids at the Parkside Community Center."

"Right."

"I've texted her, but she puts her phone away when she's working. Don't want her to panic when she realizes she's missing her supplies."

"And we don't have a driver to deliver the box?"

"Would I be here dealing with you if I had a simpler option?" Jeff put his hands on his hips and glared at me.

Never piss off the cook was a cardinal rule, so I extracted myself from the hammock. "Yes, Chef."

AN HOUR LATER, I pulled into the PCC parking lot. There were some cars there, but not any more than you'd expect on a Saturday in October. Which meant that this was one of Sunny's "pop-up" classes, where her name wasn't even listed as the teacher, and people just found out when they got there. Sometimes she waited until all the parents had dropped off their kids and let the class assistants do the first fifteen minutes, and then she stepped out and joined in. If they didn't know she was the teacher, parents weren't signing up their kids just to rub shoulders with a Starling; they were sending their kids there because they wanted to learn to cook. Joey, a member of Susana's security detail, was posted at the door, where a sign taped to the glass read: CLOSED TO PUBLIC FROM 10-2. Joey saw me coming and opened the door for me.

"The class is down the hall on the left, in the Maple Event Room." He closed the door behind me.

The other security member parked outside a door down the hall gave away the location of the room. I'd mostly gotten used to the presence of bodyguards, figuring it was easier to go with the flow than push back, and I also felt better knowing that Susana was protected.

Inside the room, Sunny was helping a girl with her stand mixer, and she hadn't seen me enter. The girl's white apron was splattered with chocolate, and she was trying to wipe away tears, but was only smearing cake batter around her face in the process.

"I promise that this kind of thing happens all the time." Susana wiped at the girl's face with a napkin. "This is a messy job. If you came away from today with a clean apron, I'd doubt your chef abilities!"

Susana still hadn't noticed me, and I shifted the weight of the boxes to my other arm. She was focused on her student, who seemed a little less mortified after Susana's encouragement. Another kid, a boy with red hair that stuck up in a few places, glanced down at his own clean apron, which was so bright white it looked like it'd never seen a kitchen. Then he stuck a finger into his mixing bowl and pulled out a glob of batter. After a few shifty glances around the room, he smeared the chocolate down the front of his apron and then got back to work.

Susana was still trying to comfort the other kid, who seemed reluctant to go back to her task. "One time I didn't realize my mixer was unplugged." Sunny took a kitchen towel and wiped the girl's cheek. "And I turned the speed all the way up to high, but nothing happened. I thought I'd blown the motor. And then I saw that it was unplugged. Guess what I did?"

"You plugged it in?" The girl offered.

"Yep. But guess what I didn't do first?"

The girl's mouth dropped open. "You didn't turn it off?"

"Yep. It took me two hours to clean my kitchen. I think there's still splatter on my ceiling!"

The girl's giggles bubbled up and her face transformed as she started to laugh. Susana laughed with her and looked so confident and at ease. She'd worn her chef's whites, which I'd seen in the closet, but never actually on her body. I had no idea how sexy she'd look in those. I set down the boxes of supplies and waited for her to notice me.

She walked between her students, peered into bowls, pointed out which pan to use, and helped other kids set the temperature on their ovens. I knew she wasn't sure she ever wanted to be a mother, but I didn't know how anyone who was so at ease talking to children, teaching them and helping them like she was, could ever be bad at parenting. She was a natural, and in her element. She was beautiful. I could see her with a child. With a baby. With our baby. I could see us with our baby, arms around each other—*what the fuck, Green. Fantasizing about being a dad? Lame.*

"You'll be mixing this way longer than you did with your brownies. Remember, with those, we just mixed until we couldn't see any dry ingredients. With a cake, you need higher speeds and longer mixing."

Susana's jacket was tight over her breasts. Did she have a shirt on underneath that? What would happen if I got her alone and undid those buttons, or were they snaps?

"But you don't want to overmix it. Too much mixing and it will be tough, just like with too little mixing. Stop as soon as you see a few bubbles pop up in your bowls."

If we had kids, would they have dark hair like hers? And freckles and grey eyes? Or would they be blonde and brown-eyed like me?

"Gabe!" Susana had spotted me from across the room. "Do you have the decorating supplies?"

Fuck, man. Get your head on straight. I gave Susana a thumbs-up.

"The supplies are here!" Susana announced to the class, and everyone cheered. "Can you help me grab an extra table?"

The teaching assistants took over as I followed her into a storage room that held folding tables and chairs.

"Thanks for coming. If I hadn't seen that text from Jeff at lunch, I would've freaked out when I went to look for that box. And the decorating is their favorite part—there might've been a mutiny if—Gabe? Why are you looking at me like that? Is something wrong?"

"Like what?" Pretty sure my face had let on that I was back to imagining Susana as the mother of my children.

"Like you've never seen me before in your life, or like I'm some kind of talking alien and you're wondering if you should call the FBI and report me."

"Sorry." I shook my head to try to chase away my intrusive thoughts, including the extra persistent one of all the things I could do with Susana that could result in a pregnancy—

"You're doing it again."

"Sorry. You just look great in your whites. I've never seen you in them."

A blush creeped up Susana's neck and settled on her cheeks, making her look even more beautiful. "I do?"

"You do." I ran my finger across her sleeve.

"Thank you." She pulled on the hem of her jacket, straightening it out.

I stepped closer, ending up just inches from her. "You look happy here. Teaching. I liked watching you."

There was that blush again. Deeper. Redder than before. "How long were you watching?"

"Long enough to see that you're a natural."

"I am?" The way she was looking at me—I could barely take it.

Nothing ventured, nothing gained. I might as well tell her what I was thinking. "I'm sure of it." I slipped my arms around her waist. Something about seeing Susana in her element had acted like a magnet, pulling me to her. I had to kiss her. Without waiting another second and risk losing my nerve or coming to my senses, I bent down and kissed her. Softly. Gently. Slowly. My lips closed but lingered on hers, testing the waters.

She slid one hand around my neck and another around my waist, and she stepped into the kiss. She opened her mouth, and I followed her lead as we tasted each other. She was both familiar and new—my heart was thumping in my chest and my hand shook slightly as I removed it from her waist and brushed my fingertips across her breast which was hidden away under her uniform. She gasped and then moaned just a little, and then she stepped back from the kiss.

"I have to get back." She was breathless and the skin around her mouth was pink, thanks to my stubble.

"I don't know what came over me."

She cocked her head as she looked me over. "Grab that little table, will you?" She pointed to a folding table resting against a wall. "And Gabe?"

"Yeah?" I pulled the table away from the wall and was glad that we'd stopped kissing before I'd gotten hard enough to make a visible menace out of myself.

"Don't be sorry. I'm not."

30

SUSANA

My back ached, my feet throbbed, and my voice was raspy from all that talking, but I felt better than I had in a long time. When I was teaching people to cook, especially kids, time flew by, and I didn't get caught up in my head or my insecurities. I was just me— a kind of me that felt authentic, confident, and happy. Gabe's visit may've had something to do with my good mood, but that was more like the cherry on top. The sense of satisfaction that'd spread through my body like warm maple syrup on a stack of buttermilk apple pancakes (my mind was apparently still in a Fall foods zone) was all self-generated.

My class went so well that the community center director and I decided that I should do a series of classes, one a month for the next few months. The kids who'd been in today's class got priority registration, and I hoped they'd all come back. They were eleven to thirteen years old, which meant they had one foot in childhood and the other in young adulthood, and I liked the surprises that brought to the table. I'd stayed late planning the menus for the next few classes, and now I was spent.

I trudged up the service stairs at Starling Manor and all I wanted was a long bath and an even longer sleep. I heard whispering voices from somewhere beyond the top of the landing which set off my warning bells. It was the whispering. I believed that if you wanted to tell a secret, or be ignored, just say something in your regular voice at regular volume. Once you started whispering, it was like sending up a flare that screamed "I'm saying something I shouldn't, so lean in, everyone!" I walked up a few more stairs but stopped two from the top. The whisperers were probably tucked inside the Secretary's Office, which was just a small room with a desk and a chair and was just to the right of the stairs.

"Did you get anything good?"

I knew that voice. The hateful lilt belonged to none other than everybody's favorite villain, Mrs. Skinner. I pulled my phone out of my bag and opened the voice recording app. I didn't know if it could pick up the conversation, but it was worth a shot.

"I'm not sure. I've got a lot of photos, but nothing that screams 'fake marriage' or 'cheater.' I think if I can get more video, we can edit something together in a way that looks bad." That voice was male, and louder than Skinner's. It sounded familiar, but I couldn't place him.

My heart was beating too quickly, and my hand had started to shake. I had a panic button app that would send a message to my security team, but I wanted to hear more of the conversation. I moved up one step and held my phone out as far as I could without extending it past the wall at the top of the stairs.

"They've had too much good press. I think it's time for another threat." Skinner again.

"I don't like the threats. That increases the security and the examination. Can't we just stick to trying to reveal them, or embarrass them?"

"We want to destroy them!" Skinner's voice had moved beyond whisper and into meltdown mode.

"I mean, I think that's a bit much," the man said.

"Mr. Hardin and I are paying you to get these pictures. We don't give a shit what you think is 'too much'. Have you put the hidden camera in their suite yet? That's how we're going to find out the truth of their sham marriage. One in the bedroom and one in the bathroom."

Hidden cameras in my bedroom? My bathroom? I wanted to vomit, and my hand was shaking so badly I could barely hold on to my phone.

"Not yet. Do you really think that's a good idea? I think we can get what we need without—"

"I don't care what you think!"

That was enough. I opened the security app and activated the call for help. I took a step back, hoping to sneak away, but it was too late. Skinner and her henchman had exited the office and headed my direction. I wanted to run, but my "freeze" response was activated again and I was no more mobile than a stone statue. And then they appeared—Mrs. Skinner and Patrick, Jeff's assistant chef. It was a special kind of betrayal to know that a member of the kitchen staff was taking secret photos of me and Gabe—there was a code among chefs, and this was a terrible violation.

Patrick blanched when he saw me, but Mrs. Skinner turned bright red, and the sweat on her brow made her look like a greasy smoked salmon.

"Why're you here?" Skinner hissed.

"I'm going to my room."

"These aren't your stairs. These are the service stairs." Skinner moved toward me, but Patrick took off down the hallway, leaving me alone with the head housekeeper.

"All the stairs are my stairs." I backed down another step, hoping I sounded more confident than I felt.

"How long were you there?"

"Where?" Maybe playing dumb would buy me a little time.

"On the stairs," she said with such venom that if words could kill, I'd have been murdered instantly.

If I could just get past her, I'd be ok. I didn't want to be in this dark stairway. One push by her and I could really get hurt. "Excuse me."

I began my ascent again and tried to get past her, but she grabbed me in some kind of tackle and I held on to the railing for dear life as she squeezed me. Good god, she must've been a python in a former life.

"No one's here to help you now, you little shit."

And she was right, until she wasn't. Help came from down the stairs in the form of Anton, who leapt three steps at a time to reach me, and it came from the top of the stairs in the form of my husband, who, by the looks of him, was about to tear off Mrs. Skinner's head.

Skinner released me as Anton rushed her, and he roughly escorted her down the stairs. Gabe hauled me into his arms like I weighed nothing and ran down the hall towards our suite with me like I was a football and he was going for the game-winning touchdown. Once in our room, he set me on the bed and frantically ran his hands over my body as if looking for bloody wounds.

"Gabe, I'm fine." My hands were no longer shaking, and my heart was slowing—as soon as he'd gathered me in his arms, I'd felt safe. I always felt safe around him, and safety was something I'd been without for a long time.

"Why did you take the back stairs?" Gabe's face was white. He looked terrified.

"They're faster? I was tired."

"We don't have security set up on those stairs. Only the front ones. You know that, Sunny!"

Tears sprung to my eyes. "I forgot. And it's my own home. Sometimes I forget I have to be careful here."

"You have to be especially careful here. We still don't know who took those pictures last summer, and—"

"I think we *do* know." My phone was still in my hand and still recording. I pushed the stop button and saved the audio file. Then I pressed play and prayed that we'd be able to make out the conversation between Mrs. Skinner and Patrick. It was a little quiet at first, but as soon as I'd moved up the stairs the phone clearly picked up their voices.

Gabe shook his head in disbelief. "Holy. Shit."

"I know, right?"

"That's Skinner and—"

"Patrick."

"Patrick? Jeff is gonna lose his shit."

"I know."

"Sunny, you're a genius." Gabe grabbed my face in both of his hands and quickly kissed me. "Send that to me. To the whole team. I have to talk to Jag. You're sure you're okay?"

"I'm okay."

"I'll be back in a few. Sam's outside the door and I'll make sure she doesn't go anywhere. Send that recording." He kissed me again, with no apologies, no shyness, no reserve. Like it was an everyday thing just to kiss me here in our bedroom. Like a regular husband and wife.

I texted the recording to the team group chat, and then I went into the bathroom—I'd triple earned that long bubble bath. I turned on the water and watched as it started to cover the bottom of the tub, but then I turned it off. This was *my* house. And Mrs. Skinner was *my* housekeeper. As much as I wanted to hide away and ignore the drama and leave the dirty work to everyone else, I needed to be there for whatever happened next with her. "I'll be back," I said to my beloved bathtub.

"The agreement says that I can't be fired!" Mrs. Skinner stood in the middle of the parlor with her arms crossed defiantly across her chest. "You have to keep me here for the full year, and it's only October!" She pointed at Patrick. "You can get rid of him, though. He's not a head staff member."

"Hey!" Patrick stood up from his perch on the loveseat, but he quickly sat back down after Jeffrey shot him a look that would make anyone wither.

The whole PR team was gathered, along with Gabe and Jag.

"Is this true, Jag?" I so hoped it wasn't true. And if we did have to keep Skinner on, could I just lock her in a broom closet for the rest of her tenure?

Jag had his phone up to his ear and put up one finger, silently asking me to wait a moment. "I understand," he said to the person on the line. "We'll meet tomorrow. Thanks again for taking my call." Jag tucked his phone away into an inner jacket pocket. He picked up a folder from a nearby end table, and flipped through some papers until he found the one he wanted. "As you all know, the fourth and final stipulation in Helen's will was that 'All Heads of Staff must remain employed for the first year after my death unless the staff members wish to resign.'"

"There you go. Good luck getting rid of me." A smirk spread across Skinner's face. "Sorry, Patty."

"Patrick, you are no longer employed by Starling Manor, effective immediately—" Jag was still talking, but Skinner interrupted him.

"See you all later. I have places to be."

"Not so fast, Mrs. Skinner." The silence that fell in the room was so heavy that it was almost suffocating. Jag's voice had been loud and sharp, and none of us were ready for the pissed-off version of Mr. Jagger. Note to self: never, *ever* get on Jag's bad side. "The authorities are on their way over, and they will need to speak to you."

"Talk to my lawyer."

"That's just the thing, Mrs. Skinner," Jag said. "If you're referring to our house attorney, she has a conflict of interest because she primarily represents Mrs. Starling. And it says in your contract, which you signed, and then signed again when Mrs. Starling took over as the primary occupant, that if you commit 'gross misconduct' or in any way threaten or endanger Mrs. Starling or the Starling name, your contract will be immediately terminated, and you will be prosecuted to the fullest extent of the law."

Skinner's face went whiter than her crisp button-down shirt. "I don't remember that part."

"I have a copy here if you'd like to see it. And if you are terminated," Jag continued, "under those circumstances, you are not entitled to your retirement account until all legal dealings have concluded, at which time—"

"I quit!" Mrs. Skinner was sweating, and the drops of moisture left slimy little trails down her ruddy cheeks. "I resign! So that means you didn't terminate me, right?" She seemed panicked.

"Well, I suppose you did beat me to the punch."

"And I have all these witnesses! I resign effective immediately!" She started to back out of the room while staring us down, as if she expected one of us to pounce and put her in a headlock.

"You'll still need to speak to the authorities, Mrs. Skinner."

"Send 'em to my room. I'm going to pack my things. You can have this hell hole." She spun on her toe and stomped the last few steps out of the parlor. "And good riddance!"

She was gone. Like, maybe really, truly gone. I felt like I could breathe. "Thank you, Jag." I suddenly felt emotional, and doubly tired. I grabbed Jag into a hug, which was not our normal mode of operation.

"It was no trouble at all." He patted my back awkwardly.

"It was a lot of trouble, and you know it. What would I do without you?"

"Why don't you head back up to the suite. We've got things covered down here."

"I'll walk you up." Gabe took my elbow as if to escort me.

"No need. I have a date with a bathtub."

Gabe hesitated, but let me go. "I'll be up once the police are finished."

· · ·

A HALF-HOUR LATER, fully relaxed and waterlogged, I flopped onto the bed. Skinner was gone. I'd never felt freer or more relaxed in my own house. Who knew that one rotten apple could make such a difference to your mood? Three cheers for being in the right place at the right time and catching the villain in the act. I never needed to think about that witch again. I could turn my mind to far more pleasant imaginings.

I was on my stomach and my plush bathrobe was more than enough to keep me warm. I wanted to fall asleep just like that, spread across the bed, but Gabe might have trouble getting under the covers later with me taking up so much room. I grabbed my phone on the nightstand and sent Gabe a text.

> Susana: All good? Out of the bath. Quiet up here.

> Gabe: Still have Skinner and Patrick here along with cops. And the team. Gonna be a bit. Need anything?

> Susana: Nope. Might fall asleep soon. Do they need to talk to me?

> Gabe: They can talk to you tomorrow. I'll be up later.

I was alone and warm and naked under the robe. Night was falling and the room was getting dark. My mind kept slipping back to the three times Gabe had kissed me that day. The memory heated me up again and reignited the twinge of desire I'd felt earlier.

I had time. Time to indulge in one of my favorite recent fantasies, which was set in the tiny cabin on the Starling property where we'd be going in December for our family holiday gathering. There was something about the cabin, which was set apart from the big house, that I'd always found romantic, and over the last month, I'd found myself fantasizing about things that could happen with Gabe in that cozy little spot in the woods.

I grabbed a pillow and slipped it under my hips, which comfortably raised my ass in the air. I slipped my hand between my legs and ran my finger across my clit, which was sensitive and swollen. I pictured Gabe in my mind—pictured what would happen if we were in that cabin with snow falling outside, and if I was naked on my stomach and on display for him:

Gabe runs his finger down my spine, starting at the base of my neck and ending on my ass. He moves his hand lower, and I squirm and try to snuggle back under the blankets.

"It's cold in here!" Goosebumps cover my body, but they aren't just from the cold. Gabe's touch electrifies me.

"You're the one who brought us to this snowy cabin in the woods. We could be back in the main house with your family, but nooo. You wanted more privacy." Gabe pulls the covers off me again and I lay naked before him, on my stomach. "And since we have all this privacy, I thought we might make the best of it." He straddles me and settles on top of my legs, not putting so much weight on me that he might hurt me but pressing down enough to pin me to the bed. He drags his nails across the skin of my back, the sides of my torso, and over my bare ass, making me wiggle and sigh.

It tickles too much when he starts to slide his fingertips over the side of my ribs, and I try to grab his hands with mine.

"You can't stop me, Sunny." He pins both of my hands above my head with one of his, and he uses his free hand to softly torture me.

He snakes his hand under my breast and pinches and rolls my nipple and I moan and press my pelvis into the bed trying to create friction between myself and the sheets. Wetness blooms between my legs, and I want his dick inside me.

"You're needy this morning, Sunny." Gabe lets go of my hands and goes back to straddling my legs, which he spreads open. "What do you need?"

I can only answer in a groan. He runs his finger over my folds with just enough pressure to make me throw my head back and cry out. He finds my clit but refuses to touch it, instead teasing the skin all around it and making me almost delirious with desire.

"Gabe," I sigh. "Please."

"What do you need, Susana? Say it." His demands make me even wetter.

I want to be fucked and fondled and flipped over. I want him to do anything and everything to me. "Please touch my clit," I whisper.

"You mean here?" He spreads my legs further and pulls my pelvis up and pushes a pillow underneath my hips, so my ass is in the air. He spreads the lips of my pussy and slides one fingertip ever-so-lightly against the side of my clit, and then he pulls away.

"Don't stop."

"Tell me what you need."

"Rub me."

"How about this?" He puts his finger back on my nub, this time on the very tip and he rubs me softly in a circular motion.

"Yes, that." I'm breathless. "Just like that. Don't stop." I'm soaked with my own wetness and his finger slides in the circle as I writhe and swivel my hips, but he never loses contact. "Faster," I beg.

"Sorry, you already told me not to stop. So, I can't stop. You're just going to have to take it like this." He keeps up the slow and steady swirl with his hand, and fuck, it's the best and worst and best again.

I push against his finger, but he won't give it to me faster, so the pressure builds slowly, and I suffer in the sweet agony of it all. "I want to come. Make me come." I'm desperate.

"Are you ready to come on my finger, Susana?"

"I want to fucking come. Please. Please, Gabe." He presses harder and sounds escape me that I can't control.

I hold my breath and—

"Sunny?"

Shit. Shitshitshit. Back to reality, and the reality was that Gabe was standing right there in our bedroom, watching me.

31

SUSANA

I'd been so into my fantasy, and so close to orgasm that I hadn't heard him come into the room. He'd probably entered quietly because he thought I was asleep and now he was getting an eyeful of me being very much awake. I'd slipped out of my robe some- where during my pleasure session, and I realized that Gabe was looking at my ass in the air, my legs spread, and my pussy on full display. The room was dark, but not *that* dark. I was frozen . . . what I wouldn't have given to have "flight" as my panic response! My clit was still throbbing and if I moved a muscle, I might explode in climax anyway, which would make things even more awkward than they already were, which was saying a lot.

"I apologize. I thought you'd be asleep. I didn't mean to invade your privacy." Gabe's voice was quiet and calm.

I was mortified, but there was no way to recover my dignity, so I gave up on the hope of coming out of this with my pride intact. And also, I had to climax. The urge wasn't going away, and knowing he was looking at me was making me even more aroused.

"Should I leave? Sam's out there, so you might want to cover up before I open the door again—"

"Don't leave." My defenses were down. I was in that space of desire and near abandon, and I was throwing all caution to the wind.

"You want me to . . . stay?" Gabe cleared his throat. He sounded unsure, but he was still there.

"If you want to." I was speaking into the mattress. This was embarrassing enough without having to look him in the eye.

"What would you like me to do?" His voice was closer. He must've been standing right by the side of the bed.

"Whatever you want to." Where my boldness had come from, I had no idea. But I was going with it. "I mean, no sex, of course—"

"Of course." Gabe's voice had taken on a husky quality and that alone might push me over the edge.

Fuck it. I'd just say it. "I really need to come, Gabe."

"Is that so?"

And with that question, the energy in the room shifted. We were no longer "unsuspecting guy walks in on girl masturbating," we were "man sees his woman spread out before him and he gets to decide what to do with her." His words made me so hot I thought I might lose it right there. I felt Gabe's weight on the bed, and then he ran his hands across the back of my thighs. He must've been sitting between my legs.

"Let me see how close you are."

I pulled my hand out from between my legs and rested it by my head. I gave over all control to him. He put a finger at the opening of my pussy, and his touch met no resistance.

"So wet," he said. "You really got yourself worked up, didn't you."

"I did." I couldn't believe we were saying these things. But I couldn't stop.

"Let me take a closer look."

I felt his weight shift and I stayed there, propped up on my pillow. Then I felt heat. The heat of his breath. Oh god. He put his fingers on my ass and his thumbs on the lips of my pussy and he pulled, gently spreading me open. All of me. He was breathing on me. Looking at me. I'd never felt so exposed and so turned on.

"So many options."

Something hot and wet entered me and pulled back. And entered me again. I cried out. He was fucking me with his tongue. He released his grip on me and moved one hand underneath me and flicked his finger across my clit. He must've been on his belly to get access like that.

"Yes. Oh god, Gabe. Please."

He kept pressing his tongue into me as he trapped my clit between two fingers, sliding up and down my swollen bud, first slowly, and then faster. I bucked against the pillow, but he rode my thrusts and kept a steady rhythm of stroking me again, and again, and again. Everything was hot and wet and I tried to close my legs against the pressure that was building inside me, but Gabe spread me wider. He replaced his tongue with several fingers from his free hand and he thrusted harder, filling my cunt and fucking me fully and forcefully with his fingers while he nipped and licked me wherever he could reach as I writhed under his touch.

I was spinning, swirling, spasming, and seeing stars. I was coming. I was coming against his fingers, on his face, into his mouth. I shuddered and screamed out and rode the wave of my climax until I collapsed against the bed in pure surrender.

I was panting. Literally panting into the sheets. I felt frozen, but this time it wasn't out of fear or panic—it was pure pleasure. My legs were still spread, my ass still in the air, and Gabe kept his fingers inside me until I'd totally recovered.

After a minute, Gabe slid his fingers out of me and caressed my ass and thighs, spreading my moisture in little trails as he ran his hands over my skin. Then he gathered my discarded robe and softly placed it across my body, covering me up.

He lay down next to me, his head next to mine, and draped an arm across me. "Hey, Sunny."

"Hi." I'd just been more intimate with Gabe than I'd been with anyone in my whole life, yet I felt so shy that I wanted to melt into the mattress and disappear. And I also wanted to kiss him. I grabbed another pillow and smashed it on top of my head. Gabe lifted the pillow and threw it on the floor. I couldn't hide from him.

"I think you came."

"God." I covered my face with my hands.

"No use hiding from me now." He pulled my hands off of my face.

His eyes were so intense this close up.

"Thank you. That felt amazing. Beyond amazing."

"How far beyond?" He traced the edge of my hairline with his fingertip.

"Really far. Sorry. I'm having trouble finding words."

"It was my pleasure." His face was relaxed, and his golden hair had fallen across his forehead and was covering one of his eyes. I brushed it out of the way so we could fully look at each other.

"I think it was my pleasure."

"I'm glad." He kissed my hand again. I still felt shy, but I also felt emboldened.

"Speaking of your pleasure. . ."

"You don't have to reciprocate. That was for you." Gabe stroked my cheek with his thumb.

"But what if I want to?"

His lips parted and he bit at his lower lip. "That's generous, but really, you don't have to—"

I pressed my hand against the front of his jeans—he was rock hard. "Tony seems to think you'd be up for the challenge."

"I'm really starting to regret making that joke."

"Would you prefer Antonio?"

Gabe laughed, rolled onto his back and put his arm over his eyes.

"I want to touch you, Gabe." I pressed my palm against his jeans again.

He groaned and lifted his hips, pushing his dick against my hand. "Ok. Just this once."

I'd imagined this for so long. What it might be like to have Gabe before me, under my control. I pulled the pillow out from under my hips and tossed it aside. I put my arms through the sleeves of my robe and untangled the belt so I could tie it shut.

"Take it off." Gabe had lowered his arm and was watching me.

"What?"

"Don't put your robe back on." He lifted his shirt a few inches and ran his fingers across his gorgeous stomach. "Please."

I paused for a moment and then slid the robe off my shoulders. Watching him watch me was such a turn-on. His eyes settled on my breasts and not taking his eyes off of them, he unbuttoned his jeans and lowered his zipper.

"God, you're stunning, Susana." He reached a hand toward me, but I caught his wrist before he touched me.

"It's my turn to touch. Keep your hands to yourself, Gabriel Green."

"Using my full name?"

Instead of answering him, I yanked the soft belt loose from the robe.

"Put your hands above your head."

Gabe raised an eyebrow, but did as he was told, putting his hands over his head. I tied his wrists together with the sash.

"Scoot over."

He was too close to the edge of the bed, so he adjusted himself and moved more toward the middle. "Any other orders?"

"Kick your shoes off."

He did so, but the rest was up to me, as he was still fully clothed. We both knew that he could bust out of that wimpy knot anytime he wanted to, but he wouldn't. He would let me be in control. I took in the sight of him. The muscles rippling in his arms, the way his chest was rising and falling quickly. The bulge in his jeans that I couldn't wait to get a hold of. I thought about slowly undressing him—taking my time and exploring every inch of his body.

But I decided that I didn't want to take my time. I was feeling impulsive and greedy. With his jeans open, I got a sneak peek at what was to come. I ran a finger down the outside of his underwear and Gabe hissed, like he was releasing pent up steam.

"Lift your hips."

He obeyed, and I grabbed the waistband of his jeans and his underwear and pulled, fast and hard, until he was naked from his waist down to his lower thighs.

"Christ, Sunny."

There he was. There was that gorgeous dick that I'd thought about for months. Now he was the one on display for me, and there was nothing he could do about it. I pushed his legs apart to give me enough room to kneel between them. He was breathing quickly. He couldn't take his eyes off me. I should've felt vulnerable as I hovered over him, totally uncovered, but instead, I felt powerful.

I brushed his balls with the fingertips of my left hand while I caressed his cock with my right. He felt hot and alive in my hand. He squirmed and wiggled as I teased him. He was so full and hard, and I wrapped my fingers around him and squeezed. He was perfection. He moved again.

"Stay still."

He grunted and closed his eyes. I flicked my tongue across his tip and little by little I took his head into my mouth, and then his shaft, moving down until I had his full length. I came up for air and went back down, sucking, licking, and using my hands to stroke him until he was so hard he was nearly throbbing.

His dick was wet with my saliva, and I slid my hand so slowly as I sucked, ignoring his urgent thrusts. He broke free from the tie holding his wrists and he dug his fingers into my hair. I twisted my hand around his shaft, and he started to whimper and buck.

"I can't . . . I'm going to . . ."

"I want you to come. Come, for me, Gabe."

He lost it. He let out a sound that was low and animal and perfect and I felt him spasm in my mouth as he released and gave me what I wanted. I kept him inside me, swallowing all he had, until he was so sensitive that he cried out, and I kept him in my mouth for a few moments longer.

He covered his face with his hands. "What did you do to me, Sunny?"

"I got you back."

"I've heard about revenge being sweet, but this takes it to a new level."

I rested my head on his thigh, taking in the view of my husband, completely vulnerable, and completely spent. "I'd say it's a touch salty, as well."

32

———

GABE

It was December 1st, and it'd been forty-seven days since that night in October. The night we had our mouths and hands on each other and we'd both had orgasms that brought us to our knees. But it'd been a one night only showing. I knew we had the rules, and we both agreed that it was just that night, but I'd be a goddamn liar if I said I hadn't wanted more. And I knew she felt the same, even if she didn't admit it to my face.

The morning after our debauchery, I woke up to an empty bed and a note on the pillow:

> *Sorry about that. Pleading temporary insanity.*
> *Was fun, but shouldn't repeat.*
> *Will return to our plan.*
> *Xoxo,*
> *Sus*

She was gone all that day and didn't get back until after I was asleep, and in the days following, she made extra efforts to not linger in bed with me. We kept our PDA going strong, so I got to touch her then, but it didn't feel like enough anymore. Day after day I tried to come up with ideas to seduce Susana—to get her to change her mind, but I wanted her to lead the way, and so far, she hadn't. But sex or no sex, I needed to get the holiday season kicked off.

The first day of December had always been Christmas Tree Day at Starling Manor. I had a gorgeous fir from a nearby tree farm, boxes of ornaments and decorations, and a staff ready and waiting to begin the set up, but I couldn't find my wife.

Helen Starling had loved the holiday season and always kicked off the decorating by lighting a candle and putting the first ornament on the tree. No matter how sick or checked out she was, she always pulled it together for that event. I'd mentioned it a few times to Susana, but she always changed the subject and we'd never really settled on a time for her to officially kick off the season.

"You're sure you haven't seen her?" I poured another cup of coffee in the kitchen while Jeff inspected a produce delivery.

"Not even once today. Jag is still searching, and security says she left her phone in the suite, so they can't track her that way."

"She was in bed earlier this morning, and no cars are missing, so surely she hasn't gone too far."

I wasn't too worried. After Skinner resigned, several of her staff also quit, knowing they wouldn't be protected in her absence, so the nasty people were gone. The atmosphere in the manor was peaceful and pleasant, and Sunny no longer had to be escorted by security in her own home.

"I might know where she is." Terra, the new kitchen assistant, was wringing a towel and seemed very nervous.

Jeff glanced up from his bag of herbs. "How would you know where she is? She hasn't been down here, has she?"

"No." Terra's cheeks went pink. "But when I had to go up to the storage room for the extra candles, I think I saw Ms. Starling in the East Wing. In a room that had a lot of mirrors."

"Her mother's old dressing room. Thank you so much." I took

one last swig of coffee, left the mug on the counter, and headed up the back stairs.

As far as I knew, Susana hadn't been in the east wing since the day last May. She tended to stay as far away as possible from anything that had to do with Helen. But Terra had been right. The dressing room door was ajar, and a sliver of light shone through the doorway and illuminated the wooden floor in the hallway. Inside, Susana sat, legs crossed, on the floor in front of a full-length mirror. She was wearing dangling earrings that sparkled in the reflection of the glass, and she had stacked several necklaces on top of each other around her neck. Scarves of every color imaginable were scattered around her as she stared into the mirror. She looked like a little girl playing dress-up.

"Susana?" I called her name from the door. "Sunny?"

Still no answer. It was like she was in a trance.

I sat down on the floor next to her and put my hand on her arm. "Are you ok?"

Susana took a deep breath but held her own gaze. "I look like her." She reached up and flicked one of the earrings and it trembled on her ear.

"Like Helen?"

"My eyes. And my mouth. Something in my face."

"I see it."

"She wore these earrings my last Christmas here. We had a ball that year and she wore a red dress and these earrings, and I remember how beautiful she was."

"Your mother was very beautiful."

"Was she?" Susana whipped her head around and looked at me, her eyes stormy. "Because you only knew her after my dad died. I think she was okay before that, but after— I just remember her being cold, and absent, and angry. And all that feels ugly."

"She wasn't always cold to me." I didn't want to contradict Susana's feelings about her mother, but I wanted her to know that there were glimmers of light.

"Tell me one thing she did that wasn't awful." Susana turned back to the mirror and started removing the necklaces.

"She set up a trust fund for me."

Susana's hand froze in mid-air. "She what?"

"She set up an account for me that matures on my thirty-third birthday. She knew that I wanted to move to my dad's property on the beach when the ownership reverted to me, and she wanted me to have enough to get started."

"You didn't tell me that."

"I'm telling you now."

She fingered the jewels in her hand and the colors of the gemstones were deep and brilliant. "I guess that's not awful. But I need to think about that."

"I understand." I hadn't wanted to hide it from Sunny, and I thought maybe Jag had told her, but I hadn't brought it up with her, and no one could take the blame for that but me. The more time ticked away in our 365-day marriage, the more I started to wonder if the dream I'd always had was starting to fade, and if another dream was taking its place. I'd been pushing it to the back of my mind, but I'd have to confront my feelings at some point. "Where did you find all this stuff?" I lifted some silk scarves and let them flutter to the ground.

"In the safe."

"There's no safe up here."

"Yes, there is. It's under that cabinet."

"I've been through these cabinets myself. They're empty."

"It has a false bottom, and there's a floorboard you can remove under that, and there's a safe under there."

"Holy shit. There were scarves in the safe?"

Susana laughed half-heartedly. "No, those were in the cabinet. The jewelry was in the safe, along with some documents, a few photographs, and an envelope with my name on it."

"Does Jag know about this? Did you open the envelope?"

"I don't think he knows, but I'm not sure. I haven't opened the envelope. I left it in there."

"How did you know about it? And how did you get it open?"

"My mom, dad, and I knew about it, but beyond that, I don't think she told anyone. I was the one who set the combination, when we moved in, and I guess she never changed it."

"Why did you decide to open it? Today?"

"I was looking for the ornament." Susana placed the necklaces back in a box and started to remove an earring.

"What ornament?" I ran my hand down her sleek black hair and then twisted it gently around my fist. She liked it when I did that.

"The ornament we used to hang before . . ." Her voice trailed off.

My mind scanned back through all my Decembers at Starling Manor, and as far as I could remember, Helen hung a different ornament every year.

"What did it look like?"

"Three birds." Susana's voice caught as emotion overcame her. "It was three starlings. It was old, and it was gifted to my grandparents when the triplets were born. Later my dad had it, and he said it represented him, my mother, and me." She sniffed, and I offered her a handkerchief. "I still can't believe you always have one of these on you." A small smile graced her lips. She wiped her eyes and blew her nose. "My mother hung it up on the tree the first year after my dad died, but I never saw it after that. She always told me it was in a safe place, but she seemed upset when I brought it up, so I stopped asking. I thought maybe it was in here, but it isn't."

"I'm sorry. I don't think I've ever seen that ornament."

Susana shrugged. "It's ok. It doesn't matter which one I hang. It's just that the holidays make me sad. They were always so great when my dad was around, but they were less great when Harry was around, if you can imagine that." She huffed and shook her head.

"Yeah. Saw that firsthand." I kissed her neck, and she leaned her head against me and kept it there. "Now that you mention it, I think Harry always chose the ornament each year, or at least handed one to Helen. She was the one who hung it on the tree, but I don't know if she made the selection." Last year's had been a crystal icicle.

"I guess we can just choose a random one. Let's get it over with." Susana returned the valuables to the safe and we made our way down to the grand parlor, where the main tree was naked and waiting for a first ornament.

A fire crackled away in the old stone fireplace and the room glowed warmly. Most of the staff had gathered around and though it was meant to be a festive event, there was a somber undertone. Susana lit the lone candle that stood on the mantle and then looked at me as if waiting for instructions.

"Do you want to pick out an ornament for us?" I asked.

Susana shook her head, so I dug around until I found a golden glass angel. Somehow it seemed fitting, and I carried it to Susana, who looked tiny next to the ten-foot fir.

"I think we're ready, if you want to hang it."

"You would pick this one, Gabriel." She let the angel dangle on her finger, and it glimmered and shone.

"You know, I didn't really hate that you called me Archie."

"You didn't?"

"Well, I did think it made me sound like a comic book character, but I got used to it"

"And I didn't mind 'Sunny' too much." She offered me a weak smile, but it disappeared quickly from her face.

She looked so melancholy that I wanted to kick myself for even pushing this tradition. It's not like it had to happen—it was just symbolic, and maybe it was time for something new.

She reached up as far as she could and lifted the angel to the tree, but then she stopped. "Wait, where's Jag?"

He'd just been in there minutes before, but he must've slipped

out. I was starting to think this was a sign that we shouldn't do this
at all.

"I think we should wait for him," she said.

A member of the security team got an alert on his smartwatch
and suddenly rushed out into the hallway, and I saw Anton pass
outside the parlor door.

"What's going on?" Susana placed the ornament back in a box
and hurried out of the room with me close on her heels.

A group of people were gathered by the front door, including
Jag, but I couldn't tell what the issue was. I tried to hold Susana
back, but she was too quick for me. She approached the group at a
brisk pace, but stopped short, causing me to bump into her back.

"What is it?" I stepped in front of her and put my arm out to
block her. The whole thing made me uneasy, and I hadn't had time
to assess the situation.

Tyler fucking Hardin was what it was. That weasel was
surrounded by members of the Starling team but didn't seem to
give a shit. Two security guards each held one of his arms, but his
feet were firmly planted, and he was speaking to Jag, his face serious. Jag's arms were crossed, and he wore an icy expression on his
face. Anton, who was hovering on the edge of the action, was a
scary dude, but I think I'd rather piss off him than Jag—Mr. Jagger
was like the father you never wanted to disappoint. I saw Jag nod
slightly, and everyone but Tyler took a step back.

"What are you doing here?" Susana pushed my arm out of the
way and walked toward Tyler.

I felt the familiar rage begin to boil in my belly, but I tried to
ignore it. There were so many people here, and my wife was safe
—*she's safe, she's safe, she's safe*—I chanted to myself like a
mantra. I expected Tyler to bark out some ridiculous insult, but
instead he stayed silent and looked to Jag as if waiting for
permission.

"Mr. Hardin has something he wishes to give you," Jag said.
"You are under no obligation to accept this gift, Susana. We can

escort him off the property if you'd like. I have seen the item in question, and if you'd like to receive it, I take no issue with it."

Tyler was still silent, which was longer than I'd ever known him to go without running his stupid mouth.

"I'll allow it." Sunny spun on her heels and headed back to the parlor, leaving all of us stunned in her wake. She may have been small in stature, but her energy was giving off major queen vibes, and it felt like she towered above all of us.

No one knew exactly what to do until Jag spoke up. "To the parlor, then, Mr. Hardin."

Tyler scuttled after Sunny, with Anton following him at an intimidating proximity. We entered the room to find Susana standing by the fireplace, the flames lighting up her face in tones of red and orange. Tyler began to approach her, and I couldn't hold myself back any longer. I took two steps for every one of Tyler's and I blocked him from getting closer to my wife.

"I don't know where you got the nerve—" I started, but I felt Sunny's hand on my arm.

"It's alright, Gabe. I've got this. But thank you." She stood on tiptoe and kissed my cheek.

Realizing I'd been dismissed, I took a step back. I was pissed at Tyler, and I was a little embarrassed that Sunny was holding it together better than I was, but I was also proud. Just when I thought I really knew her, Susana did something else to surprise me.

Tyler cleared his throat and ran a hand through his stupid floppy haircut. "I'm sorry for interrupting. I won't stay long. It's just that I knew it was December 1st, and I'd been meaning to come by, and—"

"Why had you been meaning to come by?" Susana's voice was clear and confident. Her eyes were shining and calm, and I thought she was more beautiful than she'd ever been.

"I wanted to—" Tyler started, and then he cleared his throat and tried again. "I know there's probably no way to make amends, but I wanted to try. I just wanted to tell you that I'm in a treatment program and I've been sober since—" he looked around and scratched at his neck absentmindedly, "—since the cat incident."

Susana kept her eyes on his face and showed no emotion.

"I'm seeing a therapist, and I've cut ties with my father, who's under house arrest until his trial, by the way, but maybe you already knew that. Anyway, I brought you a few things—" Tyler reached into his inside jacket pocket, but Anton pounced on him like a tiger, causing Tyler to squeak in fear.

"Arms out," Anton demanded.

Tyler, sweat on his brow, stretched out his arms while Anton patted him down in a satisfyingly aggressive manner.

"Which pocket?"

"Both." Tyler sounded like a 12-year-old boy. "I have something in both inside pockets."

Anton jabbed his hands into Tyler's jacket and came out with two items. He stepped back, and Tyler removed his jacket and sweat trickled down into his eyes.

Oh, fuck it. "Here you go." I handed him my other handkerchief.

"Thank you." Tyler wiped his brow.

I caught Susana looking at me. Were her eyes moist? She reached out her hand to me and I grabbed it, and she pulled me to her side.

"That one first." Tyler pointed to Anton's left hand.

Anton unfurled his meaty fingers to reveal a canvas mouse.

"Uh, this is for your cat. If you still have it. I'm sorry I almost —you know."

A smile played at the edges of Sunny's mouth, and she took the mouse from Anton's hand. "Thank you." She held the mouse by the tail and let it twirl in the firelight, and then she passed it to me.

"You can give her the other thing," Tyler said, and Anton handed Susana a red velvet pouch.

Her smile vanished, and she looked suddenly pale. She let go of my hand and held the gift like she knew what it was without even opening it.

"I think my dad, uh, stole this from your mom." Tyler sounded out of breath like he'd just completed a sprint. "He gave it to me the year they got married and he told me to destroy it, but I never could bring myself to do that. Anyway, I wanted to give it back. I'm sorry I had it this long."

Susana loosened the silk drawstring and opened the pouch. She shook it gently, and an ornament slid into her palm. Three birds. Three starlings, gleaming and huddled together. Tears streamed down her cheeks as she gazed at the ornament. I heard some sniffling and saw that several staff members also had tears in their eyes, and I'd be damned if Jag didn't look like he was about to lose it. A piercing meow broke the silence in the room, and there stood Mallory, apparently aware that she had a gift waiting for her.

"Oh shit!" Tyler jumped back like he'd just spotted a cobra.

I tossed the mouse across the room, and Mallory sprinted after the toy and tackled it with ferocious glee.

"I'll be going now! Merry Christmas, everyone." Tyler was out of that room so fast that the security team had to run to keep pace and escort him out of the manor.

The rest of us in the parlor waited for Susana to make the next move. Except for Mallory, who'd brought the mouse back to my feet and was loudly demanding that I throw it again.

"Get up here, you little monster." Sunny picked up the cat and crossed the room to where the tree stood, waiting. "Come on, Archie."

I went to my wife's side and put my arm around her. Mallory was trying to get out of Sunny's arms and into the tree. "This is going to be a problem, isn't it?" I said right as Mallory chomped onto a branch.

Susana gently shook our cat like she was a Magic 8 Ball. "IT IS DECIDEDLY SO." She kissed the cat on the head and handed her to me.

The Christmas tree no longer looked lonely and imposing—it looked like the possibility of wishes coming true. Susana stretched up as far as her arm could reach and gently slid the ornament onto a waiting branch. The family of three starlings looked out over all of us from their perch on the tree.

SUSANA

LAST CHRISTMAS EVE I'd eaten saltine crackers smeared with butter and drank a five-hundred-dollar Lafite-Rothschild Bordeaux Blend gifted to me by one of my clients. The whole bottle. While watching *It's a Wonderful Life*, which was completely depressing, despite its title.

This year I was snuggled under two down comforters in a cabin on my family property while my husband showered, and I was dreading the *Stars in the Snow Gala* that was just hours away. It was almost time to join the rest of my family up at the big house, but I wasn't quite ready to get out of bed. Maybe I could hide out here with crackers and wine this year, too.

I heard the water stop and Gabe started whistling as he got out of the shower. Usually I found whistling completely irritating, but something about Archie's bathroom rendition of *Carol of the Bells* was unexpectedly charming. Gabe *himself* was unexpectedly charming. We had about four months left in our marriage contract, and I was dreading losing him in my everyday life.

He'd stopped talking about his beach cottage recently, but I assumed that was so he wouldn't hurt my feelings. I didn't want to stand in the way of his dreams, but it was time to admit that I wished that his dreams included me. That was why I'd been trying desperately not to be intimate with him since that perfect night in October. I wanted to be with him, but not as much as I wanted to avoid a broken heart.

"Rise and shine." Gabe grabbed my toe that was sticking out of the covers, and I pulled it in.

"Five more minutes."

"We were supposed to be up there five minutes ago. Don't make me come under those blankets and get you."

I sat up in bed and the chilly air nipped at my nose. "Why do I have to be the only one who gets dressed at the hotel?" In a few hours I'd be whisked off to The Greyson, a stately and historic hotel that had the feeling of being nestled in the woods but was actually not far from Boston, which made it easy for the celebrities on the guest list to add it to their list of holiday events. It was where the gala was being held, and where I'd be getting ready.

"Because you're the belle of the ball, and do you really want to stuff yourself and your dress into a limo in these temps?"

"You know I don't like it when you're all rational—" My sentence was cut off by a knock at the cabin door.

"Everyone decent in there?" Indy called out. "It's freezing out here!"

I draped the comforter around me, making myself look like a marshmallow with hair, and Gabe set down the pile of clothes he was holding and secured his robe. He opened the door, letting in a blast of arctic air along with Indy and Mallory.

"This cat is terrorizing all of us up at the house. She wants her daddy."

Mallory leaped onto the hem of Gabe's robe and climbed him like a tree, ending up perched on his shoulder.

"Sorry, I slept in. I was about to get up." I offered from my downy cave.

"No problem. I needed the exercise, and I could've called, but your cat was threatening to topple all the Christmas trees if she didn't get her way."

That must've been the silver shine I saw flash from Mallory's fur: tinsel. It was then that I registered Indy's outfit: red shorts, green and red striped tights, a purple silky vest with a red thermal underneath, and a hat that looked suspiciously festive.

"Indy, are you dressed up as an elf?"

Indy shrugged. "Christmas couture. Are you ready to go over the schedule or do you need a minute?"

"We need to get dressed." Gabe pointed to his pile of clothes.

"Then hop to it. I'll wait over here," Indy headed toward the sitting area that was beyond a privacy screen, "and then we can walk back to the main house together." Indy had obviously been told to not let us delay.

So much for hiding out: the show must go on.

I STOOD STILL in the middle of the hustle and bustle of the main house, like I was a figurine glued to the base of a snow globe, and my family, the shaken-up snowflakes in the globe, fluttered around me. My family. Uncles and cousins and other relatives, and in this historic family cabin—it was a mix of magic, ghosts, and loving chaos.

This cabin, well, calling it a "cabin" was a misnomer—it was somewhere between homey lodge and woodsy mansion, but everyone had called it "The Cabin" so that's how I thought of it— had originally belonged to the Maddix family, and my grandfather and grandmother used to have gatherings here. There were so many iconic photos of the stars of the 1950s and 1960s in this cabin, which is why Embry set up last night's photo session. The photographer got shots of my uncles, my cousins, and me in some of the same situations and settings from those classic photos of yesteryear. The whole Starling PR machine was hoping to reignite both nostalgia and newfound obsession with the Starling family and legacy. It all felt pretty posed, but I had a feeling that the pictures would be spectacular and would get the job done.

We made the choice to have Gabe in some, but not all of those photos, because we all knew that after our year was up, he'd probably be out of the picture, at least officially. The spin-doctors were already working on a story about how he'd move to the coast for some kind of humanitarian reason, and they'd try to phase him out of the public eye. Thinking about that made me queasy. It felt like the closer we got to the day he'd leave, the closer Gabe and I got to each other.

"Finally gracing us with your presence?" Sebastian grabbed me in one of his signature hugs and spun me around twice before I managed to get free of his clutches. Bash pointed to the kitchen where Jeff, brought along from Starling Manor, was stacking pancakes on a platter. "Get some of those before they're all gone. My dad has already had about ten. Also, I think I want to steal your chef."

"I heard that." Jeff beckoned me into the kitchen.

"Is there a fresh batch?" My Uncle Mitch popped into the kitchen and hungrily eyed the platter.

"Save some for the rest of us!" My Uncle Miles, Simon's father, pushed his brother out of the way. They were lifelong hams and comedians, and they, along with my dad, had always kept us in stitches. But when I saw them now, it was like seeing the ghost of who my dad would've been, and it made my heart ache so much that I'd nearly broken into tears a few times. I was pretty sure they could sense it, and they were very gentle with me, letting me take the lead on hugs and conversation. I knew that they'd missed me since I pulled back from the family, and I was starting to realize how deeply I'd missed them, too. Miles planted a kiss on my head as he dashed off with his plate of pancakes, his brother chasing him with a fork in hand. They nearly ran into Simon, who, judging by the sludge he was sipping through a straw, looked like he'd chosen a green smoothie as his breakfast of choice.

"Who let the children loose in here?" Simon shot an annoyed glance at Miles and Mitch.

A clinking sound rang out in the cabin and the source of it was Shelly, game face on and knife in hand, tapping the blade against an empty champagne glass. "This isn't a toast, but I'd like your attention!"

Mitch took advantage of his brother's distraction and used it as an excuse to grab a flapjack and run. These were men who ran a billion-dollar empire, but here, they just seemed like my nutty uncles, familiar and friendly.

"The Gala starts at seven o'clock. Just a reminder that cars will be leaving here at six-thirty. Be ready, please. Except for Susana who will be prepping on site. Red carpet for everyone at the hotel rotunda, but Susana will have her entry on the ballroom stairs, so be alert to the press on site for that. Gabriel, remember that you're at the midpoint on that grand staircase so you can walk the rest of the way down with her. That way they'll get solo shots and then photos of the couple. Everyone should know your times for speeches, if you're giving one tonight, and check your phones throughout the day if your handlers have any updated notes for you, they'll be sent there."

'Handlers' made us sound like show ponies, but I guess that's kind of what we were, at least on nights like this.

"Susana, your car leaves in an hour." Shelly shuffled off to take a phone call.

Everyone went back to what they were doing, which for Gabe, was animatedly talking to Simon's mother about something probably plant related. Paula was a Master Gardener, and any time she and Gabe were in the same room together, they found it hard to talk about anything else.

He was so much more relaxed about this gala than he would've been a few months ago. Gabe had bloomed, socially, and always charmed someone wherever we went, whether it was a member of the press or a wealthy donor. And he wasn't insincere about it—if he was speaking with an interviewer, he was curious about their lives, and sometimes asked more questions than they did, which drove Shelly insane because we often got off schedule. If he was speaking to donors, he wanted to know about their business and their personal interests. Just last month he had a two-hour fireside chat with a Fortune 500 CEO about his obsession with BBC detective shows. Gabe could also be found in deep conversation with random staff members in the estates we visited. A few weeks ago, he went missing after a luncheon fundraiser and I found him helping an electrician troubleshoot some wiring issues in the basement. For a self-described loner, he was pretty social. It was another thing that endeared me to him, which gave me one more reason to dread parting ways with him this summer. I was trying to protect my heart, but I had a feeling it might already be too late.

IT WAS a half hour before I was set to walk down the hotel's grand staircase. Gabe and I had a room at the hotel for the night, even though both of us would've rather stayed in the smaller cabin out at the property. It was good to have the option, in case the night ran late, and it was also the room where I'd been primped and preened to within an inch of my life. I raised a hand to my mouth, and my hairstylist, who was putting finishing touches on the curls she'd managed to create, slapped my hand away.

"No biting your nails! We don't have time to redo that manicure."

"Sorry. Habit." I folded my hands in my lap, underneath the protective cape, hoping that it would be too hard to extract them, and I wouldn't mindlessly chomp on a nail.

The door to the room opened and Indy rushed in, fresh from red carpet festivities. They'd switched out of their elf ensemble and replaced it with a gorgeous all-black tuxedo with tails that touched the floor. The gala rules were clear: no guests could wear anything other than black or white. "How's it going here? Almost ready?"

"Ready." My hairstylist put down the curling iron and started to remove my cape.

"Wait!" Indy ran to the other end of the room and covered

their eyes. "I want to get the full effect all at once. Get her standing, spread the dress out, and get that hair placement right."

Three stylists got me up and straightened and posed, and then stepped away before telling Indy I was ready for viewing. Indy dropped their hands, and their mouth flew open. I've never seen Indy so speechless or silent, and I got worried.

I glanced down at my dress and then back at Indy. "Is it ok?"

"Ok?" Indy finally managed, a huge smile spreading across their face. "More than ok, Starling. You're a fucking masterpiece."

33

GABE

It was hard to look cool when you were sweating and pretending to look "comfortably casual" in front of several hundred guests, most of whom were famous. I was camped out on the side of the grand staircase, about halfway down, where there was a fatter step, I guess so someone trying to make an entrance down the stairs and into the ballroom could stop and wave like a queen to their adoring subjects below.

I hadn't seen Susana since this morning when they'd whisked her away to get ready for the Gala. The theme of the *Stars in the Snow Gala* this year was "Black or White." Not "Black AND White." Apparently the "or" was important. One could wear black, or one could wear white, but not both. Something about symbolizing snow and stars against a black sky.

Looking down at the guests mingling in the ballroom, I saw all the ways in which people could take one color and create a ball-gown, a weird tuxedo, and everything in-between, and it was impressive. I was in an all-black tuxedo, and though Indy said there were all kinds of designer touches in the tailoring, it looked traditional to my untrained eye. I was allowed one purple lilac bloom pinned to my lapel. I understood that I'd be the only person allowed to have any other color than black or white that evening, as Susana and I were the host and hostess, and we had to differentiate ourselves in some small way. I had no idea what Sunny would be wearing—it had been kept a secret from me.

I felt more than a little like a groom waiting for his bride to walk down the aisle, a fact that felt ironic considering the nature of our marriage. But I wasn't without the real jitters that came to an authentic groom, and I wasn't without the feelings, either. My attraction to Susana was strong, and as much as I'd try to push that away, my desire for her was very much at the surface. I tried not to think about how she looked in her long t-shirt this morning when she climbed out of bed, and how when she stood up I caught a glimpse of her bare ass, because this was not the time to get an erection.

GREEN STANDS AT ATTENTION, WAITING FOR HIS WIFE!

the photo caption could read. Or

HARD TIMES FOR GABRIEL GREEN!

Even trickier than my attraction for Susana was my affection for her. I felt like we were different people than we were last Spring when we got married, and our relationship was different, too. We trusted each other. Confided in each other. Made each other laugh. I thought about her all the time, talked to her in my head, and made decisions about things based on what I thought she might want me to do. I'd fucked up—all I needed to do for my last year at Starling Manor was keep things casual—and I'd ended up doing the opposite. I had serious feelings for Susana Starling, and I had no idea what to do about it.

Flashbulbs snapped me out of my trance and a hush spread over the room. The musicians kept playing, but they'd changed their song to an orchestral version of "Blackbird" and I followed everyone's gaze to the top of the stairs where my wife was standing. When I saw her, a wave of emotion punched me in the stomach, and I nearly toppled over. I felt hands on my shoulders, steadying me, and it was Simon, who'd appeared out of nowhere.

Susana. I'd never seen anything more beautiful in my whole life. A soft spotlight warmed her skin and she started to slowly descend the stairs, her dress trailing behind her. Her dress. It wasn't black, it wasn't white. It broke the rules by being black and white, and it broke them in a way that was so gorgeous, so perfect, it nearly broke my heart right along with those rules. Her gown was strapless, and her shoulders were bare and gleaming in the light. A scooped neckline plunged in the center, forming a graceful cut out that gave a glimpse of her sparkling skin, ending a few inches above her navel. The patterned dress was form-fitting and hugged her breasts and hips before it broke into a mermaid skirt and train that bloomed around her like a moonflower. The figures on the dress, at first, looked like flowers, but I'd quickly realized they were birds. Starlings. Her white dress was covered with stunning embroidered black starlings. The effect was mesmerizing, not just to me, but to all the guests who'd gathered to watch her magnificent entrance.

I felt a little push behind me and realized that Simon wanted me to step forward—Susana was almost at that middle step. I quickly wiped my brow with a handkerchief, stuffed it back in my pocket, and stepped out to receive my wife's hand. I couldn't take my eyes off her face, which was framed by curls—curls! I'd never see curls in her hair. All of her was lovely. Her hand trembled in mine, and I squeezed gently.

"Hey, Archie." She smiled at me.

"Hi." It was all I could say. I couldn't even speak her name.

Her lips were painted dark red, and her eyes were like a nighttime ocean studded with stars. Somehow her freckles poked through, and I'd never felt this way in my fucking life, and holy shit, was I in love?

"Ready to walk?" She tugged on my hand.

Who knew how long I'd been standing there, mesmerized. I didn't care if there were a thousand people watching us, or no one at all. Public, private, it didn't matter—I wanted to kiss her, so I did. She'd been about to take a step down to the next stair, but I pulled her back. Somehow, she moved into my body gracefully, as if we were partners in a choreographed dance. I put one hand on the small of her back and another under her chin, and I bent toward her face, pressing my lips to hers. I kissed her, and for a few seconds the whole world fell away, and I felt like I was floating.

THE REST of the night was a blur. I followed my wife around the ballroom in a daze, unable to manage conversations with anyone beyond basic small talk. I felt like I was drugged, in the most wonderful and awful way. All I wanted was to be alone with Susana before I got too scared of this magic spell I was under and went back into my emotional cave. I had to tell her how I felt.

"You ok?" She kept asking me. "You seem out of it."

"I'm ok," I kept reassuring her, but I wasn't sure she believed me.

Sunny had been sticking to club soda and mocktails for the evening, but I'd had a few gin and tonics, trying to work up the nerve to—I didn't know what. To do something, to say something.

"Are you sure nothing's wrong?" She asked me after Simon and his father Miles had finished their speeches.

"No, I'm not sure." I broke out into a sweat. "We need to talk. Now." My courage may've been boosted by alcohol, but I was glad Susana was stone cold sober. I wasn't drunk, but I was loosened up, and it felt like it was now or never.

"Alright." She looked worried as she glanced around the room. "Where?"

"Our room."

She cocked her head in surprise, as if this was more of an ask than she expected. But something in my tone must've clued her in to the fact that this was serious, so she acquiesced.

"Alright. This way."

We were near the doors to the hotel kitchen, so Susana ducked in there. I felt like we were in a movie where the person trying to pull off a heist is absconding through the kitchen, knocking over cooks and pans on their way out.

"Is something wrong?" Jeff, who was overseeing the food service, stepped into our path.

"Nothing's wrong. We just need a break. Can you let security know we're heading back to the room for a few minutes?" I said.

"Don't think I need to tell them." Jeff nodded in the direction from which we'd come. We had two security team members in our wake, both of them looking tense and hyped up.

"We're going to the room." Susana told them.

I was still mute, and I didn't know why. It was like I couldn't say anything until I got the words out that I needed to say to Susana. They were blocking my throat.

One guard got in front of us and the other stayed behind me, and we were escorted a few floors up to our suite, which I'd not seen before, and man, it was nice. But not nice enough to break me away from my mission of talking to Susana. I shut the door behind us and Susana immediately hiked up her skirt and kicked off her shoes.

"Wow. That's a relief." She took a deep breath. "You've got five minutes, Archie. If I'm up here longer than that, I'm going to take off this dress and just get in that giant tub. Wait until you see it— what?" She stopped short, obviously concerned by the look on my face. "What's wrong?"

I couldn't answer. I put my hands around her waist, but it was hard to get too close to her because I was tangled up in the train of her gown.

"Gabriel, what is it?"

I suddenly felt shy. I tried to speak. "It's—" I looked down at my feet.

"Tell me." She ducked under me so she could look up at my face. "Just tell me. I can take it."

"Okay. But don't get mad. I'm sorry. I didn't mean for it to happen," I started. She took a step back and she'd gone pale.

"What happened, Gabe?" Her voice wasn't so soft anymore.

"No, it's not like that. It's just—"

"What. Happened." She crossed her arms.

God, I was fucking ridiculous. I'd try another way. This talking wasn't going so well. "This might take more than five minutes."

She lifted her arms up and let them flop back down in a gesture of exasperation. I fished my phone out of my pocket and called Jeff, who picked up after one ring.

"You ok?" Jeff said as soon as the call connected.

"We're fine. Though I'm not sure we're coming back down tonight. Can you let the team know?"

"No problem. It's wrapping up down here anyway. Kitchen's closed and people are already leaving."

"Thanks, Jeff." I ended the call.

Susana looked like she might cry. "What's going on?"

I picked her up. I picked up Susana Starling and her giant dress. She squeaked in surprise. I carried her through the living room, past a dining table set for eight, past the wet bar. I carried her into the bedroom where a king-sized bed dominated the room. I placed her down as carefully as I could, as we were surrounded by waves of fabric and embroidered starlings blinking at me with their sequin eyes.

"What are you doing?"

I got on the bed next to her and settled in face-to-face. And then I kissed her. Just one, soft, closed-mouth, lingering kiss. When I pulled back, Sunny's lips were parted, and her breath was quick.

"What was that for?" she whispered. "If there are cameras in here—"

"There are no cameras. We're alone. And that's how I want it."

"But—"

"I want to be with you, Susana. I want to be with you . . . alone. When no one is watching. I want you. I—" the words wouldn't quite come, so I improvised. "I have feelings."

"You have feelings?" She raised her hand to my cheek, and I turned my head and kissed her palm.

"I have lots of feelings."

She took this in and then a different expression came over her face. Her eyes narrowed slightly. "What kind of feelings?"

She'd asked the question, but I was running out of words to answer.

"This kind."

34

GABE

With my face still level to hers, I pulled up her dress until it was above her waist. She gasped.

"What are you doing?"

"Exactly what it feels like I'm doing. If you want this."

She didn't pull her dress back down. In fact, she didn't move a muscle.

"I want you, Susana Starling." That was as much as I could get out and I was nearly paralyzed by fear that she'd refuse me, and by the power of my own desire. I'd never wanted anyone like this before.

"Is that so?" Her words that echoed mine from that night in October lit me up.

"More than anything."

She kept her eyes on mine and her body was still. She was resting on her forearms and her breasts pushed her strapless gown to its limit. Her legs were exposed, as were her black lace panties that I yearned to touch. A moment went by, and another. I felt her movement before I saw it—she was opening her legs. She slid them apart, inch by inch, and then she slid her heels up the bed until her legs fell open to each side. Then she let her arms relax and she fell back onto the bed and her dress inched down, revealing her dark nipples.

"I'm all yours."

My breath caught in my throat and my cock was harder than it'd ever felt. It begged to be freed from my trousers. But not yet. I raised up on my knees and took off my jacket, then kicked off my shoes. I paused for a moment and then unbuttoned my shirt as Susana watched, and then I slid it off my shoulders and down my arms. I kept my pants on, because I didn't trust myself not to plunge into her if my dick was accessible.

Her legs. Those open legs. That's where I needed to be. I stood at the foot of the bed and then climbed back on and kneeled between them. I touched the soles of her feet with my fingers, knowing that would tickle her, but she didn't jump. She just watched me. I ran my hands over her ankles, up her calves, and lingered at the tender skin behind her knees.

"Is this ok?"

"Yes." Her voice was clear. Strong. Sexy as fuck.

I kept going. I touched her knees, the front of her thighs, the back of her thighs, and then the inside of her thighs, which led right up to the place I wanted to be. I lingered at the edges of her underwear, tracing the lines with my fingertips, teasing her. "Still ok?"

"Yes."

I ran my finger along the center of her panties, stopping to twirl circles around the wet spot that had formed on the fabric. It took everything I had not to rip them off her. The more I wanted to tear them apart, the slower I made myself go. I lay down on the bed, my dick swollen and throbbing as it pressed into the mattress. I put my face between her legs and nibbled at the left strap of her waistband, and then the right strap. Then using just my lips, I bit my way over her hip bone, right to the center of her pussy, which was soaking wet but still covered by the black lace. I opened my mouth wide and covered as much of her mound with my lips as I could manage, sending hot breaths into her skin through her panties. When I pressed my mouth to her fully, she moaned and pushed her pelvis upward into my face.

I pulled my mouth away and grasped the side of her underwear. Slowly, so slowly, I scooted the fabric aside, revealing her glistening and full pussy. I loved seeing her again. Her folds were like the most beautiful flower, and I was ready to taste her again. I flicked at her clit with my tongue, just for a second, and she cried out and bucked against the air. I pressed my forearms into her legs, holding her down, and I moved my face so close that she could feel my breath against her skin. I needed full access. And no way was I going to move away from this spot. So I grabbed the lace underwear with two hands, dug my fingers in, and ripped them apart. Her panties were shredded, but we were free from them, and she was fully exposed to me, just the way I wanted her.

I teased her some more. I swept my tongue across her opening, then her clit, then her sweet lips, and then back to her clit. I changed up the order and the timing and she didn't know what to expect. I had her writhing and groaning, and we were both soaked in the wetness of her arousal. I could've kept this up for hours, but her breathing was rapid, and her noises were getting louder and more urgent. Hopefully we'd have time to explore each other for as long as we wanted, but right now, I recognized her need: Susana needed to come.

I stopped. I stopped licking her, touching her, breathing on her. She kept her eyes closed and opened her legs as wide as she could and I heard her chanting, almost.

"Please . . . please . . . please . . ." It was almost like a prayer.

I turned my right hand palm up, and slid two fingers into her. Christ, she was like hot velvet inside and I wondered if I could come just by fucking her with my fingers. I felt close to it. I slipped in a third finger to fill her, and slowly fucked her, pulling my hand out and pushing it back in. "God, Gabe." I caught her clit between my lips and alternated between sucking and licking as she threw her head from side to side. She was wildly rocking her hips and I went along for the ride, thrusting my fingers faster as she got closer to climax. With my free hand I reached up and held one of her breasts, rolling her erect nipple between my thumb and finger and that pushed her over the edge.

She cried out and her body quaked as she came against my mouth in the most spectacular eruption I'd ever witnessed. I touched her until she was so sensitive that she quivered underneath me and asked me to stop.

"I might just die if you don't stop," she sighed. "But I might die if you do."

I removed my hand from between her legs and I wiped my face with my upper arm. She tasted like the sweetest summer fruit— perfection.

I lay back beside her and put my head on her chest. Desire surged through me, but there was a peace and a satiety that came from pleasing her. I could've happily stayed there for hours, just listening to her breathe.

"Was that ok?" I asked her.

She giggled. "More than ok. That was perfect." She opened her eyes for the first time since I'd started touching her. Her gaze was soft and warm. "I want you inside me."

Those words made my stomach twist and my dick jump.

"I'm just worried about—" She stopped.

"About getting pregnant."

"I'm sorry."

"Don't apologize. I understand. I have two condoms."

"Two? Since when do you go around with two condoms?" She was smiling and her voice was less dreamy and more like her regular voice.

"Uh, since like, October? You know. Just in case we decided to make it 'more than one night.'"

"And two of them? You're optimistic."

"It's just that I know you were worried about pregnancy, so I always had two in case one was messed up or something."

"Oh." She sounded different. I looked up at her face, and her eyes were wet. "That's thoughtful. And also optimistic."

"Should I get one?"

She drew circles on my arm with her finger but didn't answer.

"We don't have to. I don't have to. This was perfect, just like this."

"Yes. Get one. Please."

I reached over to my jacket, where I had two condoms tucked into the inside breast pocket. I really did take two condoms with me wherever we went. It was habit now, and one I was grateful for. I opened one and inspected it and handed it to her for inspection.

I kissed her. And the kiss was different from any other we'd ever had. Her mouth was open and wet and soft and pressing. This was a private kiss. A kiss just for us. She pulled at the button of my pants, but there was no way she was getting them off one-handed. I saved us both the agony and hopped off the bed and stripped off the rest of my clothes. I slid the condom on as she watched, and I got back in bed.

I was nervous, but at the same time, nothing had ever felt so right. "Are you sure?" I wanted to be inside her. But I could wait.

"I'm sure." She reached down and cupped my balls and then put her fingers around my throbbing cock and squeezed. Jesus, I really might come before this even got started. "I want you to fuck me, Gabriel."

Her words unlocked something in me. I rolled on top of her and opened her legs with my knees. She grabbed my hair with both fists and kept my face close to hers but didn't kiss me. I put my tip at her opening and felt the heat of her calling me in. I wanted to dive into her and never come out.

"You're sure—"

Before I could finish my question, she closed her legs around me, moved her hands to my ass, and pushed me inside. She rocked her hips, and I moved in her, the soft heat of her pussy grasping my full length. She was still so wet from her orgasm that I slid in and out with ease and I tried to go slow, but I couldn't help building to a frantic thrusting. Her breasts bounced each time I pushed in, and she threw her head back and rode each thrust like she might come again. The pressure built up and my balls tightened, and my cock was so full as I fucked her—I lost all thoughts, all direction, all connection with the world—the only thing I had was Susana and me.

"Come, Gabe."

I couldn't hold on any longer. I pushed one of her legs up so I could go deeper. I smashed my mouth onto hers and she bit my lower lip and held me there as I started to come. She grabbed my ass and dug her fingernails into my skin. I pulled out of the kiss and buried my face in the spot between her neck and shoulder.

"You're fucking perfect," I whispered as I made a final thrust and my dick spasmed as I released into her. I moaned and bellowed and made other sounds I didn't recognize or understand, but I didn't fucking care because I was inside Susana, and it was perfection. I rode the wave of pleasure until I had nothing left to give. Sweat formed between our bodies and made us slippery, and I was trying not to think about what condition her beautiful dress might be in. She grasped the base of my dick, and I thought I heard her sigh with relief that the condom was still on. I slid out of her body slowly as she held on to me and, once out, I rolled off the condom, which was fully intact.

She was a sight to behold. Her face was glowing, her lips were swollen, and her dress was everywhere—we may have damaged some embroidered starlings in the process. I felt satisfied. Perfectly, wonderfully satisfied, but there was also a new ache of longing in my belly that I didn't recognize. My stomach felt bubbly like I'd consumed ten sodas, and I felt like I was walking on air. I was ecstatic, but I was also petrified, because not only had Susana and I officially broken our no-sex rule, but I'd disregarded my cardinal rule of "keeping it casual." My feelings were anything but casual, and I was afraid of what might be next for us. I couldn't predict it, and nothing scared me more than the unknown.

"Are you okay?" Susana looked worried, and she ran her hands up my torso, around to my back, and pulled me close to her again.

"I honestly don't know."

"What's wrong?"

I didn't want to take the magic out of the moment, but I was overcome with worry over losing Susana. I couldn't lose her. "I think I'm in love with you, Susana." I turned my head away from her and pressed my cheek into her arm. I said it. Jesus, I said it. One second. Five seconds. Ten seconds. Silence. Fuck. I'd blown it.

"No, you're not."

I turned to look at her. She was staring at the ceiling.

"I'm not what?" This was supposed to be a big moment. What was happening?

"You're not in love with me."

"If you know me so well, then why don't you tell me what I'm feeling." My heart was racing.

"No one really falls in love with me. It was just good sex. You'll change your mind tomorrow." There was a kind of coldness to her, or was it resignation? Either way, it couldn't stand.

I jumped on top of her, straddled her waist, and pinned her arms to the bed above her head. "Susana Starling. Look at me."

She had her head turned to the side. "I can't."

I kissed her neck. "Fine. But let me say that it wasn't good sex."

That got her to look at me. "What? It wasn't?"

"Nope. It was great sex."

She rolled her eyes.

"But that has nothing to do with what I just said."

"It doesn't?"

"Nope. I have real feelings for you. And they scare the shit out of me. But I'd be a liar if I hid that from you any longer, so I just wanted you to know." I let go of her arms and lay down by her side.

She rolled over on her side, the best she could in that giant dress. "Gabriel Green?"

"Yes, my lovely wife?"

"I think I'm in love with you, too."

35

SUSANA

It may have taken 234 days of marriage for me to wake up in my husband's arms, but better late than never. Sun peeked through the window of our hotel bedroom where the curtain didn't quite cover the glass, and that was the only indication that it was morning—Christmas morning.

"Merry Christmas." I didn't know if Gabe was awake, but I said it anyway.

He was behind me, big spoon-style, his arm thrown over my waist and his chin resting on top of my head. I folded perfectly into the shape of his body. Why had it taken me so long to give in to this?

"Happy Holidays." Gabe snuggled in closer, pressing his bare chest to my back.

He was wearing underwear, and I wasn't wearing anything at all. After I got out of the bath last night, I dried off, ditched the towel, jumped into bed where Gabe was dozing off, and fell asleep within minutes. But now I was awake. Awake and very aware of Gabe's erection prodding my ass. What a relief it was to enjoy Gabe—the heat of his skin, how close he held me, his breathing in my ear—and not to have to hop out of bed the moment I came to consciousness just to avoid getting too close. We'd broken the seal last night, and now all I wanted was to be closer, and to linger.

I stretched slowly and leaned into him, shifting from my side to my back so I'd be more open to Gabe. He took the hint, sliding his hand across my rib cage, and up to my breast. He circled my nipple until it was hard and then he rolled it between his fingertips which shot currents of arousal straight to my pussy.

"I like that," I purred.

"How much do you like it?"

I pulled his hand off my breast and positioned it between my legs so he could feel exactly how much.

"You really like that." He planted tiny kisses behind my ear and down my neck while swirling one finger in my wetness. "What would you like? How can I please you?" His voice could make me feel both warm and shivery at the same time.

I was overheating while goosebumps spread over my skin in waves. "You can please me by doing anything you please."

Gabe growled in my ear and brought his hand back up to my waist. "Anything?"

"Anything."

"I'll take you up on that."

I heard him reach over to the nightstand and grab something. The crackling sound a second later confirmed that he was opening a condom. He shifted to his back for a moment, and I stayed where I was, my eyes closed. The mattress bounced, and in a flash, I was flipped over onto my stomach with Gabe behind me. He put both hands on my hips and pulled backwards, forcing me up to all fours. My breasts were heavy and swung below me as Gabe roughly kneaded my ass. He pressed a knee against my upper thigh and pushed outward, opening my legs more. He spread my cheeks and let me sit like that for several seconds. I squirmed, wondering if he was looking at me, and anticipating what he might do.

What he did took my breath away: simultaneously, he pressed a finger into my asshole, and he plunged his dick deep into my pussy.

He was filling me from all angles, and I arched my back and cried out and let him fuck my ass and my cunt. I felt wild and powerful and beautifully dirty.

"Fuck, yes. Fuck."

Gabe reached around with his free hand and found my clit. He had some kind of magic fingers and my whole body quivered as he stroked me. I bucked and rocked like a wild animal, and he matched my movements and never lost contact with me. All my reserves dissolved, and I gave myself over to the instinctual indulgence of fucking him. He panted and I moaned and writhed until a cosmic shudder started in my belly and spread out through my entire being and I came harder than I'd ever come in my life. My wave of pleasure crashed down on Gabe who succumbed to it all and I felt his cock pulse inside me as he orgasmed.

"Oh my god. Holy shit." Gabe's words came out in breathless bursts as he continued to thrust into me. A few moments later we both collapsed onto the bed. Gabe gently withdrew himself.

"Condom intact?" I couldn't relax until I knew that everything was accounted for.

"All good. Safe and sound." Gabe placed the condom on top of the open wrapper and then grabbed me into a bear hug. "That was the best Christmas present I've ever gotten."

"And you didn't even have to unwrap it!"

"You're magnificent, Susana Starling."

"As are you, Gabriel Green."

He kissed my neck, my jaw, my cheek, my forehead, and then he kissed my mouth. I knew the taste of him, and he tasted like Gabe. Like home. Like love.

"We should talk," he said.

"Right now?"

"What better time to tell you how I feel about you than when you're in my arms and I just had the best orgasm of my life?"

The butterflies were back. I didn't trust myself to find the right words for the moment, so I settled for simple. "When you put it that way."

"Roll over and look at me, Sunny."

I did as he asked. God, his face. His perfect face. I couldn't bear to hope that he might say something wonderful to me.

"I'm just going to say it."

I waited and watched his face as he watched mine. I tried to memorize his cheekbones, his dark eyes, his strong nose, the way his lips curved.

"I don't want this to end. I don't want to stop being married to you after our year is up."

Did he say that? Did he really say that? Was I dreaming? Surely, I was dreaming. "But your beach house . . ." I couldn't let myself get comfortable with his words. I was never Ms. Right. This was new and strange and glorious and terrifying.

"I don't have to give up the beach house. I might just have to look at things a little differently."

I realized I'd been holding my breath. I took a deep breath in. "How differently?"

"Until you—until us . . . I didn't have anyone other than the ghosts. I'd just had that dream, which also used to be my dad's dream. I think I can still have part of that, but I can also have my own dream. I don't have to live at the beach all the time. We can talk about it, if you're open to it. But I'd like—" he kissed me softly and sweetly. "I'd like you to stay Mrs. Gabriel Green, if you'll have me."

"I can't do that."

Gabe's nostrils flared and he inhaled sharply. "You can't?"

"You know very well that you have to be Mr. Susana Starling."

Gabe rolled me onto my back and held my hands down against the mattress, easily pinning me to the bed. "That was cruel. How dare you scare your husband like that? The husband who loves you." He nibbled my neck which tickled like hell.

I tried to squirm away, but he wouldn't let me. And it hit me that he meant it. He really meant it. He hadn't backed off or backed down or changed tack. He loved me.

He stopped torturing me with tickles and gave me a second to breathe. "Fine. I'll be Mr. Susana Starling."

"And I'll be Mrs. Gabriel Green. But we'll be 'Mr. and Mrs. InDeepShit' if we don't text someone and let them know when we're coming back to the house. I think our phones have been buzzing for the last hour."

Gabe grabbed his phone. "I'll text Simon and Shelly." He tapped out a message, hit send and snuggled back up to me. "I think we should stay married longer than a year. How about you?" He said it so casually, but we both knew it wasn't a casual question.

I kissed him. "Yeah. Maybe a little bit longer."

SITTING on the floor in front of the fire, Gabe and I snuggled together. I rested my back against his chest, and he made the world's most supportive human chair, holding me up as I leaned into him. The big cabin felt festive and cozy as the only light other than firelight came from the twinkling of the Christmas tree. Our display of affection caused some raised eyebrows from my uncles and cousins, but after a few hours, several cocktails, and way too many versions of "Stars in the Snow" on the sound system, nobody seemed to care. The night was ending, and the only people left awake were the two of us, plus Simon and Sebastian. I'd never had a holiday like this, not even when I was little. I felt warm and sleepy and happy—I actually felt happy.

"When are you two heading back to the manor?" Simon asked.

"Tomorrow morning." I took a sip of my drink, which was some kind of chocolate peppermint martini made by Bash, who was the bartender for the evening.

"Don't forget we have a foundation board meeting on January 5th."

"It's Christmas, Starling! No shop talk tonight." Gabe lifted his glass to his mouth, but it was empty. "Another round, barkeep!"

"Coming right up!" Sebastian sniffed a bottle, shrugged, and started pouring liquid into a new glass.

"I'm not sure you should trust him. He might be making some kind of lethal concoction over there."

My cousin looked like he was three sheets to the wind, and the rest of us would soon follow as long as he kept serving us drinks.

"Maybe we could go to the beach house for your birthday," Gabe said.

"This March?"

"I'd like for you to see it."

"But you won't have ownership until late April, right?"

"Yes, but we can still see it. And I need to meet with the property management company anyway. Two birds, one stone."

"Why would anyone throw a stone at a bird?"

"Good point. That's an awful saying."

"I'd like to go. Anytime. It doesn't have to be my birthday."

"One Cosmic Christmas Cosmopolitan, sir." Sebastian had arrived with a bright pink drink for Gabe.

"What's in this?" Gabe sniffed the glass.

"Everything!"

Gabe winked at me and raised his glass. "Cheers, Starlings."

The rest of us raised our glasses, though Simon's and mine were empty. Gabe took a sip and nearly choked at the intensity of it. "That packs a punch, Bash."

"That means I made it right!"

"Ready for bed?" Gabe put down his drink and took my hand in his.

No more avoiding bed together. Now, instead of dreading bedtime, I couldn't get there fast enough. "I thought you'd never ask."

36

SUSANA

A pregnancy test, a surprise, and a scary letter—those were the things in store for me on my thirty-first birthday. First was the pregnancy test. I didn't really think I was pregnant, but I'd gotten into the habit of taking one every month around the time my period was due, because I didn't want to stress myself out wondering and waiting for my cycle to start each month. I'd taken one in January and February, and this was my March test. Gabe and I had never had a birth control failure, but we'd had a lot of sex, and I just wanted to double check.

While the test was taking its few minutes to process (I never sat and watched it, waiting for the lines to appear--that seemed like a recipe for a panic attack), I got dressed for the day. Usually, it was freezing and gray on my birthday, but today was predicted to be unseasonably warm, almost sixty degrees, and sunny. Gabe said he had a surprise planned for me today, but that was later, at 6:00. I chose a light sweater, jeans, and sneakers for the moment. I could change later if I needed to. For a while I'd thought that Gabe was going to take me down to the beach bungalow for my birthday, but the timing hadn't worked out and we were planning a trip later in the spring. We'd also decided to wait until our first year of marriage was done before making big decisions about our future—we didn't want to jinx anything as far as the inheritance and status of the trust and the estate, so we were continuing with our plan, which meant public appearances and charity events, but now it also meant sex. I couldn't be happier with our new lifestyle and I was sure that Gabe felt the same way.

I went back into the bathroom to check the test. I had it flipped over so I wouldn't catch a glimpse of it as I walked in. Two lines would mean I was pregnant, and one line meant I wasn't. My hand shaking, just a little, I picked up the plastic stick and flipped it over. One line. Not even a hint of a second line. Relief washed over me, but not with the intensity it had over the last few months. There was something else . . . some other feeling . . . and I couldn't quite identify it. Ambivalence? Uncertainty? Oh shit, it wasn't disappointment, was it? I didn't want to be pregnant . . . did I? I mean, sometimes I'd imagine what kind of father Gabe would be (a wonderful one, I was sure), or what our child might look like. I'd even let myself think about what would happen if we had twins. Would I rather have identical twins or fraternal? God, what was wrong with me? I tossed the test in the trash and went to face my final challenge of the morning: the letter.

I'd been thinking about the letter from my mother every day since I found it in the safe last December. I didn't even know if it was a letter—it was a sealed envelope with my name on it, in my mother's hand. But I knew my mother had loved to write letters, and I guess there was a chance it was just some kind of document. I had a feeling she'd left me a note. I'd told myself I'd open the envelope on my birthday, which could've been a bad idea if my mom had written me something nasty, but something about the idea felt right, so I stuck with my plan. It also gave me a specific time and date in the future to know that I'd open the envelope, so I was able to stop obsessing every day, wondering if I should open it, or wait. But the future had become the present—today was the day. I wanted to get this over with, so I headed to my mother's dressing room to find out what she had to say.

I OPENED the cabinet and my heart leapt into my throat. My mother's scarves were gone. The cabinet was empty. Had someone found the safe? Had Gabe come back and removed them? Was there a break-in? My hands trembled as I removed the false bottom of the cabinet, and then the floorboard. I entered the combination on the lock, and I sighed with relief when the safe opened. The jewelry was there, right as I'd left it, and so was the envelope.

I fished out the letter and was about to close the safe, but I decided to pull out a necklace. I remembered this one, though my mother rarely wore it. It used to belong to my grandmother, Sadie Starling. It was a platinum chain with a flower-shaped pendant, made of up of several diamonds of different cuts. Round, pear-shaped, and Marquise diamonds came together to make the flower, and I'd always thought it was the most romantic necklace I'd ever seen. I didn't want to put it in my pocket, but I wanted to take it with me, so I put it on. It felt delicate and light against my skin, and with it on, I felt closer to my mother, my grandmother, to all of my family. I closed the safe and sat on the floor, envelope in hand. No use in speculating any more. I slid my finger across the top seam and opened it. It was a letter. And it was in the looped, flourished hand of my mother, so familiar it was like hearing her voice. Tears sprung to my eyes when I saw the date at the top of the note: she'd written it exactly one year ago, on my birthday.

> *Dear Susana,*
> *It's your birthday. You're thirty years old, and I can hardly*
> *believe it. I remember when I was thirty. You were just two*
> *years old, and your father and I moved from our house in*
> *East Hampton to Starling Manor. We'd wanted to make a*
> *go of it on our own and hide out with our little family for a*

while longer, but it made sense to move here and embrace all that life had to offer. We wanted you to have the best of everything.

I know life didn't turn out as either of us had planned, and now it's too late for me to be the mother I should've been. I'm not doing well. My cancer has spread, and I sleep most days, and I don't think I'll be around much longer. I changed my will a while ago, and I hope you were able to take over this estate, because you are the rightful owner. I'm sorry that it required you to be married—there was some archaic language in the lifetime rights to the property that required a woman to be married if she were to fully own Starling Manor. That's why I married so quickly after your father's death. Then Harry took over, and I was unable to manage changing the rights, and after a while, I admit that I gave up. But when I realized that my time was running out, I decided to try to fight back and right some of my wrongs. I'm too cowardly to give you this letter now, as I fear I couldn't bear wondering if I'd ever hear back from you. So if you're reading this, I am gone.

I hope you are living here, if you want to, and that you found this letter. You and I are the only people alive that know of this safe and the combination. I've left some family jewelry in here, along with some photos of your grandparents and father, and some back-up legal documents, should you need them.

I hope that if you're married, that you are happy. I had a dream of your wedding, and it was beautiful. There were colors everywhere like a thousand bright birds riding on the breeze, celebrating you. I loved helping you write your vows when you were little. I've enclosed one of those that I'd kept. I hope you enjoy it as much as I have, over the years.

I was a terrible mother, but you are a perfect daughter. You were the joy of my life, and the most beautiful thing I ever

*saw. I'm sorry I failed you, and please know that I only
blame myself. Happy birthday, Susana.
With love,
Mom*

My hands trembled as I unfolded the little sheet of paper that my mother had included in the envelope. I recognized the stationery immediately: it'd been my favorite paper. It was pink with a faint rainbow print and I'd stamped it with rose stamps for extra flourish. It was just the bride's vows, written in bubbly cursive in which I'd dotted each lowercase "i" with a heart.

*I, Susana Starling, vow to be a good wife. That means I will
be smart and funny and make all the money we need. I will
read 100 books a year, and I will share them with you. I will
go for walks with you and scratch your back. We have to have
dinner with my parents every Saturday, and we will have
ten cats. I promise to love and cherish you, as long as you are
nice and kind like my dad. With this vow, I thee wed.*

I cried. I cried for my mother, for my father, and for little Susana who had no idea how dark her life would become. The tears fell and fell and fell until there were no more to come. I had to use regular tissues to blow my nose, which was an awful experience after you'd been spoiled by handkerchiefs. I felt stupid for choosing to read the letter on my birthday—my eyes would be swollen and red for hours. But I also felt at peace. For the first time in so long, I wasn't holding on to anger or resentment toward my mother. We'd loved each other. We truly had.

I HID out in my bedroom for a while after reading the letter, splashed my face with cold water, put a cool rag across my eyes, and waited for the signs of crying to disappear. I'd tell Gabe about it later, but for now I wanted to keep it private. I was famished. Gabe had jumped out of bed at the crack of dawn, wished me a happy birthday, and then took off. He said he'd be dealing with "birthday logistics" for most of the day, and that I should relax, enjoy my day, and meet him at our special lamppost at 6:00. Surely Jeff had something good going in the kitchen this morning. He had something good most days, but I had a feeling there'd be an extra treat since it was my birthday.

I heard the doorbell chime as I got to the top of the main staircase. It was a rare sound because someone usually got to the door before a visitor had a chance to ring the bell. All deliveries went to the back of the house, and we didn't have random neighbors or salesman showing up unannounced. Jag, who must've been closest to the front of the house, opened the door and let the visitor into the foyer.

It was a very blonde, very pretty, and very pregnant woman who hugged Jag like she knew him. She looked familiar—Ella! It was Ella. The woman who used to work at Starling Manor, and the woman the press reported on as being Gabe's mistress last August. I felt a pang of jealousy even though I knew I had nothing to be jealous of. I was married to Gabe. She wasn't his mistress, but she was gorgeous, in that blonde, all-American way. She was giving Brigitte Bardot vibes, which was maybe another reason I felt envious—I'd always wanted to be beautiful like that, but nature had given me black hair and freckles, but hey, I had the movie star boobs! Maybe it was the pregnancy that made me feel envious. I pushed that thought to the back of my mind.

"I need to see Gabriel." Ella's voice carried through the hall and up the stairs to where I was standing.

"He's quite busy today. May I ask what this is regarding?"

"The father of my child, that's what it's regarding." Ella put her hands on her hips and glared at Jag, obviously not in the mood to be turned away.

The father of her child? Surely, she didn't mean—I did the

calculations in my head. If she and Gabe had gotten together in August, she would be exactly as pregnant as she was now. I broke out into a cold sweat and things started to swirl around me. I crumpled to the floor. I'd been such a fool. Of course. Of course he'd been with her. How had I let myself think that this would be easy? That Gabe could love me free and clear and that we'd drive off into the fucking sunset together? I had to get out of here.

I couldn't go down the main stairs. I stood up and ran to my bedroom and grabbed my purse. I dashed for the back stairs and rushed through the kitchen where Jeff caught a glimpse of me.

"Happy birthday! I've got something here for you—Susana?" Jeff looked bewildered as I ran right through, even slamming the door on Mallory who'd try to follow me. She loved Gabe better anyway. They all did. None of them needed me.

Sam, from my security team, came jogging out the door in my wake. "Ms. Starling? Where are you going?"

"Out!" I barked. I pushed open the side door to the garage and entered the combination to the key cabinet.

"Should I get a driver?"

"I'm driving myself!" I grabbed a set of keys and clicked the fob to see which car they unlocked. Could be the truck, an Audi, a Volvo, or the trusty black Lincoln. Nope. A fucking red corvette. Of course. Of all the cars. Probably a holdover from the Hardin era. "Open the bay door!"

Sam scrambled to hit the button as I turned on the engine. I waited until I had just enough clearance to get out of the garage, and I was out of there. I sped down the back driveway and out onto the highway and headed for home. Or what used to be home, because now I belonged nowhere.

BY THE TIME I arrived at my old house, I'd calmed down a little, but not much. I felt despondent, confused, betrayed, and dumb. Why did I let myself trust Gabe? Why did I let my guard down?

Did he even know that Ella was pregnant? I unlocked my front door, stepped into the house, and shut the door behind me. The place was clean, but obviously not lived in—Mrs. Jenkins had been taking care of the house for me. She'd offered to do it for free, but after much insisting, I convinced her to let me pay her for the service. I didn't want to sell the house, not until I'd been sure that I was safe in my new life, and thank god it was still mine. The only way for me to be safe was to be alone. Gabe could have his baby with the Goddess Ella and leave me out of it.

The front door burst open and Mrs. Jenkins jumped into the living room like a paratrooper fresh from the sky and ready to battle. "Christ on a cracker, Starling, what're you doing here?"

"Visiting my own home, what does it look like?" I snapped.

Mrs. Jenkins narrowed her eyes. I'd never been snippy with her before, and she looked suspicious. She also looked gorgeous. She was dressed up, for her, in silk slacks and a short-sleeved blouse that showed off some of her tattoos. Her hair was in a glamorous side-braid and—

"Are you wearing make-up?"

Mrs. Jenkins never wore make-up. "My tats are all the color I'll ever need," she always said. "So what if I am? Now tell me what you're really doing here."

"Not until you tell me why you're so dressed up." I put my hands on my hips and may or may not have actually stomped my foot.

"Somebody's got her knickers in a twist." Mrs. Jenkins may've seen the tears that were threatening to fall, and she softened her tone. "I have an event later today. I've been trying to get out in the world a little more. Now it's your turn."

I flopped down on my couch and put my head in my hands. "It's over."

"What's over?"

"All of it."

"Too cryptic, kiddo. Need the details."

"Another woman is having Gabe's baby and I'm a total idiot and my mom actually loved me and I'm destined to be alone forever. Is that good enough for you?"

Mrs. Jenkins' phone buzzed in her hand, and she glanced at the screen. "Sounds like you're having a meltdown."

"Nuclear."

"Not the best state of mind to be in on your birthday."

"You remembered it was my birthday?"

"How could I forget? On your thirtieth we got drunk and watched *Grease* and *Grease 2*. Highlight of my year." Her phone buzzed again. "I have to take this." She stepped outside and answered a call.

I stood and paced around my house. I'd forgotten my phone back at the manor, so I couldn't even send Gabe a text to tell him to fuck off. I hated that the one person to whom I wanted to turn to and pour my heart out was the exact person who'd ripped it out of my chest in the first place.

Mrs. Jenkins stepped back into the house. "Calmed down at all?"

"Calmed down? No, I haven't calmed down. My life just got ripped out from underneath me and you expect me to be calm?" I was having a meltdown.

"Susana." Mrs. Jenkin's tone was unusually firm.

"What?"

"What's true?"

"What?" I didn't understand what she was asking.

"What's true? What do you actually know to be true?"

"Gabe probably got this bombshell pregnant, and he doesn't love me and—"

"Susana Starling." Mrs. Jenkins pounded her fist, once, on the counter, and I jumped.

"What?" I was exasperated.

"What is true?" She said each word short and sharply, like each syllable was a complete sentence.

I took a deep breath. "A pregnant woman showed up at the manor today."

"Sounds like a fact. Go on."

"And she said she was looking for the father of her baby. That she was looking for Gabe."

"Were those her exact words?"

"Yes. Well, no. Not her *exact* words."

"What were her exact words?"

"Uh—" What were her exact words? I couldn't quite remember. "Something like, I need to see Gabe. I'm here about the father of my baby."

"Sounds like that's open to interpretation, and you can't even remember her specific words. You'd never have made it in the agency, Starling."

"What agency?"

"Never mind. What else do you know to be true?"

I didn't answer her because I didn't have an answer.

"Did you see Mr. Green's sperm connect with this gal's egg? With your own eyes?"

"Gross! No." I rolled my eyes.

"Did you see him put his tallywacker in her penis fly trap?"

"You did not just say 'penis fly trap.'"

"Suck it up, buttercup. Did you see him do that?"

"No." I huffed like a petulant teenager.

"Then calm your britches. We'll figure this out."

The sound of tires on my driveway cut the conversation short.

"Who's that?"

"Maybe the owner of that sweet 'vette out there, because I know that's not yours. And don't roll your eyes at me again, little lady."

"Yes, mom." I said mockingly, but with affection that I know she noticed, because she winked at me.

She moved a curtain aside and looked out of the window. "The cavalry's here. I've got to skedaddle. See you soon, Starling." And then she was gone.

In her place, stomping into my hallway, sweaty and stern and handsome and obviously pissed, was my husband. Gabe looked at me and threw his hands into the air. When I didn't say anything, he tossed his keys on the counter and put one hand on his hip. "What the hell, Sunny?"

37

SUSANA

"What the hell right back at you, Archie." Not the most brilliant reply, but I was losing confidence in my stance. Mrs. Jenkins' question about truth had gotten under my skin, and I wasn't sure what I knew and what I didn't.

"What are you doing?" Gabe did not look happy.

"Running away." I'd decided to go with blunt honesty, and at least I knew *that* was true. I'd truly run away. Again.

"Why?" It was Gabe's turn to sound exasperated.

I realized, that on the chance it wasn't true, I probably shouldn't start right off the bat with the accusation of him impregnating another woman. The idea of him having a baby with someone else made me nauseous. "I saw Ella today."

"Ella?" He looked confused, but not shocked. "Okay. . ." He was waiting for more.

"She came to the front door of the manor this morning."

Gabe waved his hand in the "get on with it" motion.

"And she said she wanted to see you." I waited for guilt to come crashing down on his face, but he stood there looking as stupefied and annoyed as ever.

"And . . .? Why are you here, Sunny?"

"She said she was there about the father of her baby. Or something like that."

Gabe's eyes went up and to the side like he was trying to remember something or figure out a puzzle.

"She's pregnant, Gabe."

"I know she's pregnant, Susana, but what the hell does that have to do with you being here, goddamnit?"

"You knew she was pregnant?" We were both speaking English, but it felt like we were speaking different languages.

"What does it matter? Yes, I know Ella's pregnant. She and Cal have asked me to be the baby's godfather, but I can't remember if I told you that."

"Cal?"

"My best friend? Sunny—"

"Oh fuck." Ella was pregnant with Cal's baby, not Gabe's. I was a fool a million times over. I started to cry. This was way too much crying for a birthday.

"Susana, I have no idea what's—" Realization dawned on his face. He closed his eyes and brought his fingers to his temples, like I'd just given him the world's biggest headache. He took a huge, loud breath in, and let out an even bigger, louder exhale. "Susana Maddix Starling Green, did you think that Ella was pregnant with my child?"

I couldn't tell how pissed he was, but I was about to find out. "Maybe?"

Gabe closed his eyes and took another big breath. This could go a lot of ways. He opened his eyes and stepped toward me, stopping when he got about a foot away. "Cal is the father of Ella's baby."

"I'm starting to gather that." I looked at his shoes, because I couldn't bring myself to hold his gaze.

He put his finger under my chin and made me raise my head. "Susana?" he said softly.

"Yes?" Annoying tears were still slipping out of my eyes.

"I've not been with any other woman since the day you stepped back into my life. The only woman I'd want to have a baby with is you, which is good, because you're the only woman I'm sleeping with."

This was true. It was. I could feel it. But: he wanted to have a baby with me?

"I love you, Susana. And only you."

"I love you, too." We could deal with the other thing when I was back in my right mind, not barely treading water.

Gabe gathered me into his arms and picked me up. This was home. Wherever Gabriel Green was—that was where I belonged.

He held me for a long time, and then he set me back on the ground. "I don't want to rush you, Sunny, but I still have a birthday surprise to take care of, and I'm way off schedule now."

"I'm sorry."

"Don't be sorry. Just get yourself home and meet me at the lamppost at 6:00. It's 2:00 now. Have you eaten? Jeff said you ran through the kitchen like a bat out of hell."

"No, I haven't eaten."

"Well, that's not going to help your mood. I have snacks out in the Lincoln, and a driver. He's going to take you back. I get the corvette. Where are the keys?"

I pointed to my purse and he retrieved the fob.

"Are you okay? Still ok to do the birthday stuff?" Gabe looked nervous again.

"I'm ok to do the birthday stuff. I'm sorry for assuming the worst."

"We're still getting to know each other. But please know that I'm hopelessly devoted to you. You're the one that I want."

Too bad Mrs. Jenkins hadn't been around to witness the *Grease* reference.

"I have to go. See you tonight, Mrs. Green?"

"See you tonight, Mr. Starling."

. . .

I FELT balanced and calmer after I ate some food on the ride back to Starling Manor. Apparently stable blood sugar was important for a steady mood. I'd probably need to do a deep dive on why I crashed so hard into the slippery slope of worst-case-scenario with the Ella thing, but I was putting it aside for now. I wanted to enjoy my birthday, or what was left of it.

I was looking through my closet for a change of clothes when there was a knock at my bedroom door. I opened it and Indy breezed through, carrying a garment bag and shoe box.

"Uh, hi," I had no idea why they were there. Maybe I'd missed a calendar update?

"Hi, birthday girl. Thought you might want to try something new. They unzipped the garment bag.

"For what?"

"For your birthday."

"Am I going somewhere fancy? Are there photographers here?"

"Nope. Not going anywhere. Just what good would I be as your stylist if I didn't bring you a new frock on your birthday?" Something was weird with Indy's expression.

"What's going on?"

"Nothing's going on. Let's see if this fits." They pulled out a dress that I recognized immediately.

"Is that my grandmother's dress?"

"Bingo."

It was a black dress, 1950s vintage. Fitted bodice, cap sleeves, full skirt. And it was the dress Sadie Starling was wearing when she and my grandfather eloped. There were so many iconic photos of her in this exact dress, but I had no idea it still existed.

"Just had to make a few tweaks to the measurements, but you have her figure, so I thought it might be a good fit."

I pulled off my sweater, anxious to try on the dress.

"Holy shit. What's that?" Indy's mouth had fallen open, and they were staring at my neck.

"Oh, this is one of my grandmother's necklaces."

"It sure as hell is. That's the one she wore when she sang at the White House."

"It is?"

"Have you just been wearing that under your sweater all day? Is that insured?"

"Uh."

"Jesus, Starling. That's a million-dollar bauble you've got there. Be careful." Indy held up the dress, and I quickly undressed. They helped me into the dress and zipped me up. They let out a low whistle as I twirled in a circle. "Wow. You're something else."

I went over to the mirror to inspect the dress, and Indy was right. The dress was perfection and it fit like it was made for me. The diamonds sparkled and shone on my neck, and I might not have been Brigitte Bardot, but I was Susana Starling, grand-daughter of Sadie Starling, daughter of Helen Starling, and that was enough.

AN HOUR LATER, I was standing, alone, at the bench by the stables. Everything was quiet. Almost too quiet. There were usually people milling around at this time of day—groundskeeping staff, delivery personnel, or drivers, but there was no one. The light in the sky was beginning to fade and the color beyond the clouds was taking on a pink and orange hue. Where was everyone? Where was Gabe?

As if on cue, Gabe stepped out from a garden path, and with one look at him, I was starting to think that the birthday surprise he had planned was not a casual one. Gabe was wearing a slate blue Merino wool suit with a matching vest, a sharp white shirt, and a lavender tie. This outfit had Indy written all over it—I could tell because it fit perfectly, and it took my breath away. Gabe was holding a bouquet of lilacs and pink roses. *Please don't let me cry again.*

"Happy birthday." Gabe gave me the flowers and reached down to kiss me. "I want to tell you how beautiful you look, but I cannot find the words. You're stunning. Let me take a look at you." Gabe lifted my arm and twirled me around like I was a ballerina in a music box. "Wow."

"You're one to talk. You're so handsome."

Gabe smiled and kissed me again. "It's starting to get chilly, now that the sun's going down. I have something for you. Walk to the pasture with me?" He took my hand and we walked down the path toward the field. "You know why I picked this time of day, right?"

"Picked it for what?"

"For your birthday surprise. It's the gloaming!"

I laughed, which felt so good after a day filled with so many tears.

"You get to call it 'the gloaming' all night, and I won't call it 'dusk,' not even once."

"Best birthday present ever!"

"Well, I hope your actual present is better than that. There it is." He pointed to the pasture.

And there, with a backdrop of a sky kissed with violet and coral streaks and all wearing wreaths of lilacs around their necks, stood Sandy, Dapple, and Buster. My Quarter Horse, Appaloosa, and Welsh Pony. Sandy was nibbling some grass, Buster was nibbling at Sandy's wreath, and Dapple was sniffing the air as if catching the scent of something familiar. I had no words. I barely had breath in my lungs. I dropped my bouquet and ran to the fence, desperate to climb over. Screw my dress, my diamonds, my heeled shoes. Those were my horses. They were older, they had to be sixteen or seventeen years old now, but they looked perfect. Perfectly mine.

"Hold up! I'll help you." Gabe, my flowers in hand, caught up with me and lifted me over the fence.

I realized I was sobbing, and I didn't care one bit. I hoped that Gabe had a hundred handkerchiefs in his pocket, because I was going to need them all. I forced myself to walk, because I didn't want to spook the horses, but I shouldn't have worried. Dapple recognized me first and headed toward me, and Sandy followed. Buster followed Sandy, and soon the four of us were in the middle of the pasture. I kissed their faces and breathed in the scent of their necks and dried my tears on their fur. Gabe stood back, giving me space to be alone with the horses and pony.

Finally, I could speak. "How?" I asked him.

"They were living at a ranch nearby. Ella's father works there. Turns out that the woman who owns the ranch was a friend of your mother's, and she promised Helen that she'd keep them together just in case you ever came back for them."

Buster sniffed Gabe's pocket to see if he had any snacks.

"Cal was supposed to pick them up today, but he didn't show up and Ella couldn't reach him. That's why she came by. Cal accidently had her phone in his car, and he had a minor fender-bender but couldn't reach her, and it was all a mess. But I found someone to pick them up, so it all worked out."

"I don't know how to thank you."

"Believe me, seeing your reaction was all the thanks I needed. And it took a lot of people to get them here, so it wasn't just me."

"Who picked them up?"

Gabe laughed and looked a little sheepish. "Well, if you must know, I called in a favor with Tyler Hardin. Knew he had a trailer and figured he wasn't using it."

"Wow. The surprises keep coming."

"I've got another one."

"You know you can't top this one." I stroked Sandy's nose, and he nuzzled my hand.

"Wanna bet?" Gabe got down on one knee.

What was he doing? Oh god, what was he doing?

"I know you're already my wife, but I want to ask you—" He tugged on his purple tie and cleared his throat. "Susana Starling, I love you. Will you marry me again?"

My heart had never been so full. "Yes, Gabriel Green. A thousand times yes!"

Gabe stood and swept me into his arms and swung me around. "She said yes!!!" He yelled so loudly that Dapple whinnied in response. "Open the doors!"

Who was he talking to? And then, as I watched the huge barn doors swing open, I realized why it'd been so eerily quiet. It was because everyone was in the barn. And by everyone I meant Jag, Jeff, Simon, Sebastian, and both my uncles. Mrs. Jenkins, Ella, Cal, and Jane Murray from our wedding! I saw Tyler speaking to a redheaded woman I didn't know, and there were even some kids from my cooking class, some of whom were jumping up and down and cheering while two others wore beaming smiles and were pointing at a tall and slightly crooked layer cake that they'd obviously baked for the occasion. I was fresh out of tears, so I just stared. Stared at my family and friends who'd come to celebrate me.

Something caught my eye, and it took me a second to register what I was seeing. Scarves. My mother's colorful scarves. Tied to rafters and beams and hanging from the walls. As the evening breeze moved into the barn, the ends of the scarves took flight and they shimmied and waved, and just like my mother had dreamed, they looked like a thousand bright birds.

Sebastian got to me first and he captured me in a rough hug. "Happy birthday, cousin! I was getting claustrophobic in that barn, and those kids wouldn't let me eat the cake!"

"It's for her, so she has to go first!" one of my students said.

"He's impossible to control," the unknown redhead said.

"Susana, meet Alice. Dad hired her as my handler."

Alice rolled her eyes, and I felt that we could become fast

friends. "As if anyone can handle you, Sebastian. It's nice to meet you, Susana."

"Likewise. Thank you for coming! And my apologies in advance for anything my cousin says or does."

"Please specify which cousin." Simon pushed Sebastian aside and hugged me, more gently than Bash. "Some of us have manners. Happy birthday, Susana."

"Thank you, Simon. Thank you for coming." I greeted my uncles and the other guests as several staff members came from the house carrying trays of food.

Someone started some music and while I hadn't spoken to Tyler, I saw him leading Sandy, Dapple, and Buster to the stables, which was probably a good idea, otherwise Buster might devour all the refreshments.

"Did you figure out what's true, cupcake?" Mrs. Jenkins asked when she made her way to me.

I grabbed her and hugged her tightly. When I pulled away, I could've sworn I saw tears in her eyes. I didn't know that was even possible. "I think I did. Thank you. Thank you for everything."

"You're welcome. I'm always here for you. And I always will be."

I couldn't believe this was my party. My estate. My life. Gabe approached me along with Jane Murray, who had the same warm smile I remembered from our wedding last May.

"Sunny, I have one more surprise, if you're up for it."

"I don't know how many more surprises I can take!"

Gabe put his arm around me. "I brought Jane here tonight in case you'd like to renew our vows here, in front of our friends and family." There was a sudden hush over the group. This may've been a surprise to me, but the guests obviously knew that they might be here for more than a birthday party. "Nothing formal or fancy. I just want to say in front of all these people how glad I am to be your husband."

I thought about it for a second, but I didn't have to think too long. I did want to renew our vows, and tonight seemed like the perfect night.

Jane's voice was warm and soothing. "Susana, I'd love to serve as your officiant, in a non-official capacity. Do you want to marry this man again tonight?" The stars were rising in the night sky, and I was surrounded by love. I was safe, and I was home.

I took Gabe's hand in mine. "Yes," I vowed. "I do."

EPILOGUE

GABE

My feet were buried in the sand, I had a beer in my hand, and the sun warmed my face as I baked on the beach. I'd done it. I turned thirty-three, got my house by the ocean, and no longer had to work for somebody else.

"You know the sun is way stronger down here, right? I get it that you're the outdoorsy type, but you're about to be the lobster type if you don't put on more sunscreen." Susana plunked a bottle of sunblock down on my stomach. "And sex is no fun when your skin's on fire."

That was warning enough for me. I opened the bottle, filled my palm with sunscreen, and applied it to all my spots that felt a little toasty. "How's that?"

"Your shoulders and cheeks are already looking pink." Susana wore a hat and sunglasses and was camped out on a lounge chair under the umbrella while I was taking in the rays directly, just me on a towel on the ground. Old School.

When Susana swam, she wore a long-sleeved swim shirt to protect her skin, but in the safety of the shade she just wore her bikini, and it was probably wise to be some distance away from her. If I was right next to her, I'd be way too distracted by how her new green two-piece hugged her breasts and sat low on her hips.

It was June, and Susana was the official owner of Starling Manor and she oversaw all aspects of the estate. Harry Hardin had been found guilty of several counts of awful shit and was awaiting sentencing. It was a relief for both of us to know that we'd never have to deal with that asshole again. Tyler Hardin was taking over most of his father's dealings, and in his continued quest to make amends, was serving on the Starling Foundation Board. He'd already used some of his own family money to fully fund Sunny's Green Kids Grow initiative and he was looking to expand it to other regions.

My beach bungalow was small, but it turned out that it fit the two of us just fine. Well, the three of us. We'd tried leaving Mallory home when we went away for overnight trips, but apparently our little furball was quite the monster when she felt like she'd been left behind. What can I say, she was daddy's little girl. Susana was staying at the beach for a week and then she'd head back to the estate while Mallory finished out the month down here and got things settled.

Sunny and I were independent, but that didn't mean we always needed to be alone. I hired a new head groundskeeper, but I helped out around the estate when I was there. I'd also decided to keep my old cottage for myself so I could have a quiet spot to go when I needed to recharge. Sunny and I had been married for over a year, but we felt like newlyweds.

"What do you want for dinner tonight? I'll make a list for the store." Susana pulled up a shopping list on her phone and typed in a few items.

"Fish."

"Obviously. Any preference?"

"Whatever's fresh."

"I'll just drop by the fish market around four o'clock and see what they bring in with the boats. I'll build a dinner around that."

"Perfect. Just don't leave it out on the counter like last time."

"I can't believe that cat ate the whole filet!"

"That's my girl."

Susana rolled her eyes. "You've got some spots you forgot to rub in. You're looking a little ghostly."

"Don't care." Nothing troubled me right then, especially not streaks of zinc oxide smeared across my face and chest. I was in my own personal heaven. "Oh, condoms." Speaking of heaven.

"What about them?" Susana looked up from her phone.

"Add them to the list."

"Are we out?"

"No, but I don't want to find out one night that we're suddenly out, do you?"

Sunny didn't answer, and the only sounds around us were the crashing of the waves, the passing cries of seagulls, and the voices of children building a sandcastle further down the beach.

"Sunny?"

"What?"

"Gonna add condoms to the list?"

"Did you mean what you said?"

"About what?"

"Those times you've told me that I'm so great with kids. And that I'd be a good mother?" She paused and wrinkled her nose in the cute way she did when she was really concentrating. "And . . . that you want kids with me?"

"Of course, I meant that."

"Even though I didn't have the best relationship with my parents? And I've lived alone for years? You don't think I'd mess up a kid?"

"Sunny, I stand by my statement that you'd be an amazing mom." A feeling rushed over me, and I sat up so fast that I gave myself a headrush. "Are you pregnant?"

"No! I'm not pregnant."

I flopped back down and took a breath. Then I sat up again.

"Then why haven't you added condoms to the list? Do you not want to have sex with me anymore?"

"I definitely want to have sex with you."

"I'm confused."

"I just wondered, you know, what if we didn't use them?"

"What if we didn't use condoms?"

She shrugged. I couldn't see her eyes because of her sunglasses. "Yeah."

"And why wouldn't we use them?"

"I don't know. In case we, you know, were open to what might happen if we didn't."

"Susana Starling, are you serious?" My heart jumped in my chest at the idea of having a baby with Susana. And when I thought about being inside her with nothing between her skin and mine, well, something else was jumping up.

"Hold on." She pulled her beach bag closer and stuck her hand in. She swept her hand across the bottom of the bag like a fishing net trawling the ocean floor for crabs. She must've found what she was looking for because her face brightened and she pulled her hand out of the bag, fist closed around an object I couldn't see. "I love you, Archie. You're my safe place. You know that, right?"

I moved from my spot on the towel and joined her under the umbrella, kneeling in the sand by her side. "Of course I know that. And you're mine. Everything okay?"

"Everything's fine. Now, ask your question again."

"You want me to ask you again if everything's okay?"

She smiled and held out her closed fist. "No, the question before that one."

I tried to remember exactly what I'd asked. This new development had distracted me, big time. "Oh! Susana Starling, are you serious? About wanting to have a baby with me?"

Susana shook her fist theatrically and then unfurled her fingers, unveiling a miniature Magic 8 Ball attached to a keychain. "Go ahead. You asked the question; you check the answer."

I plucked the toy from her palm. If this thing said, "OUT-LOOK NOT SO GOOD," I was going to chuck it into the ocean. I held it up so we could both watch the white answer cube bounce around in the blue fluid. It wobbled and balanced and pressed against the plastic window. Its answer? "WITHOUT A DOUBT."

"Told you!" She jolted forward and pressed her soft full lips against mine, quickly reminding me of what'd started this conversation in the first place.

I scrambled to my feet and dusted the sand off my knees. "Let's go." I retrieved my towel and tossed my empty beer can into the cooler.

"Go where?"

"Back to the house."

"Right now?"

"I think that's the smart decision." I moved my towel so she could see how my erection was already pushing against my swim trunks.

She laughed and then stood up and stretched, pushing her chest out and arching her back. I had no idea how I was going to wait until we got back to the house. I wanted her right now.

She glanced again at the bulge in my swim trunks. "You have a serious boner problem."

"What makes a boner 'serious?'" I asked.

"It smokes a cigar and wears a fedora?"

I swept her off her feet and pulled her into my arms, sending a plume of sand into the air and making her squeal. Her body felt sultry and summery and smelled like salt, coconut, and jasmine. I wanted to rip her suit off her right there on the beach, but getting arrested for public indecency probably wasn't the best way to get acquainted with the locals.

Susana wiped a splotch of sunscreen off my nose. "I don't know if I can have sex with ghosts."

"You're about to find out." I carried her toward the path that led to our bungalow.

"What about our stuff?"

"We'll come back for it."

"You sure about that?" She tucked her head under my chin.

I picked up the pace. "I've never been more sure of anything in my whole life."

"I love you, Mr. Starling."

"And I love you, Mrs. Green."

ABOUT THE AUTHOR

Megan Moores writes cozy steamy romances that combine humor, edge, and happily ever afters. She holds degrees in Creative Writing and Teaching from the University of of Arkansas, and especially loves reading Romance, Nordic Noir, Police Procedurals, and Southern Gothic novels. She currently lives in Indiana with her husband, four children, three cats, and one lonely fish.

Website: https://www.meganmoores.com
Newsletter: https://meganmoores.substack.com

instagram.com/meganmooreswrites

ALSO BY MEGAN MOORES

Owls and Other Assassins